Sheila O'Flanagan is the bestselling, award-winning author of thirty books, including *Three Weddings and a Proposal*, *The Women Who Ran Away*, *Her Husband's Mistake*, *The Missing Wife*, and *All For You* (winner of the Irish Popular Book of the Year Award).

She lives in Dublin with her husband.

Praise for Sheila O'Flanagan

'One of my favourite authors' **Marian Keyes**

'Reading a Sheila O'Flanagan novel always feels like sitting down for a cup of tea with a friend . . . She writes with such warmth and empathy' **Beth O'Leary**

'A glamorous, blockbusting, empowering read . . . Sheila knows just what it is to be a woman' **Veronica Henry**

'Great characters and many twists and turns . . . A great read!' **Katie Fforde**

'A refreshing, unapologetic, funny, absorbing page-turner which left me wanting to read another Sheila O'Flanagan novel straight away!' **Emily Gunnis**

'Sheila's books always make you feel as if you've spent time with a good friend' **Carole Matthews**

'Insightful, pacy and authentic . . . Terrific' **Patricia Scanlan**

'An involving, thought-provoking novel . . . I was drawn in from page one' **Sue Moorcroft**

By Sheila O'Flanagan

Suddenly Single
Far From Over
My Favourite Goodbye
He's Got To Go
Isobel's Wedding
Caroline's Sister
Too Good To Be True
Dreaming Of A Stranger
The Moment We Meet
Anyone But Him
How Will I Know?
The Season of Change
Yours, Faithfully
Bad Behaviour
Someone Special
The Perfect Man
Stand By Me
Christmas With You
All For You
Better Together
Things We Never Say
If You Were Me
My Mother's Secret
The Missing Wife
What Happened That Night
The Hideaway
Her Husband's Mistake
The Women Who Ran Away
Three Weddings and a Proposal
What Eden Did Next

SHEILA O'FLANAGAN

What Eden Did Next

REVIEW

The right of Sheila O'Flanagan to be identified as the Author of
the Work has been asserted by her in accordance with the
Copyright, Designs and Patents Act 1988.

First published in Great Britain in 2022
by HEADLINE REVIEW
an imprint of HEADLINE PUBLISHING GROUP

First published in paperback in Great Britain in 2023
by HEADLINE REVIEW
an imprint of HEADLINE PUBLISHING GROUP

1

Cataloguing in Publication Data is available from the British Library

ISBN 978 1 4722 7271 3 (B-format)

Typeset in ITC Galliard Std by Palimpsest Book Production Ltd,
Falkirk, Stirlingshire

Printed and bound in Great Britain by Clays Ltd, Elcograf S.p.A.

Headline's policy is to use papers that are natural,
renewable and recyclable products and made from wood
grown in well-managed forests and other controlled sources.
The logging and manufacturing processes are expected to conform
to the environmental regulations of the country of origin.

HEADLINE PUBLISHING GROUP
An Hachette UK Company
Carmelite House
50 Victoria Embankment
London EC4 0DZ

www.headline.co.uk
www.hachette.co.uk

What Eden Did Next

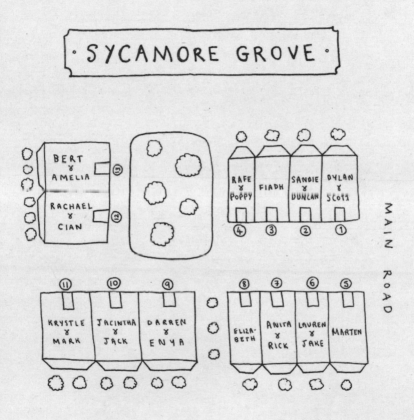

Chapter 1

Darling You,

I went to the beach before sunrise this morning and stood at the water's edge, allowing the softest of waves to break gently over my feet while I wriggled my toes deeper into the cool, damp sand. When a whisper of breeze kissed the back of my neck, I took a deep breath and stretched my arms as high as I could over my head before exhaling slowly and lowering my arms again.

It was a perfect moment.

And then, as the sun peeked over the horizon, I felt the ache of your absence and I wished you were at my side.

I wanted you to be here, scooping me into your arms and carrying me back to the house as you'd done so many times in the past. I wanted us to be having breakfast together in the garden, or even better, forgetting about breakfast and hurrying to the bedroom instead, locking the door behind us then tumbling onto the bed, laughing at our shamelessness. I wanted to see you smiling at me, to hear you whisper my name. I wanted to feel the touch of your lips on mine. I wanted to hold you and to be held by you.

I wanted us to be together again, living the life we'd dreamed of.

It was a simple dream.

It should have been possible.

And then, it wasn't.

Lila and I stayed in the house last night, but tonight we'll all be in the new hotel a little further up the coast. It opened last year and you wouldn't believe how upmarket and glamorous it is, with its chandeliers and fountains, marble floors and landscaped gardens.

It's a long way from how things used to be on this stretch of the Wexford coast, when the tourists arrived in battered caravans pulled by asthmatic cars, or rented ancient mobile homes in farmers' fields. Now it's all about the posh hotels and even posher summer houses. To be honest, I'm not sure we could ever have afforded a place of our own here. Sean and Valerie were smart to buy Dunleary when they did. It's an oasis of old-world charm among all the chic new builds.

Anyway, the glam hotel was the perfect setting for Amanda's wedding, which was fittingly glamorous too, as well as great fun. I'm writing this in—

The sharp rap on the bedroom door startled Eden so much that she almost knocked over the open bottle of washable blue ink on the desk in front of her. Conscious that the term 'washable' referred to the colour of the ink and not the ease of cleaning it up, she lunged for the bottle before it could tip its contents onto the floor, then exhaled in relief as she caught it and screwed the lid tightly closed. The tips of her fingers were now a delicate shade of blue, but the hotel's beautiful cream carpet remained an ink-free zone.

The rap sounded again.

'Just a second!' She wiped her hands on a tissue, then slid the sheet of paper she'd been writing on beneath the hotel services folder on the desk. She placed the pen beside the folder and opened the door.

The woman standing in the corridor outside was wearing a blue silk dress that almost matched the ink. It exactly matched the blue of her eyes.

'Are you OK?' she asked Eden. 'You disappeared without a word.'

'Of course I'm OK.' Eden beckoned her sister-in-law into the room. 'I was just taking a bit of time out. Relaxing.'

Michelle glanced at the undisturbed counterpane on the bed, then at Eden's still inky fingers, and raised an eyebrow.

'Not sleeping.' Eden rubbed her fingers with a fresh tissue, but it didn't make any difference. 'When the children were taken off to watch cartoons, I used the opportunity to chill out for a while. It's been a long day.'

'And an emotional one.'

'In a nice way,' said Eden as she walked into the bathroom to wash away the worst of the stains. When she returned, Michelle was sitting in the comfortable armchair, her legs curled up beneath her. Eden perched on the edge of the bed and readjusted the floral clips in her artfully messy updo. 'I'm so glad Amanda asked me to write the invitations and the place cards. Can you believe she really did get hitched? And so quickly after meeting someone?'

'It was a surprise,' Michelle agreed. 'For all of her sneering at women falling into the "marriage trap", my little sister changed her tune pretty sharpish when Bruno came on the scene.'

'She didn't really call it a marriage trap, did she?' asked Eden.

'Loads of times,' confirmed Michelle. 'When I married Gene, it was all "you're throwing your life away" stuff from her.'

'Oh, well, she was much younger then,' said Eden. 'People change.'

'Not you.' Michelle's voice was warm. 'You're the same person you always were.'

'I'm not sure about that.'

'You are,' said Michelle. 'You've always been the best, Eden.'

'And *you've* been drinking too much champagne.'

'Quite possibly.' She grinned. 'But if you can't knock back the champers on a day like today, when can you? Come on. Let's join in the fun downstairs.'

Eden glanced at her watch. 'I *was* planning on coming back down, you know. I set an alert for when the cartoons ended. There was no need to check up on me, honestly.'

'I guess . . . Well, I know you're fine, I really do. But when I saw you weren't there . . .'

Eden's mobile buzzed and she looked at Michelle as she silenced it. 'The alert. Just like I said.' She dropped the phone into her bag, then slipped her feet into her sequinned shoes.

'I have proper shoe envy looking at those.' Michelle stood up and smoothed down her dress.

'I got them in the sales,' Eden said. 'Forty per cent off.'

'A bargain.'

'I would've paid full price,' she admitted. 'I love sequins.

They always make me feel as though I've made a proper effort. And it's been so long since I've dressed up; making a proper effort is a real joy.'

'In that case, let's be joyful with the rest of them,' said Michelle as she opened the bedroom door.

Eden followed her, making sure it was firmly closed behind them.

The wedding party was taking place in a series of connected gazebos in the extensive gardens that overlooked the sea. The gardens had been a brave choice, because nobody could be sure that, even in May, it wouldn't be so cold that industrial heaters would be needed to keep the guests warm. But fate had been kind to Amanda and Bruno, and the balmy day had been ideally suited to an outdoor wedding.

'Nearly as good as Portugal,' he'd said in his after-dinner speech, to a bit of good-natured heckling from his own family, who had flown from Lisbon for the event. 'I'm very happy to be marrying Amanda and very lucky to know that she'll be in my life forever.'

Eden's throat had constricted at his words, but she'd kept her eyes firmly on him as she applauded with the rest of the guests.

Now, as she and Michelle walked along the flagstone path towards the party, she fixed a smile on her face. She would've been smiling anyway, but it was important to show everyone how happy she was today.

'Mama.' Lila left a cluster of young children and ran towards her. 'We saw Princess Fiona and we had ice cream.'

'How lucky are you!' Eden scooped her four-year-old daughter into her arms. 'Are you having fun?'

'Yes.' Lila sounded deeply satisfied. 'I love Princess Fiona.'

'She's a very good princess,' said Eden.

'Am I a princess?'

'You're *my* princess. Look at you with your lovely dress and your new shoes.'

'I want a . . .' Lila was stumped by the word, so she gestured to her head.

'A hat?' asked Eden.

'No!' Lila gave her a look of disgust. 'A . . . a . . . princess hat!'

'A tiara?'

'Yes!'

'Next time we go to a wedding,' promised Eden. 'D'you want to play with your cousins again?'

'No.' Lila buried her head in Eden's shoulder. 'I want to be with you.'

'OK.'

Eden carried her to the round table she'd been sitting at earlier. Tony and Angelina were still there, Angelina's feet propped on Tony's legs while he massaged her toes. It had been considerate of Amanda to include them, Eden thought. They were more Eden's friends than hers.

'I'm suffering for my beauty,' Angelina said as she sat up straight and put on her shoes again. 'Nobody should think that four-inch heels are a good idea.'

'They're not.' Eden grinned. 'They pull your muscles and joints out of alignment and cause back, neck and shoulder pain, as well as excessive knee torque.'

'Stop,' said Angelina. 'That's something I don't need to know.'

'Sorry.'

'My mum knows stuff,' said Lila.

'She certainly does.'

'And you've grown into a big girl, Lila,' said Tony.

'I'm a princess.' Lila gave him a satisfied look from green-flecked eyes that matched her mother's.

'A smug little madam, more like,' said Eden.

'He'd be so proud of her,' said Tony.

'Yes, he would.'

'I can't believe it's been over four years . . .' His voice trailed off.

Eden said nothing.

'Come on, Lila!' Angelina held out her arms. 'Sit on my lap for a while. Give your mum a break.'

'She doesn't need a break,' protested Lila.

'But I'd like you to sit with me,' said Angelina. 'I don't have a little girl like you to look after me like your mum does. So I'd like to borrow you.'

'Oh, OK.' Lila scrambled from Eden's lap and clambered onto Angelina's instead.

'You two should dance,' said Angelina. 'Go on.'

'Well?' Tony looked at Eden.

'Come on so.' Eden took his hand and followed him to the centre of the floor. 'We were always good for a dance.'

People made some space for them. Tony put his arm around her.

Eden smiled and leaned her head on his chest for a moment before allowing him to lead her around the ballroom floor.

Angelina watched as her husband and Eden glided past. Her arm tightened around Lila, who'd closed her eyes and almost immediately fallen asleep. She could see traces of Eden in

7

Lila's face – her high forehead and wide eyes, and the tiny dimple at the corner of her mouth. Lila was pretty in a way that Eden wasn't. But Eden was, and had always been, striking.

Angelina remembered the first time they'd met: the day Tony's best mate, Andy, had brought his new girlfriend to a barbecue on the beach. His saviour, he'd called her, only half joking, because Eden was the nurse who'd tended him when he'd arrived at A&E, his nose bloodied and his eye bruised after a tackle on the rugby pitch that had gone wrong. (Or right, he said afterwards. Brian Sewell had known what he was doing. If he hadn't crashed into him, Andy would surely have scored a try.)

Eden had laughed when he said this, and pushed her Celtic-red curls out of her eyes. She had a rich, throaty laugh that was both infectious and filthy.

'At least he's not perfect now,' she'd told Angelina. 'I'm betting he thought he was before.'

Which wasn't entirely untrue, because Andy Farrelly was a very attractive man. Angelina had fancied him herself for a while. But then she'd started dating Tony, who was on the same firefighting crew as him, while Andy had fallen head over heels with Eden. They'd become close friends, regularly meeting up, double-dating and spending occasional weekends away together. Angelina still considered Eden to be a close friend, although she didn't see her as often these days, because she and Tony had left Dublin a few years previously. It had taken Angelina some time to tell Eden of their plans, because she worried that her friend might feel in some way betrayed by their move to Enniscorthy, a mere thirty-minute drive from the hotel where the wedding was taking place. But Eden

8

had smiled, wished them every happiness and said that she'd see them as often as possible.

Their meetings since then had been more virtual than real-life. Eden rarely had time for the almost two-hour journey to Tony and Angelina's new home, and Tony was reluctant to return to Dublin unless absolutely essential. It was a shame, Angelina thought, but it wasn't anyone's fault. It was just the way things had turned out.

Her eyes continued to follow Tony and Eden around the dance floor. Eden was laughing, her eyes full of merriment as she nodded in reply to something he'd said. Her once luxuriantly red hair was now a shining unicorn grey. The appearance of grey hairs had been sudden during her pregnancy, and she'd allowed them to flourish, telling Angelina that a bit of grey was the least of her worries. A few months after Lila was born, she'd gone to her local hairdresser and had the grey enhanced so that rose-gold highlights now mixed with the silver strands. Together with the tiny pastel flowers and clips she'd woven through it, and the pale lilac and pink dress she was wearing, she looked like a kind of woodland sprite. Well, sprite was going too far, Angelina admitted, although with the weight Eden had lost and never properly regained in the last few years, she looked delicate and other-worldly. So it wasn't entirely surprising for Angelina to realise that she herself wasn't the only person watching her. Almost all of the single men, and possibly some of the married ones too, were looking at Eden as she danced with Tony.

The music stopped and they returned to the table.

'Oh, bless.' Eden looked at her daughter. 'She's finally given in to it.'

'It's been a long day,' said Angelina.

'It has. But a lovely one. Thanks for that, Tony.' Eden looked at her friend's husband. 'Now it's time for you to dance with your wife while I put this one to bed.'

'You'll come down again afterwards?' said Angelina. 'There's a baby monitoring service, isn't there?'

'I might,' said Eden. 'I'm a bit tired myself, to be honest. I haven't been out this late in ages.'

'It's not late,' said Tony.

'It is for me.' She smiled.

'Hopefully we'll see you later,' Angelina said, 'but if not, sleep well.'

'Thanks.' Eden gathered Lila into her arms and carried her back into the hotel. As she waited for the lift, she saw her mother-in-law and waved at her.

'Oh, the pet,' murmured Valerie as she came over. 'She's all in.'

'Totally,' said Eden.

'Are you coming back down?' Valerie echoed Angelina's question.

'I'm not sure,' said Eden.

'Well, if not, I'll see you in the morning,' said Valerie. 'I've a few things to tidy up at Dunleary, and then we're heading back to Dublin. Do you want to drop over for a cup of tea before you go yourself?'

'I'll see how things are,' said Eden. 'Thanks, Valerie. It was a lovely day.'

She stepped into the lift and pressed the button for the second floor, aware that Valerie was standing there watching her until the doors slid closed.

*

When she got to her room, Eden undressed Lila, who was too sleepy to even know what was happening. She laid her gently on the second bed, then covered her with a sheet. She took off her own shoes and flexed her toes before sitting at the desk again. Then she called room service and ordered a pot of hot chocolate. It arrived fifteen minutes later: a tall silver jug accompanied by two butter cookies set beside a delicate china mug.

She poured the hot chocolate, and picked up the paper she'd been writing on earlier. She took a sip from the mug, read what she'd written so far and made a face. Honestly, she thought, he doesn't need to hear all that guff about sunrises and sand and jumping into bed together. He just wants to know how the wedding went.

She crumpled the page and dropped it into the bin. Then she took a fresh sheet of paper and used her favourite Nikko G pen to write Darling You in the same elegant, swirling font as before. After that, she put away the calligraphy pen, made sure that the bottle of ink was tightly closed, and chose an ordinary felt-tip to continue in her normal, rounded handwriting.

We're back in the room after Amanda's wedding. Did you ever think you'd see those two words together? Amanda's wedding? And yet she was happy and radiant today, and she's clearly madly in love with Bruno. I'm sure she'll settle down in Lisbon no problem.

The ceremony was lovely. It was in the hotel gardens and they did a great job with the pergolas and gazebos and everything to make it look stunning. And of course those fabulous views down to the sea were the perfect backdrop for the most romantic afternoon ever.

You already know I did the invitations and the place cards, and thankfully they looked great. I have to confess, I was really stressed because I wanted it to be absolutely perfect. And even if I sound a bit Boasty McBoastface, I honestly don't think a professional calligrapher would've done any better.

I did wonder if they asked me so's I'd feel more involved. Everyone insists I'm part of the family, but they always go the extra mile so that I feel it too.

The only downside to a great day was that I kept imagining people were looking at me and thinking of us on our wedding day. Which was daft, because all eyes were on the bride, not me. And the bride was beautiful and happy. I was happy for her too. I can be happy for people who are happy themselves. Other things might be hard, but that's not.

Lila had a great time. Amanda wanted her to be a ring-bearer, but she's a bit young for that and you know what she's like, because I've told you a million times – the face of a cherub and the soul of an imp. I wouldn't have trusted her not to run away with the ring. Or swallow it. Or something. Can you imagine!!!!

Tony asked me to dance – at least, Angelina made him dance with me – and all I could think about was the last time you and I danced together and how lovely it was. It was at your mum's sixtieth. Do you remember? Tony's still a great dancer. He's completely over his injury, though he doesn't play rugby any more. Too old for it, he says.

Everyone is so wonderful to me that I feel guilty for thinking it can be a bit overwhelming sometimes. Your mum and dad are amazing. They always look out for me.

The others have Lila over for sleepovers with her cousins whenever they can. Michelle is forever texting me. She talks about you a lot, which is nice. I don't like it when people avoid using your name. Amanda isn't around much, but she keeps in touch through social media, and, of course, it was really thoughtful to ask me to do the calligraphy work.

Lila is sleeping now and I'm going to go to bed. It's been a tiring day. But a good one.

It would be even better if you were here.

But you are.

In my heart.

Forever yours,

Eden xx

Chapter 2

Elizabeth was sitting at her bedroom window sipping a cup of tea when the red car slowed down in front of her house. As she put on her glasses to see it more clearly, the car turned into the driveway of number 4. The 'Sale Agreed' sign had been taken down from the garden directly opposite Elizabeth's a few weeks earlier, but so far nobody on Sycamore Grove seemed to know anything about the new buyer.

Which was a little bit unusual, because Sycamore Grove, a small development of thirteen houses, had a vibrant Neighbourhood Watch WhatsApp group where everyone always seemed to know what was going on. Elizabeth herself wasn't interested in posting, but whenever she heard the chime that indicated a new message, she read it eagerly. The group had been originally set up by Krystle Keneally at number 11, and early alerts had focused on reminding people to close their windows at night and keep an eye out for suspicious activity. But these days the conversations were far more wide-ranging, and a simple reminder about sweeping up fallen leaves or not parking on the grass could morph into a discussion about tree bark as a herbal remedy, or wild conspiracy theories about GPS trackers. The threads were often littered with personal anecdotes and experiences, and Elizabeth, who at seventy-five came from a generation that preferred to keep their private lives private, was always surprised at how much information her neighbours were happy to share. Over the last few weeks, she'd learned that Fiadh Foley at number 3 had split up with her boyfriend; that Jacintha and Jack at number 10 were expecting their second child; and that Lauren and Jake Healey at number 6 had been left a holiday apartment by Jake's parents and his brother was furious at his own bequest of the family Volvo.

Despite being uncomfortable with all the over-sharing, Elizabeth was hooked on the gossipy posts that allowed her to know what was going on behind closed doors. But when she herself had become the centre of attention a couple of weeks earlier, she'd been overwhelmed, and touched by the kindness of her neighbours, who'd rallied around to help. Her only group post had been to thank them for their concern.

Everyone knew Elizabeth, as she'd been the first person to move into the road when the houses were first built, ten years earlier. There'd been a variety of homes to choose from, but she'd been downsizing, so went for a smaller, two-bedroomed house. Unsurprisingly, the larger properties were occupied by families, while the others were owned or rented by young couples or single people. Elizabeth was the only person over the age of fifty on the road, but she got on well with almost everyone, especially Anita and Rick, who lived next door and who regularly dropped in to see how she was. Anita worked in a high-end chocolate maker's and often brought home rejected sweets, sharing them with Elizabeth because, she said, as well as it being neighbourly, it stopped her and Rick from consuming far too many themselves.

Until they'd sold their house six months earlier, Elizabeth had also been friendly with the Ramseys at number 4, and she was curious about their successors. The new owners had been the subject of much speculation on the WhatsApp group, but despite their best efforts, nobody had been able to find out anything about them.

So she watched with interest as a young woman dressed in a grey marl T-shirt and faded denims got out of the red car and opened the front door. She was tall and slender, and wore her dark hair pulled back in a ponytail that reached halfway down her back. Given that Elizabeth's eyesight wasn't as good as it had been, along with the fact that the older she got, the harder she found it to estimate people's ages, she couldn't decide if the woman was likely to have bought the house for herself alone, if she might be moving in with a partner, or if she had family who were on the way to join her. Not that seeing her clearly would have given any indication of which scenario was most likely, but it bugged Elizabeth that she couldn't even hazard a guess.

The new neighbour was very eager to move in, she thought as she glanced at the big alarm clock beside her bed, showing that it was five minutes past eight. It was a pity she couldn't go across the road and welcome her. But hopefully she'd get the chance to say hello sooner rather than later.

Eden was getting Lila's things together when she heard the rattle of the letter box. She left the kitchen for the hallway and picked up the mail. A quick glance confirmed that it was mainly junk, which she put in the recycling bin without even opening. But she took the blue handwritten envelope with the red heart sticker on the back upstairs with her, where she opened the door to the small bedroom that had become the dumping ground for clutter. Stepping around a black bin bag full of clothes, she took an oblong lacquered box from the top shelf of the wardrobe. The old ebony box with a painted maple tree on the lid that had once belonged to her grandmother was almost filled with blue envelopes, tucked one behind the other in a tight row. Eden added the latest, unopened, to the rest, squeezing it in so that it fitted.

'Time to go, Lila,' she called as she replaced the box.

'I can't find Teddy.' The little girl appeared at the bedroom door, an anxious expression on her face. 'He's gone.'

'He can't be gone,' said Eden.

'He is.' Lila's lower lip wobbled. 'He's . . . he's missing!'

'But didn't he go to bed with you?' asked Eden.

'I don't know.'

'Of course he did.' Eden lifted her daughter into her arms while thinking that she wouldn't be able to do this for much longer. Lila had put on a growing spurt a few weeks ago. She was losing her toddler chubbiness and becoming long-limbed and gangly. And she weighed a lot more too. 'Let's call him,' suggested Eden once they were standing in Lila's bedroom. 'I'm sure he's here somewhere.'

'Teddy!' yelled Lila at the top of her voice. 'Where are you?'

Eden winced as she hunkered down and pulled out the pink-painted drawers beneath Lila's bed. There was no sign of the teddy she had slept with every night since moving into her own room. Eden had bought it for her so that she'd have something special to cuddle. Sometimes she wished she'd bought a teddy bear for herself too.

She checked the bed, feeling beneath the sheets and the

pillow as Lila's shouts grew louder and louder; then, finally, in the gap between the mattress and the headboard she encountered something soft and squishy.

'Here you are!' she cried triumphantly as she prised the teddy from his hiding space. 'How on earth did he get there?'

Lila beamed and hugged him close to her.

'Now that we're all ready, we'd better go,' said Eden. 'Granny will be waiting for us.'

She set the house alarm and locked the door behind her. As soon as Lila was strapped into the rear of the mint-green Fiat, Eden got into the driver's seat, eased onto the main road and turned towards her mother-in-law's house.

Even though it was before 8.30 in the morning, Valerie was already in the garden, pulling weeds.

'They seem to have sprung up overnight,' she explained. 'When I saw them, I couldn't ignore them.'

'Can I pick them, Granny?' asked Lila.

'Of course, sweetheart. Only the ones with the yellow flowers!' she warned as Lila scampered across the lawn. Then she turned to Eden. 'How are you? Recovered from the weekend, I hope?'

'I'm not so hopeless that I need a few days to recover from a big day out,' Eden told her. 'Besides, I didn't drink that much. All the same, it was nice to have Monday and Tuesday off.'

Valerie's eyes narrowed as she pushed her fingers through her thick wavy hair. 'You really don't have to put yourself through this, Eden,' she said. 'You don't need to work full-time, and you could get something easier—'

'I'm not working full-time,' Eden corrected her. 'But I do need the money. Besides, what I'm doing is a lot easier than

18

nursing. The hours are way more flexible and . . .' She stopped and looked at Valerie. 'Is it inconvenient for you?' she asked. 'This client is only temporary, and I'll be able to change my hours again when the job is finished. But if you want, I can say it's too awkward now and ask to change to mornings only. Or afternoons. Whatever suits you.'

'Not at all,' said Valerie. 'I like having Lila, you know that. It's important for me to spend time with her. She's part of my family.'

'Yes, but if you'd rather I—'

'That's not it.' Valerie interrupted her. 'I don't want you to overdo it, Eden. It's important you stay well, for Lila's sake as much as your own.'

'I worked a hell of a lot harder in A&E.'

'Michelle said you went to your room at the wedding.'

'For a break,' said Eden. 'While the children were watching cartoons. That's all. You're lovely,' she added. 'Every single one of you. But I'm fine, Valerie. It's been nearly five years. I've learned to cope.'

'It might be that long since it happened, but there's been so much since then. The hearing, the findings . . . it's been a lot.' Valerie pulled Eden into a hug. 'You know how much we love you, don't you? You and Lila?'

'Of course I do.'

'And I'm here for you any time,' said Valerie.

'I know. Aren't you being specially great right now?'

'I'll always . . .' Valerie cut herself off, then squeezed Eden's shoulder. 'Don't mind me. I take it all on sometimes. You take care. Have a good day.'

'You too,' said Eden. 'Bye, Lila!'

'Bye, Mum.' Lila didn't look up from the plant she was

hauling out of the flower bed. Eden laughed to herself as she heard her mother-in-law shriek. There might have been yellow blossoms on them, but Valerie's prized begonias certainly weren't weeds.

It was fifteen minutes later when she pulled into the driveway of the house on Sycamore Grove. She rang the bell, then unlocked the door and stepped inside.

'Hi, Elizabeth!' she called. 'Sorry I'm late.'

'That's OK,' said Elizabeth as Eden walked into her bedroom. 'It's only five minutes.'

'I know. But I like being on time.' Eden gave her an apologetic look. 'Lila couldn't find her teddy this morning and it took a while to unearth him. Fortunately he reappeared before she threw a complete strop.'

'That's how they are at that age,' said Elizabeth. 'My Lisa was a holy terror at four.'

Eden nearly said that Lisa was still a holy terror at fifty-four, but she didn't. Lisa Brennan was Elizabeth's eldest daughter. A barrister, married with three children, she was the one who'd employed Eden to help take care of her mother after the mugging that had left Elizabeth with badly torn ligaments in her shoulder and ankle. And it was Lisa who'd itemised all the care that Elizabeth would need, while the older woman sat in her armchair, her grey eyes resigned behind her modern and stylish blue-framed glasses.

'I'm a qualified nurse.' Eden spoke directly to Elizabeth, whose injured ankle was propped up on a stool in front of her while her arm was supported by a sling. 'I have a physiotherapy qualification too. I promise I'll do everything to help you recover from your ordeal as quickly as possible, so that I can be out of your hair and you can get back to your normal life.'

'It's such a nuisance,' Elizabeth said in exasperation. 'I managed to reach my seventies without ever being the victim of a crime. I'm always careful. And I was being careful when this happened, because I was walking along the pavement with my bag on the opposite shoulder to the one facing the road. But the young fella was on one of those electric scooters, and he simply mounted the pavement, swerved around me and yanked at it. The bag caught around my shoulder. He wrenched it free and I fell. It was over in seconds.'

'You must have got a terrible fright.'

'I didn't have time to get a fright,' admitted Elizabeth. 'It was afterwards, when I was at home and thinking about it . . .'

'And she didn't call me until the next day.' Lisa gave her mother an exasperated look. 'By then, of course, she was in agony with her shoulder, and her ankle had swollen up terribly.'

'I'm surprised you made it home on your own at all,' said Eden. 'Did nobody help you?'

Elizabeth shook her head. 'It happened in a flash and there was nobody around,' she explained. 'All I wanted to do was get into my own house. It took me half an hour even though it's normally ten minutes.'

'Well, I think you were extremely brave, if a bit crazy,' Eden said. 'However, I'm certainly happy to help out for as long as you need it.'

'Mum needs to be your prime responsibility,' said Lisa. 'You'll have to be here from morning to evening.'

Eden usually acted as a substitute care-giver, filling in for colleagues when they were ill or on holiday, so having a regular client for an entire day was a rarity for her. But she already liked Elizabeth, and the additional money for the extra hours would be welcome. Of course, she'd need Valerie or Michelle to help out with Lila for a while, but as Valerie loved having her granddaughter in the house, Eden didn't think that would be a problem.

'You seem capable, and having a physio qualification is an advantage,' Lisa continued. 'Why did you leave nursing?' She threw in the question as though it was an afterthought, but Eden knew it wasn't.

'Because of my daughter,' she replied. 'Care-giving means more flexibility for me.'

'Are you sure you have time for me if you're also looking after your daughter?' Elizabeth asked.

'Don't worry,' replied Eden. 'I have a good support network.'

'Excellent.' Lisa had sounded relieved. 'I'm glad that's sorted. You can start tomorrow.'

In the time Eden had been coming to Elizabeth, the older woman's recovery from her injuries had been steady, although she still needed a lot of help. She was determined and self-sufficient, and Eden had to remind her continually that doing things slowly but correctly was better in the long run than trying to push ahead before she was ready. Elizabeth listened, and nodded in agreement, but Eden knew she was trying to do too much too soon. Nevertheless, she was sharp and witty, and Eden enjoyed being with her.

Now, as she helped her to the bathroom for her shower, Eden asked her how the weekend party had gone. It had been very fortunate that Amanda's wedding and the time Eden had needed to take off for it had almost entirely coincided with a big birthday party for Lisa's husband. The whole family had gone to Ashford Castle for a long weekend, and Elizabeth had stayed at Lisa's home in Castleknock for a night when they got back.

'To be honest, it was exhausting,' Elizabeth confessed. 'Not being able to move around is really annoying, and I couldn't help thinking they were all looking at me, deciding I was a doddery old crock sitting in the corner and measuring me up for the coffin.'

'I'm sure they weren't,' said Eden.

'Huh.' Elizabeth snorted. 'It's what I would have thought.'

'Then you're not a very nice person.' Eden began to run the shower.

'You can't say that to me,' Elizabeth told her. 'I'm a trau-matised senior citizen.'

'You know you could get counselling if you feel upset about it all.'

'Oh, God, girl – counselling is a modern thing. I learned to suck it up,' said Elizabeth.

'I'm sure you did,' agreed Eden. 'But talking things through—'

'Listen to me, pet. I don't need any talking things through.' Elizabeth stepped carefully into the shower, using the recently installed grip-rail that Eden had suggested might be a good idea. 'Practical stuff works for me. And as for that young git who got my bag – well, a good clout around the head wouldn't have done him any harm. I hope he gets piles and can't sit down for a month.'

Eden almost choked with laughter.

After her client had showered and was dressed, Eden

helped her to the kitchen, where she made her some tea and toast. She'd been the one who'd suggested leaving a kettle, UHT milk and some biscuits in Elizabeth's bedroom for the mornings. In her experience, older people were often awake early, and as Elizabeth couldn't make it downstairs on her own, and refused to sleep anywhere other than her bedroom, Eden thought it would be good for her to be able to make a cup of tea and have something to eat before she arrived. Elizabeth had been supportive of the idea. Meantime, Lisa's two daughters, Tara and Meghan, took it in turns to call by at night to make sure she had everything she needed.

'They're good girls,' Elizabeth told Eden that first day. 'They look after me well.'

'It's nice that you have family who care about you,' Eden said.

'I'm sure I'm a desperate burden at the moment.' Elizabeth sighed. 'But hopefully it won't be for long. I looked after those girls and their brother when Lisa was a working mum, so it's payback time. Of course,' she added quickly, 'I didn't do it for payback. I did it because I love them.'

Eden was recalling Elizabeth's words now as she tidied up the kitchen to what she hoped would be Lisa's exacting standards.

'Oh, look!' Elizabeth's voice carried from the living room. 'The removal van has arrived across the road.'

Eden hung the patterned tea towel on its peg and joined Elizabeth at the window. A large van was parked outside number 4, and as they watched, the front door opened and a young woman walked out. Then the removal people began to unload the van and carry furniture into the house.

24

'Nice piece,' remarked Elizabeth as a dark green sofa was carried into the house. 'Ligne Roset if I'm not mistaken.'

Eden looked at the older woman in surprise. 'You can tell? From here?'

'I think so.' Elizabeth wiped her glasses. 'It's quite distinctive.'

'I wouldn't know who'd made any piece of furniture,' said Eden. 'I get most of mine from IKEA.'

'I worked in the furniture department of Arnotts for a few years,' said Elizabeth. 'They had some expensive stuff.'

'I think I've heard of Ligne Roset,' admitted Eden.

'Well, it's interesting that our new neighbour would splash out on it,' said Elizabeth. 'Makes me think she's living on her own. It's not generally the sort of furniture you buy when you have kids.'

'Sycamore Grove has quite an interesting mix of houses, doesn't it?' remarked Eden. 'It works for singletons as well as families.'

'It was marketed as a "unique blend of homes" when it was built,' Elizabeth told her. 'Though even the biggest house would fit into the garden of my old one.'

Eden knew, because they'd had plenty of chats in the past couple of weeks, that Elizabeth had originally lived in Raheny, in a house that had been built in the 1950s, a time when rooms were big and gardens even bigger. It had been a great family home, she had said, but too much work after the death of her husband. Francis had been fifteen years older than her, so she'd always assumed he'd be the first to pass away, and had already made plans to move somewhere smaller when that happened. Eden had been taken aback by her pragmatism.

'It was the right thing to do, but living here's not the

same as Rathmore Drive,' continued Elizabeth now. 'When I was bringing up my family, everyone knew everyone and . . . well.' She shrugged. 'Different times, of course. None of us women went out to work; we were home all day and we got to know each other very well. We didn't need a WhatsApp group to keep an eye on each other.' She took out her phone, the latest Samsung, with a big screen that made it easy to read. She opened the app and handed it to Eden.

KrystleK
Could I remind residents once again that for health and safety reasons children should not climb the sycamores. Also, they shouldn't run through other people's gardens causing damage to plants.

'In my day,' Elizabeth said, 'a mother would have opened the front door and yelled at whoever it was to get out of the tree unless they wanted a good hiding. And anyone running through a flower bed would be nabbed and marched home.'

Eden laughed as she handed back the phone. 'You're right. Times change.'

'I know. But honestly, that we have to send these passive-aggressive messages . . .'

'Passive-aggressive! Elizabeth, you might not be into the talking-things-through stuff, but you know the lingo, don't you?'

'What else have I to do at the moment except listen to the news and watch TV and doomscroll through the Twitter and learn it all?' she demanded.

'You don't say "the Twitter",' Eden told her in amusement.

'Just Twitter will do. And you shouldn't doomscroll either. You should follow cheerful accounts.'

Just then, Elizabeth's phone pinged and she read out Krystle's latest WhatsApp message.

KrystleK
Our new neighbour is moving in. I'll call to her later today, welcome her to the Grove and invite her to join the group.

'And that's another thing we did differently,' she said.

'What?'

'When someone moved in, they'd drop by to borrow a cup of sugar, then you'd find out everything about them and pass it on. Or else you'd go over and check that they had everything they needed, maybe even offer them a pot of tea.'

'Someone would actually ask to borrow a cup of sugar?'

'Or a pint of milk.'

'But why wouldn't they have their own sugar or milk?'

'It was only an excuse,' Elizabeth said.

'Right.'

'Anyway . . .' Elizabeth peered out of the window again to where the new arrival was directing the removal crew, a clipboard in her hand. 'I don't think this young lady would need to be borrowing milk or sugar. She looks as though she has it completely under control herself.'

Chapter 3

Petra McConnell did indeed have everything under control, but she wished Rafe was here to say where exactly he wanted the furniture that was being unloaded from the van. It was all very well to have stuck Post-it notes saying *kitchen* or *bedroom* on items that were very clearly meant to go in those rooms, but what about the boxes of paintings and ornaments? Not that there were many of those, but he could've made more of an effort to be here to supervise. This move was meant to be part of his new life. Yet despite his promise to arrive before the furniture, he was late. As usual.

She took out her phone. Her call went straight to his voicemail, but a moment later a reply arrived.

Rafe
Wind be long

Petra
You'd better not be

Rafe
Don't sweet

He was obviously using voice commands to send his texts, and, she muttered to herself as she peered into the box that contained crockery, she'd sweet all she liked. If he expected to arrive to a perfectly arranged house, he had another think coming.

'This?' The removal man standing at the door indicated a desk standing in the hallway.

'The small bedroom upstairs,' she told him. 'At the front of the house.'

It was the space Rafe had designated as his office. Right beside the router socket, he'd said. Almost perfect.

Petra followed the men carrying the sleek modern desk and watched them put it into the chosen bedroom. Then she went into the master bedroom, where the king-size bed had already been assembled. Rafe had always been a sprawler, lying across his bed rather than neatly beneath the covers as she always did.

The attic bedroom was Poppy's. It had two large Velux windows, making it light and airy, plenty of storage for her large collection of books and toys, and enough space for her own small desk as well as an impressive bed with a house-shaped frame over it. The frame included white net surrounds and LED fairy lights, which, Petra thought, she'd quite like for herself.

'We've finished!' The man's voice from the hallway was loud.

'I'll be right with you.'

Petra hurried down the stairs and handed a fifty euro note to the lead removal man, who pocketed it with a quick nod.

'Everything's where it should be,' he said. 'I hope you're very happy in your new home.'

'I won't be . . .' She stopped herself. The man had already taken out his phone and put it to his ear as he left the house.

She watched as the van reversed up Sycamore Grove. As it moved away, she saw an elderly lady with a younger woman supporting her standing at the front door of the house opposite.

'Nosy neighbours,' she muttered to herself. But then the young woman got into the Fiat parked in the driveway and followed the reversing van up the road, which made Petra wonder if she'd been waiting for it to get out of her way before leaving. I hope I haven't pissed off the neighbours, nosy or not, she thought as she went back into the house. It wouldn't be a good start.

Eden knew she could have manoeuvred past the removal van, but it had been just as easy to wait with Elizabeth, who was madly curious about the activity opposite. Now she stopped at the junction with the main road while a silver-grey SUV turned into Sycamore Grove. In the rear-view mirror she saw it pull to a halt outside number 4. She hadn't caught sight of the driver, but she assumed it must be the husband or partner of the dark-haired woman who'd been supervising the furniture delivery.

'She probably thinks I'm sussing her out,' Elizabeth had remarked as they stood on the doorstep watching the removal guys.

'She'd be right,' Eden said, before reminding her that she'd be back to cook her lunch. Sometimes the older woman seemed a little dispirited when Eden was leaving, but the excitement of a new arrival at the Grove had cheered her up immensely. In fact, she was a lot better today than she had been since Eden had started visiting her. Not surprisingly, she'd been a little anxious at first; Eden knew that part of it was a result of the mugging, and another part worry at how she'd feel about having a stranger coming into her house every day. But they were getting on well together now, and Eden would be sorry when Elizabeth no longer needed her.

She'd be less sorry when she finished up with her next client, she thought as she finally eased into the traffic.

Eden had dealt with many difficult people since she'd begun working with the agency, and equally difficult patients when she was nursing, but she found it hard to empathise with Phyllis Bowyer, who was very demanding and always ready to find fault.

'Can I do anything else for you?' she asked after she'd tidied the kitchen, emptied the bins, folded the laundry, swept the floors, prepared a snack and then read aloud a chapter of the blood-curdling horror novel that Phyllis had borrowed from the local library. (Phyllis always insisted on the right accent for each character, something Eden found difficult to do, as most of the novels were set in America. Phyllis had lived there for twenty years and was unfailingly critical of her attempts.)

'No.' Phyllis gave her a grudging nod. 'That's all for today.'

Eden sighed with relief as she left the house, trying to put the gory scenes of the novel out of her head.

She liked her job, and it suited her, but not every client was as easy-going as Elizabeth Green.

When she returned to make her lunch a little later, Eden saw that Elizabeth was back sitting at the living room window.

'The husband has arrived,' she said when Eden walked into the room. 'Good-looking chap.'

'I thought your eyesight was too bad to see details like that.'

Elizabeth laughed. 'Any male under the age of seventy is good-looking to me,' she said. 'To be fair, there's a few older men I wouldn't shove out of the bed for eating crisps, but I prefer to cradle-snatch these days.'

'Too much information,' said Eden.

'There's a daughter too,' Elizabeth continued. 'About six or seven, I'd say.' She sighed. 'I miss the cup-of-sugar days. I'd like to welcome them to the neighbourhood. But I guess I'll have to wait for Krystle's WhatsApp update.'

According to Elizabeth, Krystle knew everything about everybody, even things they'd rather she didn't.

'You're the one in prime position to see anyone who comes in and out,' remarked Eden.

'In those old days I was telling you about, I'd have been the nerve centre,' agreed Elizabeth. 'But technology has taken over from twitching curtains.'

Eden laughed and then asked Elizabeth what she wanted for lunch.

'A bit of fish would be nice,' suggested Elizabeth. 'There's some in the fridge.'

Eden cooked the fish while she and Elizabeth continued to talk about the relentless march of technology.

'It's good in lots of ways,' conceded Elizabeth. 'But I miss the personal touch.'

'Did you get your granddaughter to download some books for you?'

Elizabeth had complained the previous week about not being able to read the small print in books, and Eden had suggested Kindle as an alternative.

'I forgot,' she confessed. 'I'll talk to her tonight. Or you could do it for me.'

'I would, of course, but you'd have to give me your bank card, and I don't want to have that information.'

'I trust you, both with the card and setting it up,' said Elizabeth.

Eden shook her head. 'I'd rather someone from your family did it.'

'You're very professional, aren't you?' said Elizabeth.

'It's my job,' said Eden.

'And here was I thinking we were friends.'

'We are,' said Eden. 'But friends know that some things aren't shared, and your bank details are one of them. Now, are you ready for your lunch?'

Valerie and Lila were at the back of the house when Eden came to collect her daughter later in the afternoon. Lila was playing with a Lego set, while Valerie was looking through a photograph album Eden had never seen before.

'I found an old memory stick with photos on it a while back, and Michelle got them printed for me,' she told her. 'She dropped it off this morning.'

They were family photos dating back about twenty years.

'There's Andy,' said Valerie, pointing to a young boy standing on the beach, his arms aloft. 'He was about to go in for a swim. He was such a good swimmer,' she added. 'He took to the water like a fish.'

'Lila's the same.'

'Here he is at Brenna's debs!' Valerie turned the pages and stopped at a photo of a couple in formal dress. The girl, in a pale pink dress, with fair hair teased into waves and held back by a diamanté clip, looked sophisticated, but the tuxedo Andy was wearing made him look ridiculously young. 'She was mad about him,' Valerie said, then looked at Eden. 'Sorry, I didn't mean . . .'

'That's OK,' said Eden. 'I didn't know Andy when he was eighteen. And he didn't know me. I brought a very attractive guy to my debs. All my friends were mad jealous.'

'Are you still in touch with him?' Valerie's question was unexpectedly sharp.

'Of course not,' said Eden. 'I only asked him because he was so good-looking. I was very shallow back then.'

Valerie closed the album. 'I miss him,' she said.

'So do I,' said Eden.

'At least we have Lila.' Valerie glanced at her granddaughter. 'She's the image of him.'

'Sometimes,' agreed Eden. 'And sometimes she's entirely her own person.'

Valerie opened the album again and flicked through it until she reached a photo of Andy at about six years of age. He was wearing a yellow plastic fireman's helmet.

'Lila. Come here!' she called to the little girl, who came running. 'Look, here's a photo of your daddy when he was a boy. Isn't he lovely?'

Lila nodded, then buried her head in her grandmother's lap.

Eden watched them in silence.

She wished Andy was still here.

Chapter 4

After she'd settled Lila down for the night, Eden scrolled through her own digital photos of her husband. They'd taken lots over the years and her favourite was her screen saver, a selfie from before they'd moved in together. He was wearing his full fireman's kit and she was in shorts and a T-shirt. He'd asked if she wouldn't have preferred him just to be wearing a strategically placed helmet, which had reduced her to a fit of uncontrollable giggles, unable to hold the phone steady. He'd taken it from her, and she'd been struggling to keep a straight face when he pressed the button. He was laughing too. It was a photo full of joy and happiness.

She stared at it, lost in the moment, until the screen dimmed and the device automatically locked. Then she allowed herself to remember the first time they'd met, at the A&E department of the hospital where she'd worked, when Andy had shown with his face such an absolute mess she'd thought at first he'd been assaulted. When he told her it had happened on the rugby pitch, she'd remarked that that was worse than being assaulted and he'd need an X-ray to check if his nose was broken.

She forgot about him after he went to radiology, and moved

on to her next patients, a young boy who'd shoved a peanut up his nose, followed by a man with a deep gash in his forearm that needed stitches. It was a couple of hours before Andy reappeared.

'Not broken, I hear.' She smiled at him. 'Lucky you.'

'I guess. It doesn't feel like it at the moment, though.' He peered at her from his swollen eye.

'You'll be better before you're twice married.' It was a favourite phrase of her aunt's.

'Well, that'll take a while, given I'm not even once married,' he told her.

'The doctor has prescribed painkillers and anti-inflammatories,' she said with a smile. 'Don't forget to take them. They'll help.'

'OK.'

'That's you sorted.'

She was about to move on when he stopped her.

'I realise that this is a bit left-field,' he said, 'but I was wondering if you'd come out with me some time?'

'Out?'

'For a drink. Or dinner.'

'Like a date?'

'Yes.'

She'd been asked out by patients before. It wasn't exactly an occupational hazard, but it happened. She never said yes.

But this time, she did.

Eden didn't believe in soulmates. She didn't want them to exist. She had no desire to experience a connection so deep that she couldn't imagine life without it. She wasn't looking for someone to make her life complete.

But Andy did.

And it terrified her.

Because she knew it couldn't last forever. She was afraid of the day it would end. She had experience, after all, of things changing in an instant, of the people you loved not being there for you any more. Of her heart being ripped to shreds. And she'd decided back then, at ten years old, that the only person she could depend on was herself.

So the last thing she wanted was to fall in love with Andy Farrelly.

She hadn't always been afraid of love. She'd lived secure in the knowledge that she loved and was loved in equal measure. She'd thought it would be like that forever. Her teachers praised her parents for bringing up a well-behaved girl who was easy-going and got on well with almost everyone.

'Such a helpful child,' Mrs Geraghty told her mum and dad at the parent–teacher meeting. 'Always ready to put other people ahead of herself. She has an enquiring mind, but she loses interest quickly although her work is always beautifully presented. Her handwriting is unusually neat and legible for a student her age. She enjoys sport, which is important, because we encourage our children to be active.'

Martina and Matt were pleased to hear such praise of their daughter. They'd brought her up to be considerate and helpful. They encouraged her curiosity although agreed that she allowed her mind to wander. They hadn't noticed a particular neatness in her writing, but they were happy to hear it all the same. And they nodded in agreement when Mrs Geraghty talked about Eden being active – they preferred her being outdoors rather than inside playing video games or watching TV.

Whenever Eden was missing, it was the branches of the trees that overhung their garden that her parents usually checked first, because that was her favourite spot for hiding out; but the day she was to leave Galway forever, with her Aunt Trudy and Uncle Kevin, she ignored the trees and instead pushed her way through the tall bamboo that grew beside the garden shed. The bamboo, the shed and the back wall formed a hideaway that even her parents hadn't known about. When she squeezed into the narrow space that day, Mac was waiting for her. Eden knew he hadn't come through the house to get there. He'd dropped into the garden from one of the trees that Eden liked to climb. Mac was a few months older than her, lived on the same street and was her very best friend.

'I don't want to go,' she told him as she wrapped her arms around her knees and hugged them close to her body. 'I want to stay here with you and everyone else.'

Mac was sitting opposite her because the gap behind the shed was too small to allow them to sit side by side. He leaned forward so their heads were almost touching. 'I don't want you to go either. I asked my mum could you live with us.'

'You did?' Eden looked at him hopefully.

'But she said you had to live with your auntie and uncle. They're your family.'

'I wish they weren't.'

Mac took her hands in his. 'I wish you were *my* family.'

'I wish I was too.'

It wasn't fair, she thought. She'd lost her mum and her dad. Now she was losing Mac too. As he squeezed her hands, Eden heard her aunt's voice calling her.

'You have to go.' Mac released his hold and then leaned over and wiped away the tear that was sliding down her cheek. 'I'll miss you.'

'I . . .' She didn't finish the sentence.

'Where are you, Eden?! I need you here right now!' Trudy's voice was closer.

Eden took a deep breath.

'Did you hear me?' cried Trudy. 'This minute, Eden. We have to go.'

She looked at Mac for the last time. Then she crawled through the bamboo bush.

'What on earth have you been doing?' asked her aunt. 'You're filthy.'

Eden said nothing. She followed Trudy back to the house.

And when she got into the car with her aunt and uncle, she felt the protective shell harden around her broken heart.

It was on her second date with Andy that she told him about the night that had changed everything. Afterwards, he wrapped his arms around her and promised her he'd be there for her no matter what. She hadn't expected to believe him, because she hadn't let herself believe in it for years, but with Andy, she did. She allowed the shell to crack and splinter as she felt secure and protected in a way she hadn't since she was ten. And when she met his parents for the first time and Valerie drew her into a warm embrace, she felt even more secure and protected. She also felt welcome and loved.

Certainly more welcome and loved than she had with Trudy and Kevin. Eden was grateful to them for taking responsibility for her, but she knew that, in their early fifties, they hadn't expected to be the guardians of a ten-year-old girl. They'd chosen a child-free life, and until then, they'd lived it to the full. Taking Eden in had been a duty, and they'd done their best under the circumstances, but their best hadn't unlocked a hitherto unknown warm and nurturing side in Trudy, nor had it turned Kevin into a replacement father. They simply weren't equipped to become the people they couldn't be. Trudy was always kind to her niece, but her kindness was distant. She never denied Eden anything she asked for or needed, yet she never thought to buy her unexpected treats or include her in plans either. Eden's mum used to refer to Trudy as her egoistic hippy sister who couldn't be bothered with anyone or anything, but by the time Eden went to live with her and Kevin, they were managing a string of increasingly successful organic restaurants and it was the success of the restaurants that mattered most to them.

Eden knew that her mum and her aunt hadn't been especially close. Trudy was twelve years older than Martina, and despite the disapproval of their parents, had left Galway as soon as she finished school to go travelling through Europe. Having cut a swathe through the Netherlands, Belgium, Germany, Austria and Switzerland, she eventually elected to stay on the French Riviera, where her fiery red hair and emerald-green eyes marked her out among the young people who'd started to flock to the Côte d'Azur. She'd even done some modelling for the photographers who were capturing the essence of the sixties, posing in the skimpiest of bikinis against the brilliant blue backdrop of the sea, or sitting in cafés, her eyes hidden by huge sunglasses, her hair tousled in the manner of Brigitte Bardot. She'd met Kevin at a photo shoot early one morning, and by the afternoon they'd moved in together. Eventually they'd opened a bar in Antibes that quickly became the go-to place for an arty, bohemian set. They didn't bother getting married. Nor did they bother keeping in touch with home.

When they eventually returned to Ireland for a visit, ten years after Trudy had first left, the then teenage Martina had seen her sister as some exotic life form, in her trendy white flares and platform-soled shoes. At the same time she resented her deeply, because their mother, insisting on separate bedrooms for Trudy and Kevin, had moved Martina out of her own room so that Trudy could have it. Martina had been forced to sleep on a camp bed in the rarely used north-facing front room, which was always cold. She simmered with silent fury the whole time and was relieved when they left.

After that, Trudy and Kevin didn't come back to Ireland for another fifteen years, and when they did, it wasn't to Galway, but Dublin, where they opened their first organic restaurant, off George's Street. Their success wasn't instant, but business grew steadily and they added another city-centre restaurant before opening more venues in upmarket suburbs where people were becoming more and more concerned about the provenance of the food they ate.

Meanwhile Martina taught geography and biology in a secondary school outside Galway city. Matthew Hall joined the school a year later to teach maths and physics, and it didn't take long for them to become a couple. They were engaged within a year and bought a house a mere ten-minute walk from Martina's parents. Martina dropped in on Eleanor and Fred every day until they passed away. Trudy rarely came home to visit.

The accident happened on New Year's Eve. Martina and Matt were returning from a party when Matt lost control of the car and it crashed into a lamp post. His loss of control had been caused by a massive heart attack, and he was dead before the impact. Martina was killed instantly.

Because they'd expected to be out until late, Martina had arranged for Eden to spend the night with Mac and his family. She didn't hear about the accident until the following day, when Mac's mother broke it to her as gently as she could, holding her tightly and telling her that everything would be OK. But even then, Eden knew it would never be the same again, although no matter how many times she told herself that her mum and dad were never coming home, she couldn't quite believe it. Even when Trudy and Kevin arrived from Dublin to see to the arrangements, she struggled to accept what had happened. She barely spoke more than a couple of words to them, and when she realised they would be making decisions about her future, she was horrified. Her first suggestion, that she live with Mac's family, had been rejected out of hand, and her proposal that Trudy and Kevin could move into her parents' house and open a restaurant in Galway was dismissed just as quickly.

Eden often wondered why Trudy had insisted on uprooting her from her home city and bringing her to her modern house overlooking Dublin Bay when it was clearly the last thing in the world either of them wanted. Even boarding school might have been a better option, although she understood that the reality of boarding was probably wildly different from the exciting school stories she loved to read. She accepted that her aunt and uncle were doing their best, or at least their duty, by her; but she knew from the moment she stepped into the long, narrow hallway with its glossy black and white tiles and apple-white walls that it would never be home.

And even though a more tolerant relationship developed between them over the years (she stopped asking if she could have baked beans on toast for dinner, they stopped trying to make her eat snails; Trudy no longer insisted she read books by Betty Friedan and Marilyn French, Eden kept her stash of *Sweet Valley High* hidden in her wardrobe), and even though she grew to appreciate her aunt's innate sense of style and her uncle's easy-going humour, she never forgot that she'd been forced on them, and that without her, their lives would've been very different.

Then, as she was choosing her college for her nursing degree, the economy crashed, taking Trudy and Kevin's restaurants with it. Their beautiful home, which had been collateral for their loans, was repossessed. Eden couldn't understand why, when so many people seemed to be able to write off their losses, her aunt and uncle were losing everything.

'Because we did it right,' said Trudy, fighting tears as she packed their belongings into cardboard boxes. 'Because we believed in ourselves and we thought the system would help us. But this country is a sleaze-ridden hellhole. It always was. We should never have come back.'

They planned to leave again and return to the Riviera. On the one hand, Eden wasn't surprised. On the other, she couldn't see how her practically bankrupt aunt and uncle could possibly afford to live there.

'We made one good decision in the past,' Trudy told her. 'We bought a small apartment in Villefranche-sur-Mer before we left France, and we've been renting it out ever since. It wasn't part of the collateral for our loans. Nobody even knows about it. To be honest, Eden, we thought we'd move back a long time ago.'

It was because of her that they hadn't moved back, thought Eden. Because of her that they hadn't sold their restaurants sooner. Because of her that they'd lost almost everything.

'Don't be so melodramatic,' said Trudy when she said this. 'It's because of the greedy banks, not you. Besides, everything we had here was temporary. Our life there is permanent. And you'll be OK,' she added. 'You have some money of your own.'

If she had anything else to feel guilty about, thought Eden, it was that her dad had been a practical man who'd taken out a very good life insurance policy. So although her aunt and uncle were almost bankrupt, she had enough to get herself through her college years.

She'd asked if she could help Trudy and Kevin financially, but for what seemed like the first time ever, her aunt had looked at her with real affection and told her that whatever she had was hers and hers alone. And that when Matthew had named Trudy as Eden's guardian, he'd also taken out another policy to cover the costs of looking after her.

'So you don't owe us anything,' said Trudy. 'You never have.'

'I do,' Eden said. 'I owe you for giving up your life for me.'

'Family obligations are family obligations.' Trudy shrugged. 'Perhaps the crash is a good thing for Kevin and me. We never planned to be business people, but that's what we became, and it traps you, feeds on itself. We're out of it now. You can visit us whenever you like, of course.'

Eden had waited until after she graduated to go to France. By then, Trudy and Kevin had completely embraced their new life and she felt further apart from them than ever. They'd settled into a more basic lifestyle than they'd expected, but seemed to be content. Eden occasionally commented on or liked photos they posted on Kevin's Instagram account, and sometimes he posted a reply. In the photos, her aunt often recreated the poses of her youth, sitting on low rock walls overlooking the vibrant blue sea, her still-long hair almost the exact same shade of grey as Eden's was now, her complexion surprisingly youthful despite her age. Although that, Eden conceded, might be down to the filters Kevin used.

The only time they'd come back to Ireland had been for her wedding.

She hadn't seen them since then.

They'd sent flowers for Andy's funeral.

Chapter 5

Petra sent out for food. She wasn't an enthusiastic cook and didn't want to inflict her efforts on Rafe and Poppy, who were adjusting to their first day in the new house and new surroundings.

'I feel displaced,' Rafe said as he ladled some sesame chicken onto his plate. 'I thought I'd settled in Seattle and now here I am, back in Ireland. In Dublin of all places.'

'What's wrong with Dublin?' Petra chose some hoisin duck for herself.

'Nothing. I never thought I'd live here, that's all.'

'You gotta go where the work is.'

Rafe gave her a grateful look. 'You've been a brilliant help,' he said. 'Checking out the house, getting the furniture sent up, organising the school and everything. Maybe buying a place here was stupid, though. It might've been better to rent.'

'It's a good investment regardless.' Petra glanced out of the window to where Poppy was sitting on the garden swing. The blue and red swing had been a factor in Rafe's purchasing decision. Seeing it there had made him feel that number 4 Sycamore Grove could be a family home. It didn't matter that he could've bought a swing for any house, Rafe was influenced by the here and now, and the photo had been enough for him. 'You can pop back home any time,' Petra added.

'I know,' said Rafe. 'Don't mind me, I'm . . .'

She reached across the table and took his hand. 'You're doing great,' she said. 'Really you are.'

'I hope I'm doing the right thing.'

'You're absolutely doing what's right for you and Poppy.' Petra's voice was firm. 'I'm proud of you and I support you a hundred per cent.'

'But you're not here all the time,' said Rafe.

'If you need me, I'll be here in a couple of hours.'

'I don't have to be in the lab every day,' said Rafe. 'Maybe I could—'

'Too late now.' She made a face. 'You've committed to Dublin and it's great you can walk to the lab in half an hour or drive it in five minutes. You're picking holes in a decision you've already made.'

'I know. I'm an idiot.'

'Idiots don't get super-impressive jobs,' she told him. 'Director of scientific services sounds so important.'

He laughed. 'Way more important than it really is.'

'You wouldn't have come back if you didn't think it was a good move,' said Petra.

'I think, after everything, I needed to.'

Petra picked up her bottle of beer and raised it. 'Welcome back, and here's to you and your new life in Sycamore Grove. May you have nothing but the best.'

Rafe clinked his own bottle against hers. 'Thanks again for everything.'

The doorbell rang and the two of them looked at each other.

'I'll go,' said Petra.

She got up from the table and went to open the front door.

The woman on the step smiled at her, her hazel eyes bright and inquisitive, her honey-blonde hair falling around her shoulders.

'Hello,' she said as she handed Petra a bottle of Prosecco. 'I'm Krystle Keneally, the president of the residents' association. I've come to welcome you to our community.'

'Gosh, that's very kind of you.' Petra was surprised at the gift.

'We're a close-knit group here,' Krystle said. 'With only thirteen houses, we like to think Sycamore Grove is one of the most neighbourly developments in the area.'

'It's certainly the most generous.' Petra looked at the label.

'It's just a little something.' Krystle peered past her. 'Can I come in and tell you all about us? Or is this a bad time?'

'I don't mean to be rude, especially as you've been so kind,' said Petra, 'but we're having dinner at the moment, so . . .'

'I wouldn't dream of intruding on your meal,' said Krystle. 'How about you give me your phone number and I add you to our WhatsApp group. It'll keep you informed about everything that's going on in the Grove. The majority of our residents are members.'

'Oh, well, I'll . . . It's Rafe's number you need,' said Petra. 'Hold on, I'll get his phone.'

She left Krystle standing on the step and went back to the kitchen. Rafe raised an eyebrow at the bottle of Prosecco, which she put on the table. 'Neighbourhood Watch,' she mouthed. 'They want your phone number.'

'No.' He made a face.

'Yes.' She picked up his mobile and asked him to unlock it. 'I know they can be a pain in the arse, but you might need them.'

'Seriously, Petra.'

'Seriously, Rafe.'

She walked back to the front door and gave the number to Krystle, who was waiting patiently on the step.

'So it's you, your husband and . . . I thought I saw a little girl,' said Krystle as she tapped the number into her contacts, then rang it to make sure she'd got it right. 'What name shall I add?'

'Rafe. Rafe McConnell,' Petra said, then added Krystle to Rafe's contacts. 'And the little girl is Poppy. Rafe's not my husband, he's my brother.'

'Oh.' Krystle couldn't keep the surprise from her voice, but her face was impassive. Though that, Petra thought, might be entirely down to Botox. She chided herself for being uncharitable.

'He's moved back from the States,' she said. 'I'm helping out.'

'And . . . Petra's mum?'

'She passed away.'

'I'm so sorry to hear that. Was it recent?'

'Some time ago,' said Petra. 'Look, I'm sorry, but like I said, we're having dinner and . . .'

'Of course, of course,' said Krystle. 'We're a very welcoming community here. I'm sure he and Poppy will be very happy.'

Petra could tell that Krystle was itching to find out

everything there was to know about her brother and her niece, but she'd had enough of sharing information. Rafe would be pissed at her for giving as much as she had. He was an intensely private person, even more so after the last couple of years. But, she thought as she closed the front door, he was going to need support in his new life. He couldn't lock himself away with only his laptop for company forever, no matter how much he might want to.

It wasn't going to be easy for him.

Change never was.

When Eden arrived at Elizabeth's the next morning, the older woman told her that Krystle had already been to visit the new neighbours and had sent a WhatsApp about them to everyone.

'I accidentally deleted it,' she said. 'I've forgotten their name, but the young woman we saw supervising everything yesterday is his sister, not his wife.'

'And the little girl?' asked Eden as she made Elizabeth's bed.

'His,' replied Elizabeth. 'He's a widower. Which means . . .' her eyes twinkled at Eden, 'he'll be fair game to the ladies of the Grove.'

'What d'you mean, fair game?' Eden plumped up the pillows. 'Aren't most of the women here married?'

'Not everyone,' said Elizabeth. 'And not that that would stop them. Sure isn't a widower a kind of pet project for all women.'

'Why?'

'A man. Managing on his own. With a daughter!' Elizabeth exclaimed. 'So romantic.'

'Why are widowers seen as romantic heroes when a woman on her own with a kid is a bit of a burden?' asked Eden.

Elizabeth winced. 'I'm sorry. I didn't mean . . .'

'But it's true,' Eden said. 'In books and movies, men on their own with children are always wonderful, caring people doing their best – no matter how incompetently – while everyone rushes to help them out. Women with children are seen as something to take on, and the men who do that are heroes too. So they're double heroes and we're . . . not.'

'I think you're an absolute hero.' Elizabeth's tone was firm. 'But do you need help? Are you struggling?'

'Gosh, no!' Eden shook her head. 'I have a strong network behind me. I'm fine. So is Lila. It's not as though people didn't help us out, but there was no notion of the men where I live flocking around to clear my drains or put up shelves. They didn't see me as some kind of project to manage. Why should it be the other way round for them?'

'I'm sure there's a man out there who'd be only too happy to . . .' Elizabeth broke off. 'I was about to say "take you on", which means I'm agreeing with your point. Dammit.'

'It's OK, don't worry. I don't need to be taken on. I don't want to be. We're both great the way we are.'

'You're certainly great to me,' Elizabeth said. 'I love having you around.'

'Good.' Eden smiled as she plumped the pillows a bit more.

'Anyway,' said Elizabeth, 'I know we're all about the technology here on Sycamore Grove, even if I did trash the WhatsApp message, but I wondered would you mind nipping out to the shops and getting a welcome card that I could pop into his letter box. Well, that *you* could pop in, if that's OK. It's so much more personal than a text.'

'No problem at all,' said Eden.

'I'll need you to write it for me as well,' said Elizabeth. 'My fingers are still swollen and I can't hold a pen properly.'

Eden smoothed down the duvet and took Elizabeth's hand in hers. In addition to her shoulder and ankle injuries, she'd grazed her right hand badly and the cut had become infected, which had meant antibiotics and regular dressings.

'The swelling has gone down a lot,' she said. 'You could probably practise writing again, but I'd be happy to do the card for you.'

'I used to have lovely writing.' Elizabeth's tone was wistful. 'I got stars for it when I was in school.' She laughed. 'Which wasn't today or yesterday, was it? My purse is on the dresser. Take a fifty and see if you can't get some flowers as well.'

Eden fetched Elizabeth's purse and waited while the older lady took out the money and handed it to her. Then she left Elizabeth having a cup of tea and a biscuit and walked along Sycamore Grove to the nearby Spar, where she bought a card and a small flower arrangement for her client.

'There wasn't a "welcome to your new home" or even a "congrats on your new home" card on display,' she explained as she put them on the table along with Elizabeth's change. 'This is blank inside, but the picture of the house and garden is pretty.'

'It's perfect,' agreed Elizabeth. 'Will you write it for me?'

'I'll put a nice greeting inside, and you can have a go at signing it yourself,' said Eden. She sat at the kitchen table, opened her bag and took out a small pouch containing a short ruler, a pencil, an eraser and a black Stabilo brush pen. She ruled a couple of very faint lines on the inside of the card while Elizabeth watched her curiously.

'Just write "Welcome Neighbour" or something,' she said. 'It doesn't have to be perfect.'

'Of course it does,' said Eden. 'You'll like it, I promise.'

She uncapped the pen and slowly, with a heavy downstroke and light upstroke, formed the letter W in an elegant font that she told Elizabeth was called Merri Gables.

'But that's beautiful!' exclaimed her client. 'I didn't realise you could write like this. Where did you learn?'

'My aunt taught me,' Eden said as she continued with the rest of the word. 'She and my uncle ran restaurants and used to write the menus in different fonts.'

'That must have taken an age.'

She smiled as she looked up from the card. 'They switched to doing them on the computer after a while, but Aunt Trudy thought penmanship was a good skill to have. It was also her way of keeping me quiet in the house. I was more of an outdoors person when I came to Dublin first, but it didn't fit in with her lifestyle. She wasn't wrong about the calligraphy. It calms me. And occasionally I do invites and place cards and stuff like that for people and make a little money from it.'

'Do you draw as well?'

'No. Trudy was – is, I guess – quite artistic, but I don't have that spark.'

'You inherited something from her all the same.'

'I never . . .' Eden frowned for a moment and then returned to the card. 'I never thought of myself as inheriting anything from my aunt. It's more of a skill that I learned.'

'Listen, pet, you could try to teach someone how to do that all day, but you need to have a talent to make it look so great.'

'Maybe.' Eden formed each letter slowly and methodically, using the faint lines to keep them even. But Elizabeth's words had lodged in the back of her mind. That something of Trudy's talent had been passed on to her. It was a slightly unsettling thought.

Eventually she finished and handed the card to Elizabeth. *Welcome to your new home from your neighbour Elizabeth at No. 8.*

'You can sign it or not,' she said.

'It seems a pity to ruin it with my scrawl,' said Elizabeth.

'But it would be more personal.'

Elizabeth sighed and then asked for the pen.

'Not this,' Eden said. 'It's a special calligraphy pen. I have a nice felt-tip you can use instead.'

'When I started in school, we had nib pens and inkwells,' said Elizabeth.

'I like to use a pen and ink myself,' said Eden. 'There's something timeless about it.'

'Really?' Elizabeth paused with the felt-tip pen in her hand.

'Absolutely. Now, listen to me, don't try to hold it too hard; just let it flow.'

Elizabeth took a deep breath and then wrote her name beneath Eden's message.

'To be fair, it's not bad,' she said. 'And it didn't hurt my hand either.'

'You see.' Eden looked pleased. 'You're getting better. Soon you won't need me at all.'

'Maybe not,' conceded Elizabeth. 'But I'll certainly miss you.'

'D'you want me to pop over with the card and flowers now?' Eden glanced at the clock. It was approaching eleven.

'Given that you're monitoring their every move, is there someone in at the moment?'

'Give over,' said Elizabeth 'I haven't a clue. If there's nobody there, pop the card through the letter box and leave the flowers in the porch.'

'I'll do a little card for them too,' said Eden. 'Just in case.'

This time she took a business-size card from the pouch and wrote *Best wishes, Elizabeth Green* on it.

'Thank you,' said Elizabeth as Eden got up. 'You're a gem.'

Holding the flowers in one hand and the card in the other, Eden crossed the road, watched from the front window by Elizabeth. She rang the bell, and after waiting for what seemed like an age, was about to leave the flowers on the step when the door opened.

Her first thought was that the man standing opposite her was ridiculously tall. And then, that he was undeniably attractive. She remembered Elizabeth's words about every woman on the road being prepared to look after him because he was a widower. An attractive widower would make him an even more desirable catch. She'd have to ask her client exactly how many single women there were on Sycamore Grove.

He looked at her through his heavy-framed glasses.

'My client, Elizabeth, at number eight asked me to drop these to you.' Eden handed him the flowers and then the card. 'She wanted to say welcome to the neighbourhood.'

'She did, did she?' He glanced across the road.

'She's seventy-five,' said Eden. 'She told me that back in her day, you'd have dropped by looking for a cup of sugar by now.'

'A what?' He looked at her in astonishment.

'My sentiments exactly,' she said. 'But apparently it was a thing.'

'We don't have sugar in this house,' he said.

'In that case, it's just as well Elizabeth's been proactive and sent flowers instead.'

'She really bought them for me?' His expression softened. 'That was sweet of her.'

'She's old-school,' said Eden.

'Well, tell her thank you very much,' he said.

'I will.'

'Is she . . . your client, you said . . .'

'I'm her home carer,' explained Eden, and gave him a quick run-down on the reason she was with Elizabeth.

'Even here.' Now his expression darkened. 'Muggings in broad daylight! I thought we were getting away from all that, but everywhere's the same.'

Eden said nothing.

'Sorry,' he said. 'I'm a bit . . . Never mind. Anyway, she's OK?'

'She will be. I'm only with her for a few weeks, until she can look after herself again.'

The sudden buzzing of his mobile phone stopped him as he was about to speak, and he looked apologetically at Eden.

'Sorry,' he said. 'Got to take this.'

She nodded and turned away.

But when she turned back before opening Elizabeth's door, she could see that he was still standing at his, watching her.

Chapter 6

'He was surprised but pleased,' Eden told Elizabeth in answer to her immediate query when she walked back into the house.

'Did you find out anything more about him?' Elizabeth asked.

'No. I was leaving your flowers, not quizzing him.'

'Well, yes. But it gave you an opportunity.'

'Not really. His phone rang and he had to take the call.'

'That's annoying,' said Elizabeth.

'When you're better, you can drop over yourself, find out everything. He had a hint of an American accent, if that's any use.'

'It certainly makes him more interesting, though I'm sure Krystle will beat me to getting the full low-down. But – oh, Eden, I do wish I was out and about again. I'm not someone who likes sitting on her backside all day.'

'I get that,' said Eden.

Elizabeth sighed. 'It's the first time I've ever felt old. Properly old, I mean, not just a bit creaky. I was scared that thug would kill me and I kept thinking that the headline would say that I was a vulnerable elderly woman or a senior citizen or something.'

'You *are* vulnerable. *And* elderly. *And* a senior citizen.'

'Ah, but I don't usually feel that way.'

'I guess you don't,' agreed Eden. 'Anyhow, I'd have been scared of being killed too. And I'm half your age.'

'Less than half,' said Elizabeth. 'Didn't you say you were thirty-two?'

Eden nodded. 'So being anxious is nothing to do with being old.'

'I kind of get that,' Elizabeth conceded. 'But if it had happened when I was younger, I'd probably be better by now.'

'You wouldn't,' Eden said. 'Ruptured ligaments can take up to six months to heal. A tear like yours is a month or more. And yes, healing is slower when you're older, but you're doing incredibly well. As for your shoulder, you were lucky not to need surgery, so that's doing great too.'

'You're such a comfort,' said Elizabeth. 'And I mean that, I'm not being snarky,' she added. 'You know the right thing to say.'

'That's part of my charming personality.' Eden grinned at her and Elizabeth laughed, before asking Eden if she could ask her a personal question.

'Go ahead,' said Eden, although she was surprised by Elizabeth's suddenly serious tone.

'What happened to your husband?'

When Eden didn't immediately reply Elizabeth told her not to answer if she thought she was being too inquisitive.

'I bet they'll know about the widower's wife in five minutes,' she added. 'Yet you've been coming to me for weeks and I haven't wanted to ask.'

Eden took a deep breath and then exhaled slowly.

'It was a fire,' she said. 'He was a fireman and he was killed in a fire.'

'Oh, the poor man. And you poor thing!' Elizabeth was horrified. 'That must have been awful.'

'A building collapsed while he was close by. He was hit by burning debris. He was killed instantly.'

'I think I read about that in the papers.' Elizabeth frowned as she searched her memory. 'Was it a warehouse? Was another fireman badly injured?'

Eden nodded. 'Tony Marr. Andy's friend. He had a long recovery, but he's OK now.'

'I'm so sorry,' said Elizabeth. 'If I remember right, you weren't long married at the time, were you?'

'It was two weeks after our honeymoon,' said Eden.

'It must have been devastating.'

'It was.'

'Oh, Eden.' Elizabeth spoke into the silence that had developed again. 'I shouldn't have asked. You're right, I'm a nosy old bat and I should keep my big mouth shut.'

'It's OK,' said Eden. 'It'll be five years soon.'

'It doesn't matter how long ago it was,' said Elizabeth. 'Francis is ten years gone but sometimes I think of him and I still cry. At least he had a good long life. Your husband was taken too soon. That's unfair.'

'Yes, it is.'

'You told me about counselling. Did you have it?'

'Yes.' Eden nodded.

'Did it help?'

'I didn't think so at the time, but actually it did. Andy loved his job and he knew the risks. Although accidents like the one at the warehouse are incredibly rare. That's why you remembered it.'

'And your daughter?' Elizabeth's brow furrowed. 'Tell me to get my beaky nose out of your personal life if you like, but she must have been practically newborn.'

'Actually, she wasn't born at all,' said Eden. 'I was pregnant. I'd only just found out and Andy didn't know.'

'That's so sad.'

'He would've loved to have seen Lila,' Eden said. 'I would've loved him to have seen her. To have held her.'

'I'm really sorry,' said Elizabeth.

'Thank you,' Eden said. 'But listen to me, Elizabeth, it's a difficult thing for me to have dealt with, but I'm over the shock. I'm in the getting-on-with-life mode now. My family . . . well, to be honest, Andy's family, because I don't have much family of my own . . . but anyway, they've been amazing. They love-bomb me on a regular basis. Lila is adored. You don't have to feel sorry for me, truly you don't.'

'Have you . . . have you gone out with anyone since?' Elizabeth posed the question cautiously.

'No,' said Eden.

'Because you married young and you're still young,' Elizabeth continued. 'You could make a new life.'

'I don't want a new life,' said Eden. 'I'm fine the way I am.'

'I'm sure your husband—'

'Elizabeth, please.' Eden's voice was suddenly firm. 'I'm looking after myself and my daughter as best I can and in a way that suits me. The last thing we need is change. We've had enough of that already.'

'Of course,' said Elizabeth. 'I didn't mean to interfere. Or offer unasked-for advice.'

'You were being kind.'

'Intrusive is what I was being,' said Elizabeth. 'I forget you're not one of my granddaughters. I'm always offering them advice. They never take it.'

'I bet they do. They just don't tell you.'

'Perhaps.' Elizabeth nodded. 'Oh, I should've said, Tara was here and she downloaded books for me like you suggested. She made the font lovely and big and it's so easy to manage, although I'm not sure it's such a good idea.'

'Why?' asked Eden, glad that Elizabeth had changed the subject.

'Because it's so easy. I've downloaded loads. I know it's very old-lady of me, but I found ones I read in my twenties, like *The Country Girls* and *The Prime of Miss Jean Brodie*. I also downloaded a trilogy of thrillers by Alistair MacLean – Francis was big into him and he got me into those kinds of book too. Dick Francis is another. He was a jockey, so his are all thrillers around horse racing. Totally out of date now, of course, but great reads.'

'I've read *The Country Girls*, but not the others,' said Eden.

'I got Tara to download a couple of Gloria Steinems too,' said Elizabeth. 'I wasn't much of a women's libber back in the day myself – I didn't really have time to be, what with actually rearing a family – but those women were pioneers and I think I should know more. Because sometimes I think you girls today have taken some backwards steps.'

'Gee, thanks.' Eden grinned.

'Seriously,' said Elizabeth. 'Back then it was about equal opportunities and wanting to be appreciated for your brain

61

rather than your looks. But now you're meant to work as hard as men while looking great and having sensational sex all the time.'

'Elizabeth!'

'It's true,' she protested. 'I listen to Tara and Meghan talk and it's exhausting.'

'I'm not trying to have it all,' Eden assured her. 'I'm doing my best with what I have. And,' she added, 'I'm not interested in your new neighbour. Just in case you thought you could matchmake or something.'

'Darn.' Elizabeth made a face. 'I guess I'll have to come up with something else to keep me busy while I'm sitting here all alone.'

'Read your feminist books,' Eden told her. 'Then you won't want to matchmake at all.'

Much later, after Eden had put Lila to bed, she sat down with her pen and paper and began to write:

Darling You,

It's time for another update!

Elizabeth Green is a really nice woman. She feels sorry for me, but of course I'm used to people feeling sorry for me when they hear about my unfortunate past. I only told her about you, not about my parents. Otherwise it's too much for people to take in. Sometimes I wonder if I've made it all up myself. If I've really had a different life until now. They say that there are parallel universes, don't they? So there might be one in which Trudy didn't bring me to Dublin and I stayed where I wanted to be and everything turned out very differently.

And yet . . . if that had happened, I wouldn't have met you, and I can't even imagine a world where I wouldn't have met you.

Sorry, I'm rambling, saying stuff you don't want to hear. It's because I had a glass of wine when I came home. I don't usually drink when I'm alone in the house with Lila, but tonight . . . I just felt like it tonight.

Elizabeth wanted to know if I had anyone else in my life. She thinks I should rebuild and move on. Why are people obsessed with moving on? What's wrong with everything staying the way it is?

She doesn't know how much you mean to me. She doesn't know about our letters. She probably wouldn't understand. She thinks I'm alone. But I'm not. Sometimes I go upstairs and I read one of my letters to you and I know deep down that you've seen it and you're there for me. I'll always be there for you too. That'll never change.

I'm attaching a photo of Lila to this one. Isn't she gorgeous? And she's so smart too. Which one of us does she get that from, d'you think?

She was playing in the garden with Darragh last week and Michelle came out with her hands behind her back. She asked them how many sweets she was holding. Anyhow, Lila gives her this really thoughtful look and says, 'I can't see them. It would be a guess.' I thought I'd crack up laughing. Meanwhile Darragh kept yelling random numbers at the top of his voice. You'd think she was the ten-year-old, not him. (There were two sweets each. They were small. And she had a healthy dinner afterwards.)

I wish you could be here to share in her growing up.
I miss you.
I love you.
Forever yours,
Eden xx

Chapter 7

Petra's case was packed and in the hallway, but Petra herself was pushing Poppy on the swing in the back garden of number 4, allowing her niece to soar higher and higher so that eventually Rafe suggested that perhaps Poppy had had enough.

'Because she's just had lunch,' he reminded his sister. 'And I really don't want it to reappear.'

'I'm flying, Daddy!' squealed his daughter.

'You sure are. But I think your auntie would like to go home now.'

'You trying to get rid of me?' asked Petra as she gave Poppy another push.

'Never,' said Rafe. 'You've been amazing. I couldn't have managed without you.'

'I was happy to help,' Petra told him. 'And if you need anything, Rafe, anything at all, you only have to say.'

'You'll be back in a couple of weeks anyhow,' said Rafe. 'I'm sure I'll manage till then.'

'The only reason I helped with this house was so that I could have a pad to crash in when I come to Dublin.' Petra put out her hand and slowed the swing.

Rafe grinned at his sister while Poppy screwed up her face and told her father that it would be nice if Petra stayed.

'I'll be back soon,' she promised.

'I'll miss you.'

'I'll miss you too. But you won't really have time to miss me. You're starting your new school next week.'

Poppy said nothing.

'You'll love it,' Petra assured her. 'You'll make loads of friends.'

'I'm sure some of the girls on the road here go to your school too,' Rafe said.

'You could ask that woman Krystle,' said Petra. 'I bet she'd fill you in.'

'I could.' Rafe sounded doubtful.

'You need to reach out,' Petra told him.

'You sound like Jewel.'

Petra wrapped her arms around her brother. 'You can always reach me,' she said. 'Always.'

'Thanks.'

The three of them walked into the house. Rafe picked up Petra's case and followed her to the car. She popped the boot and he placed it inside for her.

She opened the driver's door.

'How is it that everything can change in a second?' Rafe ran his fingers through his thick black hair. 'You're fine, your life is sorted, you're happy, you have a family and then . . .'

'It's unfair,' agreed Petra.

'She won't remember her.' Rafe glanced at his daughter, who was turning handstands in the garden. 'Even now, there's stuff she forgets.'

Petra stayed silent.

'We have photos and videos and I make sure she watches them,' he said. 'All the same . . .'

'You don't want her to forget, but . . .' she hesitated before continuing, 'you don't want her to live in the past either. She's only six. She has to live her own life.'

'I know. I know.' He thrust his hands into his pockets. 'Being the responsible adult is harder than I thought.'

'Nobody tells you about this shit when you're young,' agreed Petra. 'That's why Mam was always saying that school days were the best days of your life, remember?'

'I didn't believe her,' said Rafe.

'Because they weren't.' Petra shook her head. 'If I had to rate the best days of my life, I'd say they were my college years. All those parties. All that fun.'

'And Mam going mad at you for staying out all night.'

'And you not getting into half the trouble I did because you were a boy.'

'Them's the breaks.' He grinned.

'Male privilege.' She smiled back at him. 'I'd better go. I promised her I'd drop in when I get back.'

'You have to give a report?'

She laughed, then shrugged.

'Take care.' He hugged her.

'You too.' She leaned out of the car window and waved at Poppy. 'Be good, sweetheart,' she said. 'Look after your dad.'

'I will.'

Petra gave her brother a final smile, then started the engine and eased the car out of the driveway.

*

'It's just you and me now,' said Rafe as he watched his sister turn onto the main road. 'We're in charge of everything.'

'Why didn't you get a job in Galway?' asked Poppy.

'Because the company I work for is in Dublin.'

'But you have an office in our house,' Poppy said.

'I'll be working in the house when you're home from school.' Rafe gave her the same explanation he'd given her twenty times already. 'When you're in class, I'll be in my office.'

'Why—'

'Please, Poppy. I'm doing my best here,' said Rafe. 'Meet me halfway, huh?'

'I'm six,' said Poppy. 'I'm the child. *You're* supposed to meet *me* halfway.'

Rafe was about to point out the definition of 'halfway', but he stopped himself. He sometimes forgot that, smart and logical though Poppy could be, she was still a little girl who'd lost her mother. And that he had to adapt to be two parents for her. Which was something he wasn't sure he was doing very well.

'How about we go get some ice cream?' It was a diversionary tactic he knew always worked.

'Cool,' said Poppy.

He locked the front door and took her by the hand. The seafront, with its wide grassy promenade, was a five-minute walk from their house, one of the big selling points as far as Petra had been concerned. 'Poppy will love it,' she'd assured him. 'It'll be home from home.'

The little girl chatted happily as they walked together in the afternoon sun. When they arrived at the row of shops that faced the prom, they joined the queue to buy whipped ice creams from the fish and chip shop that was already doing a brisk business.

'Why are they selling ice cream and fries?' demanded Poppy, as the aroma of salt and vinegar wafted towards them.

'Why not?'

'It's weird.'

'You used to have fries and ice cream at McDonald's,' he reminded her.

'That's different.'

But when he handed her the cone with its stick of Flake chocolate stuck into the ice cream, and its swirls of red and yellow topping, she licked it happily.

They crossed the road to the seafront itself, where Rafe lifted Poppy onto the low wall so that she could look down at the oily green water lapping against the rocks.

'That's where I'll be working.' He pointed across the estuary towards the low-rise glass and steel buildings of the East Point Business Park. 'It's not very far.'

'It's the other side of the water,' said Poppy.

'If our house was taller, you'd be able to see it from your window,' Rafe told her.

'I could see the sea from our house before,' Poppy said.

'I know.'

'D'you think Mom knows where I am now?'

'I'm sure she does.'

Poppy licked the ice cream around the Flake. 'I don't think I believe in it.'

'In what?'

'Heaven. Because Mom wouldn't go anywhere she couldn't talk to me from.'

'Good point.'

'Do you believe in it?'

'I don't know.' Rafe was lying. He didn't believe for one minute in any type of afterlife.

From her position on the low wall, Poppy slid her hand into his.

She didn't say anything.

Neither did he.

Krystle had seen Rafe load Petra's case into the car and watched as she drove away. She'd wanted to go out and speak to him immediately, but Saoirse had chosen that exact minute to tumble down the stairs, where, she sobbed, she'd been practising gymnastics.

That drama dealt with, she picked up her phone and composed a message to her selected group.

KrystleK
Ladies, our new neighbour seems to be on his own now. We must do our best to make sure he's coping. It's hard for a lone parent, especially a dad

The replies came quickly.

FiadhFoley
Absolutely. I'll pop by when I can

Anita
I'll drop some chocs to him next week

SandieC
Does anyone know what happened to his wife?

FiadhFoley
There's too many McConnells on Google to find out

HealeyLauren
I saw that girl who looks after Elizabeth knocking on his door. Perhaps she knows him?

Krystle frowned at the message from Lauren Healey and tapped a reply.

KrystleK
She? The girl or Elizabeth?

HealeyLauren
Elizabeth. He'd hardly know the girl would he? I bet Elizabeth sent him something. She did for me when I moved in

KrystleK
I left Prosecco on behalf of the residents' association

Anita
Prosecco! I only got a bottle of Pinot Grigio

The laughing emojis that followed Anita's message didn't make Krystle smile.

FiadhFoley
We've clearly upped our game since then!

AAtkins
How old is his little girl?

71

FiadhFoley

I saw her playing in the garden. She's a little dote. And he's very sexy, don't you think?

Krystle raised her eyebrows. It wasn't that she disapproved of Fiadh, but in the four years she'd lived next door to the house Rafe now occupied, she'd had three different live-in boyfriends. Admittedly, one of them had only lasted a couple of months, but Krystle didn't like the idea that there were transient residents of Sycamore Grove, and that there could be anything going on between residents appealed to her even less. She tapped out her reply.

KrystleK

I'll invite her for a play date with Saoirse. I wonder if she's going to the local school. I'll ask, and check if he's going to be part of the carpool

JacinthaHarmon

That'd be handy

FiadhFoley

Ah, you married women! Taking him under your wing and mothering him

Anita

I hope you don't have plans yourself, Fiadh Foley LOL

FiadhFoley

It'd be very convenient!!!!!

A clatter of laughing emojis responded to Fiadh's message. Krystle wanted to get the conversation back on track.

KrystleK
All joking aside, let's look out for him. And his little girl

Anita
Of course

SandieC
Definitely

JacinthaHarmon
Count on me

With the chat ended, Krystle put her phone back in her pocket. Nobody could say she wasn't a good chairperson and that she didn't welcome new residents. That was her job. She was happy to do it.

Ever since she'd started looking after Elizabeth Green, Eden had gone to Valerie and Sean's for lunch on Sundays. But although it was a convenient option, she didn't want it to become a permanent thing. She already depended enough on the Farrellys, and no matter how eager her mother-in-law was to be involved, Eden didn't want to take her for granted. Nor did she want Valerie to take for granted that she was always her fall-back. Nevertheless, she had to admit that today was enjoyable, because Amanda and Bruno had Skyped from their home in Lisbon, and everyone was recalling the day of the wedding, how much fun they'd had and how well everything had worked out.

'If only Andy had been there to see it.' Valerie glanced at the portrait of her son that hung on the wall behind her.

'He wouldn't have believed it,' Amanda said. 'He used to insist that I was too much trouble to marry.'

'The cheek of him,' said Eden.

Amanda laughed. 'I needed a man like Bruno to put up with me, though.'

'You sure did.' Her husband, behind her on the screen, smiled as he squeezed her shoulders.

'Anyhow, everything's going great here,' said Amanda. 'We're really happy with the new apartment.'

'I'm delighted to hear it,' said Valerie.

'Hopefully you'll visit us soon,' said Amanda. 'All of you!'

'Hey, hey, it's only a two-bed flat. It's not very big.' Bruno looked anxious.

'Not all of you at the same time,' amended Amanda. 'Eden, you could probably do with a break. You could come first.'

'She hasn't a minute,' said Valerie, as though Eden wasn't there. 'Her new client is very demanding.'

'It's only short-term,' said Eden. 'But it's full-on all right.'

'Oh, by the way, Eden,' said Amanda, 'did you see my email about the thank-you cards?'

'I'll start working on them tonight,' Eden said. 'No problem. And if you mail me the list of people you want to send them to, I can do that for you as well,' she added. 'It's a bit pointless posting them to Lisbon only for you to post them back.'

'Perfect,' said Amanda. 'I'll want some for our Portuguese friends and family, but I'll look at the list and let you know.'

When Amanda and Bruno finally finished the call, Eden told Valerie that it was time for her to go.

'Thanks again for lunch. And for everything,' she added.

'You and Lila both mean the world to me,' Valerie said. 'Andy would want us to look after you. Not that it's in any way a hardship, because I love you both so much.'

Eden hugged her, then repeated that she should get home, saying that she needed to do a bit of housework before starting on Amanda's cards.

'You're working too hard,' said Valerie. 'The home care was supposed to be something to do, not something to take over your life.'

'Caring for Elizabeth is only temporary,' Eden said. 'But if looking after Lila becomes a problem, I can always—'

'Minding my granddaughter will never be a problem,' Valerie assured her.

She walked to the door with them.

'I absolutely don't want you to fret about me looking after Lila,' she said as Eden unlocked her car. 'Sure what else would I be doing?'

'Knowing you, you've a million things on the go,' said Eden. 'You're one of those people who involves herself in everything.'

'Not so much any more,' said Valerie.

Eden checked that Lila's seat belt was securely fastened, then went back to her mother-in-law and gave her a hug before getting into the car.

Valerie stood at the door and waved as Eden backed out of the driveway.

She wished they could have stayed a little longer.

Eden had intended to drive straight home, but it was such a beautiful day that she turned towards the coast and told Lila that they were going to stay outside for a while. She parked close to the promenade and bought ice creams, which they ate sitting on one of the benches overlooking the sea.

'I like ice cream,' said Lila.

'So I see.' Eden took a wipe from her bag and cleaned the multicoloured sprinkles from her daughter's face. 'Do you want to run on the grass? I'll sit here while you do.'

'I want to walk on the wall,' said Lila.

'OK.' Eden used the wipe to clean her own hands, then held Lila's as the little girl scrambled to her feet. 'Slowly!' cautioned Eden. 'There's no need to run.'

The top of the wall was wide, so she was confident that Lila wouldn't trip, at least if she looked where she was going. Which, Eden admitted to herself, was the fatal flaw, because Lila was like Andy, utterly fearless, ready to plough ahead when other people would hold back. She remembered telling him that it would get him killed one day. Although in the end, it wasn't fearlessness that had caused his death. It was bad luck.

In the long months after the accident, there had been multiple investigations into what had happened. It seemed that everyone wanted to find someone or something to blame. Some sections of the media seemed to think that the fault lay with Andy or Tony, but Eden knew both of them had been sticklers for protocol. Andy had always done things by the book. But that didn't stop the speculation or the search for a scapegoat.

At first she read every single report, but she soon stopped. She stopped looking at social media too. The majority of people were kind, but the conspiracy theorists had used Andy's death to push their own deep-state ideas. She'd quit

Twitter and Facebook after a few weeks of it and hadn't gone back.

Valerie had also wanted someone to blame. But eventually she and Sean grudgingly accepted that sometimes accidents happened, although Eden knew that Valerie, at least, wished there was one particular person or moment she could say had been the cause of his death.

Even now, there were reports outstanding and additional reviews to be made. But Eden didn't want to know about them. Accidents were accidents because something unforeseen had happened. Like had happened to her parents. The day after the crash, she'd overheard Mac's mum say that if Matt hadn't postponed his annual check-up, his heart problem might have been identified and he'd have been on medication, which meant the crash wouldn't have happened. But when Eden repeated this to her aunt, Trudy sat down beside her and told her that not everything in life could be prevented. Who knew, she said, what might have shown up on a scan? Maybe her dad would've gone in one day and everything would've seemed fine, but the following day it might not. You can spend your life wishing that you'd done things differently, Trudy told her. But it's no way to live.

It had taken Eden time to come around to that way of looking at things. But now she did. Life was life. It was inherently messy. Inherently dangerous. You had to get on with it, like she was doing now.

She was so engrossed in her thoughts that she didn't hear what Lila was saying until her daughter tugged at her hand and repeated it. 'There's someone else on the wall.'

'There's always someone on the wall,' said Eden.

'She's going to be in the way.'

'I'll lift you down and put you back up again,' said Eden.

'She should get down. I was here first.'

'How d'you know?'

Lila hesitated.

'You've got loads of wall to walk on,' said Eden. 'Be nice.'

She arranged her face into a complicit parental smile as the little girl and the man holding her hand approached. And then the smile became one of recognition, because she saw that it was Elizabeth's new neighbour and his daughter.

'Hello,' she said as they drew near.

'Hello.' It seemed to take him a moment to place her, then he smiled. 'Elizabeth's carer.'

'Out for the day,' she said.

'Yes. Isn't it glorious?' He looked up at the cloudless blue sky.

'Utterly,' said Eden. 'That's why we're making the most of it.'

'Us too.'

'I'm Poppy.' The little girl jumped from the wall onto the promenade.

'Nice to meet you, Poppy,' said Eden. She swung Lila from the wall too. 'This is Lila.'

'I'm six,' Poppy said.

Lila hung back behind Eden.

'Say hello,' Eden told her. 'Don't be rude.'

'I don't know her,' Lila whispered.

'You do now,' said Eden. 'Say hello, it's nice to meet you.'

'Hello. It's nice to meet you,' said Lila.

'Do you want to play chasing?' asked Poppy. 'I'll probably catch you because you're small, but I'll give you a head start.'

'OK.' And before Eden had a chance to say anything, the

two girls had run onto the wide grassy space that separated the sea wall from the coast road.

'That was quick,' said Rafe.

'Nice of your daughter to ask her to play,' said Eden.

'She doesn't really know anyone yet,' Rafe said. 'So what's good from her point of view is finding someone she can boss around.'

Eden laughed. 'She'll struggle to do that with Lila.'

'You'd be surprised.'

'Truly. My daughter might seem shy at first, but she knows her own mind.' She looked quizzically at Rafe. 'Poppy's got a really strong American accent, but yours is less noticeable.'

'She was born there, but I'm Irish,' said Rafe. 'Rafe McConnell,' he added as he stretched out his hand.

Eden stared at him but didn't take it. 'Rafe McConnell?' she said slowly. 'Seriously? Rafe? Mac? Connell? Mac? You're Mac? From Galway? I'm Eden. Eden Hall. Do you remember me?' She suddenly wished she hadn't said anything, because of course it would be horribly embarrassing if he was Mac and he didn't remember her and she seemed like some demented woman who never forgot things.

But he was looking intently at her. 'Oh my God, Eden. You seemed so familiar the other day, and yet . . . It's been years, of course. I hardly recognise people I met months ago. But your eyes . . . those green flecks. They're so unusual.'

'Oh, Mac!' She was laughing now with the unexpectedness of it all. 'I never dreamed I'd see you again.'

'I was devastated when you left,' he told her. 'I didn't speak to my mum for weeks because she wouldn't let you live with us.'

'I was devastated too.'

'We have to . . . Do you want to join me for coffee? I'm sure there must be somewhere nearby, but . . .' He looked around. 'Are you with someone? Your husband? Would it be OK?'

'There's only Lila and me,' said Eden.

'There's only Poppy and me too,' said Rafe.

They looked at each other without speaking, and then Eden said that she'd love to have coffee with him but she wasn't sure about Lila and Poppy, who were chasing each other around the shrubs that dotted the grass. 'I doubt they'd want to sit still long enough.'

'We could have it here. While they're playing. If there's a takeaway place . . .'

Eden indicated the café across the road. 'They do takeaways. Mine's a cappuccino. I'll keep an eye on the girls while you go.'

Poppy and Lila were so engrossed in the game they were playing, neither noticed Rafe leaving to get the coffees. They didn't notice him return either and sit on the sea wall with Eden.

'So what have you been doing the last twenty-odd years?' she asked as she took her cappuccino from him. 'Gosh, I can't believe it's that long. But it must be. You wanted to be a footballer. I'm guessing you're not.'

He laughed. 'I ended up in biomedical research. I did a PhD in nanotechnology in medicine in Denmark, then went to a specialist facility in Seattle. When I decided to come back to Ireland, I looked around for something and it turns out that there's an amazing research lab in Dublin. I applied and got the job.'

'Wow. That sounds incredibly brilliant. The technology part I get, because you were always into that, weren't you?

The medical not so much. I remember you crying when you nearly sliced off your finger.'

'Because of the pain,' he said.

'Because of the blood.' She laughed.

'Fortunately I don't have to look at bleeding fingers,' he told her. 'Though one of my research areas is nanotechnology in wounds.'

'I'm good at wounds,' she said. 'I was an A&E nurse.'

'You did do quite a good job of bandaging my finger,' he recalled. 'I can't quite believe we both ended up in medicine. It wasn't really our thing back then.'

'We were kids,' she reminded him. 'Breaking things rather than fixing them was more our thing.'

'True.'

'I wrote to you,' she said abruptly. 'My first night in Dublin. I wrote pages and pages.'

'You did?' He looked surprised. 'I never got it.'

'Well, no. I didn't post it.' She made a face. 'It was tear-stained and crossed-out and utterly unreadable.'

'I would've liked to get it,' he said.

'I wrote again a few weeks later,' said Eden. 'I asked my aunt for money for a stamp. She wanted to know who I was writing to and I told her, and she said that you'd have forgotten me and that my life was different now and there was no point in looking back.'

'Jeez, Eden.' Rafe frowned. 'You were only what – nine? Ten? That was a bit harsh.'

'Aunt Trudy believed in telling it like it was. She was never one for sugar-coating anything. And she was probably right. We'd have written a few letters and it would've fizzled out and we would've felt guilty about it. Well, I would've.'

81

'I felt terrible that I didn't know where you were,' said Rafe. 'What my mum said was that you'd gone off for a great life with your aunt and uncle and that I had to let you go.'

Eden smiled faintly. 'It makes it sound like we were star-crossed lovers, doesn't it? But actually we just liked running wild.'

'And robbing apples from the orchard at the back of your house.'

'Oh, God, yes, those apples were lovely,' remembered Eden.

'Only because they were nicked,' said Rafe. 'I bet they were the same as anything you'd get in a shop.'

'Probably.' She laughed. 'It's really lovely to see you again, Mac. When did you start using Rafe, by the way?'

He'd been named after his grandfather, but in a school full of Micks and Kevins and Dermots, Raphael, or even Rafe, was too out of place. So from the first day he'd called himself Mac.

'When I went to Seattle,' he replied. 'It sounded more . . . more scientific. Mac was me as a wannabe United star. Rafe sounded more like a serious scientist.'

'Rafe it is so.' Eden smiled. 'I'm sorry you didn't make it to the United bench.'

'They didn't miss much,' he admitted. 'You could've made a ladies' team. You were good enough.'

'If I was, which I doubt, I wasn't committed enough. And of course things changed when I went to Dublin. Though it sounds like things changed a lot for you too.'

He nodded, but any chance they had of talking more about their personal lives disappeared as Poppy came running over and informed them that they were exhausted from their game and that Lila was ready to go home.

'Do you live nearby?' asked Rafe as they walked to the car park together.

'Artane,' she said. 'It's not as posh as Sycamore Grove.'

'Sycamore Grove isn't posh,' said Rafe.

'It kind of is,' she told him. 'Anywhere close to the seafront is considered posh around here.'

He laughed.

'Daddy works on the other side of the water,' said Poppy. 'You can see it from here.'

'Can you?' Eden looked towards East Point.

'Of course,' he said. 'It's . . . um . . . that glass building there. Looks the same as every other glass building, doesn't it?'

'It's very convenient,' she said.

'He works from home too,' added Poppy. 'For when I'm back from school. I'm going to school tomorrow.' Her voice faltered.

'Lucky you,' said Eden. 'Lila won't be going to school till next year, but she can't wait. You'll have a great time, Poppy. All the teachers around here are lovely.'

'Are they?' asked Poppy.

'Absolutely,' Eden assured her. 'You'll be very special because you're starting later than everyone else, so they'll help you out.'

'I hope so,' said Poppy.

'Definitely,' Eden said. 'I'm sure you'll make loads of friends, but I hope you'll stay friends with Lila. I know she's a bit younger than you, but it's nice for her to have a big girl friend.'

'OK,' said Poppy.

'Thank you,' mouthed Rafe.

Eden stopped at the green Fiat. 'This is me,' she said. 'Well, I'm sure I'll see you around.'

'Certainly if you're calling to Sycamore Grove every day,' said Rafe. 'Perhaps . . .' and then he broke off. 'I don't want to put you in an awkward position. I'm sure . . .'

'We're old friends,' she said. 'There's no awkward position.'

'Well, perhaps we could have a proper coffee one day next week? Catch up a bit more?'

'That would be lovely,' said Eden.

After they'd exchanged numbers, Rafe and Poppy walked to their Audi.

'She's nice,' said Poppy as she scrambled into the car. 'So's Lila, but she's a baby really.'

'You were very good to play with her.'

'It was fun,' confessed Poppy. 'Lila's a fast runner. When was her mum your friend?'

'A long, long time ago,' said Rafe. 'When I was a little boy.'

Poppy giggled.

'What's so funny?' demanded Rafe.

'You being a little boy.'

He grinned. 'I was a very good little boy,' he said. 'I did everything my mom and dad asked me.'

This time Poppy chortled.

And he laughed along with her.

Chapter 8

Petra lived in a one-bedroom apartment near Eyre Square, but instead of going straight there, she diverted to her parents' home a few kilometres away.

'Come in, pet,' said her mother when she rang the door-bell. 'How was the drive?'

'It's a motorway, Mam. You put your foot on the accelerator and go.'

Maggie McConnell made a face at her daughter and ushered her into the kitchen, where she immediately put the kettle on for a cup of tea.

'So how was it?' she asked when the tea was poured and she'd put a slice of home-made apple pie on a plate in front of Petra. 'How's he settling in?'

'Fine, I think,' said Petra. 'It's a lovely little road, very quiet and peaceful, and there's a residents' group too.' She explained about Krystle Keneally and the bottle of Prosecco to welcome Rafe to the neighbourhood.

'Well, there's posh,' said Maggie. 'It's far from bottles of Prosecco that boy was reared.'

Petra grinned and dug her fork into the apple pie.

'The woman who called around with it is like our last

neighbour, Selina Sheehy,' she mumbled through a mouthful of pie. 'All glamour and wanting to know everything about him.'

'Oh dear,' said Maggie. 'All the same, someone like Selina will keep a good eye on him.'

'As long as he doesn't keep a good eye on her,' remarked Petra.

'Is she married?' demanded Maggie.

'Yes, but that never stopped Selina, did it?'

'Indeed it did not,' agreed Maggie. 'I hope Rafe keeps his sensible head on.'

'You know he will.' Petra put her fork by the side of her plate. 'He's been nothing but sensible this last year or so. It might do him good to hook up with a glamazon for a while.'

'Petra O'Connell, I hope you're not suggesting your brother has an affair with a married woman.'

'I wasn't thinking of Krystle.' Petra's tone was appeasing. 'Just . . . someone. Anyone. He needs to have a good time. Take his mind off things. Start living again.'

Maggie McConnell looked at her daughter doubtfully. She understood what Petra was getting at, but she wished Rafe had stayed close by in Galway where she could've kept an eye on him herself. Because he was vulnerable right now. And she didn't want anyone, least of all a woman, taking advantage of him.

Eden was sitting at the kitchen table with her paper and pens in front of her, but instead of focusing on Amanda's thank-you cards, she was allowing her mind to drift back to her encounter with Rafe McConnell. When she'd arrived home with Lila, she'd gone upstairs to the junk room and spent ages searching for the photo she knew was there somewhere. It was one of them together, taken the year before her parents' accident. They were sitting side by side on the wall outside his house, both wearing shorts and T-shirts and giving a thumbs-up sign to the camera. Petra had taken it on her dad's old Polaroid instant film camera, and she'd given Eden the fuzzy black-and-white print to keep. Eden had put it between the pages of the diary she'd never bothered to write in. She'd almost thrown the diary away when she was packing to go to Dublin, but at the last moment she'd kept it.

She studied the photo again, thinking that her hair had been a total disaster area back then, but that Rafe had showed the signs of being the good-looking man he'd become. He was Rafe rather than Mac in her head now, a different person entirely to the boy she'd known in Galway. But he was a connection to her past, to a time when she'd been Eden Hall and her life had stretched gloriously ahead of her, full of promise and excitement. She hadn't believed, when Petra handed her the photo, that she'd ever lose contact with him, but she had to admit it was entirely possible, regardless of her move to Dublin, that it would have happened eventually. She knew childhood friendships didn't necessarily survive adolescence or adulthood; that was why so many people searched social media for old friends later in life, even if all reunions weren't necessarily happy ones. In her view, people weren't really searching for friends. They were searching for the person they'd once been themselves. That was why she'd never bothered looking for pages or sites relating to her life in Galway. She knew she wasn't the Eden she'd been before.

Nevertheless, meeting Rafe again had been surprisingly uplifting. She'd enjoyed talking to somebody who didn't know her as Andy's widow, but who held memories of a different Eden, a fun-loving, rebellious Eden, an Eden who hadn't retreated into herself after the double tragedies of losing her parents and Andy's accident, shedding friends and casual acquaintances, focusing only on the people closest to her. These days, excluding Andy's family, her friendships were limited to Tony and Angelina, Soledad Rodriguez and Fliss Grogan, her next-door neighbours, and Eilish Reed, one of the A&E doctors from the hospital where Eden had worked. But Angelina and Tony now lived two hundred kilometres away, and Eilish even further. She'd married an Aussie surgeon and moved to Perth shortly after Lila was born. Eilish had been on duty with her when Andy and Tony were brought into the hospital after the fire. She'd been the one to rush to Eden's side when she realised that her colleague was looking at her own husband on the trolley.

For months afterwards, Eden had kept reliving that night. She'd known immediately that Andy was critically injured. She'd wanted her training to kick in so that she could do something, anything, to help. But the truth was that even if there had been something to do, she'd been frozen to the spot, shocked at the sight of him. She'd watched him being taken away from her and had raced after the trolley, grabbing his hand and then leaning close to tell him she was pregnant. He hadn't responded. But she held onto the belief that somehow he'd known he was going to be a father.

The theme tune to the nine o'clock news made her realise that it was getting late and that she hadn't even started the thank-you cards she was supposed to be doing. She unscrewed the bottle of ink and picked up her pen.

*

Rafe had just finished unloading the dishwasher when the doorbell rang. He dropped the tea towel on the counter top and went to answer it.

A woman and a young girl around the same age as Poppy were standing on the step.

'I thought I'd drop by with Saoirse to say hello,' the woman said. 'I met your sister when I called around before. I'm Krystle.'

'Nice to meet you,' said Rafe. 'Thanks for the Prosecco, by the way.'

'You're welcome.' She beamed at him. 'We're here to invite your daughter to a play date on Wednesday afternoon.'

'That's very kind of you. She's finding her feet at the moment, so I'm not sure . . .'

'It'll be nice for her to have friends around her own age in the Grove,' said Krystle. 'Is she here?'

'She's in her room,' replied Rafe.

'Saoirse, you go and say hello to . . .' She looked enquiringly at him.

'Poppy,' he supplied.

'You go and introduce yourself to Poppy while I chat to her dad for a moment.'

Saoirse walked past Rafe and up the stairs.

'I'm sure you'll settle in in no time,' said Krystle as she made her way confidently to the kitchen. 'And we want to help Poppy settle in too. Where will she be going to school?'

'The local national school,' he replied. 'She starts tomorrow. It's all a bit nerve-racking.'

'She'll be fine. That's Saoirse's school. I'll make sure she looks after her. You'll be able to join our carpool and crocodile walks too, and that'll include her in the group.'

'That's very kind of you. I'll bring her myself tomorrow, though.'

'Of course. We only walk when the weather permits, but we're conscious of our children's well-being and the environment, so the carpool is good too. Hopefully you can be part of the rota.'

'If I can.'

His phone pinged. He picked it up and looked at the message.

Eden
I was going through some stuff earlier this evening and found this. Thought you might like it. Good to see you today

'Do you have friends and family close by?' asked Krystle as he smiled at the photo attachment.

'Not really. I'm from Galway originally, but I'm working in Dublin now. East Point.'

'Well, if there's anything at all you need, please don't hesitate to ask,' said Krystle. 'You'll find we're a very welcoming community here, and we're all willing to help each other when we can.'

'So it seems,' said Rafe.

'I can see you're busy,' said Krystle when he looked at his phone again. 'I don't want to intrude. If you fetch Saoirse, we'll be off. The play date will be from three thirty to six.'

'Thanks for asking her,' said Rafe.

He went upstairs and told Saoirse that her mum was leaving. The little girl got up from the blue beanbag she'd been sitting on and trotted down after him, followed by Poppy.

'You're Poppy?' Krystle beamed at her. 'I'm sure you and Saoirse will be great friends.'

She took her daughter by the hand and began walking down the path. Halfway to her own house, she stopped, turned back and waved.

Rafe wished he'd gone inside immediately instead of watching her leave. But, he thought, she was the kind of woman who was used to being looked at. She was tall and elegant and beautiful.

He went back inside and closed the door.

KrystleK

Hi girls, met our new neighbour and his daughter today. He seems lovely. Very reserved. Have arranged a play date with Saoirse

JacinthaHarmon

Did you find out much about him? He doesn't seem to have any social media accounts

KrystleK

He's on his own here. No friends or family

Anita

He might need some looking after. I'll drop by later in the week

FiadhFoley

I'll drop by too

KrystleK
Share any info. As the chairperson of the residents' association, it's important for me to know as much as possible about the people living here and it's unusual to have a man as a lone parent. We want to make sure his little girl is well looked after

FiadhFoley
His little girl or him?

Anita
LOL

Poppy was engrossed in her colouring book and Rafe was watching TV when his phone pinged again. This time the message was from the Sycamore Grove WhatsApp group, though he assumed it was sent by Krystle.

Sycamore Grove Residents
first of all, a very warm welcome to Rafe and Poppy @ No. 4. We hope you'll be very happy in our community. This message is to remind everyone about our Hello Summer BBQ next month. Fun and games for the children, and a barbecue for the adults (hopefully it won't rain). This year's raffle will be in aid of Cancer Research. All donations for prizes gratefully received. We look forward to seeing you.

Rafe conceded that even if he wasn't in a rush to mix with the rest of the people in Sycamore Grove, it was important that Poppy made friends. And it was good that the residents' association seemed to be so organised, though with Krystle in charge it was clear that it would be. In some ways she reminded him of Jewel, who'd coordinated their lives with total precision. Like Krystle, she'd organised play dates so that children could meet up in a safe environment. There'd been none of the casual wandering in and out of friends' houses that he'd experienced as a boy in Galway, when he'd spent almost as much time in Eden's house as he'd done in his own. And she'd done the same.

He realised that he hadn't replied to her earlier text, so he sent back a message saying that it had been good to see her too and that he was sorry he hadn't recognised her when she'd called with Elizabeth's flowers. But he couldn't blame himself. Eden had been a strong, sturdy ten-year-old who'd happily played football with the boys. The woman she was now seemed altogether more fragile, unlikely to kick a ball with enough force to totally wind you if you got in the way, as she had in the past. But her eyes, with those luminous green flecks, hadn't changed. He should have known straight away that nobody else in the world had eyes like Eden Hall.

Rafe had been devastated when her aunt and uncle had come from Dublin to take her away. He hadn't understood why his mother wouldn't let her stay with them. After all, he'd said, they were used to seeing Eden about the place. What difference would it make if she was there all the time? He'd tried to enlist Petra in his campaign, but his older sister had pointed out that they only had three bedrooms and that she already shared hers with their younger sisters and there really wasn't space for another girl. When he'd suggested that maybe Eden could share with him and Dommo, Petra had given him a withering look and told him not to be stupid.

He'd known it was stupid, of course, even then. But he hadn't wanted to believe that he was losing his best friend.

Yet when he didn't hear anything from her, he got on with his life. Malcolm Wilson, who lived a few streets away, became his new best friend and Rafe concluded it was better to have another boy as a best friend because you could laugh about things you couldn't laugh at with a girl. Their friendship had lasted through school but had fizzled out when they went to different colleges.

After that – well, he hadn't had a best friend but he'd had a lot of acquaintances, some of whom he was still in touch with through social media, although, he admitted, 'in touch' was pushing it; he saw their updates and occasionally liked their posts. Sometimes he even posted replies. But when he moved to the States and built a life with Jewel, he left behind what had gone before.

Yet here he was, back in Ireland, hoping that his daughter could have the kind of childhood he himself had had, while not being certain that kind of life even existed any more.

'Are you all right, Daddy?' Poppy abandoned her game and clambered onto his lap.

'Of course I am,' he said.

'Because you looked a bit sad.'

'Did I?'

'Yes,' said Poppy. 'I don't want you to be sad.'

'I'm not,' he said, and then, because he'd promised himself always to be honest with her, he added, 'I am a little bit, because I miss your mom. But I know she'd be happy that we have our new house and you're starting school tomorrow and that everything is great.'

'I'm scared about school,' confessed Poppy.

'That's OK,' Rafe said. 'Something new is always a bit scary. But then it stops being new and it stops being scary and you start liking it.'

'What if nobody likes me?'

'Are you a horrible, mean girl?' asked Rafe.

'No!'

'Do you have a cabbage instead of a head?'

'No!'

'Do you smell like the bottom of the trash can?'

'Daddy!'

'Then why would they not like you?'

'Because I'm new,' said Poppy.

'It's exactly the same for them,' Rafe said. 'They'll want to be sure that a new person is a nice person, and when they see how super-nice you are . . . well, they'll love you.'

'Sometimes people don't like other people even when they're nice.' Poppy rested her head against his shoulder.

'Sometimes they don't,' agreed Rafe. 'But mostly they do. So don't worry. Or, you can worry a little bit, but don't worry a lot, because I promise you everything will be great.'

'Is that a cross-your-heart promise?' asked Poppy.

'It absolutely is,' said Rafe, and hoped he was right.

He was reading the paper and Poppy was in bed when the doorbell rang again.

Another unknown woman was standing on the doorstep. He estimated she was in her early thirties, and her auburn hair was styled in a short pixie cut that emphasised her brown eyes. Her clothes were casual – stonewashed jeans and a plain white T-shirt. She was holding a rectangular food container.

'Hi,' she said. 'I thought I'd better introduce myself. I'm Fiadh, your next-door neighbour.'

'Hello. Rafe McConnell.' He held out his hand and she shook it.

'I've been working late so haven't had a chance to say hello before now,' said Fiadh. 'But I thought the least I could do is welcome you. I know Krystle has been around.'

'I got the WhatsApp,' said Rafe. 'I guess I've been formally welcomed into the community.'

'I thought I'd do an informal welcome. And give you these.' Fiadh held out the container. 'They're chocolate brownies. I made them myself.'

'That's very kind of you,' said Rafe. 'There's no need . . .'

'It's nice to be neighbourly,' said Fiadh.

'Well, so far everyone has been,' Rafe told her. 'Krystle left me a bottle of Prosecco on behalf of the residents, and she called again today to invite Poppy, my daughter, for a play date. Elizabeth from across the road sent over some flowers. Now you're here with home baking. I'm feeling very welcomed.'

'I heard about the Prosecco.' Fiadh grinned. 'That's more than I got. Clearly the residents' association has raised the bar for newcomers. Or maybe she thinks you're a Prosecco-worthy addition.'

'Perhaps she's re-gifting,' suggested Rafe.

Fiadh laughed.

'I believe you're a widower.' Her tone became more serious. 'I'm sorry for your loss.'

'Thank you.' Rafe liked that Fiadh had said the words in a kind but practical way. Not too heartfelt. Not too much sympathy.

'If there's anything I can ever do to help . . .' she said.

'We'll be fine. But thank you.'

'Well . . .' Fiadh hesitated. 'I guess I'll leave these with you.'

Rafe had started to say goodbye when it occurred to him that Fiadh was a nice person and perhaps he should try to be neighbourly in return. So he suggested she might like to join him for a cup of coffee and one of her own brownies.

'I thought you'd never ask.' She smiled broadly and followed him into the house.

She was a data analyst, she told him when they were seated at the living room table overlooking the back garden; mostly working from home, although sometimes with colleagues in the small office space the company leased near the airport.

'It suits me fine,' she told him when he asked how she liked home working. 'I'm not the world's most sociable person and my hours can be erratic, so not having to go out every day is great.'

'It was very sociable of you to drop in with brownies,' he remarked.

'I make the effort every so often.'

'Well, thanks, I appreciate it. Poppy,' Rafe looked at his daughter, who'd come into the room, 'what are you doing out of bed? You should be asleep. You have school in the morning.'

'I heard the doorbell. And voices.'

'This is our neighbour, Fiadh. She's brought cakes.'

'Ooh, really?' Poppy, who'd been eyeing Fiadh warily, moved closer to the table.

'Not now,' he said as her hand hovered over the container. 'But I'll put one in your lunch box for tomorrow.'

She gave him a disconsolate look. 'But you're having them.'

'Because we're grown up.'

'You should've put them on a plate,' she said. 'It's polite.'

'Thanks for pointing out my entertaining deficiencies.' Rafe gave her an amused look.

'What's deficiencies?' asked Poppy.

'Stuff you're not good at.'

Poppy nodded. 'You don't have practice at it,' she said. 'Mom was better.'

'Indeed she was.'

'I'm sorry about your mom, Poppy,' Fiadh said.

'It's because she died that we're here.'

'I hope you'll like it, even though your mom isn't here.'

'Mom didn't make cakes,' said Poppy. 'She made us eat healthy food. Dad still makes me eat healthy food. But he eats potato chips himself.'

'Crisps,' said Rafe. 'They're called crisps here.'

'Whatever.' Poppy shrugged.

'I should go,' said Fiadh. 'Let you get Poppy back to bed.'

'Dad, you need to take the brownies out of the box and give it back,' said Poppy. 'Otherwise Fiadh won't have somewhere for her stuff.'

'Oh, right.'

'Don't worry about it,' Fiadh told him. 'I have loads of containers. You can return it when you have time. No rush.'

'If you're sure.'

'I'm sure.' She stood up. 'I'll be off, so. Good to meet you. And you, Poppy.'

Poppy smiled at her but said nothing.

Rafe saw Fiadh to the door and thanked her again for dropping by. Then he went back into the house, where Poppy was putting the container of brownies into a cupboard.

'That was nice of her, wasn't it?' said Rafe.

'I think she likes you,' said Poppy.

'I like her,' Rafe said

'And you like Eden,' said Poppy.

'Well, yes. Eden was my friend.'

'So now you have two girlfriends,' said Poppy.

'They're not girlfriends,' Rafe said. 'They're neighbours. And now, young lady, it's back to bed for you'

Poppy said nothing. She washed her hands under the kitchen tap, then followed her father up the stairs.

Chapter 9

'I come bearing news,' called Eden the next morning as she let herself into Elizabeth's house.

'I have news too.' Elizabeth's voice came from the kitchen and Eden hurried into the room. 'I managed to come downstairs all by myself. It took a while, but I did it.'

'That's great, Elizabeth,' said Eden as she saw her client sitting at the kitchen table wearing a tracksuit. 'But don't you think you should've waited for me? To be on the safe side?'

'I'm fed up with the safe side,' said Elizabeth. 'I'm a lot better now and I'm pandering to myself by lolling around like an invalid.'

'You're not an invalid,' said Eden as she filled the kettle. 'You're recovering from a physical trauma. Did you have a shower?'

'No,' admitted Elizabeth. 'I wouldn't be able to manage that yet. I had one last night when Meghan called, so I just gave myself a bit of a once-over this morning.'

'It's good you feel so much better,' said Eden. 'Being able to come downstairs means you can cope with a bit more physio too.'

Elizabeth gave her a dark look. 'You call it physio, I call it torture.'

'Yes, well, not everything in life can be a joy.' Eden grinned. 'Would you like a cup of tea?'

'I certainly would,' said Elizabeth. 'What's your news?'

'Let's wait till the tea's made and I'll tell you all.'

Eden opened a cupboard and took out a couple of tea bags, which she put beside the red teapot on the counter. Unlike some of her other elderly clients, who preferred loose leaves, Elizabeth was perfectly happy with tea bags, but she insisted that the teapot itself was properly scalded and that the tea had brewed for at least three minutes before being poured.

Eden added the two Danish pastries she'd brought to the plate on the table. Elizabeth had already eaten her fruit, but she liked a pastry afterwards.

'So,' said Elizabeth when the tea had been poured and the two of them were sitting down. 'What's your news?'

'I know your new neighbour,' said Eden.

Elizabeth's eyes narrowed. 'Why didn't you say so when you dropped over the flowers?'

'Because I didn't realise I knew him then,' explained Eden. 'It was only yesterday, when we bumped into each other at the seafront and he introduced himself properly, that I recognised him.'

'Who is he?' asked Elizabeth. 'Someone famous?'

'No. Why should he be famous?'

'You said you recognised him.'

'Not from being famous,' said Eden. 'He was my best friend when I lived back in Galway.'

'A boyfriend?' Elizabeth's eyes widened.

'I was only ten,' said Eden. 'I wasn't thinking about boyfriends back then.'

'But now?' Elizabeth's eyes widened even more. 'Maybe you two are going to get together again and be a romantic love story. I love a romantic love story.'

'I don't think so, but it was really nice to see him again.'

'Did you find out more about why he's moved here? Or his late wife?'

'No,' said Eden. 'We're going to meet up for coffee, so I'll pass on any information then.'

'Unless Fiadh tells me first,' said Elizabeth.

'Fiadh?'

'His next-door neighbour. I saw her going into his house yesterday evening bearing gifts. Food, I think. I told you all the women of Sycamore Grove would cluster around him. Krystle was there earlier with her daughter, Saoirse. Fiadh stayed for more than half an hour. She's single, by the way, so if you want to stake a claim, you'd better do it quickly.'

'I'm not trying to stake a claim!'

Nevertheless, Eden was rattled by Elizabeth's information. She'd thought that Rafe would have had to wait to begin a social life in his new home. And that maybe she could help him. He was new to the city, after all, and she'd lived here most of her life. But it looked like Elizabeth was right and the neighbours were on his case already.

The parents at the school gates were mostly mothers. Rafe only saw one other man dropping off children, and he was tempted to go over to him and introduce himself, simply to bond with another male in a sea of women. But the man was standing beside the open door of his car, ready to drive away as soon as the children had walked through the school gates.

'It's Rafe, isn't it?'

He turned around at the sound of the voice behind him and saw a tall woman with dark hair that curled untidily around her face. She was dressed in a loose T-shirt and leggings, and was noticeably pregnant.

'I'm Jacintha,' she said. 'From number ten. I haven't had the chance to say hello.'

'I've only just moved in,' said Rafe.

'I know. I meant to call around and welcome you,' Jacintha told him. 'Is this your little girl's first day at school?'

'Yes.' Rafe's eyes were following Poppy as she walked up the path, alongside her teacher. The school didn't allow children to be accompanied to the classroom, even though he would've liked to do that for Poppy on her first day. But the head had assured him that Miss Conville would be at the gate to meet them, and she had been, greeting Poppy warmly and telling her that she was looking forward to having her in her class, where everyone was super-nice and friendly. Poppy had shot him a nervous glance before heading off with the teacher, but now she was walking confidently beside her, chatting animatedly.

'It's a lovely school,' Jacintha assured him. 'Cormac, my boy, is doing really well, and I have this one signed up for when she arrives.' She patted her stomach.

'When is it – she – due?' he asked.

'September.' Jacintha sighed. 'Not ideal, though I was getting desperate to have a second child, so I shouldn't complain. But a September birthday means she'll either be the youngest in her class, or, if I hold her back, at the older

103

end for starting school. I'd've preferred her to be in the middle. Also, I'm lugging this bump around during the heat of the summer. If we get a summer,' she added darkly. 'The long-term weather forecast is crap.'

Rafe felt himself relax into remembered conversations. The weather was always a safe topic. He made a comment about rainy Irish summers, and Jacintha nodded in agreement.

'Hopefully it'll stay fine for the summer barbecue,' she said. 'I hope you and Poppy will be there. It's a good opportunity to meet the neighbours.'

'Sounds fun,' he lied.

'It is. I hate to say that it breaks down on gendered lines, but of course it does. The women do all the organising, the men barbecue and the kids get overexcited.'

Rafe smiled.

'Anyhow, if there's anything you need, anything at all, don't hesitate to ask,' said Jacintha.

'Thank you.'

'You're welcome.'

He stood beside her indecisively for a moment, then said he had to get going. As he drove away from the school, he reflected that in his short time in Sycamore Grove, he'd talked to more neighbours than he had in his few years in Seattle. Of course, Jewel had been the coordinator of their social lives then.

He wished she was with him now.

Darling You,

It's been a busy week! Elizabeth is coming on in leaps and bounds and is itching to ditch her crutch, but I told her not to be silly, that she doesn't want to set herself back. As she's managing quite well now, I'll be doing mornings only from here on, to make sure she's had her shower and is dressed, because that's still difficult for her. Her granddaughters are staying with her this weekend, which she's very excited about. They seem to get on tremendously well – I guess Lila and Valerie will be the same in the years to come. Val is mad about her, and of course Lila loves her granny!

I've done all Amanda's thank-you cards, and even if I say so myself, they look amazing. I've sent some to her in Lisbon and am posting the rest for her here. I drew heart-shaped confetti along the side of the envelopes to pretty them up. And I have another job thanks to posting them to my Instagram page. It's become a really nice showcase for my designs, and it's good to think that people will pay actual money for them! It makes me feel like a proper creative person – some of the people who've liked my work are artists and calligraphers too. OK, that's the first time I've put in print that I'm a calligrapher. Because obviously I don't feel like a proper one. But last month I made more money from commissions than from the home-care agency. Which is a bit sad too, isn't it? That being a carer is paid so badly? Nevertheless, I'm thinking that if I promoted myself a bit more, I could cut back my carer's hours and spend time on calligraphy projects. It'd mean being home more for Lila. At the moment, she's spending far too much time at your mum's, and I really don't want to impose on her generosity.

My other big news is that I met an old friend. You'll recognise his name because I've told you about him before. It's Mac from Galway. You do remember me talking about

Mac, don't you? We lived on the same street and we were friends. He calls himself by his proper name now – Rafe. It's actually Raphael, but he hated that when we were kids.

He's moved in across the road from Elizabeth. I didn't recognise him when I first saw him (delivering flowers from Elizabeth, that's another story!), but I bumped into him again when Lila and I were walking along the seafront, and we remembered each other then. He's a widower, with a little girl a couple of years older than Lila. I'm wondering if maybe we can organise play dates for them, because they seemed to get on while Rafe and I were catching up. I don't know the circumstances of his wife's death, but I can relate to what he must be going through.

We agreed to meet for coffee sometime. It'd be nice to catch up with him. It's weird to meet someone from an earlier life I thought I'd left behind.

When she heard that I didn't have to be at Elizabeth's first thing on Sunday – Valerie obviously mentioned it to her – Michelle invited Lila and me to dinner and a sleepover on Saturday night. Lila is very excited, and so am I, because I'm going to sit back, have a glass of wine – or maybe two – and not be the one in charge for a while.

You used to be the one in charge.

I miss you.

I love you.

Forever yours,

Eden xx

Chapter 10

As Eden packed an overnight bag for her and Lila's night at Michelle's, she realised that Rafe hadn't texted her about coffee, and wondered if he'd changed his mind about meeting up again. She couldn't help feeling a little disappointed. Even though she understood the allure of putting your past behind you, Rafe was part of her happiest times. She thought about messaging him again herself, but she didn't want to appear as though she was trying to insert herself into his life. Besides, it seemed he had enough going on to keep him busy.

Elizabeth had kept her informed about the stream of visitors who'd turned up at his door over the course of the week. Krystle, again, with her daughter in tow. Jacintha, alone. Fiadh from next door, twice, also alone. Elizabeth's next-door neighbour, Anita, had dropped over with an outsize bag of rejected chocolates, and Sandie and Duncan, who shared the house at number 2, but not a bed, had called together on Thursday evening. Rafe had found time for all of them, thought Eden, but not her.

And now his sister was back. As she and Elizabeth were taking their walk around the Grove, Eden had spotted Petra and Poppy heading out in her red car. (Now that she knew that the woman she'd seen before was Rafe's sister, she recognised her. She'd always been slightly in awe of Petra.) She'd been tempted to cross the road and knock at Rafe's door while he was alone, but then thought that perhaps Petra had taken Poppy out so that he could work in peace, so she didn't.

She zipped the case closed and called to Lila that it was time to go.

Their welcome at Michelle's house in the costal suburb of Sutton was as warm as always. Lila's thirteen-year-old cousin, Iris, immediately brought her to her room to do her hair, while Michelle led Eden into the south-facing living room and handed her a glass of wine.

'How's it going?' she asked. 'Busy week?'

Eden accepted the wine gratefully. It was white and chilled, and with the glass in her hand and the early-evening sun coming through the living room's picture window, she suddenly felt as though she was on holiday.

'It's lovely of you to have us,' she told Michelle after they'd swapped stories about their week. 'Lila adores being with her cousins. It's good for her to have other kids in her life.'

'You know Iris is mad about her – she thinks of her as a younger sister. And even though Darragh is a ten-year-old boy, they get on really well together. He'll be home shortly,' Michelle added. 'He's at a friend's house at the moment.'

'It's unfortunate that there aren't many children of Lila's age near us,' Eden said. 'I arrange play dates for her, but I always have to bring her somewhere.'

'She'll make lots of friends when she goes to school,' said Michelle.

'I hope so. I don't want her to miss out. Andy and I never planned on having just one.'

'Don't worry, she won't miss out. Oh, yes, sweetheart, thanks.' Michelle nodded as her husband, Gene, walked into the room with the bottle of wine and refilled their glasses. Eden sighed with pleasure and allowed herself to relax completely. It was so lovely to have someone else take responsibility for everything.

Her sister-in-law was a good cook, and the meal she served up later was a testament to skills that Eden knew she didn't have herself. She could get by, but she couldn't create the tasty dishes that seemed no trouble to Michelle. Meantime, Gene kept their glasses filled and added male insight to the conversation he insisted was veering dangerously close to misandry.

'Of course we don't hate men,' said Michelle when he said this. 'It's simply that we're not blind to your flaws.'

'What flaws?' Gene held up another bottle of wine.

'In your case, none,' said Eden as she allowed him to refill her glass for the third time.

'I wish,' muttered Michelle, but her voice bubbled with laughter.

This was what she missed, thought Eden. The banter between husband and wife. The knowing how far you could go with teasing each other, the transition from laughter to love, to wanting to hold each other and kiss each other and . . . She took a larger-than-intended gulp from her glass, the wine went down the wrong way, and by the time she'd finished her fit of coughing, Iris and Lila had come in from the garden, where they'd gone after dinner to make daisy chains.

Lila crawled onto Eden's lap and snuggled close to her. Eden's heart filled with love for her daughter. And for her late husband. And for his family, who were looking after both of them so very, very well.

It was later in the evening and the children were in bed while the adults watched a movie on TV when her phone buzzed. She took it from her bag.

Rafe
Hey! Sorry I didn't contact you earlier. Manic week.

Eden
No worries

Rafe
I kept meaning to. But I didn't like to call late on a week night. I know you start early.

Eden
Only while I'm with Elizabeth

Rafe
I spoke to her this afternoon. We talked about you. She thinks you're Wonder Woman!

'Is everything OK?' Michelle's question broke into Eden's texting. 'You're not normally glued to your phone like that.'

Eden looked up at her. 'An old friend,' she replied. 'We haven't talked in ages.'

'Eilish? How's she doing?'

'Not Eilish. A friend who's moved to Dublin. We might meet up for coffee or something.'

'Oh, cool. That'd be nice.'

'Yes, it would.' Eden turned her attention back to her phone again and smiled as she reread Rafe's last message.

Eden
She's right. I'm totally Wonder Woman ☺

Rafe
I believe you both!

Eden
☺

Rafe
So how about that coffee? Would late-ish tomorrow afternoon work?

Eden
Sounds good

Rafe
Great. I presume you'll be bringing Lila?

Eden
If that's OK

Rafe
Poppy will like seeing her again.

111

Eden
That's sorted. Looking forward to it

Rafe
Me too. Take care.

Eden put her phone back in her bag and turned her attention to the TV again. But she'd completely lost the thread of the movie and couldn't follow the unfolding story. So she spent the next hour remembering the good times she'd spent with Rafe McConnell instead.

The aroma of sizzling bacon woke her the following morning. Her eyes flickered open and she sat bolt upright in bed before grabbing her phone and seeing that it was nearly ten o'clock. She pushed back the quilt and padded downstairs in her pyjamas. Michelle was standing at the kitchen counter buttering toast, while the rest of the family, including Lila and Darragh's friend Josh, were at the table, tucking into their cooked breakfast.

'You should've woken me,' said Eden. 'I would've helped.'

'You helped by staying asleep and out of my way,' said Michelle.

'I helped,' said Lila. 'I set the table.'

'Did you? Aren't you great? But why didn't you come into my room when you woke up?' asked Eden.

'Because I was with Iris.' Lila gave her mother a pitying look, as if to remind her that a cousin trumped a mother any day.

'Mum said you needed your rest,' Iris told her.

'She seems to have been right,' admitted Eden. 'Is there anything useful I can do now?'

'Not a bit,' said Michelle. 'Sit yourself down and I'll bring you a plate.'

Eden did as she was told, and a minute later Michelle put her breakfast in front of her.

'This is heaven,' said Eden. 'I should do it myself sometimes.'

'You haven't been able to because you've been going to your client every single morning,' said Michelle. 'It's good that you're getting a break.'

'I had a break for Amanda's wedding too,' Eden reminded her, as she dipped a piece of sausage into the runny egg.

'Yes, but all those early mornings get tiring,' said Michelle. 'So what's the story with . . .'

'Elizabeth,' supplied Eden.

'. . . Elizabeth now?'

'Much improved,' said Eden.

'And will you be assigned someone else when she's completely better?' asked Michelle.

'Oh yes,' Eden replied. 'But I won't be working the same hours. This was a one-off.'

'Good,' said Michelle. 'Because it's stressful and you don't need it.'

'Stressful for you and Valerie?' Eden gave her an anxious look. 'I asked her if I was imposing too much and she said no, but—'

'Of course it isn't too much. Mum and I both love having Lila. But we're afraid it's too much for you.'

'We? You and Valerie?' Eden was taken aback that her mother- and sister-in-law apparently talked to each other about how well she was coping.

'We agree that Andy wouldn't have wanted you to push yourself so hard,' said Michelle.

113

Eden frowned. How did they know what Andy would've wanted? He'd been very supportive of her nursing career, and nobody could deny that had had its stressful moments. He'd be equally supportive now. He'd be pleased for her. And exactly how often did Valerie and Michelle talk about her? What did they say?

'I'm not pushing myself,' she said. 'I like working as a carer. The people are usually lovely, and the situation with Elizabeth is an exception.'

'You matter to us,' Michelle said as she poured Eden a cup of tea. 'You and Lila. We want you both to be well and be happy. We know Andy would have wanted that too. You're part of our family. And that will never change.'

Eden hadn't expected Andy Farrelly to propose to her. Well, that wasn't entirely true; they'd talked in vague terms about their plans and dreams. He wanted to stay in the fire service and perhaps ultimately become a district officer or make a move into fire prevention. Eden was torn between being a clinical specialist and using her skills in research. They both agreed that at that particular moment they enjoyed being on the front line, but it might not always be the case in the future.

As they spoke of the future, Andy had looked at her and told her that he couldn't imagine one without her in it. She'd smiled at that and said that she was finding it hard to imagine life without him either.

They were overlooking the harbour at Howth while they talked, having walked as far as the lighthouse. Eden's attention was distracted by a trawler heading back to port, gulls wheeling behind it, and it took her a moment to notice that

Andy had taken a small box from the pocket of his jacket and dropped down onto one knee. When she realised what was happening, she stared at him in complete astonishment, but when he took out the ring and asked her to marry him, she threw herself into his arms with such force that they both nearly ended up in the harbour.

'And that would've been a disaster,' said Andy afterwards as they celebrated her 'yes please' in the fancy fish restaurant on the quay he'd booked earlier. 'They wouldn't have let us in here looking like drowned rats.'

It was, she thought as she gazed at the diamond ring on her finger (slightly too big, so definitely just as well they hadn't ended up in the water, or she might have lost it), the happiest day of her life.

And then they got married and she was even happier.

And then she got pregnant and she was happier again.

She wished she'd told him straight away.

She'd been waiting to set it up. To give him a surprise.

That had been a mistake.

Chapter 11

Rafe closed his laptop and stretched his arms over his head. He'd spent the past couple of hours working on a discussion paper for his upcoming virtual meeting with regional heads of the company in Germany and Sweden, and he'd finally nailed all the points he wanted to make. He liked working on Sundays, when there were no distractions and he was able to navigate his way through long documents far more quickly than during the week. Poppy was allowed to choose a movie to watch while he was busy, and if he hadn't emerged by the time it finished, she always came to find him.

He realised now that he hadn't heard a peep out of her in ages. He got up from his desk and called her name as he went down the stairs, then yelped as his bare foot stepped on a hair bobbin.

'What's wrong?' She stood at the kitchen door.

'Where were you? And why do you have to leave these on the floor for unsuspecting people to stand on?'

'Sorry.' Her look was anything but penitent. 'I was hungry, so I had some cereal, and I didn't make you anything 'cos you didn't even see me when I looked into your office.'

'Oh, sweetheart. I'm sorry.' Rafe held out his arms and she

ran into them for a hug. He carried her into the kitchen and winced. Poppy had helped herself to Rice Krispies (a trail of cereal from the cupboard to the table confirmed this); she'd also had a banana, a glass of chocolate soya milk (as much powder was on the floor as had ended up in the glass) and a slice of brown bread that she'd hacked off the loaf with a blunt knife, littering the table with crumbs. (She'd left the knife upright in the tub of spreadable butter, marking her achievement.)

'I'm glad you didn't go hungry,' he said.

'I can look after myself,' she said proudly.

'You sure can. But let's get things tidied up before Eden and Lila arrive.'

'Lila's coming to our house?'

'Yes. I told you earlier. Lila and her mum.'

'I didn't think it was today. Lila might want Rice Krispies too.'

'How about I make you both sandwiches?'

'OK.' She beamed at him, and Rafe's heart swelled with love for her.

He was both glad and relieved he felt this way.

He'd been very afraid he might not.

It was odd to turn into Sycamore Grove and not to park in Elizabeth's driveway. In fact, Eden felt so weird about it, and was so concerned that Elizabeth might see her car and wonder what she was doing, that she walked across the road to her client's house and rang the doorbell.

'Why didn't you let yourself in?' asked Elizabeth when she opened it.

'I wouldn't dream of walking into your house unexpectedly,' replied Eden.

'Fair point.' Elizabeth nodded. 'I could've been having a mad time with one of my many admirers, although as it is, I'm entertaining a female friend.'

'I don't want to be in the way,' said Eden. 'I was only dropping by to say—'

'Would you come in and stop waffling.' Elizabeth stood to one side, then smiled at Lila. 'Hello, I'm Elizabeth. I'm a friend of your mum.'

Lila, as always when she encountered someone new, was standing slightly behind Eden, but she moved forward to peep at Elizabeth from beneath her long dark lashes.

'I can't bend down and give you a hug,' Elizabeth said. 'I have a sore leg.'

'I have a plaster on my arm.' Lila held it out so Elizabeth could see it. 'I fell off my bike.'

'That must have hurt,' said Elizabeth. 'Did you cry?'

'No,' said Lila. And then she amended it to 'A little bit.'

'She was going too fast and crashed into the back wall,' said Eden. 'She was lucky to emerge with nothing worse than a few scrapes.'

'Ouch.' Elizabeth gave Lila a sympathetic smile and then ushered them into the kitchen, where a blonde woman around her own age was sitting at the table, a cup of tea in front of her.

'This is Helen,' said Elizabeth. 'We play bridge together. Helen, this is Eden.'

'I've heard all about you.' Helen beamed at her. 'If I ever throw myself over like Lizzie, I'll be asking for you to look after me.'

'Are you going to have a cup of tea?' Elizabeth turned to Eden. 'Helen brought scones too, if you'd like one.'

Eden shook her head and explained why she'd rung the bell.

'So I'm not really the reason for you being here. I'm devastated.' Elizabeth grinned. 'Though clearly very interested in how things with the hot neighbour will go.'

'It's only coffee and a bit of a catch-up,' Eden told her. 'Also, Lila is going to play with Poppy.'

'She might be my friend,' said Lila.

'I bet *she'd* cry if she fell off her bike,' said Elizabeth. 'Anyhow, Eden, I'll expect a full debrief on your date.'

'It's not a date!'

'Just remember, he's fending off the admirers.'

'We're old friends, that's all.'

'Is he an ex?' Helen looked interested.

'I knew him when I was ten.'

'Ooh, childhood sweethearts.'

'Truly not,' said Eden. 'I'd better go. How are you feeling, Elizabeth? Your leg? Your shoulder?'

'I'm grand. Would you not be worrying about me and think of your friend across the road instead. You don't want to keep him waiting.'

'She does,' said Helen. 'Always keep them waiting.'

Eden laughed and shook her head, then told Lila it was time to go.

'No need to see me to the door,' she said to Elizabeth.

'A full debrief, don't forget.' Elizabeth's eyes twinkled.

'You're incorrigible,' said Eden.

She'd only just lifted her finger from the bell when Rafe opened the door.

'I saw you pull up,' he said. 'And then I saw you go over

to Elizabeth and I thought that maybe I'd made a mistake about you coming to me.'

Eden explained why she'd gone to his neighbour as she and Lila followed him into the house. Poppy was sitting at the kitchen table, a large colouring book in front of her.

'You can colour in too, if you like,' she told Lila. 'Is that your teddy? He can watch.'

Lila looked at Eden, who told her that she was good at colouring and that it was very nice of Poppy to share her book. As Lila clambered onto a chair beside Poppy and put her teddy on the table, Poppy pushed the open book towards her and told her she could colour one page while she herself coloured the other. Lila took a yellow crayon and started on a drawing of the sun.

Meantime Rafe showed Eden his new coffee machine, an impressive piece of kit that Eden remarked wouldn't have looked out of place in a proper coffee shop.

'I know. It's great,' said Rafe. 'When you've lived in the home of great coffee, you become a complete coffee bore.'

'I'm more of a tea girl myself,' said Eden. 'My coffee machine doesn't get much use. I'm nearly ashamed to tell you that I'm quite happy with instant.'

Rafe shuddered and asked her if she'd prefer tea. 'Because I have a selection,' he told her, and took a polished box from a cupboard. 'Green, white, black, infusions . . . whatever you like.'

'Wow,' she said as she looked at the selection. 'It's actually like being in Starbucks or Costa.'

'Better, I hope,' said Rafe.

'I'm sure.' She smiled. 'Let me try your gorgeous coffee. You might convert me.'

'I will.' He poured some fresh beans into a grinder, and the aromatic smell enveloped the room.

'Can I have coffee too?' asked Poppy without looking up from her colouring.

'No.' Rafe's reply was automatic. 'But you can have some chocolate soya milk from the fridge. The ready-made stuff, not the tin. Also,' he added, 'you can have a mini muffin.'

'You said you'd make sandwiches,' Poppy reminded him.

'So I did.'

While Poppy went to the big American-style fridge and took out two single servings of soya milk, Rafe buttered some bread and, after checking that Lila didn't have any special dietary needs, added lettuce, tomato and some crispy bacon. He put the sandwiches on yellow plastic plates in front of the two girls, and told Poppy to help herself to a muffin, and to give one to Lila too.

'Petra brought them from a shop in Galway,' he told Eden. 'Not that she should've bothered, because I'm currently overwhelmed with home baking, but they're lovely. So please help yourself to one too.'

'Does she stay with you often?'

'She's got a lot of stuff on in Dublin at the moment,' explained Rafe. 'She was the one who found this house, so it's good she can stay here too.'

'Auntie Petra is cool,' said Poppy.

'Way more than me,' observed Rafe as he handed Eden her coffee. 'I hope you like it. We'll have it in the rather grandly named conservatory and leave the girls to their colouring,' he added. 'That OK with you, Pops?'

'Sure.' His daughter didn't look up.

Neither did Lila. She was intent on colouring too, her

tongue sticking out as she did her best to keep the yellow crayon within the lines.

Eden followed Rafe to the small sunroom at the back of the house.

'Nice,' she said as she sat down in one of the comfortable wicker chairs she'd already seen being unloaded from the removal van and stretched her legs so that they were in a shaft of light. She wondered where he'd put the Ligne Roset sofa.

'We're beginning to feel more settled.' Rafe sat opposite her. 'It was really weird at first, but it doesn't take long to get used to a place. And of course my neighbours have been very welcoming.'

'So I heard.' Eden explained that Elizabeth had been keeping a count of everyone who'd called in to him.

'Great.' He made a face. 'My life won't be my own with that woman across the road.'

'Ah, she'll lose interest,' said Eden. 'It's because she's stuck at home. But you'll have to behave yourself until she's completely better. No clandestine callers.'

Rafe laughed.

'So tell me all about you,' he said. 'What happened when you left Galway? How was life with your aunt and uncle?'

Eden filled him in, not dwelling too much on how lonely and out of place she'd been with Trudy and Kevin, and how guilty she'd felt when they'd lost all their money in the crash. But she emphasised how warm and welcoming the Farrellys had been, and how much she'd loved Andy.

'Lucky him,' said Rafe. 'And lucky you, too, to have found him.' He hesitated, and then asked what had happened to leave her as a lone parent.

'He died,' she said.

'I'm so sorry.'

'It was a long time ago,' said Eden. 'I'm over it now.' Even as she said the words, she felt a tightening in her chest. She was being disloyal to her husband. She wasn't over it. Over him. She never would be. But she kept her face impassive as she asked Rafe how he was managing as a single man himself.

Rafe was about to speak when there was a sudden slamming of a door, a noise from the kitchen and Poppy's voice saying hello. Lila came scurrying into the sunroom to throw herself onto Eden's lap, followed by Petra.

'You didn't tell me you were having company, Rafe,' Petra said as she stood in front of them. 'If you want me to head off again, it's no problem. Actually . . .' she gave him a sideways look, 'I could take Poppy and her friend to the park if you like.'

'Oh, there's no need for that.' It was Eden who answered, before standing up, Lila still in her arms. 'I should be heading off anyhow. It's been a busy day for us. But it's good to see you again, Petra.'

Petra looked at her in confusion.

'You remember Eden Hall?' asked Rafe. 'She lived near us in Galway?'

'Of course I do.' Petra stared at her. 'Eden Hall? I wouldn't have recognised you.'

'It's been a long time,' said Eden.

'You were just a kid when you left Galway,' said Petra. And then a stricken expression crossed her face as she remembered why Eden had left. 'Oh, God, that was insensitive of me. I'm so sorry.'

'It's fine,' said Eden.

'It was awful what happened to your parents,' said Petra. 'Really awful. You went to live with an aunt and uncle, didn't you?'

Eden nodded.

'And is this your daughter?' Petra's glance flickered from Lila to Rafe and then back to Eden.

'Yes.' Eden let Lila stand on her own two feet. 'Say hello to Rafe's sister, Lila. Her name is Petra.'

'Hello,' whispered Lila.

Petra smiled at her, and her voice softened as she said it was nice to meet her.

'She's my new friend,' said Poppy from the doorway. 'She's only little, but she's not bad at colouring.' She held up the page that Lila had been working on.

'That's actually really good,' said Rafe in surprise. 'How old is she again?'

'Four,' said Eden.

'Wow. It's very neat for a four-year-old. I'm not sure she gets that from you.'

Eden laughed. 'I know you remember me as a total tomboy, but apparently I inherited some artistic talent from my aunt.'

'What sort of art?' asked Petra.

'Calligraphy,' replied Eden. 'Not quite Picasso.'

'Of course!' Rafe exclaimed. 'The card from Elizabeth. I wondered afterwards about it, because it was personalised. I thought she'd gone to a lot of trouble for a new neighbour.'

'Card? Elizabeth?' Petra looked from one to the other.

'Will you get the card with the house on it from the shelf?' Rafe asked Poppy.

She left the sunroom and returned a few seconds later with nearly a dozen cards.

124

'Like I said, the neighbours have been welcoming,' remarked Rafe as he selected the one from Elizabeth and gave it to Petra. 'Isn't the writing inside lovely?' he asked.

'You did it?' Petra glanced at Eden, who nodded.

'I never would've thought. I remember you as a really stroppy kid who always looked like a disaster area.'

'Deep down, I still am,' said Eden.

'Oh no.' Petra shook her head. 'You've done the whole ugly-duckling-into-a-swan thing.'

'Petra!' Rafe's exclamation was horrified.

'Well it's true,' said Petra. 'Sorry, Eden, I didn't mean you were ugly before, but there's something entirely different about you now. You're—'

'Petra!' This time there was a warning in Rafe's tone.

'What?' She looked at both of them. 'Rafe thinks I'm a bit mouthy,' she said to Eden. 'But I'm paying you a compliment.'

'Noted,' said Eden. 'And now we really must go, but thanks for the offer of taking the children to the park, Petra.'

'I'm good with kids,' said Petra. 'None of my own, but I get on with the nieces and nephews. I spoil them and give them back.'

'You don't spoil me,' said Poppy.

Rafe snorted and Petra laughed.

'The best thing is that I build up so many Brownie points, they can never pay me back enough.' She winked at her brother.

'Dammit,' he said in amusement. 'I hate being beholden to you.'

'You're not.' Her voice softened and she spoke as though there was nobody else there. 'You never will be.'

125

'Rafe, Petra, we're going now,' said Eden. 'Thank you so much for the coffee. It was lovely to catch up.'

'Maybe we can do it again another time?' said Rafe.

'That'd be nice,' said Eden.

While Rafe brought Eden to the door, Petra sat in the chair she'd vacated. When he returned, she was sifting through the pile of 'Good Luck in Your New Home' cards he'd displayed on the bookshelf.

'It never occurred to me to give you a card,' she said.

'You've already given me a lot more than a card,' he said. 'I'm going to make another coffee. Want one?'

She nodded, and he went into the kitchen again, returning a few minutes later with a cappuccino for her.

'You know my preferences.'

'How could I not?'

'Anyhow . . .' She sat back in the chair and looked speculatively at him. 'Eden Hall. That's some blast from the past. Sorry if I barged in on something.'

'Don't be silly,' said Rafe. 'I couldn't believe it when I met her. We both have little girls, so . . . I thought it would be nice to catch up.'

'You used to trot around after her like a faithful puppy,' said Petra. 'And you cried for a month when she left for Dublin.'

'Maybe a week,' Rafe corrected her.

'What's her story now?' asked Petra. 'Where's the father of her child?'

He told her, and Petra winced.

'That's rough. Parents, husband . . . some people have all the bad luck.'

'She doesn't have a monopoly on it.' Rafe's jaw tightened.

'Are you going to bond with her over losing people?' Petra gave him an anxious look. 'I don't think that's healthy, Rafe.'

'I'm not bonding with her at all,' he said.

'Just . . . be careful. It's taken you time to get over everything. To be where you are now. Don't do anything stupid.'

'Oh, I'm long past stupid.' Rafe drained his cup. 'Don't worry about me, Petra. I'm never getting involved with anyone again.'

Once again, Petra drove to her parents' home after leaving Rafe.

'I wasn't expecting you today,' said Maggie. 'Is anything wrong?'

'Nothing at all. And I wasn't planning to drop by either. It's just . . .'

'What?'

Petra followed her mother through the house to the kitchen at the back.

'Rafe's met someone.'

'That was quick.' Maggie McConnell paused in the act of filling the kettle and frowned as she turned to her daughter. 'It's not the glamorous married neighbour, is it?'

'No, but . . .' Petra shrugged and Maggie sighed.

'Tell me the bad news.'

'It's Eden Hall.'

'Eden Hall?' Maggie's eyes widened. '*That* Eden Hall?'

'Yup.'

'You're kidding.'

'Clearly not.'

'How the hell did he meet her?'

Petra explained. 'Of course, it's good for him to meet people. To make friends. But Eden Hall . . .'

'They were inseparable,' Maggie recalled. 'And he was so upset when she left. Inconsolable, in fact. All the same . . .' She finished filling the kettle and flicked it on before turning to face Petra. 'They're both grown-ups now. I'm sure they've moved on.'

'She's a widow with a small kid.'

Maggie groaned.

'Exactly,' said Petra as she took some mugs from the cupboard. 'Another tragic backstory.'

'He'll be fine,' said Maggie with more conviction than she actually felt. 'He'll be absolutely fine.'

Chapter 12

Rafe and Fiadh both opened their front doors at the same time that evening in order to put out their recycling bins for the following morning's collection. She waved at him and asked him if he'd wait for her for a moment. He shrugged and did as she asked while she went back into her house, leaving her door open.

'I made extra.' Fiadh reappeared with another food container, this time filled with slices of rocky road, and held it out to him.

'You really don't have to go to the trouble of baking things for me,' said Rafe.

'I do it for myself. This was my first go with them and I didn't quite get the quantities right. You'd be doing me a favour by taking them.'

'In that case, thank you. If you hang on a second, I'll give you back your other container.'

'Sure.' Fiadh stepped over the low wall that separated their gardens and followed him to his front door. She paused on the step before Rafe, a little uncertainly, invited her in.

'Was that Elizabeth's carer I saw leaving your house earlier?' she asked casually as she sat at a bar stool in the kitchen.

'Eden? Yes.'

'Are you looking for someone to look after Poppy? I didn't think those senior care people did that.'

'Turns out I know her from way back,' replied Rafe.

'What a coincidence.' Fiadh tucked a stray lock of hair behind her ear.

'Yes. Ah, here it is!' He finally found the container he'd been looking for. Petra must have put it away, because he was sure he'd left it on the counter top.

'I believe Elizabeth thinks she's wonderful,' Fiadh said.

'I haven't spoken to Elizabeth, but I know Eden is a very capable woman,' said Rafe as he handed her the container. 'Thanks again for the brownies. Poppy loved them. And for these too. It's very kind of you.'

'Let me know what you think,' said Fiadh. 'I bake to manage my stress.'

'Oh?'

'My job can be pressurised,' she said. 'And with my mad hours it can get on top of me sometimes. My doctor told me I needed other things in my life.'

'Always listen to your doctor.' Rafe smiled at her.

'The problem with baking as stress relief is that it adds the kilos. So it's good for me not to eat them all.'

Rafe raised an eyebrow. Fiadh was tall and slim and he couldn't see a spare kilo on her at all. But he didn't say anything, and after a moment, she told him she'd better get home.

'I've a project to finish before the morning,' she said. 'Having the option to work from home is all very well, but it does mean you work twice as much.'

He nodded in agreement.

130

'At least it's just me,' she said. 'I don't have to take anyone else into consideration. It must be more difficult with a child. If you're ever stuck for someone to keep an eye on her, let me know. I did a lot of babysitting when I was at school and in college, so I'm happy to help out if you need it.'

'You're very kind,' said Rafe.

'No problem.' Fiadh got up from the stool. 'Have a great evening, Rafe.'

'You too.'

He saw her to the door.

He was about to close it after her when he spotted Elizabeth sitting at her front window. It took him a moment to realise that she was wearing enormous earphones. They made him think of stakeout movies where the cops were spying on someone.

He raised a hand in acknowledgement. She raised hers in return.

Elizabeth had decided to sit in the living room at the front of the house rather than her comfy armchair at the back, because Rick Flaherty was mowing his lawn and the sound was penetrating the earphones and interfering with her enjoyment of her podcast. It was about an unsolved murder, and she was very much enjoying the procedural nature of it. She'd even gone so far as to make notes. Not that she'd be able to solve the case when half the police force had failed, but she wondered if her conclusions would end up being the same as theirs. Because although the podcast labelled the case unsolved, the police had a chief suspect and weren't looking for anyone else. Elizabeth thought that perhaps she could be a modern Miss Marple, finding a solution when nobody else could.

When she glanced up again, she saw that Jacintha Harmon was walking up the pathway to number 4. She wondered at what point Rafe would tire of the steady stream of neighbours calling to his door.

She gave it another week.

She said as much to Eden the following morning.

'Isn't it odd that it's women who are usually portrayed as fragile or emotional or needing a man to protect them,' she mused. 'We're brought up on the fairy tale of the handsome prince coming to rescue us. Whereas in real life, it's mostly women who rescue men.'

'You might be right,' said Eden, as she unloaded the dishwasher.

'I rescued my own husband, but I never let him know.'

'How?'

'I met him when we were both working in the civil service,' Elizabeth said. 'I was in the typing pool. He was a higher executive officer. We thought they were really clever and important, and so did they, but that was a myth. Some were smart, of course, but the typing pool girls were equally smart, if not smarter.'

'You were one of the smart ones, that's for sure.'

Elizabeth smiled at her. 'But I knew I wasn't going to do much better than the typing pool. I was twenty when he came in with the stuff he needed typing. He was thirty-five.'

'Gosh, he was quite a bit older, wasn't he?' said Eden. 'Was it love at first sight?'

'Not at all,' said Elizabeth. 'It was him looking to see who he could get to do a rush job for him. He should've dealt

132

with our staff officer, but she'd gone home early with a migraine and I was the first person to spot him looking like a lost sheep, wondering who to ask.'

She smiled again as she remembered. Given the noise of the women pounding the keys of their Remington typewriters, it was unsurprising that Peggy Dawson suffered from migraines, and that nobody had seen Francis come in.

'He was looking for the quickest typist,' she told Eden. 'I had seventy-two words a minute.'

'Is that quick?'

'On a manual typewriter, with the keys sticking? You're damn right it is,' said Elizabeth. 'Anyhow, I told him I'd have it ready by four thirty. Which was fifteen minutes before he needed it.'

'And did you?'

'Naturally.'

'And he was so grateful he married you?'

Elizabeth laughed. 'No, but he bought me a Hermès scarf from Switzers.'

'Switzers?'

'A posh department store. It was at the end of Grafton Street. Where Brown Thomas is now. I used to press my nose against the windows and yearn to be able to buy the clothes there. Even a scarf was out of my reach back then.'

'So was the scarf a thank you for your work or an invite on a date?'

'A bit of both, I suppose,' said Elizabeth. 'We went for a coffee in Bewley's after work one evening. We had sticky buns and talked about the meaning of life.'

'Seriously?'

'Hey, sticky buns constituted a great date back then. Francis was a decent man. He felt he was being overlooked for promotion because he wasn't married.'

'Surely not.'

Elizabeth frowned. 'It was supposed to be by seniority – which was daft as well, because that meant people who were there longest got moved up the ladder regardless of ability – but being married did make a difference. I remember being surprised at a particular appointment, and then Peggy said that it wasn't surprising at all, the man concerned had six children to feed.'

'Oh.'

'Francis's career was stalled. He needed a wife.'

'You didn't marry him for his career, though, did you?' Eden looked at her in astonishment.

'Not entirely,' said Elizabeth. 'I liked him. He was kind and generous and . . .' She exhaled slowly as she gazed into the distance. 'I knew I could have a good life with him.'

'But you didn't love him!'

'In the end I did,' she said. 'And his family, who were desperate snobs, were proud of him.'

'And that's how you rescued him.'

'Absolutely. He was going nowhere until he married me, but twenty years later his photo was in the paper as part of a delegation to America for St Patrick's Day. He's standing in the Oval Office with Ronald Reagan and Charlie Haughey, and it was the proudest moment of my life.'

'So . . .' Eden spoke carefully, because she didn't want to insult Elizabeth, 'do you think your whole life was about helping him out?'

'Not a bit of it.' Elizabeth laughed. 'He gave me stability and children. I gave him ambition.'

'But couldn't you have done well in your job too? If you were a super-duper typist?'

'Not back then,' said Elizabeth. 'Whatever about getting Francis promoted, there was no hope for the women, especially the typists. It was like we could only do one thing. It's different now, and rightly so, but I did the best with what I had. And I was happy.'

'I guess we all make choices,' said Eden.

'You've had to make them too,' said Elizabeth. 'Different choices because of your circumstances. And they'll affect how you think in the future.'

'Of course. But I still won't be looking for anyone to rescue me. Even less to rescue anyone else,' she added.

'Yet that's what my neighbours are doing for your Rafe,' Elizabeth said. 'Trying to mother him and chivvy him and make sure he's in the best place to do well for himself.'

'He's not my Rafe.'

'You're the only one who knew him when he was younger,' said Elizabeth. 'And when we've known someone from child-hood, we know more about them than anyone. So he's more your Rafe than anyone else's.'

Eden shook her head.

'Regardless,' said Elizabeth, 'they all have their own motives for pitching in. Fiadh Foley is definitely on the lookout for a new man in her life, and she's been plying him with home baking. Sandie Carroll might be living with Duncan Gillespie, but it's only house-sharing and she dropped by number four with a big pot of something last week. And even if Krystle and Jacintha aren't sizing him up as husband material, they're keeping a good eye on him.'

'You're hilarious.' Eden smiled. 'There I was at the start

thinking that you were shaken and stirred by your ordeal, but all it's done is turn you into the Oracle of Sycamore Grove.'

'Not really.' Elizabeth shook her head. 'I'm simply making observations. And all I'm saying is that he's being well looked after.'

'Good. Because I don't have time to look after him,' Eden told her. 'I'm far too busy looking after myself.'

Darling You,

Elizabeth was in a funny mood today. She's obsessed about the fact that the women on her street are calling on Rafe every day. She thinks the single ladies are eyeing him up as husband material, as though we do that all the time when actually we have better things to be getting on with. (I've said 'we' there. I mean they, of course, because I don't feel that being a widow is exactly the same thing.) Mind you, it's unlikely Elizabeth would be eyeing him up if she was a younger woman herself – she's very independent, even if she did have to give up her job as a shorthand typist when she got married.

She told me all about her working life, and when we were having our tea afterwards, I remarked that shorthand sounded so old-fashioned and quaint. So she turned on the radio, took down everything the newsreader said, then read it back to me. It was unreal! The rows of symbols were lovely. I'm wondering if I can incorporate them into my calligraphy work.

I sent Amanda her thank-you cards and she's delighted with them. They're pretty amazing, even if I say so myself. I'm going to upload some pics onto my Instagram account.

Hopefully it'll lead to more commissions. I'd like to turn the calligraphy into something bigger, but the reality is that it's easy for people to do their own stuff on their computers, so it's probably always going to be niche.

I missed you more than ever today.

I miss you every day.

Forever yours,

Eden xx

Chapter 13

Eden hadn't seen Rafe since their coffee at his house, although he'd sent her a couple of cheery emoji texts hoping she was well. She'd replied with cheery emojis of her own, but wondered if, since they'd had the obligatory coffee, he'd rather not keep up their friendship. After all, she thought, as she walked with Elizabeth around Sycamore Grove's green, they were different people now, even if seeing him made her feel as she had when she was ten, as though the world was a happy place and that all she had to do was go out there and have fun.

'Are you all right, Eden?' asked Elizabeth. 'You seem distracted this morning.'

'I'm sorry.' Eden jerked her thoughts into the here and now. 'I was daydreaming. But,' she added, 'I was keeping an eye on where we were going. I wouldn't have let you trip or anything.'

'I know that,' said Elizabeth. 'I'm very confident when I'm walking with you.'

'Soon you'll be confident walking on your own,' said Eden. 'You'll be back to your day-to-day living in no time.'

'How are you getting on with your new clients?' asked Elizabeth. 'Are they nicer than me?'

Eden laughed. 'All my clients are lovely, but I'm only caring for one other person at the moment. He's a very gallant gentleman.'

'Ooh. Gallant! That's a word I haven't heard in a while. Why does he need care?'

'I can't discuss my other clients,' said Eden.

'You're so discreet.' Elizabeth made a face. 'I want gossip from you.'

'You wouldn't want me to talk about you to anyone else, would you?' asked Eden.

'No,' Elizabeth admitted. 'But I miss gossip. My best friend, Agnes, passed away in the first wave of the pandemic. We used to talk for hours every day. Helen's been really good to me, but I miss chatting with Agnes.'

'I'm so sorry,' said Eden. 'I'm glad you stayed safe.'

'As safe as I could be,' said Elizabeth. 'When they talked about it mainly being dangerous for old people, it's a bit of a dagger to realise that you're the old person they mean! Most of the discussions made me feel I was lucky to be alive at all, given that I was apparently low-hanging fruit that'd probably fall off the tree regardless.'

Eden couldn't help laughing, even though the older woman's annoyance coated her every word.

'You may laugh,' said Elizabeth sternly. 'But one day you'll be low-hanging fruit yourself. The trouble with young people,' she continued as she warmed to her theme, 'is that you think you know what old people are thinking. But you don't. You're making assessments based on how we're portrayed, not how we are. Because inside I'm the exact same Elizabeth McGrath who started off in the typing pool full of hope and ambition. And although my ambition has been blunted, I still want to go places and do things.'

'Like what?' asked Eden.

'A round-the-world trip,' replied Elizabeth. 'It's one of those things I've kept putting off, but maybe next year I could do it. It's a good reason to get fit again.'

'That sounds like a great idea. Who would you go with?'

'I'm not sure,' said Elizabeth. 'It was something Agnes and I talked about, but now . . .' She sighed and looked at Eden. 'Don't put things off, Eden. Grab life while you can. No sense in waiting.'

It was good advice, thought Eden, but not always that easy to follow.

'I could go with Helen,' mused Elizabeth. 'But I'd probably kill her if I shared a room with her. She's pernickety.'

'Pernickety?'

'Fussy,' amended Elizabeth. 'Maybe a few of us could go. My bridge club ladies, perhaps. I'll ask them.'

'D'you have many friends in the bridge club? I haven't seen anyone other than Helen.'

'Loads, but I told them not to call around while you were here. No point in having everyone at the same time. I like to manage my social life.'

Eden laughed. 'It sounds better than my own.'

They'd just finished their stroll around the green and were approaching Elizabeth's driveway when Rafe's silver SUV turned into the road. He parked outside his house and waited beside the car as they approached him.

'Hello, ladies,' he said. 'How are you?'

'We've been walking around the Grove,' said Eden.

'Lovely day for it,' said Rafe. 'I'll have to get back into walking myself. My exercise regime has been shot to pieces ever since I came back to Ireland.'

'I definitely need to exercise more too,' said Eden. 'Though in all honesty, running after Lila can be a good workout in itself.'

'So can running after Poppy,' agreed Rafe.

'How's she doing?' asked Eden.

'She's settling in,' replied Rafe. 'I was on carpool duty earlier, so she's had a chance to make friends.'

'They got you into the carpool pretty quickly,' remarked Elizabeth.

'It's for Poppy's sake,' explained Rafe. 'I want her to feel part of things. But Sycamore Grove generally has embraced us with open arms. I've already had a babysitting offer from Fiadh, and both Krystle and Jacintha have offered to help out if I need it.'

'Good to see them rallying around,' said Elizabeth with a sideways look at Eden. 'When I'm back to my best, you can give me a shout too if you need help at short notice. I'll be honest and say that it'd be more an afternoon thing for me. I go to bed early.'

'That's very kind of you,' said Rafe. 'Only after you're better, though.' He paused. 'You wouldn't like to help me out in another way, would you? Both of you?'

'How?' asked Elizabeth.

Rafe explained about the amount of baked goods that the neighbours had dropped in. 'Which is very kind of them,' he added, 'and I appreciate it, but it's far more than Poppy and I could ever get through, leaving aside the fact that I don't like her to have too many sweet treats.'

'I love sweet treats,' said Elizabeth. 'Though I'm not sure how the ladies will feel if you pass them to me instead of eating them yourself.'

'Just a few,' he said.

'Go on then.'

They followed him up the driveway and into his house, where he wrapped brownies and pieces of rocky road in kitchen towel for them.

'I really shouldn't,' said Elizabeth. 'But I absolutely will.'

'Same here,' said Eden. 'I don't often give Lila sweet treats either, but one or two won't harm her, and they do look fabulous.'

'Poppy's mom was into clean eating,' said Rafe.

'I'm sorry for your loss,' said Elizabeth. 'What happened to her?'

'D'you know, Elizabeth, I'll tell you some other time, if that's OK.'

'Of course it is,' said Eden before Elizabeth had time to respond. 'Come on, Elizabeth, I'll be late for William if I'm not careful. Let's leave Rafe to get on.'

Rafe shot her a grateful glance as she led Elizabeth out of the house.

KrystleK

Hi ladies. I see Elizabeth has made it in to Rafe's 🏠 She was there for an age. Her carer was there too

Anita

She's been dying to call over 😊 She sent him flowers

JacinthaHarmon

Of course, she's another single lady 😊😊😊

SandieC

ROTFL – I didn't know me and Fiadh had competition

Anita

And Fiadh has the advantage of being next door to the hot hunk

FiadhFoley

I'm just being neighbourly 😊

SandieC

☺

KrystleK

We should drop by Elizabeth's too and make sure she's doing OK. We were good when she first fell but when the carer started coming it didn't seem necessary

FiadhFoley

I bet Elizabeth will get all the gossip out of him ☺ I certainly haven't.

Anita

Me neither

KrystleK

He's very reserved

SandieC

I like that in a man 😊

JacinthaHarmon
How's the baking going, BTW?!?

FiadhFoley
It's very acceptable at number 4, that's for sure

Anita
So are the broken chocolates

SandieC
And my carrot cake

FiadhFoley
Jaysus girls, are we losing the run of ourselves or what?

SandieC
All's fair 😊

KrystleK
No cat fights, ladies 😒 I do hope he comes to the summer BBQ

Eden apologised for being five minutes late when she arrived at seventy-nine-year-old William McEnroe's home. Her latest client dismissed her tardiness with a good-natured wave of the hand. William was recovering from heart bypass surgery, but although frail, he was invariably in good spirits.

'Fit as a fiddle,' he said to every enquiry she made about his health.

And actually he was quite fit, despite the surgery. His main hope was to get back to playing golf, and he was assiduous in following both her instructions and those of the consultant. He was unfailingly polite, with a certain old-world charm about him, and never complained, even when he was struggling.

'You're doing great,' she told him now as she looked at his scars. 'Honestly, I've had younger patients than you who've made much slower recoveries.'

'I'm not recovered yet,' said William. 'Three months, the doc said.'

'You'll see a big difference before that,' she assured him. 'Have you been called to the cardiac rehab clinic?'

He nodded. 'I got a letter the other day.'

'Excellent.' She filled the kettle for their cup of tea. 'And your god-daughter is still calling by?'

'Yes. I don't want to put too much of a burden on her, though. She's really kind to drop in on me at all, and she has her own family to look after.'

'How about your son? Have you heard from him lately?'

'He called me yesterday. The timing is awkward.'

William's only child, Ethan, lived in New Zealand.

'Still, it's good to be in touch.'

'I wish he was closer,' said William. 'Not because of this aul' heart thing, just because it would be good to see him more often.'

'It's hard,' agreed Eden.

'Mustn't grumble, though,' said William. 'At least I'm still standing.'

'And you'll be standing for a few more years yet.'

She handed him his tea and a plain biscuit from the tin. 'Just the one,' she said. 'No sneaking more when I'm gone.'

He grinned. 'You're a hard woman.'

145

'I have them counted.'

She turned on the TV. It was tuned to Sky Sports. William was happy to watch any sport, and she left him settled down in front of it for the afternoon. Then she drove to Valerie's and picked up Lila before heading home. Lila had already had lunch, so Eden simply gave her milk and a banana while she made a sandwich for herself. Afterwards, she brought the little girl to St Anne's Park, where she ran around happily until she suddenly sat down and said she was too tired to run any more.

'Can we have a dog?' she asked when Eden picked her up to carry her back to the car.

'Oh, honey, we can't have a dog right now,' Eden said. 'We're out too much. It wouldn't be fair.'

'Other people have dogs.'

'Maybe sometime,' said Eden.

'Huh.' Lila buried her head in her mother's shoulder.

Eden wasn't sure if 'huh' meant 'OK' or 'this isn't over yet'. She had a horrible feeling it might be the latter.

After Lila had gone to bed, Eden spread her pens and inks on the kitchen table and got to work on her latest commission, another that had come through her Instagram feed. This time it was invitations to a gender-reveal party. Monique had sounded very excited about both her pregnancy and the party when they'd spoken over the phone.

'It's a small get-together,' she'd told Eden. 'Family and close friends. About twenty of us. So I want the invites to be personalised and lovely.'

They'd agreed a design and Eden had promised to get them to her before the end of the following week. As she worked on the cards, sitting at the table with one of her favourite playlists providing soft music in the background, she wondered, as she always did, about her client and her life, and felt privileged that her work would be part of a happy occasion.

Eden already knew that Monique's baby would be a girl. Monique hadn't been able to keep it to herself, even though she was holding out before telling her family.

'There won't be anything on the invites to spoil the surprise, though, will there?' she'd asked anxiously, and Eden had hastened to reassure her that the invitations wouldn't give the game away.

When her gynaecologist had offered to tell Eden the gender of her baby, she'd said yes, even though she and Andy had always agreed that they'd want it to be a surprise. But without him there, she'd needed to know. That night, she'd written him a letter to tell him they were going to have a baby girl. The following day, on three different occasions, she'd seen the name Lila. She'd been utterly convinced that Andy was telling her that that was the name he wanted for their daughter. And so, despite Valerie suggesting that perhaps Andrea, after her dad, might be more appropriate, Eden had insisted on Lila. Valerie then said that Andrea might be a good second name. Eden had given in on that.

Chapter 14

As Elizabeth's improvement continued on a daily basis, Eden's hours, which had already been reduced, were cut back a little more. Now she didn't come until her client was up and dressed, and she usually found Elizabeth sitting in the small sunroom off her kitchen, reading the paper on her iPad.

'Sitting in the sun helps,' said Elizabeth. 'We've been lucky with the weather lately. I think that's helped me recover, to be honest.'

'Quite possibly,' agreed Eden.

'The sunny days are having an effect on you too,' remarked Elizabeth. 'You seem much cheerier.'

'Goodness, I hate to think that I've seemed miserable to you.'

'It's not that,' said Elizabeth. 'It's . . . well, you're normally in great form, but you're very self-contained. As though you're holding yourself in. Lately you've been more open. Perhaps it's not just the sun.'

'Maybe it's that you're feeling better and everything seems cheerier as a result,' said Eden.

Elizabeth smiled and said nothing.

Eden was about make Elizabeth's cup of tea when her

phone buzzed with a message from Rafe to say that he was working from home, and as he could see her car parked outside Elizabeth's, he wondered if she'd like to drop by for a coffee when she was finished. She replied that she couldn't because she was going directly to William's afterwards. When she said this to Elizabeth, the older woman suggested that since they were about to have tea themselves, she should ask Rafe to come over to them. A couple of minutes later, he was at the door.

'More goodies.' He held out a food container.

Eden gave him an amused look and asked if they were his own home-baking efforts.

'Jacintha Harmon's,' he admitted. 'Salted caramel squares. If I ate everything that's sent to me, I'd be needing an intervention by now.'

'I'm not sure if my health manager will allow it,' said Elizabeth as he opened the container and told her to take one. 'I've put on a few kilos while I've been convalescing, and she's been talking to me about diet and nutrition.'

'Oh, nonsense,' said Rafe. 'Both of you can afford an extra kilo or so.'

'That's very pass-remarkable, young man.' Elizabeth gave him a stern look as she chose a square. 'You don't comment on women's weight.'

Eden chuckled as Rafe looked abashed.

'How are you getting on?' Elizabeth asked. 'Both with work and the neighbours?'

'Work is good, and you already know that the neighbours have been amazing,' he said. 'Poppy's made friends with Saoirse Keneally and the sisters from number 13 – Gemma and . . .'

'Colleen,' supplied Elizabeth. 'Both nice children.'

'It's good there are kids her own age around,' remarked

Eden as she poured tea for herself and Elizabeth and coffee for Rafe. She then helped herself to a salted caramel square, which was, indeed, delicious.

'Poppy got on well with Lila,' he said. 'Maybe we should set up a play date.' He gave her a rueful look. 'I can't believe I know all about setting up play dates now. They weren't a thing when we were small.'

Eden nodded. Back when she and Rafe were friends, there had been nothing structured about their leisure time. It had been entirely random, except for football matches and training sessions. And as the school pitches were beside the orchard that backed onto Eden's house, it was no big deal for her to get to them herself.

'Eden has a new calligraphy job,' Elizabeth said. 'It's another example of how times have changed.'

'Oh?' Rafe looked at her.

Eden told him about the gender-reveal party.

'They were popular among a certain set of moms in Seattle,' he said. 'Not that I ever went to one.'

'You didn't think of it for Poppy?' asked Elizabeth.

'It wouldn't have been my decision to make,' said Rafe.

Both women realised that his words had been carefully chosen. But it was Elizabeth who broke the silence by changing the subject entirely and asking if Rafe planned to be at the summer barbecue.

'It's ages away, isn't it?' he asked.

'Time will fly by. And Krystle will want to make dozens of lists so that she can control us all.'

Rafe laughed. 'She'll never control you.'

'Because I'm old enough to be her mother and she knows better.'

'Well, if I'm around, I guess I'll show up. I'm planning to bring Poppy to her gran in Galway for a week or two when school ends, and she might stay there a little longer. It's possible I'll tie that in with a trip back to the States. So it all depends.' He shrugged.

'Do you have family in the States?' asked Elizabeth.

He shook his head. 'It'd be a work-related visit.'

'All work and no play,' Elizabeth said. 'You need to make sure you have time off. That's one of the massive advantages my generation had over yours. Once you walked out the door from work, that was the end of it. Nobody could contact you in a million different ways. When I moved into my first house, I didn't even have a landline, and the public telephone box was a mile away.'

'There's a certain charm to that,' agreed Rafe. 'Though I'm not sure I could cope.'

'Me neither,' agreed Eden.

'In the spirit of all work and no play, though . . .' he looked at her enquiringly, 'I wondered if you'd like to have dinner with me at the weekend.'

'Oh!' It was Elizabeth who made the exclamation. 'How lovely! A date.'

'Well, not a date exactly,' said Rafe. 'Just . . . you know, dinner. Old friends catching up.'

'How many times do you two need to catch up?' demanded Elizabeth. 'Haven't you had the catching-up coffee already? Aren't you catching up again now? For heaven's sake, Rafe, ask the girl on a proper date.'

'Elizabeth!' cried Eden. 'Stop with the . . . Well, I'm sure we have much more to catch up on. It's fine.'

151

'Where were you planning this non-date?' asked Elizabeth. 'Somewhere fancy, I hope?'

Eden covered her eyes with her hands while Rafe laughed.

'I guess somewhere fancy is the only way of retrieving the situation,' he said. 'Fiadh mentioned that there was a nice restaurant near the seafront. How about there?'

'Fiadh was probably hoping you'd ask her there yourself,' remarked Elizabeth.

'I don't think—' Rafe began, at the same time as Eden said she'd be quite happy with a coffee and a bun somewhere.

'I did actually ask you to dinner,' he reminded her. 'So buns don't cut it. I could make reservations for Saturday evening. What d'you think?'

'She's dying to say yes,' Elizabeth said.

'Of course I'd love to go to dinner with you,' said Eden. 'I just have to work out the babysitting arrangements for Lila. My family are great, but I don't usually need them to look after her in the evenings. I'm not sure how that would work out.'

'Ah, well that's where I can help.' Rafe looked pleased with himself. 'Petra will be in town again and she's happy to babysit.'

'Doesn't she want to go out herself?'

'She was the one who suggested that I did,' said Rafe.

'With me?' asked Eden.

'She didn't specify anyone in particular,' he told her. 'But I thought of you.'

'It's definitely a date,' said Elizabeth.

'Call it what you like,' said Rafe. 'But it would be lovely to have dinner, Eden. There's twenty-odd years to chat about.'

Eden was still considering babysitting arrangements.

'Would we be out very late?' she asked. 'I'm thinking of Lila's bedtime . . .'

'If she's anything like Poppy, she'll fall asleep wherever she is. You can scoop her up and bring her home and she won't even notice,' said Rafe.

'Always providing you go home,' said Elizabeth.

'For heaven's sake!' Eden gave her a dark look that was, nevertheless, both amused and exasperated. 'I'm not staying over at Rafe's. There wouldn't be room. Not with the girls and Petra there too.'

There was a moment's silence as all three of them dealt with the thought that there would be plenty of room if Eden and Rafe shared a bed. To cover her confusion, Eden got up from the table and put the cups in the dishwasher, rearranging the crockery already there to make room for them.

'I have to go,' she said as she busied herself with putting a tablet in it and switching it on. 'Mr McEnroe will be waiting for me.'

'You haven't said yes to Rafe's dinner date yet,' Elizabeth pointed out.

'I kind of assumed it was a done deal,' Eden said.

'In that case, d'you want me to collect you and Lila on Saturday and bring you to number four?' asked Rafe. 'I'll text you the time for dinner.'

'Sounds good to me, Eden,' said Elizabeth.

'It sounds good to me too,' said Eden. 'I'll get back to you on the babysitting. Not that I wouldn't be perfectly happy with Petra doing it, but I need to have a think about what's best for Lila.'

'Poppy would love to have her,' said Rafe.

'I'll let you know,' promised Eden. 'Thank you so much for the invitation.'

'Thank you for saying yes.' Rafe smiled at her. 'Everyone – including Petra – has been on at me to get out and about. And now I am. With my oldest friend. So it works out all round.'

'It does.' Eden picked up her bag. 'Elizabeth, I'll see you tomorrow. Rafe, I'll confirm with you about Lila.'

She didn't give them time to say anything else, but hurried out of the house and got into her car.

Darling You,

A weird thing has happened. Rafe McConnell, the childhood friend I told you about, has asked me to dinner. He dropped over to Elizabeth's for coffee and he asked me then. She jumped in and called it a date, which I suppose it is in a way, even though I can't imagine going on a date with anyone. Why would I, when I have you? But the idea of dinner is seductive. Not seductive in a sexy way. Seductive in the way of going out as a grown-up without Lila in tow. It's not that I haven't ever gone out without her, but usually it's only for coffee with one of the neighbours. Or, at a push, lunch. I haven't been to dinner in the evening . . . gosh, I can't remember the last time. Was it when you and me and Angelina and Tony went to that place in Blackrock and we were chatting so much we missed our stop on the Dart and had to wait for one coming in the opposite direction? Or was it when you and I went to the little Italian off Dawson Street? Why can't I remember? Why is it so vague in my mind?

154

We had such good times, didn't we? I miss Angelina and Tony not being close by any more. Chatting via Zoom and Skype isn't the same.

Anyhow, I've said yes to Rafe because I really and truly want to get dressed up and sit at a table and have an adult conversation that has nothing at all to do about children. Having said that, perhaps that's exactly what he wants to do!!! He has a daughter called Poppy. Did I mention that before? She's six. He seems to be doing a great job as a dad but he might want advice on bringing her up here. Not that I have any to give him. I just muddle along, depending on your mum and Michelle and hoping to God I'm getting it right. Anyhow, I really don't want to talk about children on a night out. I want to go to dinner and talk like you and I used to talk, about all sorts of stuff. About movies and politics and science. Remember all the things we wanted to do together? And all the things we did. I'll never forget you trying to persuade me to go rock-climbing with you! It was the one and only thing I refused to do. I did the parachute jump (never again) and I did the parasailing thing too (equally never again), but I couldn't face climbing up a cliff with a rope. It was bad enough on the indoor wall. Funny, isn't it, the things that become the last straw. And funny too, though not funny ha-ha, funny sad, that it was work that killed you and not any of your crazy sports.

I'm telling you about Rafe's invitation because I wouldn't keep you in the dark about something like that. But there's no need to worry. Despite Elizabeth's best efforts to call it a date, it really is nothing more than friendship. And going out to a nice restaurant would be such a treat.

It's OK to treat myself, isn't it?
I wish you were with me right now.
Forever yours,
Eden xx

Eden was pleased she hadn't contacted Rafe to confirm Lila would stay with him, because Michelle texted during the week to ask if she'd like a sleepover with her cousins on Saturday night. Eden's reluctance with Rafe's suggested arrangement wasn't that she hadn't confidence in Petra's ability to look after two children, but leaving Lila with Michelle for the night was a much better option. It meant (and Eden admitted to herself that this was entirely selfish) that she could happily have a couple of glasses of wine, something she rarely, if ever, did when she was alone with her daughter. Which did make her worry that she had the wrong idea of what a night out should be, because she shouldn't need wine to make it great. But she'd been capti-vated by the thought of sitting at a table and someone pouring wine for her and the whole notion of being out with no strings and no responsibilities. If Lila stayed over with Michelle, that was exactly how it would be. So she texted her sister-in-law and said that Lila would love to spend the night at hers, and Michelle texted back to say that her brother Gavin's children, Jonas and Amber, who were ten and seven, would also be there, so Lila would have a great time.

Eden
Are we all dumping our kids on you? Are Stephanie and Gavin out on Saturday too?

Michelle
They've been invited to a reception at the Mansion House
🍷 Not sure exactly what for, but Steph is madly excited
and has blown a fortune on a Dries Van Noten dress in BT

Eden
Are you sure you don't mind having them all?

Michelle
You know me, I love when they're all together 😊 I'll be
doing Sunday brunch too, very casual, cold meats and salads

Eden
Sounds great

Michelle
Mum said you were busy with invites to a party. At least
having Lila out of the house will give you some peace and
quiet 😊

Eden replied with a thumbs-up. She had no intention of
telling Michelle that she'd be out to dinner. It wasn't that
her sister-in-law would mind, but she felt odd about saying
that she was meeting a man they didn't know. Michelle – and
the rest of the family – might get the wrong idea entirely.

Chapter 15

On Saturday afternoon, Eden went to the hairdresser, bringing Lila with her. Her daughter watched in fascination as Nastaszja mixed the colour for her mother's hair – Eden was having her rose-gold highlights refreshed for her night out.

'Can I have pink in my hair too?' asked Lila.

'When you're older.'

'I don't want it when I'm older, I want it now.' She made a face.

'Your hair is lovely the way it is,' Eden said. 'And look, I brought new bobbins for you. Nastaszja is going to cut yours and plait it for you and put these in. You'll be gorgeous.'

Lila looked at the star-shaped neon-green bobbles and gave Eden's plan a grudging acceptance.

'But I won't forget pink,' she warned.

Both Eden and Nastaszja had to cover their mouths with their hands to stop themselves laughing.

When mother and daughter were finished, they studied themselves in the mirrors and agreed that both of them were fabulous. Nastaszja had reprised the style Eden had worn to Amanda's wedding, although this time without the floral clips, which Eden thought were too fussy for what was really only a casual dinner. Meantime, Lila's plaits were perfect and her bright bobbins were visible from the other side of the salon.

'Thank you,' said Nastaszja as Eden handed over a generous tip. 'Have a lovely night tonight.'

'I'm staying with my cousins,' Lila told her.

'I hope you have a lovely night too.'

Eden smiled at Nastaszja, then bustled her daughter out of the salon. It was a fifteen-minute walk back to the house, and she stopped at the newsagent's on the way to buy Cornettos for both of them.

'This is the best day,' said Lila.

'And you'll have great fun tonight.'

'I know.' Lila licked her cone. 'You can stay with us if you like.'

'It's OK,' said Eden. 'It's cousins' night. Auntie Michelle and I will have another night.'

'Why is the sky blue?' As she so often did, Lila changed the subject completely, and Eden spent the rest of the walk home answering her daughter's increasingly difficult questions about the sun, moon and stars, and wishing she'd paid more attention in school.

'You're looking very glam,' said Michelle when Eden called to the house with Lila a few hours later.

'We had a girls' day,' explained Eden. 'We had our hair done and Lila got new bobbles, didn't you, pet?' But Lila had already run through the house to the back garden, where her cousins were jumping on the trampoline.

'It seems such a waste for you to go home and work with that lovely do,' said Michelle.

'Oh, I'm meeting my friend who's moved back to Dublin,' said Eden. 'So it won't entirely go to waste.'

'That's great.' Michelle smiled. 'You deserve a lovely night out.'

Before her sister-in-law had time to quiz her about the evening, Eden looked at her watch and said that she had to go. 'Because I do need to do a bit of work before catching up with the gossip.'

'There's nothing like a girlie gossip night to cheer you up,' agreed Michelle. 'Have a great time.'

'I will.' Eden didn't correct Michelle's assumption that her friend was a woman. 'Thanks again for taking Lila.'

'My pleasure,' said Michelle. 'And don't rush to come over tomorrow. Like I said, it's brunch. Have a lie-in.'

'This is the second time you've given me the opportunity of a lie-in recently,' Eden said. 'I don't want to presume . . .'

'You're not,' Michelle assured her. 'Besides, you've taken my kids from time to time too, don't forget. So don't worry about a thing, and don't do anything I wouldn't.'

'Of course not,' said Eden.

When Michelle had texted about Lila's sleepover, Eden's immediate response had been to let Rafe know. His reply had been a smiley face followed by an admission that the arrangement now suited him, as Poppy had also been asked to a sleepover, at Saoirse Keneally's. Which now left Petra free to have a night out in Dublin herself.

Rafe
And really, you were right about them maybe falling asleep, especially Lila, as she's younger. So it's probably best all round, although it would be nice for them to have a sleepover together sometime. What d'you think?

Eden's first thought was, in fact, that Rafe always capitalised and punctuated his texts perfectly. Very few people of her acquaintance did that any more, except perhaps her Aunt Trudy. She sent a reply saying that she was sure Lila would love a sleepover with Poppy and then suggested that she meet him at the restaurant, given that there was no need to call to his house first.

After that, she spent some time deciding what to wear for her first dinner out in a very long time. She knew that the seafront restaurant was modern and edgy, with a casual but up-to-date vibe. Which, she reckoned, as she surveyed her wardrobe, meant that nearly everything she possessed was in some way unsuitable. In the past, her go-to casual look had been slim-fitting jeans with a plain T-shirt and jacket teamed with colourful accessories; but even with her weight loss over the last few years, her jeans now were mom jeans, designed for running around in comfort rather than looking chic, while her jackets were functional rather than stylish. At least, she thought, she still had lots of cheerful jewellery.

Her newest item of clothing was the dress she'd worn to Amanda's wedding, but that was entirely unsuitable for this particular dinner. In the end, there really was only one choice, and that was her only other dress, the red V-neck she'd bought on her honeymoon in Sicily five years earlier.

She'd worn it once.

She and Andy had stayed in a quietly luxurious hotel outside Catania for their honeymoon, and she'd seen the red dress in the window of a small shop in one of the nearby streets. Even though it was very simple, it was beautifully cut and looked effortlessly elegant. With its uncomplicated design and pretty pearl buttons down the front, it looked equally elegant on, and even Andy, who had zero interest in clothes, had whistled appreciatively when he'd seen her in it.

'I've married the most beautiful woman in the world,' he told her as he put his arm around her and kissed her, much to the delight of the sales assistant.

Eden felt beautiful herself when she wore the dress to dinner in a small restaurant right on the edge of the sea. Soft lights were strung up over the outside dining area, candles flickered on the tables, and even the ubiquitous violin player walking between the tables was welcome rather than an irritation.

'You know I'll love you for the rest of my life?' said Andy as they walked barefoot along the beach afterwards.

'And I'll love you forever,' she said in return.

She wiped away the tear that had slid down her cheek at the memory. This was why she hadn't worn the dress since. It reminded her too much of a time when everything had seemed perfect. When she'd found her place in the world and was happy with it. And when the rest of their lives together had stretched out forever. Perhaps it wasn't the right choice for tonight after all.

'It's only a dress.' She said the words out loud as she took it from the wardrobe. 'A piece of clothing. That's all. And it mightn't even fit you.'

But it did. Perfectly. Just as it had fitted her perfectly then.

Although that night she'd worn her vibrant red hair loose around her shoulders, and she'd looked younger, prettier and completely in love. As she slipped out of the dress again, she told herself that it was good that her hair was a different colour, because she wasn't the Eden who'd walked barefoot on the beach any more. She was different too. And she could see that a dress was just a dress and not a symbol of the life she'd lost.

She left it hanging on the wardrobe door and went downstairs to work on the gender-party invites.

At 5.30, with the final card complete, she stopped working and put her pens away. She ordered a taxi for later, made herself a cup of tea and took her time about drinking it, then went up to the bathroom to put on her make-up.

Sitting in front of her mirror transported her back to the past again, although this time it was a very different past. She was in her teens and living with Trudy and Kevin. Having gained a reputation as being a bit stand-offish and studious, she'd been surprised when Mark Mason had asked her out. Although she'd been using cleansers and Clearasil for ages and had started using tinted moisturiser when she turned fourteen, Eden had never been one of those girls who crafted a perfect face for going out. Make-up was forbidden during school hours, but as soon as the final bell sounded, many of her schoolmates immediately took out cosmetic bags loaded with Rimmel, No. 17 and Maybelline. A few even owned Mac and Bobbi Brown. For her date with Mark, she'd gone to Boots and bought foundation, eyeshadow and lipstick. She'd been in her bedroom, trying out her look, when Trudy had walked in with a pile of folded school shirts and asked what she was doing.

'Making a mess of my face.'

'You're trying too hard,' said Trudy. 'Come here. Let me.'

Eden allowed her aunt to take charge. Whenever she was front of house at one of their restaurants, Trudy was always striking and glamorous, and Eden wanted some of that glamour for her first date.

The look Trudy did for her was more understated than Eden had expected, but was perfect nonetheless. Her aunt substituted the pink lip gloss Eden had chosen with a golden apricot of her own that exactly suited her colouring, and expertly smudged her eyeshadow to produce a dramatic smoky effect.

'Thank you,' said Eden as she gazed at her reflection.

'You're welcome,' Trudy said. 'Keep the gloss. Have a good time. Don't do anything stupid.'

Trudy regularly told her not to do anything stupid.

She never did.

Now, she remembered all the tips her aunt had given her as she applied foundation, eyeshadow, mascara and blusher. She finished with a distinctive carmine lipstick that she'd had in her make-up bag for years and that almost exactly matched the red of her dress. She was pleased with the result. The woman who looked back at her now was very different to the one at Amanda's wedding. Less ethereal, more decisive.

It's me like before, she thought as she appraised her work in the mirror. Even if my hair is the wrong colour.

She opened the wardrobe again and took out her sequinned shoes. Perhaps they were a bit dressy for dinner with Rafe, but they were the only pair of heels she now possessed. Besides, her first dinner out in ages deserved heels and sequins, and as it would be a car-to-bar scenario this evening, she could afford a little bit of discomfort to ensure she looked good.

The last time she'd worn this dress she'd teamed it with flip-flops.

They were still at the back of her wardrobe.

Chapter 16

Rafe decided to walk to the restaurant, but misjudged how long it would take and arrived twenty minutes early. He ordered a gin and tonic and sat at a window table overlooking the bay. When his drink arrived, he took out his phone and searched for Eden's Instagram. She really was talented, he thought, as he looked at samples of her calligraphy. She'd always been good at their school art projects, but he'd never taken much notice because back then he'd thought of art as a girlie kind of thing. And he'd never seen Eden as a girlie sort of girl.

His stomach lurched. Perhaps this Eden was very different to the Eden he remembered. Casual coffees were fine, but maybe dinner had been a bad idea. What if they had nothing in common any more? Intense though their childhood friendship had been, it was only a tiny sliver of their lives. Maybe a couple of hours would make them realise that they could never replicate that friendship. Maybe they shouldn't even try.

He closed the Instagram app and opened his own photos. Jewel smiled out at him. Different in so many ways from Eden, with her poker-straight blonde hair and her luminous blue eyes, yet with the same inner core of strength. Seeing her caused his stomach to knot. He took a deep breath and released it as slowly as he could.

He sensed rather than saw a movement at the entrance to the restaurant and looked up. Eden was standing there, radiant in red, her eyes seeking him out.

He stood up as she approached the table and kissed her on the cheek.

'You look stunning,' he said. 'Love the shoes!'

'Thanks. You've cleaned up well yourself.'

He was wearing jeans and a V-neck jumper in soft green wool, his go-to casual outfit.

'Would you like a drink before we order?' he asked. 'I'm having a gin and tonic, but they do cocktails if you prefer.'

'Why not?'

She chose a Bellini.

'I feel like that moment on the last day at school,' she said after she'd had a sip. 'You know, when you've been let loose and you've nothing to worry about.'

He grinned. 'I remember that feeling. Being free and irresponsible and not having a care in the world.'

Eden raised her glass. 'To not having a care in the world.'

He clinked his own glass against hers.

'Not a care in the world.'

Their conversation over dinner was light-hearted and general, touching on their personal lives but never delving too deeply. Eden appreciated that as much as Rafe. And although she would have liked to ask him more about the loss of his wife, she knew from experience that sometimes you didn't want to talk about it. To relive it. To go through it all again so that the person you were with could feel good about asking and letting you share your feelings. Sometimes you wanted to keep it all to yourself.

'I'm still surprised we both ended up in medicine,' she remarked when they reached the coffee stage. 'Obviously very different career paths and specialities, but you're inventing ways of helping to treat people, and in my nursing life, I'd be trying to actually put them into practice. Not that I ever expected to inject anyone with a nanobot or whatever,' she added.

He laughed. 'But when you do, I'll be the one to invent it.'

'I've left that behind,' she told him. 'I'm happy doing home care instead.'

'Elizabeth's a pet,' he said.

'She's lovely,' agreed Eden. 'Not everyone's as easy-going, but I enjoy what I do now.'

'Do you miss nursing?'

'Sometimes,' she admitted. 'But this way I can choose my hours, so it's a much better set-up for me. And I'm lucky with my in-laws, of course. Valerie, Andy's mum, is besotted with Lila, and Michelle, his sister, is great with her too.'

'And your own family?' he asked.

She looked at him in confusion.

'I meant your aunt and uncle.'

Eden replied that they now lived in the south of France and didn't really keep in touch.

'That's a shame,' said Rafe. 'It would be nice for you to visit.'

'Oh, I doubt they'd want me there,' said Eden. 'They're living their lives.'

'Nevertheless . . .'

'You never know, but it's not high on my priority list,' she said.

'Touchy subject. Sorry.'

'Ah, not really. It's just me being prickly. They did their best and I . . . well, I didn't want to be with them, so I made it harder than it needed to be. We've never quite overcome that.'

'You were a child,' he said. 'It was a difficult time for you.'

'I could've made more of an effort.'

'Do you really believe that?'

'With hindsight, yes. But they weren't easy to live with, and when I met Andy and his family, no effort was needed at all to get on with them, so I definitely thought the fault was entirely with Trudy and Kevin. I can appreciate the sacrifices they made for me now, but it's too late to be close.'

'Fair enough.' He nodded at their empty glasses. 'Would you like another drink before we go?'

'It's been wonderful to have a guilt-free evening with alcohol,' she said. 'But I'm done now, thanks.'

He nodded, then signalled for the bill.

There was a short debate about paying, but Rafe insisted that tonight was his treat and eventually Eden conceded.

'Will I order a cab, or would you like to walk along the seafront?' he asked when they were outside. 'It's a lovely evening.'

The sky was clear and not yet completely dark, while the hint of summer breeze was warm. It seemed a shame not to enjoy it. Eden looked down at her high heels.

'Oh,' said Rafe. 'Maybe not.'

She smiled, then opened her bag and took out the flip-flops she'd put in earlier.

'Just in case,' she said as she slipped them on.

They turned towards Howth and began to walk, Eden

169

holding her sequinned shoes by their narrow heels. There were lots of other people out that evening, many walking or running along the prom, while groups of teens and young adults were sprawled on the grass. Their laughter and conversation carried on the air, but Eden and Rafe themselves didn't talk. The silence between them was an easy one, and both were lost in their own thoughts.

It wasn't long before they reached the wooden bridge at Dollymount.

Rafe stopped and looked at her enquiringly. 'Can we walk along here? I don't know where it goes.'

'To a lighthouse and the beach,' she said. 'Mad busy during the summer, of course. There's a golf course too,' she added, and then grinned at him. 'But at night people generally come here to . . . well, you know.'

'Oh,' he said. 'Right. Let's leave it till daylight in that case.'

'Good idea.' She looked along the coast road. 'I'll bag a taxi. It's time to get home anyhow.'

'I'll use my app.'

'Don't bother. There are always loads – here!' She stuck out her hand as she saw the green taxi light on the top of an approaching car. It slowed down.

'Will we share?' asked Rafe. 'The driver can drop you off first, then me.'

'If you don't mind a little detour, that'd be great, thanks.'

He got into the back seat beside her and she gave her address to the driver.

They sat in companionable silence for the fifteen minutes it took to reach her house. As the car pulled up outside, she turned to him.

'I had the most fabulous time,' she said. 'Would you like to come in for a nightcap?' She made the offer without thinking, asking him as a friend, but almost immediately realised how it could be misinterpreted. But he said yes before she could change her mind.

Eden's home was a small house in the middle of a terrace, opposite a row of busy local shops. The terrace itself looked like an afterthought, squashed in later than the larger houses nearby, as though a builder had suddenly realised he could use an awkward piece of leftover land more profitably. But the tiny gardens were all well maintained, and a small wreath of dried summer flowers circled the brass knocker on Eden's front door.

'Come in.' She unlocked the door and deactivated the alarm.

The layout of the house was compact, with a short hallway leading to a kitchen-diner at the end. The hall was painted in a muted green, with grey floor tiles that continued into the kitchen. Rafe was surprised to see that it and the dining area were decorated in bright primary colours, the most prominent being a cheerful primrose yellow

'Yellow makes the space feel bigger,' said Eden when he commented on how uplifting the colours were. 'Plus we get the sun here in the morning, so it's lovely to come down to. In the evening, I open the doors to the living room and let more light in that way. But if it's a dark and gloomy day, the yellow instantly cheers me up.' She smiled at him. 'What would you like? Wine? Beer? Coffee? Instant, I'm afraid; I don't have a super-duper machine like yours. I'm having water myself,' she added. 'I need to rehydrate or I'll be hopeless in the morning. I'm out of practice at nights out.'

171

He smiled. 'Me too. But if you have a non-A beer . . .'
He broke off. 'Probably not. Don't worry.'

'It's not a worry. My cellar is stocked with non-A drinks.'
She opened the fridge and handed him a Heineken Zero,
then filled a glass with sparkling water for herself. He walked
from the diner into the living room. The decor here was
more muted, although Eden had chosen a two-seater sofa
and a tub chair in different shades of pink as a contrast to
the neutral walls. Wool throws and cushions in more shades
of pink and rose were scattered on the sofa, while the walls
were covered in paintings and photographs. Only one of
them, as far as Rafe could see, was of Eden and her husband,
and that was a wedding photo, hung next to the window.

'It was a lovely day,' she said as she stood beside him.
'Fabulous weather.'

'He looks like a nice guy.' Rafe turned to her. 'Which is
a daft thing to say, isn't it? Making assumptions about someone
because of how they look. But . . .'

'We all do that,' Eden said. 'The moment we meet. First
impressions count. Mind you, my first impression of Andy
wasn't quite as heroic as he turned out to be.'

She told him about their meeting at the A&E unit, and
their subsequent dates, and of how she'd fallen in love with
him almost straight away.

'Sometimes I think I was looking for love,' she said. 'You
know, I wanted the right person to come along and . . . oh,
I dunno, protect me or whatever. I was on my own in Dublin.
I had friends but nobody close. I missed having someone I
could share things with. Someone like you.'

'I wish you'd written to me,' said Rafe.

'Aunt Trudy was right,' said Eden. 'At some point you'd

have got bored with the letters, especially as I probably would've done nothing but moan.'

'I don't think so,' said Rafe.

'Who knows?' Eden shrugged. 'Better that we have great memories of our friendship now. Can you imagine if we'd met after some awful postal bust-up? Or even worse, one of us ghosting the other?'

'You're so practical, Eden,' he said. 'You don't have to be. Not with me. We're still best friends.'

Afterwards Eden couldn't remember if that was the moment he'd reached out and touched the side of her face. And if it was then that she'd touched his in return. She couldn't remember when exactly he'd pulled her close to him and kissed her, or whether it was she or Rafe who'd undone the pearl buttons on the front of her dress. She couldn't remember sliding it from her shoulders, letting it fall to the floor in a puddle of red.

But she remembered pulling him onto the sofa. She remembered the touch of his hands on her body. She remembered kissing him, and thinking that he tasted like nobody she'd ever kissed before. She remembered the weight of him on her, and the feel of him moving inside her, and she remembered every single moment of the joy that exploded in her when the two of them came together.

She remembered what it was like to be loved.

When she shivered, he pulled the woollen throw around her and held her tightly.

'OK?' he murmured.

'Absolutely.'

She didn't say anything else. She allowed herself to drift in the security of his arms. The memories returned: the two of them running through the fields together, climbing trees together, playing football together, hiding behind the shed together. Never once influenced by being a boy and a girl. Just people who got on well. She remembered crying in her bedroom at Trudy and Kevin's because she knew that Trudy was right about writing to him, that she was living too far away now for their friendship to matter. She remembered how much she'd missed him.

And then she'd found love and friendship with Andy and nothing else had mattered.

'You're the first,' she said into the silence.

'The first?'

'Since Andy.'

He chose his words with care. 'It's an honour.'

She was silent again, and then gurgled with laughter.

'What?' he asked.

'I've never been told that having a shag on the sofa was an honour before.'

'Were there many? Before Andy?'

'Actually . . . no,' she confessed. 'I'm a bit lacking in that department.'

'Not from where I'm lying,' he said.

She laughed again. 'Sorry. I don't know why I'm laughing. I guess it's nerves.'

'No need to be nervous.'

'You certainly weren't.'

'You're not my first,' he told her. 'Since Jewel. There were three others. Two were one-night-only things. The third . . . I was reaching out for someone, but it was a mistake. Neither of us was what the other needed.'

She snuggled closer to him. 'It's hard to know what you

174

need, isn't it? It's hard not to feel . . . well, guilty, I suppose. Guilty for enjoying yourself with someone else when you once promised there'd be nobody else.'

'And then you have to say that they'd be happy for you,' Rafe said. 'You have to persuade yourself of that.'

'Andy would want me to be happy,' said Eden. 'I'd want him to be happy too. But . . . oh, I don't know . . . maybe a bit less happy. I mean, happy, yes. Just not the same sort of happiness. That's terrible, isn't it? Makes me sound so selfish.'

'Understandable, though,' said Rafe.

'Would Jewel have wanted you to be happy?' asked Eden.

'Jewel wanted everyone to be happy,' said Rafe. 'She was the most . . . she wanted . . . Happiness was her thing. After everything she'd gone through, it was the most important emotion in the world for her. Maybe more important than love.'

Eden waited for a moment before asking him the question she'd avoided before. What had happened to Jewel? How had she died?

Rafe adjusted the woollen throw so that it was binding them close to each other.

Then he told her.

'She worked as an administrator in the same lab as me in Seattle,' said Rafe. 'I was always surprised she wasn't a researcher, because she had a razor-sharp mind and knew so much about everything. We met a few times in the cafeteria. She was very reserved, particularly about her personal life. I didn't spot it at first, but the more I talked to her, the more I realised that her conversation always related to other things. She loved music and dance and reading and culture.'

Underneath the throw, Eden was beginning to feel that Jewel was too good to be true. And that made her feel uncomfortable. She thought of Rafe's one-night stands and his relationship that had petered out into nothing. Was that because no woman could measure up to someone as perfect as Jewel?

'I asked her to come to a concert with me. It was a fundraiser with lots of really good acts and I thought it might be her thing. She didn't say yes straight away. She said she had stuff to organise first. But then she agreed and it was fabulous. We had a great time.'

How often, wondered Eden, did you make love with someone and then listen to them talk about their late wife? How often did anyone want to hear about a previous partner at all? Yet she did.

'I'm probably boring you,' said Rafe. 'I don't talk about this much, to be honest. I'm—'

'It's OK,' she interrupted. 'Tell me.'

'Her upbringing was . . . difficult,' continued Rafe. 'Her parents were members of a very strict church. One that preached ultra-traditional values. Considered women to be the property of men, didn't believe they should have money of their own, or jobs of their own, that sort of thing.'

'Seriously?'

'She was married when she was sixteen. He was thirty years older than her.'

'What!' Eden sat upright, the throw falling from her shoulders. 'Is that even legal? Are you sure this so-called church wasn't a cult?'

Rafe shrugged as he pulled her close to him again and rearranged the throw. 'She didn't call it a cult, but it sounded pretty controlling to me. Girls were taught how to cook and sew and keep house. Men went to work and were supposed to be looked after.'

'But she managed to leave him?'

'She ran away,' said Rafe. 'Or escaped, as she told me. She worked bars and restaurants and saved all her money.'

'And they never found her?'

'Eventually he did. Someone posted her photo on social media and he tracked her down. She got help from a women's centre and escaped again. Then she made her way to Seattle.'

'How did she get the job in your lab?'

'She was super-intelligent,' said Rafe. 'She was also afraid to go out much. So when she wasn't working, she was studying.'

Eden exhaled slowly. Why was life so hard for women sometimes? Someone as intelligent and brimming with goodness as Jewel should've been encouraged to use her talents to the full. Instead, her upbringing had been harsh and restrictive, and she'd died far too young.

'And you started going out together and everything was great. And then . . . Was it cancer?'

'No,' said Rafe.

'You don't have to tell me,' said Eden when he stayed silent. 'You didn't come here to be quizzed about your late wife. I know what that's like. I shouldn't have asked. I'm sorry.'

'She was murdered,' he said.

Eden stared at him in shock.

'She was at a corner store one afternoon,' Rafe continued. 'Picking up a few bits and pieces. Keeping herself to herself. A man walked in and shot her. Then he shot himself. It was Darius. Her husband. Though ultimately I discovered that it wasn't a legal marriage, because she would've needed to have parental consent and a judicial order in her home state to marry, and of course she had the parental consent but no order. And they'd married in her so-called church so it was never even registered. Nevertheless, she always called him her husband.'

'Poor Jewel. Poor you.' Eden put her arms around him and held him close. 'But . . . the timeline . . . I'm a bit confused. Had she married you by the time Darius caught up with her? When was Poppy born?'

'Poppy is *his* daughter. Jewel was pregnant by him twice previously but lost the babies both times after he abused her. It was when she found herself pregnant with Poppy that she ran away again. Jewel and I never married. She was afraid that somehow Darius would hear about it, find her again and try to take Poppy from her. I sometimes wondered if she couldn't bear the idea of being married at all. She was so damn strong despite everything she'd gone through, and our relationship was really normal. She didn't bring her past to it. Except Poppy. Although Poppy knows I'm not her biological father, she's always thought of me as her dad, and as far as I'm concerned, she's my daughter. I was made her legal guardian before we left the States.'

'It must have been a terrible time for you,' said Eden, after she'd taken a few minutes to process Rafe's story.

'I'm not going to lie. It was.'

'Why wasn't it all over the papers?' She gave him an apologetic look. 'I googled you after we met again. The only thing I saw was your professional biography at the lab.'

'It was in the local papers but not a big story,' said Rafe. 'I was mentioned as a "family friend" and Poppy's name was kept out of it. There are lots of murders, lots of family dramas in America. Jewel's wasn't anything out of the ordinary.'

'I can't believe you've even said that.'

'And yet it's true.'

'How on earth are you managing to cope?' asked Eden.

'That's why I came back,' he told her. 'That's why I'm here. To start again. To leave the past behind.' And then he tilted her face so that he was looking straight at her. 'Although a different past has caught up with me instead. You.'

He stayed the night, but got up early the next morning. When Eden's eyes fluttered open, it was to the sound of the shower. He was using the bathroom shower and not the one in the en suite of the master bedroom, because they hadn't slept in the master bedroom. She'd hesitated at the top of the stairs for a moment, then opened the door of the spare room. It was always ready for guests, although the bed was a double and not king-sized as her own was. She'd felt a little squashed as she'd lain beside Rafe, him sleeping, her wide awake, thinking about Jewel, thinking about Andy and thinking about Rafe, not really sure how she felt. But eventually she'd drifted off, and now she got out of bed, dressed in shorts and a T-shirt and went downstairs to make breakfast.

'I'm sorry if I woke you,' said Rafe when he came into the kitchen a few minutes later. 'I have to get back because I don't know what time Poppy will come home.'

'Not at six a.m., that's for sure,' said Eden. 'Have some coffee and toast. I forgot earlier that I have a bag of ground beans, so I can make you a decent cup in the cafetière. There's fruit and cereal too, if you like.'

179

'Coffee is fine,' said Rafe. 'Thanks.'

'Eat something,' said Eden. Then she shook her head. 'Sorry. I shouldn't be telling you what to do.'

'It's OK.' He walked over to her and put his arms around her. 'I spent the night in your house. You can order me around.'

'I really can't,' she said.

'I'm sorry if I upset you with Jewel's story,' he said. 'It's why I don't usually talk about it. People find it weird and tragic and then they find me weird and tragic too.'

'It's certainly tragic,' agreed Eden. 'But it doesn't make you weird or tragic at all. In fact it makes you a bit of a hero. You became the legal guardian to her child. That's immense, Rafe.'

'I was the only person Poppy had,' said Rafe. 'I've been a dad to her for most of her life. It's not immense. It's what anyone would do.' He exhaled slowly. 'Though I have to admit that I was scared at first. I worried that I'd stop loving her because her father had murdered her mother and robbed me of the woman I loved. But Poppy . . . Poppy is Jewel's daughter, and I always thought of her as my daughter too, and I'll never stop loving her.'

'I'm glad.'

She put her arms around him, and then he was kissing her, and she was kissing him, while his hands slid beneath her T-shirt and she unbuckled the belt around his jeans.

'You're OK with this again?' he asked.

'Absolutely.'

Perhaps, over time, they'd make love in every room of the house, she thought after he'd gone.

Or perhaps not.

Because the idea of Rafe in the same bed as the one she'd shared with Andy was too difficult to imagine. No matter how wonderful he currently made her feel.

Chapter 17

Rafe arrived home a little after 7.30. He eased the key into the lock as quietly as he could, but when he walked into the kitchen, Petra was already sitting at the table, reading the paper on her tablet and eating one of the muffins that Fiadh had dropped over the previous day.

'Hi,' he said. 'I thought you'd still be in bed after your night out in the city.'

She looked up from the tablet. 'It wasn't a late night and I woke up early. You're up early too.'

He shrugged.

'Or didn't you go to bed?' She raised an eyebrow.

He didn't answer as he switched on the coffee machine and took a tin from the cupboard.

'Late dinner?' she said.

He tamped down the coffee and slid the portafilter into place.

'Long chat afterwards.'

'I'm guessing it was more than a chat.'

'Are you judging me?' he asked. 'Are you moralising?'

'Of course I'm not moralising! For feck's sake, Rafe, who do you think I am? Our grandmother? Or maybe our great-grandmother, because Granny McConnell is one of the most liberal people I know and she certainly wouldn't moralise. I'm questioning your judgement, that's all.'

'Because I went out with someone I know and like?'

'You knew Eden when you were kids!' cried Petra. 'She's a grown woman now. It's not the same thing at all.'

'Just because we were children doesn't mean our friendship wasn't real,' retorted Rafe. 'As for now – we have things in common. It's nice to share them.'

'All night?' Petra gave him a dark look.

'OK, OK, maybe sleeping with her wasn't the wisest move. But we both wanted it, so why the hell not? And it was great to sleep with someone I care about.'

'Care about, yes,' said Petra. 'I don't want you to dig yourself into a hole you can't get out of, that's all.'

'Why should that happen?'

'Because she's as vulnerable as you!' exclaimed Petra. 'That's what you have in common! Lord knows, Rafe, losing your husband in a terrible accident has to be equally traumatic as losing the woman you love to her crazed ex.'

'Possibly not equally traumatic.' Rafe took his coffee to the table and sat opposite his sister.

'No. You're right.' Her voice softened. 'But listen to me, Rafe, the two of you have gone through tough times. And you're not over it yet. You don't know if she is either.'

'I've done a lot of things to get over it. I've moved back here, for God's sake!' He shook his head. 'And it's nearly five years since her husband died. People get over things in five years.'

'They do,' conceded Petra. 'It's been less time for you, though. All I want is for you not to do something stupid like entangle yourself with someone already damaged.'

'How d'you suggest I live the rest of my life?' demanded Rafe. 'Sit around and wait for some mythically perfect person to show up?'

'I'm not saying that.' Petra gave him a despairing look. 'Of course I want you to find someone. But someone new. Someone you can start over with.'

'I can perfectly well start over with Eden if that's what I want,' said Rafe. 'I'm not trying to do that. We're . . . It's casual.'

'I'd like to believe you. But don't let yourself fall for her because you think she's a connection with the Rafe you were before all this happened. Because she reminds you of the past.'

'You'd prefer it if I hopped into bed with the cake-baking woman next door?' he asked. 'Who I'd be living beside if it all went pear-shaped?'

'Don't be stupid, Rafe.'

'I'm not. Eden and I went to dinner, had a good time and ended up in bed together. It's not a big deal.'

Maybe not to her brother, thought Petra. But it might be a very big deal to Eden Hall.

HealeyLauren

Hi all. I saw hunky Rafe being dropped home in a cab at the crack of dawn this morning

SandieC

Seriously? Was he out all night?

HealeyLauren
I dunno. But it didn't look as though he was coming from work. Does he work shifts?

FiadhFoley
He does a lot from home. And there's Poppy to consider

Anita
His sister is there at the moment

FiadhFoley
I might drop in . . .

Anita
Again????

FiadhFoley
You can talk!

HealeyLauren
Be nice, ladies

SandieC
Ho hum

Anita
All the Single Ladies . . . LOL

Eden arrived at Michelle's with a bouquet of flowers she'd bought in the supermarket.

'They're lovely,' said Michelle. 'You didn't have to.'

'I saw them and I couldn't help myself. How were things last night? Did the children behave?'

'As you'd expect.' Michelle smiled. 'A few squabbles, but overall they were grand. They're playing on the trampoline at the moment.'

Eden could already see the heads of the children as they bounced higher and higher.

'Tea?' asked Michelle as she put the flowers in a vase.

'I'm fine, thanks. And thanks for doing brunch too. You really are a superwoman.'

'I like it,' said Michelle. 'Perhaps in a few years I'll try for a paying job again, but at the moment I'm happy playing at being a full-time mom and housewife.'

'You're certainly not playing at it.'

'Well, no.' Michelle smiled. 'I am the crème de la crème of moms and housewives. My darling husband doesn't know how lucky he is,'

'Yes I do!' Gene walked into the dining room. 'And you can't possibly take a paying job. Who would I get to do my paperwork instead?'

'You should pay Michelle for all the work she does for you,' said Eden.

'What's mine is hers,' said Gene. 'She doesn't need paying when she can access my accounts whenever she likes.'

Michelle gave him a gentle prod in the ribs and told him to go outside and keep an eye on the kids while she set the table.

'How was your evening?' she asked Eden.

'Fine,' said Eden. 'Enjoyable.'

She felt her face flush. Having sex for the first time in years had been more than enjoyable. It had been absolutely wonderful.

186

'It's always nice to have a night with a girlfriend,' said Michelle. 'Put the world to rights over a bottle of wine.'

'It wasn't quite like that,' said Eden.

'You didn't put the world to rights?'

'No. I mean I wasn't with a girlfriend.'

Michelle paused, a knife in her hand.

'Don't tell me you stayed home after all!'

'No, I went out. I just didn't meet a girlfriend.'

'But you said you were meeting your friend who'd moved to Dublin. Didn't you?'

'I did. But my friend is a man, not a woman. I knew him when we were kids.'

'You told me it was a woman.'

'You assumed it. I didn't correct you. It was a catch-up with an old friend who happens to be male. I hadn't seen or heard of him since I was ten years old. We bumped into each other a few weeks ago and he asked if I'd like to have dinner with him sometime, and so last night I did.'

'But you totally misled me about it.'

'I'm sorry.'

'Do you plan to meet him again?'

Eden remembered the feel of Rafe's fingers on her thighs, the scent of his body next to hers and the comfort of his arms holding her close. I hope so, she thought. I really hope so. 'We haven't arranged anything,' she told Michelle. 'All the same, it was nice to chat with him. We've both been through the mill in the last twenty-odd years.'

'How has he been through the mill?'

'He lost his wife.'

'I'm sorry to hear that. How?'

'She was murdered.'

187

'Jesus Christ, Eden.' Michelle dropped the knife and Eden picked it up.

'They were living in America at the time.'

Michelle looked at her in open-mouthed silence while Eden told her about Jewel's killing. She continued to refer to her as Rafe's wife and Darius as her ex.

'So you left your daughter, *your and Andy's daughter*, with me last night while you had a date with an old friend who you felt sorry for because his wife was murdered, but you didn't think it might be a good idea to fill me in?'

'I didn't know what had happened to Jewel until last night, so what would I fill you in on? Besides, you offered to have Lila for a sleepover. It shouldn't matter who I was with.'

Michelle recommenced placing cutlery on the table.

'It doesn't, of course.'

'And yet you're annoyed at me.'

'Worried for you,' she said.

'Why?'

'Because . . . because you don't really know this guy at all. His story could be complete fantasy. He might—'

'I *do* know him,' said Eden. 'I grew up with him. He's a nice man and I enjoyed having dinner with him. It's not a big deal.'

'You still should have told me.'

'Perhaps.' Eden sighed. 'You *are* annoyed. I should go.'

'No,' Michelle said. 'It's fine. Stay.'

'It was just dinner.' Eden hoped the untruth wasn't written all over her face.

'Right.' Michelle placed the last knife in its place, and then walked out of the room.

Darling You,

Something else has happened. And I don't really know how to tell you about it or even why it happened. Because you won't want to know. And yet you have to know. I have to tell someone. It seems wrong to tell you, but you're the one I confide in. You're the one I tell everything to. If I didn't have you, if I couldn't pour my heart out to you, I don't know how I'd cope.

I told you about meeting my old friend Mac McConnell. Rafe. I told you he has a little girl, Poppy, a couple of years older than Lila. I didn't tell you I was meeting him for dinner last night. It was so lovely to go out with someone different. Ever since Angie and Tony moved to Enniscorthy, it seems all my socialising is with Michelle or Stephanie or your mum. Which is great, but it's nice to go out with people who aren't Farrellys.

Anyhow, we went for a walk afterwards and then Rafe came home with me.

Oh, Andy, I had sex with Rafe. I'd forgotten how much I missed someone making love to me. I say making love, but I'm not sure that's what it was for either of us. I think it was more of a release. Of something pent up inside us. He's gone through a difficult time with the loss of his wife, so as well as our childhood friendship, we had a lot in common.

That's not why I slept with him, though. It just happened. It was the first time since you and it was very different. Not better. Not worse either. Just different.

Michelle was pissed off with me when I told her I'd met him. I didn't say anything about the sex, although she must have suspected. I get the impression that she doesn't like the idea of anyone or anything new or different in my life. It's a little bit like I'm betraying you and what we had together. And maybe, for her, it makes it all the more real that you're gone.

I understand why she'd feel like that. I feel it myself. To be honest, it's hard even for me to think I'd want to go out with anyone but you. To be with anyone but you.

Because, despite the lovely evening, despite the sex, Rafe isn't you.

You needn't worry. She needn't worry. Nobody will ever take your place.

Rafe is lovely, but I'm not in love with him.

How can I be when I still love you?

Forever yours,

Eden xx

Chapter 18

Rafe texted that evening to ask if she'd had a good day. Eden replied saying that after their lovely morning it had been full-on at Michelle's, that Lila had been hyped up all afternoon and that she'd only just got her to bed.

Rafe
Petra made me feel like a teenager who'd stayed out without permission when I got home.

Eden
☺ ☺

Rafe
After she left I went to the seafront with Poppy. Missed seeing you and buying ice creams. Poppy missed Lila too. She's made friends on the road but she likes Lila a lot. Perhaps we can organise that play date?

Eden
Lila would like that

Rafe
They could have theirs . . . we could have ours?

She took a while before responding cautiously.

Eden
Maybe

Rafe
No pressure. It was so good to be with you. In every sense.

Eden
It was good to be with you too. I had a wonderful time.
Talk later. Ex

She wasn't sure of the etiquette in signing off texts to a man she'd slept with the night before. She didn't know if *Ex* was too friendly, or not friendly enough. She wondered if there was a designated emoji she should have used instead.

Michelle was still peeved with Eden for not telling her about her date with Rafe. Over the last five years, she and her sister-in-law had shared everything, and she couldn't understand why Eden was being secretive now. Or perhaps she could. It wasn't, Michelle told herself, that she disapproved of Eden going out with a man. But she absolutely had concerns that she'd gone out with someone who'd been involved in a murder case. After all, Eden only knew Rafe's side of the story. There could be a lot more to it than he was saying. And Michelle felt a responsibility to ensure that someone who'd been through so much herself didn't get suckered in by a man who didn't necessarily have her best interests at heart. In any event, the most important person in all this wasn't Eden at all. It was Lila. Andy's daughter. As her godmother, Michelle had a responsibility towards her too. And as she took that responsibility seriously, she felt perfectly entitled to monitor Eden's love life very carefully indeed.

Eden made herself a cup of tea, then opened her laptop and saw an email that had arrived in the new account she'd recently linked from her Instagram and Pinterest pages.

Hi, I saw your work on Instagram and I'd like to discuss a time-limited project for a client with you. Please call if interested. The message was signed *Vanna West*, and there was a mobile number beneath.

Eden preferred specific requests to vague enquiries. Usually people talking about projects were looking for ways to get something done for free. But Vanna West's comment about a client piqued her interest, and so, even though it was Sunday evening, she dialled the number. Unsurprisingly, she was diverted to voicemail. She left a message asking Vanna to call her back, then allowed herself some time to scroll through sites dedicated to calligraphy pens. She already had a good selection, although she tended to stick to a favoured few, but she'd grown to love different pens and enjoyed browsing even though browsing often led to buying. She didn't care that she might rarely use some of her purchases. She felt a joy in unboxing them, in rolling them between her fingers, in trying them out.

After half an hour, during which she had to make herself stop clicking on the 'buy' button more than once, her mobile buzzed. There was no caller ID.

'Eden Hall,' she said.

'Hi, we spoke by email earlier.' The voice at the other end was brisk and efficient, yet the woman's tone was warm. 'I'm Vanna West.'

'How can I help?' asked Eden.

'Like I said, my client has a project and asked me to source someone who could work on it for her. It's small, relatively speaking, but will need special care and attention. I was checking out various people. I liked your work. And I like that you got straight back to me.'

'Thank you.' Eden didn't want to say that people more in demand than her probably wouldn't have bothered calling back so quickly.

'Are you located in Dublin?' asked Vanna. 'Could you come and see me tomorrow afternoon? Around two?'

'Where?'

'Dalkey,' replied Vanna.

Dalkey was a chic town on the other side of the city.

Eden did a quick calculation. She would be finished with William McEnroe by 12.30, and if she drove directly to the train station, she could catch a Dart to Dalkey, which would give her plenty of time to get to the house, unless it was too far from the station to walk.

'We're ten minutes by foot,' Vanna replied when she asked. 'Fifteen tops.'

'I'll be there,' Eden said.

'Great.' Vanna sounded pleased. 'Look forward to seeing you.'

Eden realised as she put her phone on the table that she was presuming Valerie would be able to keep Lila. Hopefully Michelle hadn't said anything to make her mother-in-law think that Eden was taking the Farrellys for granted while she lived some hedonistic lifestyle of her own. But if Michelle had mentioned her evening with Rafe, it certainly hadn't affected Valerie, who told Eden she'd be delighted to keep Lila with her for the afternoon.

'You're getting very posh with your clients in Dalkey,' she said.

'I think it's a PR office or something,' said Eden. 'The person I spoke to said it was a small project for a client of hers.'

'It's a nice place to have an office,' said Valerie. 'I hope it works out. It's lovely to have a hobby that earns you money.'

'I've been wondering if I couldn't do a bit more of it,' said Eden. 'There've been quite a few enquiries through my Instagram account lately. It's just a question of finding the time.'

'You're quite stretched as it is,' Valerie agreed. 'Especially with the extra hours you took on to look after the woman in Sycamore Grove.'

'Am I imposing too much on you?' asked Eden. 'My carer's hours have been cut back now Elizabeth's on the mend. That's why I thought I had time for the calligraphy.'

'Of course you're not imposing,' Valerie assured her. 'And I'm happy to take Lila whenever you like. All the same, you don't want to spread yourself too thin. I know it was a hard-fought battle, but surely the payout you finally got after the accident means you're provided for, at least for the time being.'

'Most of that went into a fund for Lila's education,' Eden reminded her. 'The rest won't last forever. I need my job and I like it. Being a care-giver is very rewarding, even if it's not well paid.'

'Are you sure you're OK financially? Andy would never have forgiven me if I let you struggle.'

'The only time I struggled was immediately after the accident,' Eden said. 'But I didn't have to worry, because you and Sean stepped up to the plate and helped me out when I could have been in a really tricky financial situation. I'll be eternally grateful to you for that.'

'We would never have let you get into difficulty,' said Valerie. 'You went through so much. It was awful.'

'We all went through a lot.' Eden didn't want to revisit the days when Andy's actions had been scrutinised and there were suggestions that he'd taken shortcuts that had led to his own death and Tony's injuries. It had been her darkest time, but the Farrellys had been nothing but supportive, even though it had been difficult for them too. 'I'm doing fine now,' she added. 'I have great people around me.'

'You know how important you are to us, don't you?' said Valerie. 'And how much Lila means to me?'

'Of course I do. You've proved it to me time and time again.'

'We're here for you.' Valerie hugged her. 'Any time at all.'

Elizabeth was eager to hear all about Eden's date with Rafe. She ushered her into the kitchen and put the kettle on to boil before Eden even had time to ask how she was and what needed to be done that day.

'Tell me everything,' she demanded when the tea was ready and they were sitting at the table. 'I'm dying to know.'

'I've never done a debrief of a date with anyone in my life, and I'm certainly not going to do it now, even for you.' Eden's eyes flickered towards Rafe's house. His car hadn't been in the driveway when she arrived. She supposed he was at the research lab.

'Where did you go, though? Was the meal nice? Did you have a drink afterwards? Did he leave you home?'

'It was fine,' said Eden.

'You know me well enough by now to know that "fine" doesn't cut the mustard,' said Elizabeth.

Eden laughed.

'You have a lovely laugh,' said Elizabeth. 'It's really joyful, with a touch of naughtiness to it. Did you do anything naughty with your Rafe?'

'Not my Rafe.' Eden took a cookie from the plate on the table.

'So . . . you won't see him again?'

'I really don't know,' replied Eden.

'You need time to process it.'

'I do?'

'Actually, no.' Elizabeth grinned. 'You should go for it and have a good time. But whatever works for you. I'm just an old dear who thinks life is galloping along so quickly that everyone with more of it in front of them than behind them should grab it with both hands.'

'Easier said than done when you have a family to think of.'

'It's you and Lila,' said Elizabeth. 'Whatever you grab, she'll benefit too.'

'Not entirely. There's a lot of Farrellys to consider as well.'

'In what way do you have to consider them?'

'They're Lila's family. Andy's family. And my family. My sister-in-law was put out that I left Lila with her when I went out with him.'

'She shouldn't have been. You can't live your life to please her or them.'

'That's not it. It's . . . Oh, I don't know, Elizabeth. Nothing is simple, that's all. Anyhow,' she continued. 'I've more news for you than a date. I might be getting another calligraphy job, and it's very mysterious.' She went on to tell her about Vanna West's phone call and her visit to Dalkey later that afternoon. 'I thought it would be an office but when I Google Mapped the address I couldn't see anything but high walls and trees. It could be someone with a lot of money to spend.'

'I hope it's a proper job and not some kind of scam,' said Elizabeth. 'You never do know, do you, when people contact you on the internet. But I'm guessing internet scams aren't generally run out of mansions in Dalkey.'

'It doesn't even have a street number, only a name,' said Eden.

'You'll have to tell me all about it.'

'I will,' promised Eden. 'Now, let's give your shoulder a little TLC.'

Although Eden had passed though Dalkey a number of times, she'd rarely had a reason to go there. As she walked along the twisting road from the station, she was enchanted by the views of the sea through the tall trees that swayed in the afternoon breeze. When she reached a high stone wall that shielded a secluded house from the road, she knew she'd arrived. She followed the wall for a hundred metres or so until she reached double gates with an intercom set into an iron post.

She pressed the button, and when a voice answered, she said her name.

It was five minutes to two.

She waited until the gates swung open, then walked up

the gravel driveway to a house that reminded her of the illustrations in the children's books she used to read; the same books she'd saved to read to Lila when she was a bit older.

It was an old-fashioned building with a sloping red roof and tall chimneys. Leaded glass windows were framed by climbing flowers, while ceramic urns either side of the short flight of steps leading to the front door overflowed with multicoloured blossoms. At the top of the steps, two seated lions, carved in granite, guarded the pillar-box-red door.

It was like stepping back in time

As she mounted the steps, she heard the throaty roar of a very modern motorbike and a figure in black leather rode down the driveway towards the gate. Although she only got a brief glimpse, the face behind the open visor of the helmet looked familiar. She was still trying to place him when the door opened, and she fixed a smile onto her face.

The young woman standing in the hallway was very tall, with brown eyes and black braided hair that fell almost to her waist.

'You must be Eden,' she said. 'I'm Vanna. Thank you for coming.'

'No problem,' said Eden. 'You have a lovely house.'

Vanna smiled as she beckoned her inside. 'Not mine,' she said. 'My client's.'

Eden hadn't forgotten that Vanna had called on behalf of a client, but neither had she expected to be visiting the client's home; she'd assumed the house was Vanna's own.

She followed her into a wide hallway. A large chandelier hung from the ceiling and half-open doors either side led to other rooms. Vases of fresh flowers on occasional tables set alongside the walls filled the hallway with summer scents.

Vanna led the way to a room near the end of the hallway. It was smaller than Eden had expected, although it overlooked the bay and she could see the sparkle of the sun on the water in the distance. There was a table in the centre with a high-backed chair behind it, but the room was dominated by a pink velvet chaise longue beside the window.

'This is the quiet room,' said Vanna. 'I thought you might like to work here.'

'Work?' Eden looked at her in surprise. 'We haven't agreed on anything yet.'

'You're right, I'm sorry,' said Vanna. 'What I meant was that I wanted you to do some samples for me. And then we'll see if your vision matches my client's.'

'You didn't tell me I'd have to do something for you. I'd have brought my pens and ink.'

'I didn't think.' Vanna frowned. 'I'm not sure if—'

'It's OK,' said Eden. 'I have pens that don't need ink in my bag. But I like using ink best.'

'I'll keep that in mind,' said Vanna. 'Why don't you sit down. What we wanted was for you to design an invitation. Something that says "You're invited to a party" in different fonts. Maybe half a dozen? So that we can get an idea of how it would look. We want it to be fun but elegant.'

'You know, I could've done all this from home and shared it online,' said Eden.

'Yes, but this way there's only one copy, and it's physical,' said Vanna.

Eden felt as though she was in the middle of a spy movie.

'It would be helpful if you gave me an idea of what kind of party it is,' she said as she opened the satchel she'd brought with her and took out her pens and some paper as well as

200

her favourite book of alphabet scripts. 'A birthday? An anniversary? A celebration?'

'A celebration,' said Vanna after a short pause. 'But maybe a birthday too.'

'For a young person or an older one?'

'Young. A woman in her thirties.'

'I'm so glad you said that.' Eden gave her a sudden smile. 'I'm in my thirties myself.'

'I'll be thirty next year,' said Vanna. 'I've decided it has to be young.'

Both of them laughed and Eden felt herself relax.

'Is there any special theme you want to incorporate?' she asked. 'Does your client have anything she particularly likes? Flowers, jewellery, cars, motorbikes,' she added, thinking of the figure she'd seen earlier.

'Music,' said Vanna 'She likes music.'

'OK.' Eden sat behind the table and laid her pens neatly beside the paper. 'How long do I have?'

'How long do you need?'

'An hour?' Eden knew it wouldn't take her too long for each font, but she needed to think about it first.

'Would you like some water?' asked Vanna.

'That'd be great.'

'I'll get it, and then you can start.'

She left the room. Eden stood up again and walked to the window. Perhaps her potential client was a musician. And then it came to her: the familiar face behind the visor – surely it had been Bono, the lead singer of U2. She felt her heartbeat quicken. Bono lived in Dalkey, didn't he? Could the client actually be the man himself? But Vanna had said that it was a woman. In her thirties. That wouldn't be Bono, obviously. Or even his wife. But maybe it was someone in the family. Or maybe Vanna had given her disinformation, to put her off the scent.

'Just like a spy movie,' she murmured to herself. 'What have I let myself in for?'

'Here you go.' Vanna came into the room with a jug of iced water and a tall glass. 'I'll leave you to it. But if there's anything you need, just text me.'

'OK. Thanks.'

Eden poured herself a glass of water and sat behind the desk again.

She needed to put thoughts of spy movies and famous musicians out of her head and think about what she was doing. She needed to get the sense of a thirty-year-old woman who liked music and lived in a beautiful old house and was going to have a party.

She stared in front of her.

It was nearly fifteen minutes before she took up a pen and started to form letters.

Rafe came out of his front door at exactly the same time as Elizabeth opened hers. She waved at him and he crossed the road.

'How are you doing?' he asked.

'Almost back to my best,' said Elizabeth. 'Eden is such a good carer and she's an even better physio. It's torture,' she added, 'but it's made a big difference.'

'Good.'

'She enjoyed her date with you,' said Elizabeth.

'That's good to hear.'

'Are you going to ask her out again?'

'Are you gossiping?'

'Yes,' said Elizabeth. 'I'm an old woman. I'm entitled to gossip.'

He laughed.

'Be nice to her,' said Elizabeth. 'If you're not going to see her again, be kind. If you are, treat her well.'

'I'll keep that in mind,' promised Rafe. 'Oh, look, here's Fiadh.'

'Hi, guys! I made some lovely almond slices last night,' said his neighbour as she approached them. 'I'll share them with you both.'

'Oh, God, Fiadh, please no. I mean, by all means share with Elizabeth, but everyone has been so kind that my house is like a bakery at the moment.' Rafe held up his hands in mock horror.

Fiadh laughed and suggested that he might like to join her for lunch in the garden instead. 'Because,' she told him, 'I bought far too much from the deli earlier and I hate throwing out food.'

'You're a popular man,' remarked Elizabeth as Fiadh walked back to her house, having refused to take no for an answer.

'I'm a novelty,' he said.

'I think you're more than that for everyone here,' Elizabeth said. 'Enjoy your lunch.'

Chapter 19

Having finished her sample designs, Eden sipped at her glass of water while Vanna studied the fonts.

'I used two very traditional ones,' Eden explained. 'Then two modern, and two that I'd call fun but elegant. I was thinking about the music element and how to emphasise that.'

'I see.' Vanna nodded as she looked at the samples. 'They're all great.'

'Of course we don't have to go that way. We can keep it very plain if your client prefers.'

'Can you wait here?' asked Vanna.

'Of course.'

She left the room. Eden stood up and looked out of the window again. She wondered if Vanna's music-loving client was in the house, making a judgement on her work without even meeting her. She wondered about the Bono connection again too, although she was beginning to suspect that she'd made a mistake about the man on the motorbike, and that he was probably a courier leaving packages at the house.

It was nearly ten minutes later when Vanna reappeared and asked Eden if she'd accompany her. Eden got up from behind the table and followed her out of the room and across the hallway. Vanna opened one of the doors and ushered her inside, but Eden stopped on the threshold, dazzled by the absolute whiteness of the walls and curtains, and the white grand piano in the centre of the room. The colour came from the rugs – all in various shades of green. Eden recognised the striking and familiar look. It had been the cover image of the country's bestselling album of the previous year. An album that had won a Grammy for the artist, who had previously received an Oscar nomination for her theme song to a Best Picture winner.

Amahle Radebe, composer and singer, was sitting on the stool beside the piano. She stood up, a petite woman in a black tracksuit. Her jet-black hair was short, and she pushed her purple-rimmed glasses onto the top of her head as she approached Eden.

'Oh, wow,' said Eden. 'I didn't think it would be you. I love your work.'

'Thank you.'

'Your song "Forever Yours" is my favourite of all time.'

'Thank you again,' said Amahle.

'We played it at our wedding,' said Eden. She gave Amahle a nervous smile. 'Sorry, I'm blathering. I've never met a famous person before.'

Amahle grinned. 'I'm well known, but I don't consider myself famous. Which isn't false modesty. It's just that I don't really buy into it, you know? You can be famous for a few weeks and a nobody afterwards. You've got to take it all with a grain of salt.'

'Oh, but you are!' protested Eden. 'The awards, the sales, everything!'

'At the moment,' agreed Amahle. 'You never know when

there'll be someone else. Anyhow,' she turned to the piano and picked up the papers that Vanna had brought her, 'I like these a lot, and this one in particular.'

Eden smiled in delight and then explained to Amahle how the process of choosing a design and printing the cards worked.

'But I want them all handwritten.' Amahle looked disappointed.

'It's not a problem, but it's a lot more expensive to have it all done by hand,' Eden said. 'You can do it on a computer for less.'

'The expense isn't really the issue here. And I'm not sure you should be actively discouraging your customers from going for the bespoke option.'

'Well, no. I guess not.' Eden glanced around the room again. She noted the framed awards on the walls and remembered the millions of records that Amahle Radebe had sold. She recalled the woman's story – the daughter of an Irish mother and a South African father, she'd won a Feis Ceoil music competition at ten years old, singing Miriam Makeba's sixties hit 'Pata Pata' and then the Irish classic 'The Foggy Dew'. But nothing had been heard of her more widely until a memorable appearance at Glastonbury ten years later, followed by the fastest-downloaded album that year. Suddenly her face was everywhere. Her concerts sold out, and without being ever-present on social media, she became an international star.

And here I am, thought Eden, standing in her house in Dalkey, talking to her about invitations to a party.

'Is it to celebrate another Grammy?' she asked.

'They're not announced till next year, and I don't know if I've been nominated yet,' Amahle said. 'But I'm celebrating that my single "You Me Again" was a massive hit, plus the fact that it's my thirtieth birthday. I'm not usually good at celebrating things,' she added, 'but I thought that this year I should go all out.'

'And why not?' Eden beamed at her. 'I'm sure it'll be great. I'd be honoured to do the invitations for you.'

'It's a little more than invitations,' Amahle said. 'I'll be gifting something small to everyone who comes, and I want them to get it with a little scroll that has a few lines from one of my songs chosen specially for them. I need you to write those for me too.'

Eden asked for more information about the timetable and the number on the guest list.

'It's an intimate party,' said Amahle. 'So around sixty. And I'll need to give my guests plenty of notice for September.'

'OK.' Eden's idea of intimate was about a dozen, but she supposed things were different in the world of celebrity. Because no matter how much she might deny it, Amahle Radebe was definitely a celebrity.

'Vanna will talk to you about the details and your fee. She'll also get you to sign a NDA, of course.'

'NDA?'

'Non-disclosure agreement. So that you don't talk about it to other people.'

'Of course I wouldn't.'

'People say that and then . . .' Amahle shrugged. 'I need to make certain.'

A few weeks ago I was sitting in front of the TV in my jammies trying to decide the next Netflix series I was going to watch, thought Eden. On Saturday night I went to dinner with a man. Then I had sex with him. Twice. Now I'm standing in Amahle Radebe's house talking about signing a non-disclosure agreement. This is not my life.

And yet somehow, today, it was.

This time Vanna brought her to a bright, airy room with large windows that overlooked a vegetable garden. It was laid out as a modern office, and she went to the desktop computer on the large glass desk in order to print out the NDA.

'It's nothing scary,' she told Eden as she handed her the pages. 'Just that we'll flay you alive and boil your bones in oil if you breathe a word to anyone.'

Eden read through it, although she didn't really know what she was looking for. However she did notice that she'd be liable for damages if she spoke about her work or revealed anything she'd learned about Amahle Radebe.

'There's a contract for the calligraphy too.' Vanna printed off another document. 'I hope this is OK for you.'

This time the first thing Eden saw was the fee, which was significantly higher than she'd ever charged anyone in her life before. When she pointed this out, and said that she hadn't discussed a price with Amahle, Vanna smiled.

'We're paying for your discretion as well as your work,' she said. 'And for you to meet the deadline. You'll see from this contract that if you don't fulfil it in time, you'll be liable again.'

Eden nodded, but she was still gobsmacked at the money. Even though Amahle had said it wasn't a problem, her personal experience was that the more well-off a prospective client was, the more discount they wanted. Some even offered to promote her work on their own social media if she did stuff for free. Nobody had ever voluntarily agreed to pay more than she'd charged before.

'Did you ask around?' She looked up at Vanna. 'You know, to compare pricing? And to compare calligraphers too?'

'I did some background research,' said Vanna. 'I liked your story, though. And, like I said, both of us liked your work.'

Eden had given her reasons for taking up calligraphy on her website, saying that it had been a life-saver when she was going through her hardest times, and that it had brought her both tranquillity and joy. She said that she wanted to bring joy to everyone she worked for.

'I'm glad you chose me,' she said. 'I promise I'll do a great job. You won't regret it. We need to choose a font and a design. I can send some to you based on what I showed Amahle today. It would be good to get that settled as soon as possible.'

'Perfect,' said Vanna. 'Is there anything else?'

'Not from my side of things,' said Eden.

'Good. We'll be in touch.'

Vanna showed her to the front door. As she was about to leave, Eden turned to her again.

'Could I just ask one thing?'

'Of course.'

'Was that Bono I saw earlier?'

'The NDA covers everything you learn while you're here.' Vanna's voice was amused. 'I'm not going to answer that question, because it's not just about Amahle.'

'Fair enough.'

But Eden was smiling as she walked to the train station.

Bono and Amahle Radebe in one day. How often could anyone say that?

*

Valerie and Lila were making daisy chains in the garden when Eden returned.

'How did it go?' Valerie asked.

'I've got the job.' Eden beamed. 'It's for a party and the client wants me to do the invitations. All by hand, no printing.'

'Goodness, that'll take some time.'

'It's a fantastic job with lots of work, and they're paying very well.' Eden flopped onto the grass beside them. 'It's definitely worth it.'

'I'm glad to hear it. And if you need some time to yourself, just let me know and I'll look after our little princess.'

'You're a star, Valerie.'

'D'you like my ti-ar-a, Mama?' Lila tilted her head so Eden could see the floral circlet on her head.

'You're definitely a princess,' said Eden. 'I'll take your photo.'

'With Granny.'

Lila and Valerie sat side by side while Eden took the snap.

'She's the image of Andy at that age,' said Valerie when she showed it to her. 'It's uncanny.'

Eden smiled, then glanced at her watch and said they'd better be off.

'Would you like a cuppa first?'

'Ah, no, you're grand,' replied Eden. 'I've a few bits and pieces to catch up on, so I'll take Lila home.'

Valerie walked them to the front door and gave Lila another kiss before waving them away. Then she went back into the house. Her husband, Sean, was in the den with his iPad.

'I didn't say a word,' she said when he looked up. 'But I soooo wanted to.'

'I hope she goes for it,' said Sean.

'Of course she will,' Valerie said. 'Sure she'd be mad not to.'

Eden realised that in her excitement to get to Dalkey, she'd forgotten to leave anything out of the freezer for dinner. She was checking the contents of the fridge when the doorbell rang. Making a note that it was probably going to be omelettes tonight, she went to answer it.

A delivery man stood there, his face almost completely obscured by a colourful bouquet of flowers.

'Eden Hall?' he asked.

'Yes.'

'Have a nice day.' He handed the bouquet to her.

She took the flowers into the kitchen and put them in the sink while she opened the card.

Thank you for a wonderful evening and a wonderful morning too. Hope we can do it again. Rx

She inhaled the scent of the flowers.

Then she took out her phone.

Chapter 20

'What has you here so early?' asked Valerie the following morning when Eden rang the bell. 'Not that I mind, of course.'

'Stuff to do before I get to Elizabeth's,' said Eden. 'Are you sure it's OK?'

'Of course.' Valerie gave Lila a hug and told her that her grandad was in the kitchen and needed a hug too. 'Didn't you say your hours with Elizabeth had been cut?'

'She still needs me in the mornings,' Eden said. 'But I haven't taken on anyone else later, so that I can concentrate on the calligraphy job.'

'Oh go on, tell me who it is. You know I won't breathe a word,' said Valerie.

'I can't.' Eden had no intention of breaking the NDA. In any event, she wasn't at all sure that Valerie would be able to keep the secret. Almost immediately, she congratulated herself on a wise decision when her mother-in-law told her that she'd been talking to Stephanie the previous evening and had mentioned the job to her.

'Steph says she hasn't seen you in ages.'

'We've both been busy.'

'Don't ever get so busy that you don't have time for family,' said Valerie.

'Not a chance,' Eden assured her as she picked up her bag. 'Thanks again, Valerie.'

Rafe opened the front door before Eden's car pulled in to the kerb.

'You made it,' he said as she walked up the driveway. 'I wasn't sure you would.'

She followed him into the kitchen. He looked more dishevelled than she'd last seen him. Today he was wearing a navy T-shirt and grey shorts, his hair messy and his feet bare.

'I should've sent you a basket of baked goods instead of flowers,' he remarked as he indicated the large Sachertorte on the counter. 'Lauren dropped it in last night. I still have caramel squares and banana bread from Jacintha and Amelia to get through too. And the only way I got out of almond slices from Fiadh was agreeing to have lunch with her yesterday.'

Eden raised an eyebrow.

'It wasn't a . . . it was a Caesar salad in her garden, that's all. She works from home. And she tried to offload the almond slices on me anyhow.'

'Do they seriously think you're starving, or are they engaged in a Sycamore Grove bake-off?' Eden grinned.

'Whatever it is, I wish they'd stop. Or at least coordinate their efforts. Please take some cake for Elizabeth when you go over. Take some for yourself too.'

'I couldn't possibly rob more cake. There'd be a target on my back if they found out. And yours too if they knew you were giving it away. Besides,' she added, 'I honestly don't eat a lot of cake.'

213

'You used to love it when we were kids.'

'Apple tart from stolen apples,' she reminded him. 'Never sweet cake or cream cakes.'

'Your mum made great apple tart.'

'Are we going to spend our time talking about cake?' she asked.

'Have you a better topic?'

'Strangely enough, yes,' she said, and put her arms around him.

They were lying side by side in his bed, Eden's head resting on his shoulder, when the doorbell rang.

'Crap!' He jumped up and pulled on his shorts and T-shirt before hurrying out of the bedroom. Eden heard him open the front door and then the sound of voices. She got out of bed and quickly dressed, then peeped over the banisters to see Krystle Keneally in the hallway.

'Poppy left it in the car earlier,' she was saying as she handed Rafe a child's sky-blue cardigan. 'I should have checked she had everything before letting her out, but they were all so hyper about the visit to the petting farm that it was hard to keep track. I hope she won't be too cold.'

'She'll be fine,' said Rafe. 'Besides, the weather forecast is good. Don't worry.'

'All the same . . .'

'You can't be on top of everything, and Poppy is a demon for leaving stuff behind.'

'Thanks,' said Krystle. 'I thought it better to give it to you now rather than wait until I pick them up, in case she or I forget again. How d'you think she's settling in at school?'

214

'Pretty well, thanks to Saoirse taking her under her wing,' said Rafe.

'Of course they'll be off for the summer holidays soon,' Krystle said. 'You'll probably need some help looking after her. Amie – Amelia – does some child-minding during the summer months if that's helpful, and our residents' association organises lots of different things for the children too. Actually, if you're not rushing off to work, I brought our newsletter for you. It has all the info you'll need. I like to print things out as well as put them on our website.'

Before Rafe had time to say anything, Krystle walked past him and into the kitchen. Eden, who was still observing the encounter from the landing, struggled to hold back her fit of the giggles, even though she was now trapped in Rafe's house and was due at Elizabeth's soon. She hoped Krystle would leave whatever information she'd brought with Rafe and leave. But when five interminably long minutes had gone by and she still hadn't made a move, Eden decided she'd better take matters into her own hands.

She adjusted her clothes, brushed her hair, then tiptoed down the stairs and opened the door to what she hoped was a second bathroom. Fortunately, she'd guessed correctly. She flushed the toilet and washed her hands before stepping into the hall and walking into the kitchen.

'Sorry I took so long.' She smiled at Rafe, who was standing opposite Krystle. 'I hope you like the samples, but there's no obligation to use them for your . . . house-warming.'

His eyes opened wider at her words, and Krystle, who'd turned to face her as she started speaking, looked both excited and puzzled.

'A house-warming!' She turned back to Rafe. 'How fabulous.

215

I'm looking forward to it already.' Then she looked at Eden again and frowned. 'Aren't you Elizabeth's carer?'

'Eden is also an old friend of mine,' said Rafe. 'When I was thinking of the house-warming, I asked if she could help with designing invitations.'

'It's my hobby,' Eden said.

'She did a lovely card for Elizabeth,' added Rafe.

'I didn't know that,' said Krystle. 'But I remember now that someone mentioned you knew each other.'

'From way, way back,' said Eden, even though Krystle's remark had been made to Rafe and not her. 'I'd better head across to Elizabeth now, Rafe, if you don't mind. It was good to chat to you this morning. Let me know what you decide.'

'I'll see you out.'

Krystle stayed where she was while Rafe followed Eden to the front door.

'A house-warming!' he hissed. 'I don't want to have a house-warming.'

'It was all I could think of on the spur of the moment,' she whispered. 'I couldn't stay holed up in your bedroom any longer, and I needed an excuse for being here. You don't have to actually have a house-warming.'

'Now that Krystle knows about it, I probably don't have any choice.'

Eden laughed. 'It can be payback for all the cakes.'

'Maybe it would be fun.' His tone was unconvinced. 'But only if you really do the invitations and come along.'

'We'll see,' she said. 'Now, I really have to go. Elizabeth will be waiting for me.'

'OK,' he said. 'I'm so glad you came this morning.'

'I'm glad too,' she said. 'Oh, and by the way . . .'

216

'Yes?'

'Your T-shirt is inside out.'

She winked at him and walked across the road.

'It's all go over at number four this morning,' remarked Elizabeth as she let Eden in. 'I saw you turn up earlier, and then Krystle.'

'Elizabeth Green, you are the nosiest neighbour ever.' Eden hung her jacket on the peg in the hallway.

'I'm not,' protested Elizabeth. 'I was up really early and I like sitting in the living room looking out, that's all. I've always done it. I don't gossip.'

Eden gave her an amused look.

'Seriously. I don't!' cried Elizabeth. 'Come on, tell me. Why were you there?'

'He's thinking of having a house-warming,' Eden told her. 'He asked me about doing some invitations for him.'

'That's exciting!' said Elizabeth as she sat down and propped her leg up on the footstool. 'At least, it will be if he invites me.'

'I'm sure he will.'

'So . . . did he ask you to call early to discuss a party?' asked Elizabeth.

Eden slowly rotated her client's ankle, and the older woman winced.

'Sorry. I know it's still painful. All the same, your flexibility has improved a lot.'

'Stop changing the subject,' said Elizabeth. 'Why did you go to Rafe's before coming here?'

'He sent me a lovely bouquet and I wanted to thank him.'

'Ooh – that's what I call properly romantic.'

'It was a very nice gesture,' agreed Eden.

'More than a gesture,' said Elizabeth. 'Especially if it brought you running.'

'I didn't come running,' said Eden. 'And we're just old friends.'

'It's more than that,' said Elizabeth. 'There's a chemistry between you two. It's obvious.'

'I like him,' admitted Eden. 'We had a lovely time together and I wanted to see him again.'

'So . . . is this going to go further?' asked Elizabeth.

'You know what you said before?' Eden looked up from her massage. 'About women being the ones to look after men? Well, I'm not going to be that woman. I've enough to look after already.'

'What if you look after each other?'

'Elizabeth, you're from a different generation, so I don't expect you to understand no-strings sex,' said Eden. 'But it's a thing.'

'So there was sex.' Elizabeth grinned. 'Gosh, I wish I'd had loads of it with no strings when I was younger. In my whole life I've only ever slept with one man. Can you imagine! I could've missed out on the most mind-blowing organisms and not even know.'

'Orgasms.' Eden stifled a smile.

'Oh, yes. Sorry. I always get that wrong. Either way, I probably missed out. Because Francis was a lovely man, but a bit . . . have I got this right? . . . a bit plain vanilla.'

Eden couldn't help herself. She doubled up with laughter and had to wipe the tears from her eyes before she could even look at Elizabeth and nod.

'I like vanilla,' Elizabeth said. 'But sometimes I think a bit

218

of a crunchy Magnum or a raspberry ripple would've been nice too.'

'Elizabeth, I can't keep going with this conversation.' Eden could hardly keep a straight face.

'I don't know why it's so funny,' said Elizabeth. 'And you've got me thinking. Maybe I should look out for a bit of something myself. It's been more than ten years, after all. And I did quite like it back in the day.'

'I truly can't believe we're even talking about this.'

'Was he good?' asked Elizabeth. 'Rafe?'

Eden stopped laughing. She looked at Elizabeth from her green-flecked eyes.

'Yes,' she said. 'He was. Very.'

Elizabeth smiled at her. 'In that case, I hope you keep enjoying it. And that it doesn't get all messy and emotional if that's not what you want.'

'I'm not an emotional person any more,' said Eden as she moved to work on Elizabeth's shoulder. 'I left that behind a long time ago.'

KrystleK
Hi, ladies, Rafe is thinking of having a house-warming party

Anita
Oh brilliant, when?

KrystleK
He didn't say. But it would be fun, wouldn't it?

HealeyLauren
Nice that he wants to get to know the neighbours. Did he ask your advice?

KrystleK
Not initially. He was discussing invitations with Elizabeth Green's carer when I dropped over with a cardigan Poppy left in my car

SandieC
What's Elizabeth's carer got to do with anything?

KrystleK
Apparently she's a designer of some sort and he wants her to do invitations

SandieC
Gosh, he's going all out if he's sending invitations!!!! I'd've sent a WhatsApp

KrystleK
I suppose she offered. Apparently she's an old friend

FiadhFoley
How old? How friendly?

KrystleK
I dunno

FiadhFoley
He said nothing about her when we had lunch yesterday

SandieC
Lunch?!?

FiadhFoley
A salad in my garden – very relaxed

SandieC
Anything more we should know?

FiadhFoley
My lips are sealed 💋

When Eden got to William McEnroe's, she found him in an uncharacteristically grumpy mood. She didn't try to lift him out of it, but simply made sure he'd taken his tablets before preparing his lunch. When she'd first started coming to him, he'd asked her to eat with him, but she told him that she always made a meal for herself and Lila later, so didn't have room for anything during the day too. Nevertheless, she sat down for a cup of tea. (That was one of the downsides of being a carer. The cups of tea were endless.)

'Do you play chess?' His question came out of the blue.

'Me? No,' she replied. 'I know the moves, but I don't know any strategies or anything.'

'I'm bored and I'm missing my golf,' said William. 'If I could play chess, that'd keep me occupied a bit more.'

'Sorry I can't help,' said Eden. 'Does your son play?'

'Have you forgotten he's on the other side of the world?'

'You could play him online,' she told him.

'It's not the same.' But he looked thoughtful.

'Anyhow, I'm sure it won't be long before you're on the golf course again,' she said.

'I wouldn't have the energy for it right now.' He made a face. 'I was really active before this stupid heart thing.'

221

'And you will be again.'

'Ah, don't mind me, I'm just feeling sorry for myself.' He pushed his plate with its half-eaten meal away.

'William, you're the least sorry-for-yourself person I've ever met,' said Eden. 'You're entitled to have a down day. And entitled to be tired, too. But you'll bounce back, I can tell by looking at you.'

He smiled at her. 'You say the nicest things. That's what I miss, you know, now that I'm older. Women saying nice things.'

'You must have some women friends who say nice things to you,' said Eden.

'Not really.' He shook his head. 'The women I knew were all Pamela's friends, not mine. And I've sort of lost touch with them. They called around a lot at first, but . . . well, I don't think I was very welcoming, to be honest. I didn't want them in my face day in and day out. Now I see that they were only trying to help.'

'How long ago did Pamela pass away?' asked Eden as she took his plate of fish pie and covered it with cling film, deciding that he might like to finish it later.

'Four years,' said William. 'It's like yesterday. It's so unfair how quickly time passes when you get older. I was watching the news last night and they were talking about Bill Clinton. I remember him being elected president and I remember him visiting Ireland. Pam and I went to see him speak. I knew it was a good long time ago, but I was thinking maybe fifteen years at the most. It's closer to twenty-five! That's a quarter of a century. I'll be a hundred in less than a quarter of a century, always providing the renovated ticker holds out.'

'And our president will send you a birthday card.' Eden smiled at him.

'Live every moment, young lady.' William looked at her from his faded blue eyes. 'Live with no regrets.'

His words were still in her head as she worked on Amahle's invitation cards that evening. The thing was, she thought, as she allowed the pen to form the lines and curves of the letters, she *did* live without regrets. Even though Andy had been killed, she didn't regret marrying him. It had been the single best thing to have happened to her, and she was thankful that they'd had their short time together. And because she didn't regret Andy, she couldn't regret that she'd had to leave Galway and come to Dublin to live with Trudy and Kevin. Because if she hadn't, they wouldn't have met. And yet, she thought, as she increased the pressure on the downstroke of the letter N, if she hadn't left Galway, would she and Rafe . . .

She lifted the pen and got up from the table. It wouldn't have been Eden and Rafe. It would have been Eden and Mac. And Mac would probably have gone to the States anyway and left her behind. So there wouldn't have been any Eden and Mac. It wouldn't have happened.

But she couldn't help daydreaming of what might have been if they'd stayed friends and become lovers. Maybe he wouldn't have gone. Or she'd have gone with him. And they might have married and had children of their own. Lila would have been someone else. Eden turned the tap on full, allowing the water to gush out angrily and fill the kettle. She wouldn't change a single thing in her life if it meant not having Lila.

Her daughter was her world.

Her phone buzzed. She dropped the tea bag she was holding into the purple mug on the counter top.

223

Rafe

When d'you think I should have my house-warming 🔥

Eden

You're going to have one?

Rafe

My next-door neighbour, Fiadh (almond slices and Caesar salad), asked me about it. Apparently everyone's very excited. Obviously there's a WhatsApp group I'm not part of that they use for girlie gossip.

Eden

😊😊 Don't be sexist

Rafe

I'm not, but they're definitely over-sharing with each other. Anyway, I don't do house-warmings and I don't do parties.

Eden

Maybe it's time to start

Rafe

They're having some kind of neighbourhood BBQ shortly. That'll be enough socialising for them, surely.

Eden

Have your party first – it'd be a social scoop 😊

Rafe

If I have it at all, it'll definitely be after the BBQ. Right now

I'm thinking of heading to Galway with Poppy for a few days. School breaks up this weekend and it would be nice for her.

Eden
The weather forecast is brilliant for the next fortnight. I'm sure it'll be lovely

Rafe
Would you like to come?

Eden looked at the message for longer than usual before replying.

Eden
I can't. I've to be at Elizabeth's and I haven't booked time off

Rafe
I'll probably go for a week, but you could come for the weekend and be home by Sunday night.

Eden
I'd have to find a hotel . . .

Rafe
You could stay with us at Dommo's. D'you remember Dommo?

Of course Eden remembered Rafe's older brother, who had already seemed very grown up to her when she was younger.

Eden

I can't possibly stay at your brother's house

Rafe

You can. It's a B&B.

Eden

Is it OK if I think about it?

Rafe

Of course. There's no pressure. The girls would have a lovely time. Sorry, that sounds like putting on pressure now! Whatever you want, Eden. It's up to you. Let me know.

Not going back had been a cornerstone of Eden's life ever since she was ten. Putting Galway out of her mind had meant putting everything that had happened there, both good and bad, out of her mind too. But Rafe had changed that. She'd thought more about her childhood in the last few days than in all the intervening years.

But would going to Galway move things on from no-strings sex?

Would she be able to do that?

Did she even want to?

Chapter 21

Petra and Dommo met in a café near Galway's Spanish Arch. The number of visitors to the city was steadily increasing as the summer drew on, and from their outside table, brother and sister watched the ebb and flow of tourists as they took photos and selfies at the old city wall.

'So Rafe and Eden are spending a few days with you and Becky. I thought you'd be booked up by now,' said Petra as she stirred her coffee.

'We are. But there's plenty of room on the house side.'

'Are they sharing?'

'Not that it's any of our concern, Petra, but no, and he was very specific about it.'

'I don't know if I'm relieved or not to hear that.' She put the spoon on the saucer. 'Oh, Dommo, I wish he'd found some bright, cheerful, baggage-free woman who'd lighten up his life rather than getting involved with Eden Hall.'

'He's a single dad, she's a single mum; they have a lot in common.'

'I know I'm probably being silly, but he's been through so much, it'd be nice if he'd found someone without any issues.'

'We all have issues.' Dommo shrugged.

'Even if she's over hers, I'm not so sure about him,' said Petra. 'He might seem fine on the surface, but he was a mess after Jewel was murdered and I very much doubt he's put it completely behind him. If that's even possible.'

'So what's worrying you? That he's bad for Eden or that she's bad for him?'

'I don't bloody know!' Petra groaned. 'I just worry that they might be bad for each other.'

'It's his life, Petra. You can't interfere. You have to let him make his own mistakes.'

'He's already made a lifetime of them,' muttered Petra. 'He needs someone to look after him, not the other way around.'

'Didn't you say there's a whole army of women on his road looking after him?' asked Dommo.

'That's true.' Petra acknowledged her brother's point with a slight smile. 'He sent me a photo of his kitchen after a batch of deliveries. It was like an artisan food hall.'

Dommo laughed.

'Maybe I'm getting myself in a knot over nothing,' Petra admitted as she finished her coffee. 'Hopefully it'll all be fine and this thing with Eden will fizzle out.'

'You're stressing over it because you're the eldest girl,' Dommo told her. 'Eldest daughters always feel a sense of responsibility towards everyone.'

'Because we're left with the babysitting and the looking-after when we're young,' agreed Petra. 'While you, eldest son, went about your life without a care in the world.'

'I'd like to say you're wrong, but you're not.'

They sat in silence for a moment.

'Another coffee?' asked Dommo.

'Make mine a decaf this time,' said Petra. 'I probably don't need a caffeine hit on top of everything else.'

When Eden told Valerie about her trip to Galway, her mother-in-law was taken aback.

'You're going away on your own?' she said, her eyes wide.

'With Lila, of course,' said Eden.

'I'm delighted you're having a little break, but you always said you'd no interest in seeing Galway again.'

'Not when I was younger,' agreed Eden. 'All the same, everyone raves about the west, and Galway's my home city, so I should see it for myself as a grown-up.'

'If you leave it for a week or two, I could go with you,' suggested Valerie. 'We could make a girls' weekend of it.'

'It's not that I wouldn't welcome your company or want to visit with you some other time,' replied Eden. 'But the opportunity came up for this weekend and I decided to take it.'

'Opportunity?'

'A friend's brother has a guest house near Barna,' said Eden. 'I'll be staying with them.'

'Does your friend have children? It's always nice for mums to get together.'

'A girl, a little older than Lila.' Eden was aware she was doing exactly the same with Valerie as she had with Michelle by not correcting her assumption that her friend was a woman, and she was well aware that Valerie would be just as put out as Michelle at the thought of her spending time with an unknown man. But she wasn't in the mood for the same debate again, so she said nothing. In any event, it was none

229

of Valerie's business who she went away with. (Although she'd never kept anything from Valerie before. Her life was usually an open book as far as her mother-in-law was concerned.)

'I hope you'll have a great time. Don't forget to send me some photos.'

'Of course.'

Valerie took a deep breath and beamed at her. 'OK, so I have some news too. I wasn't going to tell you until everything was finished,' she said, unable to keep the excitement out of her voice. 'But while we're talking about getaways, we have brilliant news about Dunleary.'

Dunleary was the seaside cottage in Wexford that they'd bought shortly after Andy was born, and it was where Eden and Lila had stayed the night before Amanda and Bruno's wedding. Andy and his siblings had spent every summer there when they were younger. As soon as the school holidays started, Sean and Valerie would pile them into their big estate car and drive the hundred and fifty or so kilometres to the cottage, where they'd remain until the new term began. Sean himself stayed in Dublin during the week because he didn't fancy a daily two-hour commute each way, but he always arrived at Dunleary on Friday afternoons and didn't return to the city until Sunday night.

In more recent years, Sean and Valerie had stayed there at regular intervals, and for long spells during the summer, although they always invited the family to join them, which they did at different times. Eden and Andy had often spent weekends at Dunleary, especially during the summer, and whenever they did, they discussed their own plans to move to the Wexford coast in the future. They'd agreed it was something they'd like to do when they started a family, when their priorities about their lives and careers would change.

'Are you heading off for a few weeks?' Eden asked her mother-in-law now. 'I wondered when you might. The weather's perfect for it.'

'No,' said Valerie. 'Well, no, but yes.'

Eden looked at her enquiringly.

'Sean is *finally* retiring!' Her mother-in-law clapped her hands in delight. 'We're going to move there permanently.'

'Oh, wow.' Eden's eyes widened. 'That's so exciting.'

'Isn't it?' said Valerie. 'I'd hoped we'd do it a few years ago, but when they offered him an extension to his contract, he didn't feel he could refuse. But now the contract's up and he's ready for a quieter life.'

'You both totally deserve it,' said Eden. 'When will you move?'

'As soon as the renovations are complete,' replied Valerie.

Eden knew that Valerie and Sean had been getting the windows in the house replaced, because Valerie had told her so when she'd asked about the builder's equipment piled against the wall when they'd stayed for the wedding.

'They must be nearly finished by now,' she said.

'It's not only the windows,' her mother-in-law told her. 'There's more. And I need to talk to you about it, Eden.'

'Me, why?'

'Because . . . well, because with all the changes we're making – and some of them are very, very exciting – we want you to come and live with us.' Valerie's eyes shone. 'We want you to be part of our new life at Dunleary.'

It took a few seconds for her words to sink in, and then Eden looked at her in complete astonishment.

231

'*Live* with you?' she said. 'You mean, move to Wexford myself? With Lila? Permanently?'

'Exactly.'

She stared at Valerie wordlessly.

'We realise that it would be a lot trickier for you in Dublin without us,' continued Valerie. 'After all, you depend on me a lot to look after Lila for you. It was one of the things we had to think long and hard about before making the final decision to move.'

'You shouldn't have even considered that,' said Eden. 'This is your life and your time, Valerie. It's up to me to worry about Lila.'

'Don't be silly,' said Valerie. 'You're both a massively important part of our lives. Andy would want us to prioritise you, so of course you were a major consideration. I know you don't talk about it any more, but that house you're living in was meant to be a first step on the ladder. You're always complaining about the traffic on the main road and people parking outside your gate when they go to the shops. You deserve something bigger and better. You and Andy talked so much about moving to Wexford yourselves, and now you can. This ticks all the boxes. It's a *wonderful* environment for Lila and it'll give you the chance to concentrate more on the things you like doing and give up the stuff you don't.'

'But . . . but you're talking about me sharing your home,' Eden said.

'You wouldn't really be sharing it.' Valerie beamed at her. 'The extra work we did – we've added a self-contained extension. It's perfect for you and Lila. It will be your new home.'

Eden was speechless.

'You'll have your freedom, but we'll be able to watch out

for you,' continued Valerie. 'Andy would love to think that you made the move you always wanted to make. I know you were upset when Angelina and Tony did it after the accident. This way you'd be close to her again too. It's so perfect.'

'Angelina and Tony moved to Enniscorthy to be near her mum,' Eden said. 'I was upset at her leaving Dublin, but I totally understood.'

'And Enniscorthy is only thirty minutes from Dunleary.' Valerie gave her a triumphant smile.

'It'd be nice to be close,' agreed Eden. 'But we're still friends no matter what.'

'Yes, but you don't meet up very often, do you? Angelina said it to me at the wedding. She was so happy you popped over to see her the day before. I nearly told her about our plans, but I kept my mouth shut.'

Eden couldn't help feeling that Valerie was running her over with a steamroller. As though her mother-in-law had thought it all through for her. Which, actually, she had. To be fair, she was making some good points. But she couldn't seriously expect Eden and Lila to move into Dunleary and share a home with her and Sean, self-contained extension or not. And how would the arrangement work? What sort of rent did they expect? Was there a separate electricity meter for the extension so that she knew what her bills would be? Did it have its own kitchen?

'We wouldn't dream of asking for rent,' said Valerie when she put these questions to her. 'After all, Eden, this works two ways. We're there for you, you're there for us. But we won't be on top of each other, I promise.'

'All the same, I couldn't possibly—'

'We'll work it out,' Valerie said. 'Don't worry.'

'What about the rest of the family?' asked Eden. 'I'm sure they think you've simply been giving Dunleary a facelift, not adding a complete extension for me to live in!'

'We haven't said anything to them yet, but I bet they'll be thrilled at the idea,' said Valerie. 'Nothing will change for them. They can join us whenever they like.'

'It's extraordinarily generous of you,' Eden said after she'd processed the idea of being surrounded by random Farrellys whenever they wanted a holiday by the sea. 'And there are some massive advantages. But I'm not sure that it's really practicable, Valerie. Lovely as it is to visit you, you'd soon get tired of us under your feet all day.'

'But you wouldn't be.' Valerie shook her head. 'That's why this is a good idea. Let me show you the plans. It'll put your mind at rest.'

She disappeared out of the room while Eden sat at the table and tried to absorb what her mother-in-law was proposing. Dunleary had always been a place where multiple families lived together, but that was for short periods during the holidays. Living with Sean and Valerie all the time would be . . . well, thought Eden, it would be impossible. No matter how lovely the idea of fulfilling her and Andy's dream of moving to the country was, this was an absolute non-starter.

'Here we go.' Valerie returned with a sheaf of architect's drawings, which she rolled out in front of her. 'This is it.'

'Gosh, Valerie, it's a lot more work than it seemed when we were at Amanda's wedding.'

'I didn't want to say anything then.' Valerie smiled. 'It's a totally self-contained wing. It has its own kitchen and bathroom as well as two bedrooms and a sitting room. And look here . . .' She pointed at the drawing. 'You can use this as a study and do your calligraphy there. After all, if you're getting these well-paid projects now, you'll need somewhere nice to work. Let's face it, the kitchen table isn't the best place for your growing empire.'

'You seriously haven't done all this just for me, have you?' asked Eden.

'For you and for Lila,' said Valerie. 'And, of course, for Andy.'

Eden caught her breath.

'The architect told us that lots of houses have self-contained annexes now,' continued Valerie. 'Sort of future-proofing them for when and if the owners might have people living with them. Or, when we're older, we could move into it and you could live in the main house. Instead of me looking after Lila, she could look after me!' Valerie laughed. 'Obviously it's not something we need to do now, but who knows? And who better to have with us than a professional like you?'

'It's all really lovely, but it's a lot to take in.' Eden was digesting the fact that Valerie's plan included a time when she and Sean would need home care, and that she was looking to Eden to provide it. 'I have to think about it. And of course I have an actual care-giving job at the moment. I know lots of people do long commutes, but—'

'That's the brilliance of this idea!' cried Valerie. 'You could sign on with a local agency in Wexford if you want to keep working as a care-giver, or you have the option of concentrating on your calligraphy instead because you'll be getting rental from the house in Artane. Whatever you choose, I'll be able to take care of Lila. It's the perfect solution.'

The perfect solution to a problem she hadn't known existed,

thought Eden, as Valerie rolled up the plans again. The perfect solution to a problem her mother-in-law had just devised.

'You've certainly given it a lot of thought,' she said.

'You know Andy would've wanted us to make sure you and Lila were well looked after,' Valerie told her. 'This way, you will be.'

Eden couldn't get Valerie's news, and her offer of a home, out of her mind. Sitting in her own living room, where the only view was of her pocket-handkerchief-sized front garden and the row of shops across the road, she wondered if she was being silly in thinking that moving in with her in-laws would be a terrible mistake, especially as she and Lila would be living in their very own self-contained annexe. And Valerie was right that a move to Wexford would fulfil the dream she and Andy had had of raising their family in the country. Admittedly this wouldn't be the way they'd imagined it, but life didn't always turn out as you expected. She had plenty of experience to prove that.

Valerie was also right in saying that it would be a wonderful environment in which to raise Lila. Her daughter would have the freedom of the huge garden, as well as easy access to the beach and the sea, all of which she loved. Although . . . Eden frowned . . . she hadn't seen a separate front door to the new extension. That would mean her parents-in-law would always know when she was home and when she was out.

She also had to remember that Dunleary would still be a home for the rest of the Farrellys too. No matter what Valerie said, Eden wasn't at all sure that they'd want her to move in with their parents. Although perhaps they'd be behind the idea that Eden was the right person to look after them when the time came. She released a slow breath at the thought. She hadn't ever contemplated not being involved with the Farrellys, but a future tied to them while Sean and Valerie grew older and older wasn't one she'd visualised.

Eden had once believed that the closeness of her husband's family was the ideal, and how most families should be. But over her time as a nurse, and then a carer, she'd realised that families came in all shapes and sizes. Some were hotbeds of intrigues and alliances. Some had long-running feuds the origins of which were lost in the mists of time. Some parents disapproved so thoroughly of the choices their adult children had made that they broke off all contact with them. Some children thought of their parents as a burden. Some family members simply tolerated each other. Some actively disliked each other. There were a million different ways of caring and not caring, but Eden had loved knowing that she belonged to a big family who did everything together and looked out for each other, even if sometimes it was a little claustrophobic.

Living with the Farrellys for the rest of their lives would be more than a little claustrophobic, though, wouldn't it?

She curled her feet under her on the sofa as she recalled her experience of living with Sean and Valerie in the weeks immediately after Andy's death, and again for a time after Lila was born. She'd needed and depended on them on both of those occasions, but had been glad, in the end, to get back to her own house. How long would she last at Dunleary before wanting to come home? Or how long would it take for them to get fed up with having her around all the time? But of course Valerie would never get fed up with her, because she had been Andy's wife.

And if I live with her, I'll be Andy's widow forever, she realised. He'll always be the invisible person in the conversation.

Although Eden was very aware that Andy remained a silent presence in her own life, she couldn't help feeling he was even more present in Valerie's. His mother spoke of him as though he'd simply gone away for a while and could return at any minute. Often when she talked of him, it was to show his approval or disapproval of something she wanted Eden to do. She'd framed this proposal as something he'd approve of, and Eden couldn't help thinking that having her late husband make judgements, via Valerie, on her day-to-day life would be more than she'd be able to bear.

Her phone buzzed and her heart skipped a beat as she thought it might be her mother-in-law with even more reasons why the move would be a good one. But it was Rafe, to tell her that everything was organised for their trip to Galway and that he was delighted she'd decided to come.

'Great,' she said, when he'd gone through the details with her. 'I know Lila will love it.'

'I hope we all will,' he said, before ending the conversation.

And here was another complication, thought Eden. One that she hadn't even let herself consider before now. How would her new relationship with Rafe McConnell fit into her living in Wexford? She didn't even need to ask the question to know that the answer was 'not at all'. Because even if he was prepared to drive almost two hours to see her, Valerie would hardly welcome him into her home.

Her home. There it was again. Dunleary could never truly feel like Eden's own home. It would always be Sean and Valerie's. And living with Andy's parents would make it impossible for her to have a relationship with anyone else.

238

She hadn't considered new relationships over the past five years. How could she, when she was still in love with her husband? And even though she was calling what she had with Rafe a relationship, it was mainly a physical thing. But she certainly wouldn't be able to have no-strings sex in comfort in Dunleary!

Her phoned buzzed again. This time she groaned when she saw the caller ID. Michelle got into the reason for her call straight away, saying that she'd just come back from Valerie's and her mother had told her about the Galway trip.

'When did you decide on this?' she asked. 'You've always been dead set against going back to Galway. I couldn't believe it!'

It took Eden a moment to shift her thinking from the thorny question of Dunleary and Wexford and switch to her visit to Galway with Rafe.

'The opportunity came up and I took it,' she told Michelle. 'It was a spur-of-the-moment thing.'

'That's so unlike you.'

'What is?

'Making decisions on the spur of the moment. Mum said you were going with a friend. It wouldn't be your friend from the other night, would it?' Michelle's voice took on a slight edge as she asked the question.

'Why not? His brother runs a B&B.'

'You're seriously thinking of going to Galway with some guy you knew over twenty years ago?'

'I'm *from* Galway.'

'Like that ever mattered to you before.'

'It's a weekend away. There's no ulterior motive.'

'What about Lila?'

'What about her?'

'Is she going on this trip with you?'

'Of course she is.'

'So you'll be doing whatever you're doing with this guy while she . . . Well, what are your plans for her?'

'For crying out loud, Michelle, I won't be doing anything to upset Lila. Don't forget Rafe has a daughter of his own.'

'Lila is my god-daughter,' said Michelle. 'I'm entitled to ask about her welfare.'

'She's *my* daughter and if you think for one second that I'd do anything that wasn't in her best interests, you don't know me very well.'

'You said this guy's wife had been murdered.'

'Yes.'

'How d'you know he didn't do it?'

'Oh, for God's sake, Michelle!'

'It's a reasonable question. The husband is always the prime suspect, for the very good reason that the husband is often the guilty party.'

'He didn't kill her. It was a shooting in a grocery store.'

'That's what he told you. But how can you be certain?'

'Listen to yourself,' said Eden. 'You're barmy. Besides, he wouldn't have been given custody of Poppy if they thought he was a murderer.'

'Why would they need to give him custody if he's her dad? Because they had suspicions about him?'

Eden gritted her teeth. She shouldn't have said anything about Rafe having custody of Poppy. She really didn't want to talk about his private life to her sister-in-law, but she knew Michelle wouldn't let it go. So she explained that Poppy wasn't Rafe's natural daughter but that he'd raised her as his own. And then, deciding that she might as well give Michelle the whole story, she added that it had been Poppy's natural father who'd shot her mother.

'Oh. My. God.' Michelle was horrified. 'I can't believe you're getting involved in this . . . this melodrama!'

'It's not a melodrama,' objected Eden.

'Jeez, Eden, give me some credit. It's completely fucked-up is what it is.'

'From one perspective,' agreed Eden. 'But right now, Rafe's a lone parent looking after his little girl, that's all.'

'And have you had this crazy story confirmed by an independent source?' demanded Michelle.

'No. I trust Rafe. I know him.'

'You *knew* him,' said Michelle. 'When you were a kid. Big, big difference. And I wouldn't be taking my responsibilities as Andy's sister and the guardian of his daughter seriously if I didn't ask these questions.'

'I'm her mother and I'm perfectly happy that Rafe is a good, truthful person. Oh, and you're Lila's godmother, not her guardian.'

'Says the woman who's happy to leave her with me for days at a time.'

'I've never left her with you for days at a time.'

'What about when we went to Longford? Who looked after her then?'

'I had food poisoning! I was in bed for forty-eight hours.'

'Exactly. And who stepped up to the plate? Yours truly. I'm always there for you, Eden. Always.'

'Well, you can be here for me by saying that it's perfectly fine for me to visit my home city with a friend.'

'A friend you're shagging.'

241

'And you know that how?'

'I'm not naïve, Eden.'

'Look, it's a perfectly innocent trip. You don't need to worry about either my morals or Lila's safety. Or whatever it is that's biting you.'

'It's just concern about you.'

'It's not necessary.'

'It is,' said Michelle, and her voice softened. 'You were such a fragile little thing when you met Andy. So quiet and anxious and needy. He changed you. *We* changed you. After he died, you couldn't get out of bed for a month. It was the same when Lila was born. It's not surprising you struggled, but we rallied around because that's what families do. We care about you, Eden, and I'm certainly not going to let you mess up your life and Lila's over some bad judgement.'

'It's *my* life!' Eden reminded her. 'And Lila is *my* daughter. I'm bringing her away for a damn weekend whether you like it or not.'

'Calm down,' said Michelle. 'Believe it or not, Eden, the only thing I care about is you and Lila. I don't want you doing something that would take her away from us.'

'What are you even talking about?' demanded Eden. 'I'm not taking her away from you! We're going to Galway for two nights, that's all.'

'But if you get further involved with this guy, who knows? He could manipulate you into moving to Galway, and that would break Mum's heart. Andy would be devastated.'

'Andy is dead!' The words came out more forcefully than she'd intended. She swallowed hard. 'I wish he wasn't, but he is, and I'm doing my best to be a good mother to our daughter. We haven't been away together before. I need to do this. So please stop giving me grief about it. And if you want to talk about somebody moving away, has Valerie said anything to you about Dunleary?'

'No. Why?'

'Chat to her. It's a far more interesting topic of discussion than my morals.'

She was shaking as she put the phone back on the table.

She'd never had a conversation with Michelle like that before.

She'd never even disagreed with her.

And if she took up Valerie's offer of a home in Dunleary, she'd never be able to disagree with any of the Farrellys again.

Eden was ready and waiting when Rafe's SUV pulled up outside her house a little after midday on Friday. She opened the front door as he and Poppy both got out of the car. Poppy ran up the driveway, past Eden's Fiat, and asked if she could go inside and get Lila.

'Of course,' said Eden, and then smiled at Rafe. 'Hi.'

'Sorry I'm late. I'd forgotten what a palaver it was getting her ready to go anywhere,' he said as he gave her a kiss on the cheek. 'We have to double-check she has everything. And then check again. And then there's always the whole "Where's my whatever-it-is?" just as we're about to leave.'

Eden grinned.

'I hope you're more organised than me,' Rafe added.

'Totally ready.' She raised her voice and called for Lila, who came to the door dragging her bright orange Trunki case behind her.

'Cool case,' said Rafe. 'Let me put it in the car for you, Lila. You can get in the back seat beside Poppy.'

Lila followed Poppy to the car, Rafe behind them, while

243

Eden set the house alarm and locked the door. She was about to walk to the SUV too when a familiar car pulled up and Michelle got out. Eden caught her breath and hurried down the driveway.

'Is everything OK? Why are you here?'

'Everything's fine – why wouldn't it be?' Michelle took a bag from the car. 'I'm glad I caught you. I thought you weren't heading off until later.'

'I don't remember mentioning a time,' said Eden.

'You must have done,' said Michelle. She looked at Rafe, who was leaning against the Audi. 'Hi,' she said. 'I'm Michelle. Eden's sister-in-law.'

'Pleased to meet you.'

'Eden tells me you're old friends.'

'We are indeed.'

'It's nice for her to meet someone she knew when she was a kid,' said Michelle. 'Times were tough for a while, but she's doing great now.'

'Um . . . Michelle, I'm still here. You don't have to talk about me as though I wasn't,' said Eden.

'Sorry.' Michelle kept her gaze on Rafe. 'You were living in the States, I believe.'

'Yes,' said Rafe.

'And you're staying with family in Galway this weekend.'

Eden felt her jaw clench as Rafe nodded and said that they were.

'Well, take care of my niece, she's very special,' said Michelle. She held out the bag she'd taken from the car. 'This is why I came. I was in the shops earlier and I saw this and knew Lila would love it, especially for a weekend away.'

Eden peeked inside at the navy blue T-shirt dotted with multicoloured sequinned stars.

'She certainly will,' she told Michelle. 'Thank you.'

'I would've brought something for . . . I'm sorry, what's the other little girl's name?'

'Poppy,' said Eden.

'I would've brought something for her too if I'd thought of it. I wouldn't like to think that she'd feel left out. That you weren't looking after her too.'

'Poppy will be fine,' said Rafe. 'And Eden isn't coming to look after her, you know.'

'I didn't mean that was why you invited her.' Michelle's tone was guileless. 'Just that girls can feel aggrieved very easily.'

'Not Poppy,' Rafe said. 'Anyhow, Eden, we'd better go if we want to miss as much of the weekend traffic as possible. On a glorious weekend like this, the whole country will be on the move.'

'Yes, we're going to Wexford with Mum and Dad later,' Michelle said, as though he was still talking to her. 'Iris and Darragh are really looking forward to it. It's a pity you're not coming, Eden.'

'There'll be plenty of other occasions,' said Eden.

'Indeed there will. Especially if it becomes your forever home. Mum told me all about it. It's a brilliant idea.'

'We'll see.'

'You couldn't do better.'

'We'll see,' repeated Eden. Then she opened the passenger door and got into Rafe's car. 'Have a great time in Dunleary,' she told Michelle. 'I'll give you a shout when I'm home.'

*

'What was all that about?' asked Rafe when they were finally on the road.

'Michelle was put out that I decided to come away with you without consulting her first.' Eden shrugged.

'You're supposed to consult your sister-in-law before doing something?' Rafe was incredulous.

'Andy's family have been great to me, but they sometimes forget that I can manage fine on my own. To be fair, I wouldn't have managed at all in the beginning without them,' she added, 'so I know where they're coming from, but it can get tiring.'

'I bet.'

'They're grand really.'

'I didn't realise there was a town called Dunleary in Wexford.'

Eden told him about the holiday house that Sean and Valerie now planned to retire to.

'But what did she mean about it becoming your forever home?'

'It's Michelle being Michelle,' said Eden as she glanced at the two children in the back seat. 'And Valerie being Valerie. I'll deal with it.'

'Whatever you say.' Rafe shrugged.

They drove in a silence only broken by the track of the movie Poppy and Lila were watching in the back seat, until, close to Athlone, Lila piped up with a request to go to the loo, followed shortly by Poppy, who demanded they stop urgently. Fortunately the next service area was only a few kilometres away, and when they arrived, Eden hustled both girls into the restroom. While she monitored their extravagant hand-washing routines, a young mother with two children of her own gave her a complicit smile as she guided her daughters into a cubicle. Eden supposed that the other woman thought she was mum to both Poppy and Lila. The idea unsettled her.

She and Andy had agreed that they should have two children. Andy thought two was enough, and Eden's main wish had been for their son or daughter not to be an only child. She hadn't liked being an only child herself, and had often wondered if this had been a choice her parents had made, or if they'd planned to add to the family eventually.

It was probably because she was on her own back then that Rafe had mattered to her, she thought, as her glance flickered in his direction. He was the brother she'd never had, though given that she'd now slept with him, she clearly didn't think of him in a brotherly way any more. And now she was going to spend a weekend with him but probably not sleep with him, which was a bit ironic.

She glanced at him again, but his eyes were fixed firmly on the road ahead. She took out her phone. No messages from anyone.

She heaved a sigh of relief.

An hour later, they'd reached Galway city and were driving along the coast road towards Dommo and Becky's house close to the pretty town of Barna.

'I don't recognise any of it,' Eden said to Rafe as she looked out of the window. 'I don't remember anything except Orchard Close. And the truth is, my memory of that is probably faulty.'

'Haven't you photos?'

'Nope.'

'At all?' He gave her a surprised glance.

'A few,' she conceded. 'Some of me and Mum when I was a kid. A handful of us on holidays . . . Neither of my parents was much for going abroad, so most of them are places along what's now the Wild Atlantic Way rather than anywhere exotic. We used to go camping a lot. But truthfully, one camping site looks much like another to me.' She shrugged. 'I know Dad took more when he got his digital camera, but he rarely printed them, and the camera itself must have got lost in my move to Dublin, because I never found it.'

'Oh, Eden.' This time Rafe's glance was sympathetic. 'All those memories.'

'They were probably only more photos of places I wouldn't recognise,' she said.

'It'd be nice to have them, though.'

'I made lots of new ones,' she said. 'Not so many with Trudy and Kevin, but Andy and I were forever taking selfies. And I take loads of photos of Lila. Now the metadata tells you everything about the photo, so . . . happy days.'

'And do you go to exotic places with her?' asked Rafe.

'If you consider Wexford to be exotic.'

'But you don't go away on your own together?'

'There's nowhere I want to go,' she said, and turned her face towards the window again.

Dommo and Becky's house was a couple of kilometres inland. It wasn't, as Eden had expected, one of the older single-storey buildings that were so common in the area, but a modern two-storey house on a hill, with picture windows that overlooked a large garden to the front. The house itself was whitewashed, with a grey slate roof and balconies outside the upper rooms that faced towards the ocean.

'Wow,' she said. 'This is impressive.'

'Your money goes further in the west,' said Rafe as he drew the car to a stop. 'Poppy and I stayed here when we first came back. I was tempted not to move to Dublin at all, but even though I can do some of my work remotely, I also need to be in the lab. All the same, when I look at this and compare it to Sycamore Grove . . .'

'And Briarwood Terrace.' Eden got out of the car. 'I wonder Aunt Trudy could bear to leave.'

'Ah well, it was the seventies or so, wasn't it?' said Rafe. 'I'm not sure Connemara had embraced the kind of delights that the Côte d'Azur had to offer back then. Though on days like today, with the sun shining and a warm breeze, the Atlantic Ocean beats the French coast any time.'

Eden laughed. 'How right you are. Come on, girls, out you get.'

Poppy and Lila scrambled out of the car, Poppy leading the way to the front door and pressing firmly on the bell.

A few seconds later, a dark-haired, dark-eyed woman wearing a white top over patterned leggings opened it.

'Auntie Becky!' cried Poppy. 'We're back!'

'So you are, *a stór*, and it's lovely to see you,' said Becky. 'And this must be your friend.' She hunkered down in front of Lila. 'What's your name?'

'You know her name,' said Poppy impatiently. 'I told you on the phone. It's Lila.'

'You're very welcome too, Lila,' said Becky.

She straightened up and smiled at Rafe and Eden. 'Come in, come in. You made good time for a Friday afternoon.'

Eden felt immediately at home as she followed Rafe into the bright, welcoming house, where polished wooden floors were covered in ethnic rugs, and paintings of local landscapes decorated the walls.

'This is the guest side,' said Becky. 'Come on through to the family house.'

She led them along a wide corridor to another part of the house that was equally warm, welcoming and colourful.

'You know where you're going, Poppy, don't you?' she asked.

Poppy nodded, and bounded up a narrow staircase, followed by Lila.

'This is our room,' she announced as she flung open a door. 'Well, it's mine, but we're sharing.'

'And you're in the next room, Eden,' Becky said. 'Rafe is at the end of the landing.'

'You said this is the family side,' said Eden. 'Are you sure we're not inconveniencing anyone?'

'Not a bit of it,' said Becky. 'Dommo and I have the master bedroom opposite Rafe.'

Were there no children? wondered Eden. Or were they older, and away at college? She didn't ask, but instead opened the door to her room, which had a small balcony with a view over the side garden. The silver shimmer of the sea was visible in the distance.

'It's lovely, thank you,' she said.

'There's an en suite,' said Becky, 'though the children have to share a bathroom.'

'I have my own bathroom at home,' Poppy, who'd followed them, informed her.

'You'll just have to rough it here so,' said her aunt. 'Rafe, you know the lie of the land. I'll leave you all to freshen up and see you downstairs later.'

'Great, thanks,' said Rafe. He turned to Eden. 'OK?' he asked.

She nodded.

'See you shortly,' he said, and left her to it.

Eden unpacked as quickly as she could before checking to see how Lila was getting on. Her daughter had stuffed her clothes into a drawer of the dresser in the room she was sharing with Poppy.

'You probably want to change into a fresh T-shirt and shorts,' suggested Eden as she took the crumpled clothes from the drawer and began to fold them. 'Would you like to wear the new tee Auntie Michelle bought you?' She held it up for Lila's approval.

Lila nodded enthusiastically, then pulled the sequinned top over her head before scrambling into the cotton shorts Eden handed to her. Poppy insisted on changing too, and then the two of them clattered down the stairs, leaving Eden to continue folding clothes before returning to her own room and putting on a fresh T-shirt and shorts herself.

A tap at the door told her that Rafe was there.

'You all right?' he asked when she opened it.

'Yes. This is lovely.'

'So are you.' He leaned towards her.

She broke away before the kiss became anything more than a brief touch of their lips.

'We should go down and see what the girls are up to.'

'They'll be fine.'

'All the same,' said Eden, 'I don't want your sister-in-law to think we're up to no good while she's been turned into an impromptu babysitter.'

'I take issue with your definition of "no good".' Rafe grinned and took a step towards the landing, but Eden put her hand on his arm to stop him.

'Do they have children?' she asked. 'We're taking up a lot of bedroom space.'

'No,' replied Rafe. 'I don't know if that's a choice or not. They were together a few years before they married. Becky's older than Dommo – not that it makes a difference, but perhaps it influenced any decisions they made.'

'She doesn't look a day over thirty.'

'She's forty-three.'

'You're kidding!'

'Maybe it's because of her business.' Rafe grinned.

'Oh?'

'She can tell you about it,' said Rafe. 'I don't want to use up all the conversation.'

'Idiot.' But Eden smiled.

'That's me,' said Rafe, and put his arms around her.

This time she let herself melt into his kiss.

Poppy and Lila were drinking fruit juice when Eden and Rafe walked into the large kitchen.

'Tea?' asked Becky.

'Coffee,' said Rafe. 'I happen to know you have a machine nearly as good as mine.'

'It arrived safely, did it?' Becky smiled at him. 'Of all the things that most worried you in moving to Dublin, your coffee machine featured the highest. He bought a load of fancy furniture,' she said, turning to Eden. 'Stored it all in our big shed. But he kept the coffee machine in his room.'

'It does seem to be his pride and joy,' agreed Eden. 'I'll have tea, thanks.'

'Breakfast tea, Earl Grey, green or an infusion?' asked Becky.

'Oh, crikey, there's a choice.'

252

'Of course.' Becky looked amused. 'We run a guest house. Every taste is catered for.'

'I'll have the bog-standard tea, please,' said Eden.

'In that case, I'll make a pot.' Becky took a large patterned teapot from a shelf. 'Girls, if you want to play in the garden, you can. But no pushing too high on the swings.'

'There are swings?' Lila's face lit up.

'Like I said,' Becky smiled at Eden, 'we cater for every taste, even the children.'

'Thanks for having us,' said Rafe when they were sitting around the long wooden table. 'Especially at such short notice.'

'It was lucky you asked about this weekend,' said Becky. 'My sister and her boyfriend are coming to stay for a couple of days soon, so we wouldn't have had the space. Anyhow, Eden, tell me about yourself. Rafe said you and he were pals when you were kids. That's so cute.'

If the McConnells were anything like the Farrellys, Eden was pretty sure that Becky already knew everything there was to know about her, but she gave a brief résumé of her childhood friendship with Rafe, and an even briefer one of her move to Dublin.

'And then your husband passed away?' Becky's eyes were full of sympathy.

'Yes. It was a hard time. But I'm doing well.'

'Eden works as a carer, but she also does calligraphy,' said Rafe. 'She has a brilliant top-secret commission for someone mega-famous.'

'Really?' Becky looked at her with interest.

'I knew I shouldn't have said anything to you,' said Eden, giving Rafe a dig in the side. 'I had to sign an NDA,' she added. 'They'll cut out my tongue if I talk about it.'

'Ooh, that's so exciting!' cried Becky. 'Well, not the cutting-out-your-tongue part. But the whole NDA thing.'

'I know.' Eden laughed. 'It's a whole different world.'

'She's very talented,' said Rafe.

'And you?' Eden looked at Becky. 'Rafe said you have your own business.'

'Yes,' replied Becky. 'Natural cosmetics. I use seaweed from the Connemara shore to make creams and lotions.'

'Really?' said Eden. 'I got a lovely set as a present last Christmas. It's called Cuan.'

'My range!' Becky clapped her hands in delight. 'Which set did you get?'

'It was a hamper from my parents-in-law,' said Eden.

'Oh, excellent choice. Lots of nice goodies in that.'

'I love them,' admitted Eden. 'I honestly think they've improved my skin. I hope it's not rude to say that yours looks fabulous.'

While the two women continued to talk about skincare and seaweed products, Rafe got up and wandered into the garden. He passed the two children, who were happily playing on the swings, and walked towards two large warehouses carefully screened from the house by tall trees. He could hear music coming from one of them and he pushed the door open.

Inside, his brother looked up from the metal he was polishing.

'How's it going?' asked Dommo.

'Good,' said Rafe.

'Settled in?'

'Yes.'

'The girlfriend and her daughter too?'

'Yes. What are you working on?'

'A tree,' said Dommo.

Rafe nodded. As well as running the guest house with Becky, and being part of the Cuan Cosmetics business, Dommo was a metal sculptor who exhibited his work in various galleries throughout the country.

'Going well?' he asked.

'Pretty good. I'll be easing off for the summer season, getting back to it when things slow down.' Dommo put his tools to one side and wiped his hands on a cloth. 'How're you?'

'I'm grand,' said Rafe. 'Glad to be out of Dublin for a while.'

'We'll make a country boy of you again, science man,' said Dommo.

'That might be pushing it,' said Rafe, and the two of them laughed.

Chapter 22

When Rafe and Dommo returned to the house, they found the two women still talking at the kitchen table.

'I hope you're not gossiping about me,' said Rafe.

Eden told him that he wasn't in Sycamore Grove now, and that she and Becky had been chatting about home businesses and ways to make them work. 'Because,' she added with a smile, 'who knows how mega I might be after my super-duper calligraphy contract, and it's good to get advice from someone as successful as Becky.'

'My over-achieving family,' said Rafe. 'I'm such a disappointment.'

'You know quite well that Mam likes saying "my son the medical scientist" when she talks about you,' said Dommo. 'I'm only the B&B man.'

'Who has exhibitions of his sculptures,' said Rafe.

'I don't remember you guys being this competitive,' said Eden.

'Because I was his big brother and could win any competition by beating him up,' said Dommo as he gave Rafe a gentle dig. 'Sorry.'

After more good-natured banter, Rafe suggested that his

brother and sister-in-law probably had stuff to do and that he and Eden should bring the girls to the beach.

'I know it's almost evening,' he said, 'but there's hours yet before sunset and it's still glorious.'

Poppy and Lila were happy to abandon the swings for the seaside, and a short while later they were scrambling on the rocks that surrounded a small cove near the house, while Eden and Rafe sat together and watched them.

'Mum texted to ask if we'd like to go to hers for lunch tomorrow,' said Rafe. 'Would you?'

'At Orchard Close?' Eden looked at him.

'Yes.'

She hesitated.

'You don't have to,' he said.

'I really would like to see your mum again,' she said. 'I'm not quite so sure about Orchard Close.'

'You don't have to decide now.'

'I do,' she said, more firmly this time. 'And yes. I'll go with you.'

As he leaned towards her, there was a loud cry from Poppy, who'd tumbled off the rock she was climbing. Fortunately her pride was hurt more than anything else, but Rafe decided they'd been on the rocks long enough and it was time for a swim.

The two girls made their way into the sea, shrieking as the cold water hit their legs. Much to Rafe's astonishment, Lila threw herself onto her stomach, her arms and legs thrashing confidently.

'I've been bringing her swimming since she was a tot,' said Eden. 'And, of course, when we go to Wexford with the Farrellys, she's in the sea all the time.'

'How come you didn't change your name?' asked Rafe. 'Why did you stay Eden Hall?'

'Work reasons mainly,' replied Eden. 'And . . . well, it might sound a bit mad, especially as I'm so close to Andy's family, but I wanted to keep the connection to my parents.'

'It doesn't sound mad at all,' he said.

'Thank you for suggesting this.' She nodded to where the two children were splashing each other. 'Poppy is good for Lila.'

'And you're good for me.'

He put his arm around her and kissed her, until the girls called for them to join them in the water.

Dommo and Becky were awaiting the arrival of more guests that evening, and suggested to Rafe that he and Eden might like to book a local restaurant for later, saying that they'd keep an eye on the children. But Eden, not wanting to impose on them, proposed they get a takeaway that they could eat in the garden, as the weather was so balmy.

'Always providing we can find one,' she added.

'We're in Galway, not the ends of the earth,' said Rafe. 'Of course there's takeaway. What would you like?'

'I have a list of places I recommend to the guests,' said Becky. 'Italian, Indian, Chinese, Japanese, European . . . whatever you fancy.'

'Are you going to join us?' asked Eden. 'Is there anything you'd like? It's my treat.'

'That's very kind of you, but don't worry about us,' said Becky. 'We've got lots to do. You're the ones on holiday, so feel free to go with whatever suits you. We might pop out and join you for a glass of wine later.'

In the end, they chose Italian, and the pizzas that arrived were the best Eden had ever tasted.

Dommo donated a bottle of wine from the cellar (as he cheerfully called the basement), and as they sat with a glass each after the meal, while the girls once again played in the garden, Eden remarked that they really could be in Italy right now.

'You don't get this wild Atlantic seaboard in Italy.' Rafe gestured towards the traditional Connemara stone wall that marked the boundary of the garden and the road to the ocean beyond. The sun was still above the horizon, its pale orange glow reflected by the high waves that crashed onto the shore.

'Next stop America,' murmured Eden.

'There's actually a signpost near the beach,' Rafe said. 'New York four thousand nine hundred kilometres.'

'And Seattle?' asked Eden. 'How far away were you there?'

'About seven thousand,' he replied.

It was less than two hundred and fifty kilometres from Dublin to Galway, she thought to herself. And yet it had taken her over twenty years to come back. And then she thought again of Wexford, which was closer to Dublin still, but somehow an entire world away.

'We've been really lucky with the weather,' remarked Rafe after they'd eventually put Poppy and Lila to bed, exhausted from their day.

'And lucky with your brother and sister-in-law too,' said Eden. 'She's an absolute pet, and of course, I'm not scared of him any more.'

'You were scared of Dommo?' Rafe looked at her in astonishment.

'Not scared really. Just in awe. He was so tall and powerful and grown-up, at least in my head.'

'He's a total softie.'

'I know,' she said. 'Becky told me all about how he's taken on so much of the B&B stuff so she can develop the cosmetics business. She's a real powerhouse.'

'I don't know her that well, to be honest,' admitted Rafe. 'I was away when they got together.'

'She has a pharmaceutical degree and was always interested in the benefits of natural products and the idea of setting up her own business,' Eden told him. 'But she inherited the B&B from an aunt and wanted to keep that going too. Guests often buy the cosmetics, so they complement each other, though if the business keeps growing, they'll have to make a decision about it, because it'll be impossible to do both.'

'You found all that out in half an hour?'

'That and lots more.' Eden grinned. 'But if I told you all of it, I'd have to kill you.'

'Why aren't all women working in the secret service?' asked Rafe. 'Or running the world?'

She laughed.

He put his arms around her, then kissed her.

Out of the corner of his eye, he saw Dommo watching him from the kitchen window.

It was almost midnight when they left the garden. As they tiptoed past the girls' room, Eden heard Lila whimper gently. She put her head around the door and saw her daughter sitting up in bed, rubbing her eyes.

'Hey, honey,' she whispered as she walked softly over to her. 'Are you OK?'

260

'No.' Lila's voice was tearful. 'I lost Teddy.'

'Here he is.' Eden picked the teddy bear up from the floor where he'd fallen and handed him to her.

'Sing to me,' said Lila.

Eden glanced towards the door, where Rafe stood silently. 'See you later?' she mouthed.

He nodded.

'Come on then.' She gathered Lila into her arms. 'Let's get you back to sleep.'

Lila's favourite song was 'Feed the Birds' from the musical *Mary Poppins*, a song that Eden's own mother had sung to her. She was still humming softly when Rafe came back a short time later. He gave her an enquiring look and she shrugged helplessly, even as Lila opened her eyes and asked why she'd stopped singing.

'Don't worry,' he whispered. 'I'll be back.'

Rafe closed the door and went downstairs again. The light in the kitchen, which had been off earlier, was now on, and he looked into the room. He was surprised to see Dommo sitting there, a laptop open in front of him.

'What are you doing?' he asked.

'Becky's accounts.'

'At this hour?'

'You know me. A night owl.'

'Doesn't she mind you sneaking downstairs in the middle of the night?'

'She's out for the count.' Dommo closed the laptop. 'What about Eden? Isn't she expecting you to knock on her door?'

'Lila woke up a short time ago,' said Rafe. 'Eden's getting her back to sleep.'

'The joys of parenting.' Dommo closed the laptop. 'This can wait. D'you want to have a quick beer outside?'

'Better make it a non-A if you have it,' said Rafe. 'I'm not good with beer on top of wine.'

The brothers walked into the garden with their beers and sat on one of the benches.

'Cheers.' Dommo clinked his bottle against Rafe's.

The last time he'd sat drinking beer with his brother, recalled Rafe, was when he'd first come back to Ireland. Dommo had tried to talk about Jewel and what had happened, but Rafe hadn't wanted to discuss it. Now, though, he told Dommo how helpless and enraged he'd felt when he'd heard the news. And how guilty at not having been able to protect her.

'You did your best,' said Dommo.

'Not good enough.'

'You can't stop bad things happening in life. And it sounds to me like Jewel was a clever, resourceful woman who'd done fantastically for herself. What happened was terrible, but it wasn't her fault, or yours; it was all down to that guy.'

Rafe said nothing.

'What about Eden?' Dommo put the question as casually as he could.

'What about her?'

'Another woman with a tragic past. Are you trying to protect her too?'

'She doesn't need my protection.'

'And yet you tried when you were kids. When her folks were killed and you wanted her to move in with us.'

'Oh, for God's sake, why does everyone keep banging on about that? It was more than twenty years ago.'

262

'But you still keep trying to help.'

'I'm not trying to help. We're friends, that's all.'

'More than friends, Rafe. That wasn't a just-friends kiss you gave her earlier.'

'OK, so we wouldn't have separate rooms if the kids weren't with us. But we're not . . .'

'Not what?'

Rafe wasn't sure what he wanted to say.

'How do you feel about her?'

'When did you get so into talking about feelings and stuff?' Rafe gave him an irritated look. 'As I recall, any time we expressed our feelings when we were younger, you'd tell me I'd feel this all right, before thumping me.'

'I've matured.' Dommo grinned. 'I try not to thump people indiscriminately. But if it makes you feel better, I can always throw a punch at you again.'

Rafe laughed.

'It was Petra who asked me to talk to you,' Dommo confessed. 'To, you know, get you to open up. She worries about you. She's afraid you've got some kind of mad chivalrous notions about Eden.'

'Neither of you has to worry about me,' Rafe said. 'Eden and I are having fun together, that's all. Overall, I feel pretty good with where things are right now. Only to be improved if you get me another beer.'

Dommo went off to do as he was asked.

When Lila was finally asleep (it had taken three full renditions of 'Feed the Birds' to get her off), Eden tucked the teddy bear beneath the light summer duvet and rose quietly from the bed. She glanced at Poppy, who hadn't moved even while she sang. Poppy's body was like a starfish on the bed, her own duvet pushed down around her ankles. Eden covered her as gently as she'd covered Lila. Poppy stirred a little but didn't wake.

Eden looked at the two of them, one fair, one dark. She remembered how uneasy she'd felt at seeing the woman at the motorway services, knowing that she was thinking of them as a family. She wondered why that had upset her. Why she didn't want anyone thinking Poppy was her daughter too. Poppy was a lovely child and brilliant with Lila, who adored her.

They'd make a good family together, she thought.

She wasn't sure if that was what she wanted.

She wasn't sure if that was what Rafe wanted either.

Eden turned away from the children and tiptoed out of the bedroom, leaving the door slightly ajar. She walked along the corridor to Rafe's room, but when she didn't see him there, she returned to her own.

She was surprised not to see him there either. She hesitated for a moment, then opened the window and stepped onto the narrow balcony. The night air was warm, the breeze soft, and there were more stars visible in the sky than she was used to seeing from her Dublin home. She remembered Uncle Kevin once telling her that her mum and dad were stars now. For a long time afterwards, she would stand at her bedroom window, looking for the ones she thought might be them. When Trudy found her gazing upwards one night, she told her that Kevin had been talking utter nonsense and that Eden should know better. The thing was, she *did* know better, but she liked the idea that two of the twinkling lights were her mum and dad. And when Andy died, she couldn't help standing in the garden, eyes raised, reminding herself that both she and he were star stuff; that the elements that made up the people they were had been formed in the heart of distant suns. And so even if Trudy was correct, she wasn't entirely accurate.

The thought had always comforted her.

She was distracted by a sudden movement in the garden and leaned forward to see Rafe and Dommo sitting side by side on one of the garden benches, each with a bottle of beer in his hand.

They were too far away for her to hear more than snatches of the conversation, but although she knew she shouldn't try to eavesdrop, she couldn't help straining to hear their words.

'. . . friends . . .'

'. . . about her?'

'. . . throw a punch . . .'

The sound of laughter drifted up to her, followed by silence. She smiled. It was good to see Rafe at ease with his older brother. She watched as Dommo got up from the seat and walked towards the house, while Rafe stayed where he was. She wondered if she should join him. But then Dommo returned with two more bottles of beer and sat beside his brother again. Eden strained even more to hear what they were saying.

'. . . a couple of kilos already with all the treats . . .' said Rafe.

She smiled again. She didn't need to be beside him to know he was talking about the army of women in Sycamore Grove who were bombarding him with food.

'. . . sweet loving,' said Dommo.

'. . . to rampage through the neighbours.' Rafe laughed. 'Like a TV show.'

More laughter. More amused conversation. And then Dommo's words were carried clearly by a sudden gust of wind, his tone serious.

'Does Poppy miss her?'

She didn't hear Rafe's reply.

'Do you?'

This time she heard his answer.

'Every single day.'

'And Eden? Does she help?'

His reply was low and inaudible.

'Petra told me you were never getting involved again.'

Eden held her breath as she strained to hear what Rafe said in reply, but the direction of the wind had changed again and she couldn't hear any more of their conversation. She stepped back into the room, closed the window behind her and went to bed.

She was sitting on a rock, seawater lapping at her feet as she gazed into the pool left by the outgoing wave. Barnacles clung to the side of the stone and the red fronds of an anemone swayed with the movement of the water. She sensed him behind her but didn't turn around. She waited for him to put his hands over her eyes and ask 'Guess who?' as if she didn't know already.

Instead she heard the whisper of her name.

'Eden.'

She saw his reflection in the pool.

'Andy.'

The incoming wave shattered the image.

'Andy?' she said again.

'No,' he whispered. 'It's me, Rafe. It's fine. Go back to sleep.'

Her eyes opened.

She heard the click of her door.

She sat up in bed.

'Are you there?' she asked.

But there was no reply.

Lila came into Eden's room at six the following morning telling her it was time to get up and play.

'Have a snuggle beside me for a little while first,' Eden murmured, and was relieved when her daughter clambered into the bed.

But although, amazingly, Lila fell asleep again, Eden didn't. She lay on her back, gazing at the ceiling, wondering if she'd dreamed Rafe opening and closing her bedroom door in the middle of the night, and if she'd actually spoken Andy's name aloud. She recalled the remarks she'd partially overheard him make about Jewel. Did he dream about her the way she did about Andy? How did he really feel about what had happened to her? How much of a presence was she in his life? She realised that until now, she'd looked at their relationship entirely from her own point of view. She hadn't really considered his. And she suddenly understood why Dommo and Petra worried about him. It must be hard to accept that the person you loved had been murdered. Harder perhaps than losing them in a tragic accident. She hadn't totally recovered from what had happened to Andy. Rafe couldn't possibly have recovered from what had happened to Jewel.

They were both struggling with their different pasts.

Maybe their present was a terrible mistake.

*

267

She slid out of her bed and was in the shower when Lila woke again and padded into the bathroom to join her. The day she was able to have a shower on her own without Lila wanting to either chat or get under the water with her would be one of the best days of her life, Eden thought, as both of them got soapy beneath the spray. And yet she'd miss it too.

She told herself that she spent too much of her life being impatient in the present and hankering after the past. She resolved to try to live in the here and now a bit more. Even if the here and now was Lila using up most of her favourite foam spray.

The shower soap's invigorating verbena scent followed her as she headed downstairs for breakfast with her daughter. Eden felt uncomfortable with Becky serving her in the guest dining room, but the other woman told her not to be silly, that she was used to cooking and serving everyone and that it was easier to do this than to have visitors in the kitchen. Rafe, when he and Poppy came down a little later, swung his sister-in-law around in his arms and told her she was a gem.

'How are you this morning?' he asked as he sat down opposite Eden.

'Fine, thanks.'

'Did you sleep well?'

'I heard you at the door. I . . .'

'It was later than I expected. I was in the garden with Dommo. Sorry.'

'It's fine.'

'Are you still OK to come to lunch at Mum's?'

'Of course, if she's all right with having us.'

'She can't wait to see you again,' said Rafe. 'She was full

of questions about how you are and what you've been doing.'

Coping, thought Eden, that's what I've been doing.

Just like you.

They went to the beach again that morning, and while the children were paddling in a rock pool, Eden turned to Rafe and asked why he hadn't come into her bedroom.

'You were half asleep,' he said.

'I was dreaming of Andy.'

'That's why I didn't come in.'

'Did I say his name?'

He nodded.

'I don't dream of him that often.'

'When Jewel was first killed, I dreamed about it every single night,' he told her. 'But not so much now.'

'Though you think of her every day.'

He looked at her in surprise.

'I heard you talking to Dommo,' she confessed. 'Only snippets. I wasn't really trying to eavesdrop.'

'He worries about me.' Rafe dug his feet into the warm sand. 'They all do.'

She nodded.

'I guess you're used to that too,' he said.

She nodded again.

'Although they tell you to take your time, people would prefer you to get over things as quickly as possible,' said Rafe. 'Jewel was an important part of my life and it's not easy to put what happened to her out of my head completely.'

'Of course not!' exclaimed Eden. 'It's the same with me and Andy.'

'We're life's flotsam and jetsam,' he remarked after they'd sat in silence for a moment. 'Bobbing aimlessly on the waves, being washed up on the shore.'

'Certainly our families seem to think of us like that,' Eden said. 'Perhaps it's time to have a sense of direction. To land wherever we want to.'

'Eden Hall.' He gave her an admiring look. 'I'll have to remember that for the next time Petra or Dommo tells me I'm drifting into something.'

'Do they seriously think that?' she asked.

'I don't know what they think, to be honest.' Rafe shrugged. 'I've never been in a situation where people were worried about me before.'

'And are they more worried about you and me than you and Jewel?' she asked.

'I think they worry that I don't know what I'm doing,' he admitted. 'But right now, I'm not worried about anything at all.' He stood up. 'Come on, last one in is definitely the jetsam.'

And they ran, shrieking, into the water, followed by their children.

Eden stared out of the car window as they drove towards the city. She still didn't recognise her surroundings, but her memory was finally jolted when they reached a roundabout that led inland from the coast. She recalled the large grey house that stood at one of the exits. Now renovated, it had been run-down in her day, and the children often told each other that Witchy O'Sullivan lived there. The soot-black cat usually stretched out on the branches of the huge chestnut tree of the grey house proved it.

The tree had been cut back, and the house remodelled and repainted. The rainbow and unicorn stickers now clearly visible on one of the upstairs windows showed that it had become a family home. There was no sign of a black cat either in the tree or anywhere else.

Rafe turned one corner and then another, and suddenly Eden recognised the road where she'd lived. It, too, had changed over the last twenty-two years – there were more cars parked on the street and in the driveways, and a lot of the homes had been given complete makeovers. When Eden had lived there, they'd all been identical, with white-painted walls and mock-Tudor beams over the front porches. Many homeowners had since dispensed with the beams, glassed in the porches, widened their driveways and extended the back of the houses too.

Rafe pulled up outside a house halfway along the road. Eden instinctively glanced across to the other side, where her childhood home stood. The new owners had embraced the general efforts at refurbishment and removed the beams, as well as replacing the original windows and front door.

'Come on, Mama.' Lila nudged her, and she realised that she'd been in a daze. Rafe was standing on the pavement, waiting patiently for her.

She opened the door and stepped onto the street.

'All right?' he asked.

'Yes,' she said. 'I'm just . . . It's so weird to be here. Everything's different. And yet it's the same too.'

'I know.' He put his arm around her shoulders and squeezed.

She turned away from her old home and followed him up

271

the path to his own door, as she'd done so many times in the past. He rang the bell.

Eden remembered Maggie McConnell as very tall, with dark eyes and clouds of dark hair that she often held back in brightly coloured scrunchies. But the woman smiling at her now was around her own height, and her bobbed hair was the same shade of grey as Eden's own. Yet her brown eyes were still the same, warm and welcoming, with a hint of mischief.

'*Fáilte, fáilte*. Come in, come in!' she exclaimed. She swung Poppy up into her arms and then kissed Rafe on the cheek before turning to Eden. 'Eden Hall. It's really you. Don't you look wonderful!'

'Hello, Mrs McConnell,' said Eden.

'Call me Maggie,' said Rafe's mother. 'It's a joy to see you again. And who's this?' She smiled at Lila, who was hanging behind Eden.

'This is Lila.' Eden introduced her. 'Say hello to Mrs McConnell.'

'She says her name's Maggie,' whispered Lila.

'You can call me Auntie Maggie.' The older woman smiled at Lila. 'Aren't you the prettiest little girl.'

'Nana!' Poppy was outraged. 'You said I'm the prettiest girl.'

'You're the prettiest girl with brown hair,' said Maggie. 'Lila's the prettiest blonde. Although she's more of a strawberry blonde,' she said to Eden. 'Like you were in the day.'

Eden put her hand to the mass of grey and rose-gold curls that she'd pinned up earlier. 'I think I was more carroty,' she remarked.

'You had lovely hair, just like your Aunt Trudy,' Maggie

told her. 'She was stunning as a young woman. Anyway, why are we standing in the hallway talking about hair? Come on into the kitchen.'

'Nana!' yelled Poppy, who'd run ahead of them. 'Nana, there's a bouncy castle in the back garden.'

'So there is,' said Maggie. 'I wonder how it got there.'

'You put it there!' Poppy's eyes were shining. 'Is it for me? For us?'

'If you're good girls,' Maggie said. 'Take off your shoes before you get on it. And no pushing!'

Poppy opened the back door and ran into the garden, followed by Lila, who'd lost all sense of shyness at the sight of the bouncy castle.

'There was no need for that.' Rafe gave his mother an amused look.

'I thought it was a nice idea,' said Maggie. 'She can work off her excess energy, and sure the cousins will be over later, so it's something to keep them all happy. Besides, I got it from Barney McKeown; he rents them out and this is the smallest one he has. Nobody ever wants it. He gave it to me for a good price.'

'You're such a softie.' He slid his arm around her waist and kissed her on the cheek. 'And you spoil your grandchildren something rotten.'

'I didn't spoil my children,' said Maggie. 'I'm entitled to ruin the next generation altogether.'

They both laughed, while Eden stood at the kitchen door looking around her. The house was both familiar and changed. The McConnells had added a big kitchen and dining extension to the back that took full advantage of facing south. But the deep alcove in the dining area, where Mr McConnell had built a shelving unit for the children's collection of sporting trophies and other awards, remained. She recalled Rafe proudly putting his under-10s soccer trophy on the middle shelf, alongside Petra's swimming medals. Now the shelves held books and ornaments. Eden wondered where the trophies had gone.

'So, Eden, would you like a tea or coffee or anything else before lunch?' asked Maggie.

'Water is fine, thanks,' replied Eden.

Maggie took a bottle from the fridge and filled a glass. She handed it to Eden and then asked Rafe what he wanted.

'Water will do me too,' he said.

His accent had softened in the last twenty-four hours, taking on the gentle burr of the western seaboard, and here, at home, it softened even more. Eden smiled to herself at the sound of it.

'Well now,' said Maggie when they were sitting at the kitchen table. 'How have you been getting on since I last saw you, Eden?'

Eden glanced at Rafe. She didn't know how much he might already have told his mum about her. But he simply gave her an encouraging smile. So she told Maggie that she'd gone through a bit of a rocky patch, but that now she was a lone parent who also worked as a carer, and that she was lucky with the great support her family gave her.

'And how are Trudy and Kevin?' asked Maggie. 'I remember when they came to collect you. Such an awful time for everyone. Trudy was so scared.'

'Scared?' Eden gave her a startled look.

'She said to me that she was useless with children. That she hardly knew you. That she was afraid you'd hate her.'

'Oh.' Eden was even more startled.

274

'She asked me for tips on how to look after you and I told her to let you be yourself and not to interfere.'

Well, thought Eden, Trudy had certainly taken that advice to heart. She'd never interfered even when Eden felt she should.

'We weren't the closest,' she confessed to Maggie. 'Though that might have been as much my fault as hers.'

Even as she said the words, she realised that she'd never really believed that before. She'd always blamed Trudy for not being the person she wanted her to be. For not doing things the way her mother had done them, even though she'd sometimes felt smothered by the intensity of Martina's love for her. But Eden knew she'd always focused on the things Trudy hadn't done, or had done badly. She'd forgotten about the freedom that her aunt had given her. Not just the freedom to socialise, but the freedom to have her own opinions, to disagree with her, to want to do things differently.

'You'll make mistakes in your life,' Trudy had once told her. 'The important thing is to own those mistakes. To know you made them and why. To accept the consequences. And to learn from them. Nobody is perfect, Eden. Not you, not me, not your mum or your dad.'

At the time, Eden had felt bitter that Trudy had criticised her parents, as though by saying they made mistakes she was in some way blaming her dad for having crashed the car and killed her mother. His mistake, she seemed to be saying, and the fact that he and Martina had died was merely a consequence. Nothing to get upset about.

It wasn't what she had meant. Eden could see that now. Perhaps she'd seen it back then too. But she hadn't wanted to accept that her aunt might have been right about anything.

'You OK?' Rafe looked at her.

'Yes. Just remembering my time with Trudy. I didn't want to move to Dublin, so I guess I was hard to live with.'

She hadn't thought of herself as being hard to live with before either. She'd thought it was Trudy and Kevin who were the difficult ones.

'Well, you all must have done something right, because you've turned into a lovely young woman and a good mother,' said Maggie.

'I'm glad you think so,' Eden said. 'But all I do is muddle along.'

'Not at all,' said Rafe. 'You do a million things well. You're a great mum and a wonderful carer – Elizabeth speaks really highly of you – and you have your hush-hush celebrity calligraphy work too.'

'Hush-hush celebrity?' Maggie looked enquiringly at Eden, who explained about the hobby that was turning into something profitable.

'Oh, I remember you making Christmas cards one year!' exclaimed Maggie. 'They had a cut-out Santa on the front and you'd sprinkled them with glitter. They were lovely.'

Eden smiled as the memory rushed back. Making a card had been an arts-and-crafts project in school and her mother had been so enchanted with the one she'd brought home that she'd asked her to make more for the neighbours. She had regretted the request when the silver glitter had taken on a life of its own and appeared all over the house for weeks, but the cards themselves were a great success.

'Your mum was very arty too,' said Maggie. 'She had a real eye for pretty things.'

'I don't remember,' confessed Eden. 'And I don't really see myself as arty either.'

'I wouldn't have either until those cards,' Maggie agreed. 'Before then, you were a total tomboy. Then you were a tomboy with glitter.'

They laughed. Eden felt herself relax. She'd always felt at ease in the McConnell house, and now, after the initial strangeness of it, she was settling into it again.

'It's warm chicken salad for lunch.' Maggie stood up. 'I'll get on with it while you two relax.'

'Can I help?' Eden stood up too, but Maggie put her hand on her shoulder and pushed her gently back into her seat. 'Not a bit of it,' she said. 'You're a guest, and it's lovely to have you.'

'Maybe I should help?' suggested Rafe. 'I'm not a guest.'

'Yeah, but I want to get it done with the minimum of fuss,' Maggie told him as she opened the fridge. 'So you can sit there and *lig do scíth.*'

Eden smiled at the Irish expression to take a break and rest.

Rafe's mother was about to speak again when the kitchen door opened and a young woman walked in laden down with shopping bags.

'Noelle.' Maggie smiled at her. 'I didn't think you were coming today. Guess who's here.'

The young woman looked at Eden and shook her head. Eden, in turn, looked at Noelle.

'I used to wheel your pram,' she told her. 'I pretended you were my own baby sister.'

'It's Eden Hall,' Rafe said. 'From over the road.'

'Eden.' A smile broke across Noelle's face. 'Gosh, I only have the vaguest memories of you.'

277

'I remember you really well,' said Eden. 'I loved lifting you in and out of the pram. Your mum used to have heart attacks watching me as I staggered around with you. You look great.'

'You too.' Noelle walked to the fridge, took out a juice and poured it into a glass. 'I heard you and Rafe had met up in Dublin. I didn't know you were going to visit.'

'That's because you never listen to anything we say,' teased her mother.

Eden was wondering exactly what she'd heard and what the McConnells were saying about her when the door opened again and another woman, carrying a toddler in her arms and followed by a small girl, walked in.

'Joy!' exclaimed Rafe. 'You came.'

'Well, of course I came.' His younger sister smiled at him. 'Mam said there were other children and a bouncy castle. As well as you. And . . .' she looked at Eden, 'your best friend, Eden Hall. How are you? It's lovely to see you again.'

Although there was only a year between them, Eden being the older of the two, she and Joy had never been close friends. This was partly because Joy had shared a birthday with Marcella Murphy from two doors down, which conferred best-friend status on her, and partly because Eden had always been regarded as Rafe's friend. Nevertheless, they'd sometimes played in groups together, and the two girls had got on well.

'It's lovely to see you too,' she said. 'And your children are so cute!'

'Donnacha,' Joy said as she set the toddler down on the floor. 'And Florrie, who was four last week.'

At that point, Lila and Poppy ran into the kitchen demanding something to drink, and immediately wanted to bring Donnacha and Florrie outside with them. The kitchen door opened again, and this time Richard, Rafe's dad, joined the group. He gave Rafe a hug, and as Eden stood up to greet him, he kissed her on both cheeks, telling her it was lovely to see her.

It was like the Farrellys, she thought. That same loud, boisterous and loving family dynamic that Andy's family had. The dynamic she'd always loved and craved for herself. One that had been utterly unthinkable with Trudy and Kevin.

She felt herself relax into it.

'So where are you guys staying?' asked Noelle, as she pulled out a chair and sat down.

'We're at Dommo's,' Rafe said. 'Eden and Lila are only here till tomorrow. Poppy and I will be staying till the end of next week.'

'Are you two a couple?'

'Of course not!' cried Eden. 'We're . . .'

'Old friends,' supplied Rafe.

'You were a pair of demons when you were young,' said Maggie. 'Are you sure it's just old friends now?'

Rafe gave her a dark look.

'It'd be cute, though, wouldn't it.' Joy grinned. 'Childhood friends meet up and—'

'Put a sock in it,' said Rafe. 'Men and women can be friends, you know.'

He was making it perfectly clear, thought Eden as she listened to the chatter going on around her. She wasn't a replacement for Jewel. There were definitely no strings. Despite the hot sex, they were no more than friends.

And then, as she sat with the others at the table, she felt the weight of Rafe's hand on the top of her leg. She looked straight ahead as his fingers reached the edge of her shorts, gently brushing against her bare skin before he lifted them away again.

'More water?' asked Maggie.

'Yes, please,' she said.

He came to her room again that night. She was lying in bed, reading a book that she put to one side when he opened the door.

'Am I interrupting?' he asked.

'It's a page-turning thriller,' she told him. 'Any minute now there's going to be another dramatic twist.'

'Would you rather I left you to it?'

'Old friends let other old friends finish their exciting thrillers.'

He gave her an appraising look.

'We're more than friends.'

'That's not what you said at your mum's.'

He exhaled slowly, and this time his look was more measured.

'I didn't like to say we were . . . well . . . Not in front of my mother.'

'We're mostly friends,' she agreed. 'Premium friends.'

'Is that OK with you? Do you feel—'

'Shut up, Rafe,' she said, and dropped the book onto the floor. He got into the bed beside her and pulled her beneath the covers.

'So . . . I feel a little bit like we're doing this in my parents' house,' she whispered. 'Sort of illicitly.'

'I know.' He grinned. 'It adds a bit of spice, doesn't it?'

'Just don't start the headboard banging,' she warned. 'I

don't want Poppy and Lila running in thinking awful things are happening.'

'I can bring you to the heights of pleasure without making a sound,' he assured her.

She chortled, and then gasped as his hands slid along her body.

'Maybe you can,' she murmured. 'But I'm not sure silence in these circumstances is my forte.'

Chapter 23

The next morning, Rafe drove Eden and Lila to the train station.

'It's a pity you can't stay,' he said. 'The girls were having fun, and so was I.'

'It was lovely,' she agreed. 'Last night was particularly enjoyable.'

'Yes, it was,' chimed in Poppy, who'd insisted on coming to the station too. 'Me and Lila liked the karaoke.'

Becky had organised it for them, and the two girls had spent hours singing together in the den.

'Mum texted me,' Rafe said. 'She was delighted to see you again.'

'It was lovely to see her too.' Eden's voice was full of warmth. 'She's exactly the same person I remember. So's your dad. Your sisters . . . I wouldn't have recognised them. They look great,' she added quickly. 'Noelle is so grown-up and glamorous. And Joy is such fun. You have a great family, Rafe. I loved meeting them.'

'And Poppy loved having Lila here, didn't you, sweetheart?'

'Lila's my best friend,' said Poppy.

'So all's well in our worlds,' said Eden.

'More than that, I hope. I want everything to be perfect.'
'It absolutely is.'

He smiled and leaned towards her and kissed her, and the taste of him stayed with her all through the journey back to Dublin.

She was happy, she thought that evening as she took out her pen and ink and continued working on Amahle's cards. She was happy she'd gone to Galway, she was happy to have seen her old house again, and that she'd seen the McConnells too – even if she'd been taken aback at how grown-up Noelle now was. Not that she shouldn't be, of course, she was in her late twenties, but, thought Eden, it was funny how you imagined that places you hadn't been and people you hadn't seen pretty much stayed the same, even when you yourself had changed. And yet even though Orchard Close was different, and even if Rafe's family were older, the essence of being there, the comfort she'd remembered as a child, hadn't changed.

The comfort of being with him hadn't changed either.

Even if other things had been added to the mix.

She put down her pen and picked up her phone.

Eden
Missing you already

Rafe
Same here. And Poppy is missing Lila.

Eden
We'll see you again soon

283

Rafe

Of course. Am meeting Petra in town shortly.

Eden

Have fun

Rafe

Will do. Take care. Rx

When her phone buzzed a moment later, Eden decided that Michelle must have some kind of alert set up to warn her every time she was in contact with Rafe McConnell. She was tempted to ignore her, but decided it was better to speak to her sister-in-law now rather than put it off.

'Hi,' she said.

'You're back.'

'I've been back ages. We got a train this morning.'

'Oh. I thought you wouldn't be home till later.'

'I didn't tell you what time I was going and I didn't tell you what time I was coming back because it doesn't matter.' Eden couldn't keep the exasperation out of her voice.

'Did you have a good time?' asked Michelle.

'Yes. Lila loved being at the beach with Poppy, and it was lovely to see Mrs McConnell again.'

'Rafe's mum? What's she like?'

'Like all mums,' said Eden. 'Like Valerie, although not as . . .' She'd been going to say 'domineering', but that was unfair. Valerie wasn't domineering, although she did set the agenda for everyone. So instead she said 'bubbly', which absolutely wasn't the right word.

'She was bubbling over at lunch all right,' said Michelle.

'Her only topic of conversation was the move to Dunleary and the extent of the building work. Imagine keeping that from us the way they did! And imagine that they're adding on an extension just for you. It's so exciting. It's good for them and it's good for you too. Everyone was fully behind the idea, and I'm sure you're thrilled.'

'*Everyone* was OK with it?' Eden was surprised. Because she'd been thinking about it on the way home on the train, and she couldn't imagine that all the Farrellys would be comfortable with the idea of her and Lila living in their parents' house. She said this to Michelle.

'It's not like they're handing it over to you. Mum said she suggested you rent out your place as long as you were with them. We all agree it's the perfect solution. You're there with babysitters on tap. And it's ideal for Mum and Dad to have you with them too. Not that they're in any way infirm at the moment, but as they get older, it could work out very well, given your nursing experience.'

'You've thought it through.'

'We had a long discussion. Lots of opinions were aired, but they were mostly positive. You should've been there. The others were surprised to hear you'd gone to Galway for the weekend, given how against it you've always been in the past. But I told them you were staying with a friend. I didn't tell them it was a man,' she added. 'You said you're just friends, and I accept that it's good for Lila to have a girl around her own age to play with. So I'll take you at your word that it's nothing more.'

Eden touched her lips with the tips of her fingers, remembering Rafe's kiss. And she remembered his hands as they moved softly along her body. She caught her breath.

'I'm sorry if it seemed like I was interfering.' Michelle's voice was conciliatory. 'I'm concerned for you, that's all.'

'I understand where you're coming from, but your concern is utterly misplaced.'

'I don't want you to be hurt.'

'I could never be hurt any more than I was when Andy was killed,' said Eden. 'Or than by those horrible speculative newspaper reports. Or that damn photographer who took those photos at the funeral. Or the journalist who covered the inquiry. Nothing and nobody can hurt me like that again, Michelle. You don't need to worry.'

'I suppose not.' Michelle sighed. 'OK, let's put this behind us and focus on Mum and Dad's great news and how fantastic it is for them. And how fantastic it will be for you and Lila too. Will I see you later in the week?'

'I'm sure you will.'

Galway had been a short break. But she was back in the heart of her family now.

And Rafe was over two hundred kilometres away, in the heart of his.

Rafe took yet another selfie of himself and Poppy on the beach and sent it to Eden. It was the last of the many he'd already sent during his week away. Each time she replied with a 'missing you' message and sometimes with a selfie of her own.

But she hadn't yet replied to his latest when he saw Petra walking along the strand.

'Bunking off work?' he asked as she joined him.

'I started at six this morning, so I think I've done enough,' she said. 'How're things?'

286

'Great,' he replied. 'Poppy was about to build the biggest sandcastle of the week. She's done bigger and bigger ones every day.'

'They're *fortresses*,' Poppy told Petra. 'You can watch me.'

The two adults sat on the dry, almost white sand while Poppy began filling her bright yellow bucket nearer the sea.

'She loves it here,' observed Rafe.

'You could always move back.' Petra picked up a handful of sand and allowed it to trickle through her fingers. 'You said before that you only needed to be in your office a couple of days a week. You could divide your time between Dublin and Galway.'

'Not successfully,' said Rafe. 'There are times I need to be in the lab too, and that's not something that can necessarily be planned. Besides, I wouldn't want to leave Poppy here while I was in Dublin. It wouldn't be fair to her or to . . . well, whoever I left her with.'

'Joy said she'd be happy to have her,' said Petra.

'You've talked to Joy about me and Poppy?' Rafe stared at her. 'What the actual f—'

'We were chatting,' said Petra quickly. 'That's all. She was saying what a good time Poppy had with her kids the other night and how easily she fitted in. And Poppy said something about not wanting to go home because she loved Galway and . . . Well, Joy wondered if it might be a good idea for you to base yourself back here.'

'It's a terrible idea.'

'But you have to admit that Poppy loves the place.'

'So do I,' said Rafe. 'It doesn't mean I want to live here. I could've stayed, but I didn't.'

'I know you've said the job means you have to be in

Dublin,' said Petra. 'But I'm sure it wouldn't be impossible to live here if you wanted. Employers are much more flexible these days.'

'Why does everyone suddenly want me in Galway?' demanded Rafe. 'You never tried to get me home from Seattle, and that was a lot further away.'

'You had Jewel then,' Petra pointed out.

'I have a life in Dublin now,' said Rafe.

'Does it include Eden?' Petra kept her voice casual.

Rafe's jaw tautened.

'I mean, it's fine if it does,' she added.

'And why is everyone obsessed with Eden?' he asked. 'We get on well. I care about her. That's all.'

'I'm not obsessed,' said Petra. 'Though I can't help wondering if you're putting her ahead of what's good for you and Poppy.'

'I thought my family would be pleased for me to have someone new in my life,' said Rafe. 'I thought you'd see it as a sign of me moving on. Settling in. But it's clearly only with a person you approve of, and you don't approve of her.'

'If she's right for you, she's right for you,' said Petra. 'I don't want it to be a case of out of the frying pan and into the fire, that's all. I don't want you falling for Eden simply because you knew her once and it's an easy thing to do.'

'Sounds like a perfectly good reason to fall for anyone. If that's what I'm doing. As for the frying pan and the fire – her circumstances are a million miles away from Jewel's, and it's been a long time for both of us since we lost our partners. We're not children, Petra. Please don't treat us that way.'

'So there is an "us"?'

Rafe shrugged.

'It's early days.'

'I want you to be happy,' Petra assured him. 'I just don't want your happiness to be more complicated than it needs to be.'

'I've gone through the complicated part of my life.' Rafe stood up and brushed the sand from his shorts. 'Everything now is simple by comparison.'

He walked towards Poppy and sat down beside her. He filled one of her plastic buckets with damp sand, then turned it over. She gave him an approving thumbs-up.

Petra stayed where she was and watched them.

Darling You,

It's been an eventful couple of weeks. I meant to write to you a few times, but I've been so busy with the invitation cards for my hush-hush client, I haven't had time. I'd almost finished them yesterday when Lila came rushing into the kitchen with a bottle of juice. She tripped and sent it all over the afternoon's work. It was really hard not to scream at her, because I'd promised I'd have them all done by tomorrow. And of course Lila was upset and cried for ages and I had to spend time telling her it was OK, even though I was raging at her . . . It's not easy to work with a child in the house.

Which brings me on to the next bit of news and how it might affect me. Your mum and dad are retiring to Dunleary! They're doing it up and adding a self-contained annexe. They want me and Lila to live there with them and rent out Briarwood Terrace.

I'm not at all sure it's a good idea, but when Lila dumped the juice over the cards, my first thought was that it wouldn't have happened in Dunleary, because Valerie would've kept her out of my way. And although calligraphy isn't my actual full-time job, I'm being paid a lot for this and I have to have it done right and on time. (I spent all day today working on it. Lila was at your mum's.) Naturally Lila gets irritated when I ask her to be quiet when I'm working, and I feel bad if I get annoyed with her. Thing is, I'm getting quite a few requests now, and if I take them all, I'll definitely need some extra childcare for Lila. It would be a lot easier if I was living in the same house as Valerie, even if that does turn her into an unpaid child-minder, which I really don't want to do no matter how much she says that she loves it.

It's not all about the work and looking after Lila, of course. As your mum pointed out, moving to Wexford was our dream too. She says you'd approve of the plan. You probably would. Your whole family is behind it, although I thought Gene and Stephanie, as the in-laws rather than original Farrellys, might have some reservations. I wasn't at the round-table discussion, so I don't know what was said. I'd've liked to see their actual reactions rather than hearing about it via Michelle and your mum, both of whom insist that nobody objected at all.

I quite can't believe your parents started building an extension for us to live in without saying a word to me first. I love Sean and Valerie, I really do, but how can I live my own life if I'm living with them?

Speaking about living my own life . . . I've a confession to make.

I went to Galway with Rafe McConnell. You remember Rafe. The guy I slept with. (I'm guessing you won't forget that I slept with a man who isn't you!!!)

The weekend wasn't a romantic break, in case you're thinking that. Lila and Poppy (his daughter) were with us and we stayed at his brother's B&B. OK, I can't lie to you – I slept with him again. I've missed sleeping with a man, and Rafe . . . I can't believe I'm writing to you about another man, Andy, I really can't . . . but Rafe is a good person.

We've agreed that we're more than friends, but not anything . . . well, I guess we're friends who have great sex (sorry, sorry), but we're not, you know, emotionally involved.

All the same, he makes me happy.

I never thought I'd feel properly happy again after what happened to you, but when I'm with Rafe, I am. I have confidence in him. I trust him. I have fun with him. We had lunch at his mum's house and it was all lovely and relaxed and so free and easy. I felt like a different Eden there. A more light-hearted Eden. Maybe even a more positive Eden.

I'm not sure I could carry on seeing him if I was living in Dunleary. It would be all wrong, wouldn't it? Can you imagine your mother's face if he showed up?

Oh, Andy, I wish I had a time capsule so that I could go back to when we were together. To those few hours when I knew I was pregnant and when you were alive and when I believed and hoped that my colleagues could save you. And that our future still stretched out before us.

I'm telling the truth when I say that no one could ever take your place.

I will always be

Forever yours,

Eden xx

Chapter 24

AAtkins

Hi Rafe. Sorry to disturb you on your holiday but are you planning to be back soon? I'm organising a trip to the zoo and I thought Poppy would like to come

RafeMcC

That's very kind of you. We were to be back at the weekend but I have to make a short work-related trip to the States first. So it'll probably be the following weekend before we return. That might be too late for you.

AAtkins

Unfortunately. We're going on Tuesday

RafeMcC

Next time maybe.

AAtkins

Are you enjoying your break?

RafeMcC
Yes. Galway is lovely.

AAtkins
Look forward to seeing you home again soon

RafeMcC
Thanks. And thanks for the invite too. I won't mention it to Poppy or she'll want to come back for it. See you soon.

AAtkins
Take care

Rafe put his phone back in his pocket and went to look for his daughter. It was true she'd be disappointed at not going to the zoo, but she was having a great time in Galway. She'd even stopped missing Lila.

He hadn't stopped missing Eden.

KrystleK
Does anyone in the group know when Rafe is back?

AAtkins
There's a coincidence! I was in touch with him a short while ago. Not till the weekend after next ☺

KrystleK
He should've arranged to have his lawn mowed before he went away – there are dandelions popping up all over the place ❀

293

JacinthaHarmon

Jack's mowing ours on Saturday. I'll ask him to do Rafe's too. He won't mind

KrystleK

That's not the point. Everyone has a responsibility to maintain their property

AAtkins

I think he planned to be back sooner. He has a work trip or something

FiadhFoley

Any chance Jack could mow mine too Jacintha? I'll pay him in cookies

JacinthaHarmon

I'll ask

FiadhFoley

☺

KrystleK

I know this isn't an official summer party group chat, but I hope you're all on track with what you have to do?

AAtkins

Of course

JacinthaHarmon

Yes

FiadhFoley

Would it be OK if I brought wine instead of making a dessert? I'm really busy right now

SandieC

I'll do yours for you Fiadh

FiadhFoley

☺

After her near disaster with the invitation cards and her rush to get them completed on time, Eden was surprised when Vanna didn't immediately send her the addresses for the envelopes. Instead, she asked Eden if she could address them at Amahle's house later in the week. For security reasons, Vanna said, as though she was afraid that Eden would somehow manage to monetise knowing where some of Ireland's best known musicians and celebrities lived. It might be something that would happen in other countries, Eden conceded, but not in Ireland, where, generally speaking, most people probably knew already and cared less. Nevertheless, she told Vanna she had no problem in coming to the house, but asked if it would be possible to bring Lila too, assuring Vanna that her daughter knew how to sit quietly when she was working.

'Of course,' Vanna replied. 'And she doesn't have to sit quietly; she can play with Rosario's son. He's about the same age.'

Rosario was Amahle's housekeeper, and Lila instantly got on with her little boy, Dion, thrilled by the opportunity to play in the extensive garden with its fabulous tree house. The tree house was built around the trunk of a massive oak tree rather than high in its branches, and was perfectly safe for children. Rosario kept them plied with home-made lemonade, and Eden didn't have to worry about anything except her work.

'It's all fabulous,' said Amahle when she looked at the pile of invitations and envelopes that Eden finally placed in front of her. 'Would you be able to do menus for me too? I'd like people to be able to take them home as keepsakes. I know they'll probably throw them in the bin,' she added, 'but I think it's nice to do.'

'I can certainly design them, but it would definitely be a lot quicker to do those on the computer,' Eden pointed out. 'It would also give you a bit of flexibility about food options, because we could change them up to the last minute.'

Amahle looked at her thoughtfully. 'That's a good point.'

'You'll need place cards too,' Eden reminded her. 'I can do those individually.'

'OK,' said Amahle. 'Print the menus and write the place names. You'll need special cards for that, won't you?'

'They're easy to get,' said Eden. 'I'll put a little musical design on them for you.'

'You're a gem,' said Amahle. 'I haven't really considered the food yet, but I want to give things musical names . . . you know, like An Orchestra of Fresh Fruits, something like that.' She made a face. 'That sounds incredibly naff, doesn't it? I'm supposed to be a creative person. I should come up with something classier. Fruit Jazz, or Calypso Cake.' She smiled. 'You're right about the menus if I keep changing my mind on what I'm calling stuff. Are you sure you can do them at short notice?'

'No problem at all. Just let me know when you're ready.'

'How about I pay you a retainer?' suggested Amahle. 'So that you can prioritise my work? I'm not saying you can't do something else, but if you do, take into account that mine is more important.'

'There's really no need,' said Eden. 'I'm a working mother. I'm good at managing my time.'

'All the same.' Amahle got up from the desk and called Vanna's name. Her assistant walked into the room.

Amahle explained what she wanted to do, and mentioned the amount of the retainer, another sum that made Eden's eyes widen. She felt obliged to tell Amahle that, once again, it was higher than she needed.

'I'm paying you to focus on my job,' said Amahle. 'And to continue doing what you do with maximum discretion. It's worth it to me to have trust in someone, and I have trust in you.'

'I always thought that rich people were super-careful with money,' confessed Eden. 'I thought you'd be trying to keep the costs of your party low.'

'I'm not trying to throw money away,' agreed Amahle. 'But this is a big deal for me personally, so I'm happy to splash the cash a little. Besides,' she added, 'I believe that people should be paid properly. My dad's favourite expression is "a labourer is worthy of his hire". Or her hire in your case. Why would I not pay what you're worth?'

'Because a lot of the time people don't,' said Eden. 'Think of all those huge corporations where the CEOs are billionaires but the workers are on minimum wage and they move the business around so they can locate in the cheapest places possible. They don't need to do that. But they do it anyhow.'

'My dad lost his job when new owners took over the hotel where he worked and fired half the staff,' said Amahle. 'It was all done as part of a renovation project. It's true that the hotel was beautifully restored, but staff like Dad, who'd given so much time and energy to the place, were replaced by cheaper workers.'

'I'm sorry,' said Eden. 'What did he do there?'

'He was a waiter,' Amahle replied. 'A really good waiter.'

'And now?'

'He and Mum run a tea shop in Arklow,' said Amahle. 'She does the baking, he does the serving.'

'How lovely,' said Eden.

'Yes, it is. I own the tea shop, so I'm their boss.' Amahle grinned. 'I make sure they send me profit-and-loss statements and all sorts. It does really well, though. It's in a wonderful location and gets a lot of tourist trade.'

'You're a one-woman empire,' said Eden.

'I got my chance and grabbed it with both hands,' Amahle said. 'Nothing more.'

'You have a talent. Your voice is amazing.'

'Thank you,' said Amahle. 'But no matter how talented you are or how hard you work, success also needs a certain amount of luck. I've been lucky too.'

'Why are you putting yourself down?' asked Eden. 'You've been smart. You control your own career. You have a business with your parents. You can't say it's all luck.'

'Are you giving me a motivational talk?' Amahle looked amused.

'I wouldn't dream . . .'

'You're right,' conceded Amahle. 'Women do sometimes put themselves down. We call it luck when actually it's good judgement. So yes, Eden Hall. I'm talented and I have good judgement, I'm totally in control of my career and I deserve to win the Grammy. Hiring you was definitely good judgement on my part,' she added. 'Because you're talented and own your own career too. So here's to us and our creativity and brilliance.'

Her words, so genuine and direct, made Eden smile. And the feel-good emotions they generated stayed with her for the rest of the day.

Elizabeth filled Eden in on the Sycamore Grove summer barbecue preparations when she called for the physio session at the end of the week. She said that everyone was hoping that the weather would hold long enough for the barbecue not to be a washout.

'Because we've had nearly a month of sunshine now,' Elizabeth pointed out. 'And even if some days have been a bit on the chilly side, there hasn't been much rain. It's overdue.'

'Hopefully it'll stay fine,' said Eden, as she flexed Elizabeth's ankle. 'Gosh, this is so much better now, isn't it?'

'Hands of an angel.' Elizabeth smiled at her and Eden laughed.

'You'll be able to dance at the barbecue.'

'My dancing days are behind me,' said Elizabeth. 'I'll show my face, have a drink of lemonade and come home.'

'That sounds a little party pooper-ish.'

'Ah, look, nobody's interested in me,' said Elizabeth.

'Rubbish. Haven't the residents called in to see you while you've been laid up? Doesn't Anita drop in chocolates every week?'

'Because I'm the elderly neighbour,' Elizabeth said. 'They feel obliged to look out for me. They don't want Sycamore Grove to be mentioned on the news as a place where my mouldering body was found after a dodgy smell started coming from the house.' She winked at Eden to show that she was joking. 'You might be right, though,' she added. 'I've been a bit institutionalised since the mugging. It's like a lockdown all over again. I want to go out, and yet I've got used to being at home.'

'In that case, the barbecue is a good idea,' said Eden. 'And my aim is to get you fit to dance.'

'You're a tyrant, you know that? Nobody is going to dance with me.' Elizabeth hesitated, and glanced sideways at Eden. 'I could ask Rafe. I'm sure he'd dance with me out of pity. If he's back in time.' She pursed her lips. 'Krystle got her knickers in a twist because he didn't say how long he'd be away and there are weeds growing in his grass.'

Eden raised an eyebrow.

'Krystle takes her chairwomanship of the residents' association very seriously,' said Elizabeth.

'He went to the States, then Vancouver for a demonstration of . . . well, something,' said Eden. 'He'll be back soon. Meanwhile, Poppy is staying with her aunt in Galway.'

'You're certainly up to speed with his itinerary.'

'I went to Galway with him,' she said.

She told Elizabeth about her stay at Dommo and Becky's B&B and how lovely it had been to be with Rafe.

'So you two are an official item now?' Elizabeth beamed at her. 'That's fabulous!'

'Not really.'

'Not really fabulous or not really an item?'

'Not really anything,' said Eden. 'It's complicated.'

'Oh, God, there's nothing more annoying than people deciding that things are complicated,' complained Elizabeth. 'You like him. He likes you. What's complicated about that?'

'I might not be staying in Dublin.' Eden went on to explain about Sean and Valerie's proposal, emphasising how great it would be for Lila.

'And do you want to do this?' asked Elizabeth.

'Well, my first thought was to say no, because I don't really want to live with the in-laws. But Andy and I had planned a move to Wexford eventually. We thought it would be great for our children. So perhaps Lila deserves it.'

'Lila deserves to be with a mother who loves her. Which you definitely do, no matter where you live. The rest . . . Well, it sounds a little to me like everyone is looking at you as a potential long-term carer for your parents-in-law,' said Elizabeth.

'There is a bit of a quid pro quo going on,' agreed Eden.

'You're a professional care-giver,' Elizabeth said. 'They shouldn't be trying to get your services for free.'

'They're giving me a lovely home to live in,' Eden pointed out.

'Or are they trying to force you into it?'

'A bit,' conceded Eden.

'What would happen to your no-strings sex?'

'I can't let sex get in the way of making important decisions.'

'Shouldn't that be a . . . you know . . . a deal-breaker?'

Eden laughed.

301

'There have to be deal-breakers. Or deal-makers,' said Elizabeth.

'I know. But no-strings sex shouldn't be one of them.' Eden began to tidy away her equipment.

'Are you sure there aren't any strings?'

'We're calling ourselves premium friends. So perhaps some strings, but I'm sure they're easily broken.'

'Really?' Elizabeth looked disappointed.

'Honestly, Elizabeth. I've more in my life to worry about than sex.' Eden zipped up her bag. 'I'd better go. I don't want to be late for William.'

'How's he doing?' Elizabeth could see that Eden didn't want to talk about Rafe any more.

'Improving, same as you.'

'Is he as nice as me?'

'He's lovely, but he's an aul' fella who thinks I'm a chit of a girl, and he can't bear me ordering him around. Except when it comes to organising his dinner.'

'The way to a man's heart,' agreed Elizabeth. 'What interests does he have?'

'He likes sport. And chess.' Eden swung her bag onto her shoulder. 'It's a pity I don't play. That would keep him occupied.'

'Francis and I used to play,' said Elizabeth. 'If William ever wanted a game . . .'

'Are you asking me to ask him?' Eden looked at Elizabeth in surprise. 'A chess date?'

'Only if he was interested.'

Eden wasn't sure that putting clients in touch with each other was a part of her job. Or if it was even ethical.

'I suppose I could mention it,' she said.

'Great,' said Elizabeth, and beamed at her.

When Eden mentioned Elizabeth's suggestion to William, his eyes lit up.

'I'd love to play her,' he said. 'It'd be nice to have a game against someone.'

'I'll talk to her and see when would work.'

'Any time for me,' said William.

'It'll probably be sometime next week.'

'I'm looking forward to it already.' William smiled.

'And that,' said Eden, when Michelle dropped by unexpectedly that evening, 'is how I've turned into a matchmaker.'

'Is there no end to your talents?'

'It'll probably be a friendship based on the one thing they have in common,' admitted Eden. 'But it'll be good for both of them. Probably more for William than Elizabeth,' she added. 'Because she's right about one thing – women generally are better at looking after themselves than men. Even with her injuries, she's kept herself busy. Well, busybodying more than anything, I guess. She knows everything about everybody on that road. William hardly even speaks to his next-door neighbour. Not that I'm much better myself; I haven't talked to my neighbours in ages. I need to get out more.'

'You're just back from Galway.'

'It was good for me to see my childhood home. But that's it really.'

'And how is Rafe?' Michelle's tone was studiously bland.

Eden explained about his trip to Vancouver and the States.

'Will you be seeing him when he comes back?'

'Possibly.'

'Mum is a bit worried you haven't said anything more about the move to Dunleary,' Michelle said. 'She and Dad are hoping you'll move at the same time as them.'

'I'm still thinking about it, but moving with them is absolutely impossible,' said Eden. 'I'm really busy with work and everything.'

'Work? What's going on in your work that's so important?'

'Elizabeth and William, for starters. I want to keep caring for them until they're both fully recovered, and I'm not going to commute from Wexford every day. I'm also doing the party stuff for Am . . . my VIP client, which means occasional trips to Dalkey too.'

'But you *will* move?'

'It's not as straightforward as that. But I'm seriously considering it.'

'I'm sorry if it appears I'm hassling you.' Michelle's voice softened. 'It's just that it's such a no-brainer for you and Lila as well as for Mum and Dad. You'll be living your dream.'

Moving to Wexford *had* always been a dream, thought Eden as she mulled over their conversation after she'd put Lila to bed that evening. But she and Andy had only mentioned it one summer when they were all at Dunleary. To listen to Michelle and Valerie, you'd think they'd talked of nothing else. As if it was the most important thing in their lives. Andy's family needed to stop thinking they knew everything about them.

Yet she was certain that everything the Farrellys did, even if it was sometimes stifling, was done out of love and a desire for her to have the life she would have had if Andy had lived.

For a very long time, that was what she'd wanted too. She'd mourned the life that had been taken from her when Andy died, in the same way she'd mourned the life that had been taken from her when she'd left Galway as a ten-year-old. And yet, she thought, who knows how those lives might have turned out. Circumstances changed. People changed. It was impossible to pretend otherwise, although it was only in the last few weeks that she'd truly realised it.

Returning to Galway and seeing her childhood home had made that clear.

She'd been a different Eden there. Not the Eden she would have been if she hadn't left, but a more light-hearted, fun-loving version of the woman she was now.

Because of Rafe?

Or were there other reasons?

Later that night, she broke her own rule and poured herself a glass of wine before scrolling through her phone and finding an old video of a summer in Dunleary with Andy. She watched as her late husband mocked his father with a list of fire regulations for the garden barbecue as they sat at a long outside table with the rest of the family for dinner – a dinner she remembered well, because at the time it had all felt so continental, with the red-and-white-checked tablecloth and Valerie's jugs of home-made lemonade, bowls of fresh salad and baskets of crusty bread. She remembered how committed to this family she'd felt and how grateful she was to them, and how in love she was with Andy.

It didn't seem like more than five years ago, she thought. It was hard to believe how quickly time had gone by. How quickly her life was going by.

She finished the glass of wine without even noticing and then, because there was only a small amount remaining in the bottle, she poured what was left into her glass.

She'd told Michelle that the reason she didn't want to move to Dunleary yet was so that she could continue to care for Elizabeth and William. That wasn't entirely true. The main reason she didn't want to move right now was because she'd be too far away from Rafe. Too far away from having fun with him and tumbling into bed with him and putting herself and her own pleasure first. There was nothing wrong with that, but she wondered how she'd feel if what was between them came to an end and she had to live yet another sort of life alone. Because if she told the Farrellys she wasn't going to Dunleary so that she could stay in Dublin and have sex with Rafe McConnell, she was pretty sure she'd be burning her boats with them.

Would she have jumped at their offer if Rafe wasn't around? Or would she have been just as aware as she was now of the potential pitfalls of living with them?

Rafe was complicating things. And yet he was such a lovely complication. But there was no guarantee he'd be around forever. Who knew what might happen in the future. If Eden had learned one thing, it was that you couldn't depend on people, or things, to stay the same.

Although she could depend on Valerie. Her mother-in-law would never change.

She drained her wine glass and sat at the kitchen table, a sheet of paper and one of her felt pens in front of her. She picked up the pen and drew two columns, heading them *Pros* and *Cons.*

The pros were obvious.

1. Private accommodation in a beautiful house
2. Huge garden leading to the sea
3. Constant babysitting for Lila
4. A gentler pace of life
5. Big financial benefit

She took more time over the cons.

1. Sharing living space with Sean and Valerie
2. Unexpected Farrelly family visits
3. Change of job (though maybe that's also a pro)
4. Potentially caring for Sean and Valerie (but surely not for years yet)
5. 250 km from Dublin
6. 250 km from Rafe
7. No chance of a private life

She'd thought the distance from Dublin – and Rafe – was the most difficult one. But as she wrote the last line, she realised it wasn't. Because it was true that she'd have no private life at all at Dunleary. No matter where she went or what she did, Valerie would know.

It would be like living with Trudy and Kevin all over again, she realised, before recalling that her aunt and uncle had hardly ever asked her where she was going or what she was doing. That unlike Valerie, who seemed to think she was always on the brink of needing help, Trudy and Kevin had assumed she was getting on with things perfectly well on her own.

And I resented that too, she thought, as she put the cap back on her pen. I'm such a contrary person. Nothing makes me happy!

She couldn't live in Dunleary, though. It had nothing to do with Rafe. Or the no-strings but premium friendship. She had to be her own person and do her own thing.

She had to be strong.

She had to do this for herself.

Chapter 25

Eden told Rafe about Valerie's offer when he FaceTimed her from Vancouver, where he'd gone after a couple of days in Seattle to meet his former colleagues.

'So that's what Michelle meant about it being your forever home,' he said.

'Yes.'

'You should've said. This is a big deal, Eden.'

'It is if I go.'

'And will you?'

'I've decided against it,' she said. 'It's a lovely idea in many ways, but I don't want to live with Sean and Valerie.'

'Oh good,' said Rafe. 'Because I'd miss you a lot.'

'Idiot,' she said. 'I'd miss you too. How much longer will you be away?'

'A week or so,' he said. 'I was anxious about Poppy, but she's being spoiled rotten by everyone in Galway, so actually all I should worry about is that she'll be insufferable when I get back.'

'I can't wait to see you,' said Eden.

'Same here,' he said. 'Gotta go. My meeting's starting.'

*

It was a couple of days later when Valerie asked Eden to come to Dunleary with her to see how it looked now that the renovations were nearly finished.

'Nearly finished?' Eden was surprised. 'They must have been working twenty-four/seven.'

'They're hard workers all right,' agreed Valerie. 'They knew we were keen to get in before the end of the summer.'

Eden still hadn't told Valerie that she wasn't going to move there, but she thought this might be a good opportunity. Because she could point out to her mother-in-law how difficult it would be for them to share the space and how, great though the idea was on paper, it wouldn't work in practice.

'Bring Lila too,' Valerie said. 'She should see her new home.'

'Valerie, you know I haven't said yes to this,' Eden told her. 'I'm not bringing Lila and getting her all excited about something that, I'll be honest with you, I'm not convinced is right.'

'Wait till you see it for yourself before making any decisions,' said Valerie.

Eden said nothing. But instead of dropping Lila with Michelle as Valerie suggested, she asked her next-door neighbour, Fliss, if her teenage daughter would be able to babysit for a few hours.

'Leave her with me,' said Fliss. 'I haven't looked after her in ages. And we're going to have a picnic in the garden later anyhow.'

With Lila safely next door, Eden headed to Valerie's and the two of them drove to Dunleary together.

When they arrived, Eden got out of the car and stared at

the building in front of her. It was clear that the work was almost complete – the original windows had all been replaced, there was a new front door, and all that needed to be done to the new extension was the exterior paintwork.

'Doesn't it look great?' Valerie unlocked the door and Eden followed her inside, their footsteps echoing through the empty hallway as they walked towards the kitchen at the back.

'Oh my goodness!' she exclaimed. 'This is amazing!'

The room, which Eden had previously thought of as very traditional, with its pine cupboards and terracotta tiles, had been updated with sleek contemporary units, a polished concrete floor, a new gas range and a large patio door that allowed the room to be flooded with light. Dunleary was still an oasis, but it was now an oasis of modern style rather than old-world charm.

'It was always a bit dark in here before,' remarked Valerie.

'It's fabulous,' Eden said. 'And you clearly found the best builders in the world to get all this work done in such a short space of time.'

'This is nothing.' Valerie smiled. 'Let's look at the new wing.'

She led the way into the hall again and this time pushed open a door that hadn't been there before.

'This way,' she said.

Eden stepped into a short corridor that opened onto a bright living space. She stood in the centre of the room and stared at the impressive sea view through the enormous sliding window that took up an entire wall.

'Wow,' she gasped. 'It's stunning.'

'Like it?' Valerie looked pleased with herself.

'I didn't visualise it like this from the plans,' Eden said in awe. 'It's a candidate for home of the year.'

The drawings she'd looked at certainly hadn't conjured up the true picture of this cleverly designed space, almost as big as her entire house, bathed in light and infused with a sense of the outdoor beauty that surrounded it.

'And here are the bedrooms.' Valerie ushered her further into the extension. The bedrooms were identical, although one opened onto a small patio (obviously yours, Valerie said). They shared a well-equipped bathroom.

'The kitchen is smaller than I'm sure you'd like,' admitted her mother-in-law as she continued the tour. 'But it's got everything, although you'll have to share the washer/dryer with us. But that's in the outside utility room anyhow. And here's the study.'

'Oh.' Eden looked at the quirky space. Two narrow windows rose the height of the walls and formed an alcove in which Valerie had positioned a modern desk and office chair. The natural light was almost perfect for working in, but there was an Anglepoise lamp on the desk too, as well as a wooden in-tray with a sheaf of plain white paper, and a large blotter, carefully centred. Valerie had remembered how much she loved blotters, thought Eden, as she ran her fingers over it. She'd gone all out to make it welcoming for her.

'There's still some painting and finishing work to be done,' Valerie acknowledged. 'But it should be completed soon. And then it's all exciting stuff like buying furniture and accessories. We have a budget for that, but of course you can pick whatever you want.'

'I couldn't possibly—'

'We can afford it,' Valerie interrupted her. 'Sean will be getting a great pension and we have savings too. Like you, we'll be renting out our house in Dublin, at least in the short term. We'll probably sell it eventually.'

'It's totally fabulous,' said Eden. 'I wasn't expecting anything like this.'

'I knew that when you saw it you'd love it,' said Valerie with satisfaction.

'I do,' admitted Eden. 'But Valerie, I can't simply move in here rent-free and—'

'Now, stop with all that,' said Valerie. 'I know you, Eden. You don't want to be beholden to us. You said that before, remember? When we helped you out after the accident? And Andy told me you said the same thing when we loaned you the deposit for the house in Artane. But this is what families do. They look out for each other. And we all want to look out for you and Lila. You're my precious son's wife and she's the beautiful daughter he didn't get to see. We need you to be part of us, to honour him.'

Eden swallowed the lump in her throat.

'What better place to raise her?' said Valerie as she stood beside the desk and looked out of the alcove windows. 'This is somewhere he loved. It's your opportunity to have what you always wanted. A home by the sea.'

She'd been so sure she didn't want this. So sure that the cons outweighed the pros. But the extension was breathtaking and very private, even if it didn't have its own front door, and even if she had to share Valerie's utility room. Briarwood Terrace, with its tiny rooms and equally tiny garden, simply couldn't compete. Waking up to the sound of the sea would be very different to waking up to the constant hum of traffic. And working in peace and quiet in the custom-built study would be a world away from sitting at her kitchen table with Lila looking for attention or spilling juice all over her hard work.

Andy would agree.

And he'd tell her that yes, she was living their dream.

She walked through the extension again. She could see herself here, cooking in the galley kitchen, relaxing in the living room, working in the study. She could see Lila here too, enjoying the freedom that the enormous garden gave. Yes, Sean and Valerie would be beside them, but it wasn't exactly the same as living in the same house, was it? They wouldn't be on top of each other all the time.

There were thousands of reasons to say yes to this move.

Did they outweigh the one to say no?

Rafe FaceTimed her that night. It was early afternoon in Seattle, where he'd returned after his trip to Vancouver.

'I'm in West Montlake Park,' he said as he turned the camera to show her. 'It was one of my favourite places here.'

'It looks lovely,' she said. 'A sort of bigger version of the Clontarf prom.'

He laughed.

'A much bigger version,' she amended. 'As befits the States. How did everything go for you?'

'Good,' he said. 'They're working on new nanobot technology in the Vancouver lab. It's very exciting. I'm doing a lot with the team there. They'll need me back a few times; we can't do everything remotely.'

'Would you go back there to live?'

'I lived here in Seattle, not in Vancouver,' he reminded her.

She acknowledged the difference.

'But would you leave Ireland?' she asked.

'I've only just got back.'

'I went to Dunleary today,' she said. 'It's . . . amazing.'

'Amazing like you want to live there?'

'Oh, Rafe – it would be so good for Lila. Maybe even so good for me . . .'

'I see,' he said.

'You don't, not really.'

'I think I do. You're still connected to these people. To your late husband's family. They matter more to you than anything.'

'It's not that. I have to think . . . I have to make the best decision.'

'You told me you'd already decided.'

'I might need a little more time. To be absolutely sure.'

'OK.'

'It's not about you,' she said. 'It's about me. And Lila.'

'I'm very clear that it's not about me,' he told her. 'I don't want it to be.'

'Oh, Rafe! Don't think—'

'I'm not thinking,' he assured her.

'Look,' she said. 'How about you and I take a little time out? Until I get my head together.'

'I'm not going to interfere in what you want,' Rafe said.

'I just have to . . .'

'Decide,' he said. 'But you shouldn't be deciding based on me. Only on you.'

'I know.'

'Take your time out. I won't get in your way. I won't contact you at all.'

'I didn't mean it like that,' said Eden. 'Honestly.'

'It's fine,' said Rafe.

'I'll call you.'

'Whenever you like,' he said, and ended the conversation.

Chapter 26

Elizabeth was more excited about the neighbourhood barbecue than she cared to admit. The reason she was excited was that William McEnroe was joining her. Ever since Eden had arranged for them to meet to play chess the previous month (she'd gone above and beyond, actually driving Elizabeth to William's house and collecting her again afterwards, rather than letting her get the bus), they'd spoken at least once a day. William phoned in the mornings to ask how she was, and then in the afternoons they continued their chess games by Skype. When he felt confident enough to take the bus to Elizabeth's house for the first time, she cooked him a healthy lunch and they chatted until late in the afternoon. That was when she asked him about coming to the barbecue.

'I won't be able to participate very much,' he said.

'You can keep me amused. That's participation enough,' Elizabeth told him.

And he agreed.

So as she sat at her window and watched the preparations on the green, she was feeling more cheerful than she'd done at any time since her accident. She no longer needed home assistance, although Eden was now giving her a few private physiotherapy sessions. Eden had been initially uncertain about this, although she agreed that more physio was a good idea, but Elizabeth insisted she didn't want anyone else, and so Eden had agreed to come once or twice a week before her visits to William McEnroe.

Elizabeth was glad that she was beginning to regain the independence she prized so dearly, and she felt the benefit of the physio, but she also liked having Eden drop by. She and the younger woman had forged a friendship, and she hoped that they'd stay in touch after her physio finally ended. She'd thought it would be because Eden and Rafe would get together, making Eden a regular visitor to Sycamore Grove, but the couple were, as the younger woman had told her 'on a break'.

'But I thought you were getting on so well,' Elizabeth wailed. 'What about the sex?'

'I worry about your obsession with sex,' Eden told her.

'I'm not obsessed,' insisted Elizabeth. 'But I am obsessed with you having a good life, Eden. And I thought—'

'Remember what we said before?' asked Eden. 'I'm not looking after him, he's not looking after me, and neither of us is rescuing the other.'

Elizabeth said nothing in return.

There was nothing to say.

Poppy was also watching the preparations for the barbecue, her nose pressed against the window while she gave a running commentary to Rafe about what was going on outside.

'People are bringing tables out of their houses!' she called. 'And balloons. There's balloons, Dad.'

Rafe was engrossed in rereading the paper on personalised

therapeutic chromallocytes that had been presented at the Vancouver meeting, and he'd tuned out Poppy's stream of chatter.

'Daddy!' She stood beside him and jogged his arm. 'Can I go outside and help?'

'Jeez, Poppy, I didn't see you there. You scared me.'

'Scaredy-Dad.' She giggled. 'Can I help?'

For an insane moment he thought she was talking about his nanorobotic paper, but then he looked out his own window and saw the activity on the green. Krystle Keneally was standing beneath one of the sycamores, her sunglasses perched on her head and a large clipboard in her hand as she directed operations. The male neighbours were following her instructions without question while the children ran around with balloons.

'OK,' he said. 'But don't get in anyone's way.'

'I won't!' She kissed him and ran down the stairs.

Rafe turned back to his paper, but his concentration had been broken and he eventually closed the lid of his laptop and looked outside. The noise from the green had been added to by music that was playing through loudspeakers attached to the trees. He recognised Ariana Grande's 'Dangerous Woman', a favourite of Jewel's, who'd been a big fan. She'd played it on his sound system the first time she'd come home with him, singing along as she'd peeled her T-shirt over her head, put her arms around him and pulled him close.

The thing about Jewel was that despite her upbringing, despite the horrors of her life with Darius, despite having to run away, despite having to start all over again, she hadn't let it define her. She'd succeeded in putting it in its place. Her past was her past, she'd told him, and her only intention was to live the best way she knew how.

319

That was what she'd done.

That was what he wanted to do too.

To honour her memory.

He took a deep breath, then hurried down the stairs and went outside to join the neighbours.

William arrived at Elizabeth's house a few minutes before the official start time for the barbecue. He wore a short-sleeved yellow polo over a pair of extravagantly checked trousers, which, he told Elizabeth, as he presented her with a bunch of flowers, were the smartest he had, even if they were part of his golf gear.

'You look amazing,' said Elizabeth, who was thinking that her sunglasses would help shield her from the canary-yellow shirt.

'Until I met you, I was faffing around the house in my tracksuit,' he admitted. 'It was Eden who told me I needed to up my game a bit.'

'Thank you for bothering.' Elizabeth smiled, took the flowers from him and went into the kitchen, where she put them in a vase on the windowsill.

'There seems to be a lot of activity out there already,' said William.

'Let's join it,' said Elizabeth. 'I'll introduce you to the residents of Sycamore Grove.'

'Right you are,' said William.

They left the house arm in arm.

Krystle was keeping an eye on Rafe McConnell, who was chatting to Duncan Gillespie. Duncan lived at number 2 with Sandie Carroll. Krystle didn't quite believe that Sandie and

Duncan were simply housemates, and had once asked Sandie, jokingly, if the two of them had ever slept together. Sandie had completely ignored her, which made Krystle feel that her thoughts on the matter were spot on.

Her gaze moved across the clusters of neighbours to Sandie herself, who was deep in conversation with Fiadh Foley. The two single women of Sycamore Grove together. Krystle wondered which of them might end up in bed with Rafe McConnell first. Because she was one hundred per cent certain that someone would. It was impossible to have a good-looking available man in their midst without either of the unattached women making a play for him. In fact, she thought, as she continued to look around her, it wouldn't surprise her if one of the attached women made a play too. There were plenty of rumours about the state of Rachael and Cian Hanrahan's marriage. They'd been together for fifteen years and had three children, but there'd been recent talk of a short-lived affair between Cian and a work colleague, although nobody could confirm it. Nor could they confirm rumours that the book club Rachael allegedly went to once a week didn't actually exist. Krystle pursed her lips. Rachael was currently in close conversation with Scott Simmons, although that didn't mean anything, as Scott and his partner Dylan were Sycamore Grove's same-sex household, something that made Krystle proud. She liked thinking she was the chairperson of a diverse residential group.

Her attention was suddenly drawn towards Elizabeth Green, who was walking towards her accompanied by a man Krystle didn't know. She chastised herself for not knowing, and for not having called to see Elizabeth like she'd meant to. But, she said as she greeted her neighbour, Elizabeth had been very occupied with her carer, hadn't she, and Krystle herself hadn't wanted to bother her.

'Don't worry about it,' said Elizabeth. 'I'm fine now. Well, almost fine. This is William, by the way.'

'We haven't met, have we?' Krystle leaned forward and air-kissed William.

'No. I'm Elizabeth's chess buddy,' he said.

'Oh, really? I didn't know you played, Elizabeth.'

'Not well,' Elizabeth admitted. 'But William is keeping me occupied. Well done, Krystle, on your organisation. Everything looks fantastic, as always. I'm sure you've been very busy.'

'Thank you.' Krystle smiled in satisfaction. 'Fail to prepare, prepare to fail is my motto. As soon as our Easter egg hunt is over, I start planning for this.'

'If anything needs doing, ask a busy woman,' said Elizabeth. 'It makes the subscription to the residents' association worth every penny.'

'Thank you,' said Krystle again. 'I hope our newest member thinks so too.'

Elizabeth followed her glance to Rafe, who was now in a group with Anita, Jacintha and Fiadh.

'You've seen quite a bit of him, haven't you?' Krystle asked. 'Coffee mornings and the like. And that carer of yours in and out to him too.'

'We've only had elevenses once or twice,' protested Elizabeth. 'As for Eden, they're old friends, you know.'

'I haven't had the opportunity for a proper chat with him,' said Krystle. 'He's always so busy. The most conversation we've had has been when the children are being picked up or dropped off.'

'I know he appreciates the support of the neighbours,' said Elizabeth. 'Everyone has rallied round.'

'We're all very aware that he's raising a little girl by himself,' agreed Krystle. Her voice lowered. 'Poppy told Saoirse that her mother had been killed in a robbery. What a terrible thing for them to have gone through. No wonder they came back from America.'

'I don't know anything about that,' said Elizabeth. 'But it's his private business, isn't it? And he's doing a great job with Poppy.'

'Absolutely. I didn't mean to imply otherwise. Maybe I should go and break up that group for now. We don't want him monopolised, do we?'

She strode across the grass and William turned to Elizabeth. 'Who's this Rafe chap who's causing such a stir?'

Elizabeth told him. 'I knew there was a bit of a story about his wife, poor man, but despite everyone thinking I'm a nosy old biddy, I never asked. He and Eden had a bit of a thing going, but it seems to have fizzled out,' she added. 'Which is a pity.'

'If it's meant to be, they'll fix it,' said William.

'I know.' But Elizabeth's brow was furrowed as she led him towards the drinks table.

Chapter 27

Rafe was enjoying himself. Poppy and the other children were being entertained by a magician Krystle had arranged, as well as the enormous bouncy castle erected at one corner of the green. (Rafe couldn't help wondering how parents had amused their children before the arrival of bouncy castles. They were an essential piece of outdoor kit.) Without having to worry about Poppy, he'd had fun grilling burgers with Mark and Jack, the husbands of Krystle and Jacintha respectively. Mark was an NFL fan, so they were able to bond over chats about the Seahawks, while Jack was an engineer with an interest in nanotechnology, which led to an interesting conversation about technological advances in medicine. But now their task was to serve the burgers and hot dogs they'd been cooking for the past hour, and Rafe was whistling tunelessly as he popped them onto the plates the neighbours held up in front of him.

'You look as though you're having fun,' said Elizabeth, the last to approach.

He grinned at her. 'Burgers and beer. My dream day. How are you keeping? I haven't spoken to you in ages, sorry.'

'You've been busy, I'm sure.'

'Not so busy that I couldn't pop by.'

'Maybe it's not as interesting for you without Eden.' Elizabeth kept her tone as neutral as possible. 'She's only coming to me for occasional physio now.'

'We haven't talked for a while,' said Rafe. 'Burger or sausage?'

'One of each.' Elizabeth held out a couple of plates.

'Glad to see you're eating well.'

'One is for my gentleman friend over there.' She indicated William, who was sitting on one of the chairs. 'Eden told me she'd gone to Galway with you, by the way.'

'Did she?'

'Yes. She had a good time.'

'I'm glad to hear it.'

'What's gone wrong with you two?'

'Nothing.' Rafe put the food tongs he'd been holding onto a plate. 'We're taking some time out, that's all. We were seeing a hell of a lot of each other.'

'Is it because of this Wexford thing?'

'If the move is good for her, she should go.'

'She thinks it's good for Lila,' said Elizabeth.

'It probably is.'

'Oh, for crying out loud, Rafe!'

'What?'

'Someone needs to tell her she'd be making a terrible mistake.'

'We don't know that.'

'We damn well do,' said Elizabeth. 'I've heard her talk about Valerie and Michelle and how they manipulate her.'

'That's a bit strong.'

'They make her do things she doesn't want to do all in

325

the name of a man who died five years ago. That sounds manipulative to me. And now they want her to live with them.'

'Eden told me that the extension they've built for her is stunning and it would be a fabulous place to live.'

'Not her place, though,' observed Elizabeth.

'Who knows?' said Rafe. 'Anyhow, she wanted time to make decisions and I'm giving it to her. Which is a good thing, Elizabeth. Because much as her family want to look after her, my family are trying to look after me and stopping me doing something stupid like getting involved with a woman who's gone through a difficult time and needs to make her own mistakes if she wants to.'

'There's a difference,' said Elizabeth.

'There is?'

'Your family might be interfering in your life, but it's her late husband's family who are interfering in hers. And I'm not entirely sure they have her best interests at heart. They might think they do,' she added, 'but I'm not convinced.'

Rafe said nothing.

'I don't want to interfere either,' said Elizabeth.

'You're doing a very good job of it all the same.' He gave her a half-smile. 'Listen to me, Elizabeth. If there's something in Eden's life that needs sorting – and I can't help feeling there might be even more than this Wexford thing – she needs to sort it herself.'

'Maybe,' said Elizabeth. She added some potato salad to her plates and then looked at him again. 'If there's a leak in your bathroom, do you care who fixes it as long as it's fixed? Nobody needs to take the moral high ground here, Rafe. You can fix it if you want.'

'Perhaps in the old days,' he said. 'Perhaps then men went to women who'd asked for time and space and took them in their arms and crushed them with a kiss and made everything OK, but that's not the way things happen now. I'm certainly not going to take some stupid action that'll make me look like an entitled twat.'

'I suppose you're right.' Elizabeth sighed. 'Maybe I wanted you two to fall in love, but it's entirely up to you.'

'We don't need to fall in love,' said Rafe. 'We need to sort out our lives.'

'You need to communicate,' said Elizabeth. 'Not be on a break.'

'You're very gung-ho about all this for someone of seventy-five,' said Rafe.

'Because when you get to seventy-five, you've a long lifetime of mistakes to reflect on. Not just your own, other people's too. I don't want her to make one even if it's her right. I don't want you to either.'

'Sometimes saying nothing is best,' Rafe told her.

'Maybe,' Elizabeth conceded. 'I'd better get back to William, who's very good at saying nothing. His problem is a distinct lack of sociability.'

'Fortunately, with you at his side, that's not really a problem at all.'

'Don't laugh at me,' warned Elizabeth.

'I wouldn't dream of it,' said Rafe.

Then he smiled at Fiadh Foley, who held out her empty plate and asked for seconds.

Darkness had fallen by the time the party broke up, although some neighbours joined others in their gardens to keep things going. Rafe had shrugged off invitations to have a beer with Jack or wine with Sandie and Duncan, or even a coffee with Anita and Rick. He told them that he'd probably go to bed, not being much for late nights any more.

Poppy, along with Krystle's daughter Saoirse and young Sophie Hanrahan, was camping out with the Atkins family. Amelia had erected a big tent in the back garden and the children were being allowed to sleep there. Poppy was almost overcome with excitement when Rafe, after ensuring that Amelia would call him straight away if there were any problems, had said that she could go.

'You're the best dad in the world,' she told him.

He was basking in the glory of being a great dad as he opened a can of beer and sat down in the calm of his own back garden. The day had been more fun than he'd expected, and Poppy had really enjoyed herself. That was the most important thing, he said to himself as he took a welcome gulp of beer, that Poppy was happy. That she felt she was fitting in. That she'd adjusted to her new life.

He took out his phone. There were plenty of meaningless notifications, but nothing from Eden Hall. Not that he'd expected anything. He thought about the conversation with Elizabeth – though 'lecture' was more accurate – and shook his head. He liked his older neighbour, but she was wrong about this. He'd been wrong about Eden himself. He hadn't realised how much her late husband and his family still mattered to her. The only person who'd been totally right was Petra, who'd insisted that Eden was more trouble than she was worth.

Big sis knows best, he murmured as he got up and fetched another beer from the fridge. He knew he'd had too much to drink over the course of the day; the beer had taken the edge off everything, but he didn't care. It was as well Poppy was camping out with the Atkinses. He wasn't in a fit state to be in charge of a small child right now.

'Hey, Rafe!' The voice was a loud whisper. He looked around.

Fiadh's head was visible over the garden wall. She held up a bottle of wine.

'Help me finish this, will you? I nicked it when we were tidying up.'

'Sorry, but this is my last.' He held up his beer.

'Keep me company while I put a dent in it?'

'Well . . .'

'I'll join you.' And in a surprisingly agile move, Fiadh pulled herself onto the wall and then dropped down into Rafe's garden.

'You could've killed yourself,' he remarked.

'Not a chance.' Fiadh grinned. 'I've had too much to drink. I would've fallen like a cat, all soft and squishy.'

Rafe laughed and got her a glass for her wine.

'So,' she said as she pulled up a chair, 'you've been properly integrated into the Sycamore Grove network now. Everyone loves you.'

'It was nice to meet all the husbands and boyfriends,' said Rafe. 'Until now I'd only spoken to the women.'

'Are we such a disappointment to you?'

'Not at all. You've been absolutely wonderful. It was good to meet the guys, though.'

'And here was I thinking you were captivated by my conversation this afternoon.'

He'd spent a lot of time talking to Fiadh after he'd finished serving food. She was good company.

'You were utterly captivating,' he assured her.

'Good.' She grinned and filled her glass with wine, wincing as some splashed over the side. 'Oops,' she said. 'I'm not being very elegant here.'

'You're fine.'

'I thought you'd be over at Jacintha's,' she said. 'Your new homies are there.'

'I decided I'd had enough,' he told her. 'And then it was so warm I thought better to sit out here. Which I couldn't without a beer, so . . . no willpower.'

'I like a man with no willpower.' She winked at him. 'What do you think of the neighbours?'

'Everyone's been great to me,' said Rafe. 'Even though I apparently lowered the tone by not mowing my lawn. I'm thinking of getting one of those robot ones you can schedule, so that it doesn't happen again.'

'Seriously?'

'Nope. I'm not that anal.'

They sat in comfortable silence for a moment, then she reminded him of his promise to have a house-warming.

'I hardly think I need bother now. I've met everyone and they've met me.'

'But what about your specially designed invitations courtesy of Elizabeth's carer?'

'They're not done yet. I haven't seen her in a while.'

Fiadh gave him a thoughtful look but didn't ask the question that was foremost in her mind.

'Send around a WhatsApp,' she suggested. 'I have a few ideas about a theme. What about Caribbean Night? Multicoloured cocktails matched with multicoloured clothes. It means the men could wear their tropical shirts.'

'Tropical shirts?'

'All men have tropical shirts! You could serve jambalaya for the food.'

'Could be fun.'

'And you could sound more enthusiastic,' Fiadh said. 'It's important to make an effort, especially when you have your daughter to consider.'

'She seems to be doing well with most of the other kids. She makes friends easily.'

'It's not the kids you have to think about. It's the parents.'

'I get along OK with them too. Amelia Atkins asked Poppy for the camp-out sleepover tonight. That's a good sign, surely?'

'Sleepovers for Poppy are one thing,' said Fiadh. 'But you have to think of yourself too.'

'None of the mums have asked me for sleepovers.' He grinned at her, but instead of laughing with him, she gave him a serious look and then gently asked about his late wife. 'There's been a bit of talk,' she said.

'What sort of talk?'

She told him.

'Yes, Jewel was killed in a shooting,' he said. 'It was a tragedy, but I don't want it to overshadow Poppy's life or mine.'

'We all think you're fantastic,' said Fiadh. 'Such a terrible thing to happen and yet you're coping marvellously with Poppy all on your own.'

'There are millions of lone parents doing their best,' he said. 'It doesn't matter what the circumstances are. I'm nothing special.'

'I suppose you're right.' She nodded as she refilled her glass. 'But you're the lone parent here on Sycamore Grove, and we all care about you.'

331

'That's very kind.'

'Seriously. We want to support you however we can. So don't be afraid to ask for help if you need it.'

'I won't.'

'It's hard when you're alone,' she said. 'People aren't meant to be alone. Maybe for a while, but then . . . everybody needs somebody.' She leaned forward. Her face was inches from his. Her perfume, sweet and musky, hung in the air between them. 'Just let's . . .'

The kiss took Rafe by surprise. She tasted of Pinot Grigio and maraschino cherries, and her hair smelled of coconut. His desire for her was suddenly overwhelming, and he put his hand behind her head, drawing her even closer as he kissed her in return, while her own hand slid slowly down his torso until her fingers rested on the waistband of his shorts.

He released his breath slowly when she swung her leg over his so that she was sitting on his lap. He could feel the heat of her sun-kissed skin as she wrapped her arms around him. Her fingers slid lower. His lips found hers and he tasted the maraschino cherries again.

He slid his hand beneath her floaty top, tracing slowly upwards until he reached her bra. He opened it in a single fluid move.

She undid the button on his shorts, shifting her position on his lap so that she could undo the zip more easily. She began to ease it downwards.

'This is the perfect way to end the day,' she murmured.

Rafe tensed and broke their embrace, gently lifting her from him. He stood up.

'Inside?' she asked.

He shook his head.

She looked at him enquiringly.

'I'm sorry,' he said. 'I can't.'

'It feels like you can.' She grazed him with her fingernails. He shook his head again.

'Sorry, but no.'

'You've got to be kidding me.' Her eyes glittered in the moonlight.

'I'm sorry. I really am.'

'Jeez, Rafe, it's not . . . We're having fun, that's all. A post-barbecue bonk. No pressure. What's the problem?'

'There's no problem.'

'There is or you wouldn't have stopped.'

'I . . .'

'Is there someone else?' she demanded.

He shook his head. 'You're my next-door neighbour. You've been incredibly kind and generous towards me. But this is a bad idea.'

'No it's not. It's a great idea.'

'Tonight it is, tomorrow it won't be.'

'Tomorrow will be every bit as good, I promise.'

'You're a really nice woman,' he began.

'Don't insult me by calling me nice.' Her voice shook.

'All I meant was—'

'Call me wonderful. Call me fabulous. Call me a bitch if you like. But don't ever use that wishy-washy non-word about me.'

'Fair enough. You're beautiful. You're kind. You're caring. I don't want to fuck that up by—'

'Having sex won't change anything.'

'Having sex changes everything,' said Rafe.

Fiadh sighed as she readjusted her skirt, then ran her

fingers through her hair. 'I thought this would be great,' she said.

'You don't really want to jump into bed with me,' said Rafe.

'I bloody well do.' Fiadh glared at him. 'I haven't had a decent ride in months. And I wasn't thinking about bed. I was thinking about here.'

'I'm sorry, but . . .'

'What?' she asked. 'Is it me? Is it you? Actually, don't answer that. You'll say it's you.'

'Because it is. Look, Fiadh—'

'Don't make excuses,' she said. 'Don't say anything at all. Let me leave with my dignity, such as it is, intact.'

He shrugged helplessly.

'We won't talk about it any more. Ever again.' She opened the back door and walked into the kitchen. 'I'll leave through the front. I nearly dislocated my hip getting over the damn wall.'

He followed her in. Sitting on the counter was a food container with a blue lid.

'That's yours,' he said. 'D'you want to take it?'

'I want to hit you over the head with it.'

'Feel free,' he said.

She laughed suddenly, then gave him a pensive look. 'You've been through a really hard time, but you have to move on, Rafe.'

'I *have* moved on,' he said. 'This isn't about moving on.'

'What then?'

'I guess . . . I guess it's about where I'm moving.'

'Are you trying to keep me dangling for the future? When whoever it is you *do* want to have sex with turns you down.'

334

'It's not that. But sleeping with you then not sleeping with you and having to live beside you would be awkward.'

'You could keep sleeping with me.'

He gave her a rueful smile.

'Oh, all right.' She took the container from him. 'I hope you find what you're looking for.'

'I hope you do too,' he said.

She stepped outside, then turned back to him.

'I won't bother you with any more ideas for the house-warming,' she said.

He nodded and closed the door behind her.

Eden was in her pyjamas, sitting on the sofa with her legs curled up beneath her and turning the pages of the photo album Valerie had given her when they'd visited Dunleary to see the extension. Her mother-in-law had produced it just before they left; the photos were all prints of Eden and Andy at the Wexford house. They looked young and happy and in love – which, of course, they were, but Eden's heart had sunk at yet more photos of her husband given to her by Valerie. How many did she have, for heaven's sake?

'I've never seen a better-matched couple,' Valerie had said when she'd handed it to her. 'Not even among my other children. You and Andy were unique.'

They certainly had been, thought Eden. Although perhaps they'd never had the chance for things to go wrong between them. Their future had never been written. All that was left was their perfect past.

A past she'd never be able to forget if she moved to Dunleary, even if the house had been remodelled and changed. And a past that would be with her every day, because Valerie wouldn't allow it to fade. Andy was ever present in Valerie's heart and his name was always on her lips. Although he was in her own heart too, thought Eden, as she reached the end of the album for the third time. He always would be, no matter where she lived.

She picked up her phone and scrolled through her messages. She hadn't deleted his last ones to her, a thread of reminders about schedules, requests to pick up random shopping, forwarded jokes. Mundane messages reflecting their day-to-day lives, and all the more meaningful to her for that.

I'm as bad as Valerie, she thought as she looked at them. Even though she said she wanted to move on, she kept allowing herself to be pulled back by him. And she would always be pulled back if she moved to Dunleary. She knew that, yet after seeing the place in all its renovated glory, she was ready for it to happen. She'd been seduced by it again. Seduced by the idea of living there. Seduced by the dream that she and Andy had once had. Besides, Valerie and Sean had gone to so much trouble for her. She owed them.

If she said no to them, she'd also be saying no to Andy.

But she'd said no to him a million times when he was alive.

She'd said no to his plans to travel around Europe on his motorbike.

She'd said no to subscribing to a beer delivery service.

She'd said no to having a baby before she was thirty.

She had never told anyone that Lila was a mistake. She'd been shocked when she realised she was pregnant, and it was the absolute shock of it that had stopped her from saying anything to Andy straight away. She'd needed time to process it. And then she'd wanted to wait for the perfect moment to tell him.

The perfect moment never came.

She closed the photo album and picked up her phone again.

She looked at the messages from Andy.

She took a deep breath before deleting them.

Rafe was lying on the Ligne Roset sofa in the living room. He'd bought it specifically so that he could stretch out his full length on it, but the truth was that the kitchen-diner had become the heart of the house and he rarely used the living room. But it was a good place to be tonight, quiet and calming after the bustle of the barbecue and the disaster of his encounter with Fiadh.

Petra would be mad with him, he thought. She would have approved of Fiadh, who was a good woman (he mentally edited out the word 'nice') and clearly knew how to have fun. His sister would've pointed out how much more suitable she was than the neurotic Eden Hall, with her dreams of her late husband and her unhealthy attachment to his family.

That was one thing he'd never had to worry about before. Jewel had cut herself off from her parents, and after her death they'd wanted nothing to do with Poppy. Though perhaps his own family were a little more like the Farrellys than he'd care to admit. After all, he was lying here thinking about his sister's approval for a relationship he wasn't going to have.

You're not the boss of me. He used to say it to her when they were younger and she was left in charge. *You're not the boss of me and you can't make me do stuff I don't want to do.* But childhood was all about other people making you do things you didn't want to do, and taking decisions on your behalf. He'd railed against it then, but he couldn't help thinking that right now it would be lovely to have someone swoop in and tell him what to do. To make decisions for him. To be the adult in the room.

He was tired of being the person in charge of everything.

He got up from the sofa and went into the kitchen. He switched on his coffee machine and opened the fridge to take out some milk. To his surprise, he saw his phone sitting on the middle shelf between the butter and a bowl of salad he'd brought back from the barbecue. He frowned. He must have put it there when he'd taken out his beer earlier.

That's why I need a grown-up in the house, he said to himself as he took it out. To stop me doing stupid things like this. He tapped the phone to check it was still working. The home screen lit up and he saw the preview of the message.

Eden
Are you awake?

Chapter 28

Eden had given up on expecting a reply to the text she'd sent over an hour earlier, so she was surprised when her phone pinged. She picked it up and looked at the screen.

Rafe
Yes.

Eden
Am I disturbing you?

Rafe
No. I was chilling. Actually, my phone was chilling. It was in the fridge. That's why I didn't get back to you sooner.

Eden
Your phone was in the fridge? 😐

Rafe
Long story.

Eden

Do you want to tell it to me?

There was a pause before the dots indicating he was typing appeared and his message arrived.

Rafe

By text? In person?

Eden

I can't come to you. Lila is asleep upstairs

Rafe

I'll come to you if that works. Poppy is having a camping sleepover.

Eden

Are you sure? It's late

Rafe

Yes. Give me a few minutes.

Eden

OK

She set down her phone, then took the photo album upstairs and put it in the wardrobe alongside the lacquered box of letters. After that, she changed into a light top and shorts before standing by the front window so that she could open the door before he rang the bell and woke Lila. Her heart was beating faster. She took a few deep breaths and waited.

It was nearly ten minutes later when a car stopped outside. 'You took a taxi?'

'I had a few drinks at the barbecue earlier,' he explained 'A confusion over tins of beer and mobiles is possibly why the phone ended up in the fridge.'

'You've told me the entire story within five seconds. That's not the way to build up suspense.'

'Sorry.' He stepped into the hallway, expecting her to walk towards the kitchen, but she didn't. She closed the door behind him and stayed where she was, her back against the wall. Her hair was loosely pinned up, and the slim-fitting top hugged the contours of her body. He reached out and touched the side of her face. She put her hand on his shoulder.

'This isn't the way to build up suspense either,' she said, and kissed him.

In the taxi on the way over, he'd considered being cool and aloof, but now he was kissing her back, and the thought went through his head that this was like Fiadh a couple of hours earlier, except that it wasn't like Fiadh at all, because Eden felt so different in his arms, and her lips tasted of wild strawberries while the scent of her hair was fresh and minty.

'We should probably move from here,' she gasped. 'I don't want to wake Lila.'

He lifted her up and carried her into the kitchen, where he sat her gently on the table.

'Are you sure you want to do this right now?' he asked.

'Yes.'

She slid her shorts down over her hips. The turn-up caught on the tips of her toes and she kicked the shorts away, which made both of them laugh. Then she pulled her top over her head, and he did the same with his T-shirt, and she said that maybe it would be better if they didn't do it right here, because if she had sex on the table, she'd never be able to have breakfast there with Lila again.

He looked at the open door of the utility room and once again he lifted her up. He carried her as far as the washing machine, placing her gently on it before they came together, hot and breathless and exhilarated.

'Doing the laundry will never be quite the same again either,' she murmured afterwards, as a thread of perspiration slithered between her breasts.

He ran his finger slowly along it.

'Thanks for dropping by tonight,' she said.

'You want me to go now?'

'No!'

'Oh good. For a moment there I thought you only wanted me for my body. Given that we're on a break, you know.'

'Your body is a good enough reason to forget about the break.' She smiled. 'But never the only one. Would you like some coffee? Sorry, that sounds so . . . so . . .'

'So?'

'We've just shagged each other senseless on the washing machine of all things, and now I'm offering you a cup of coffee. The first bit was all wild abandon and porno movie. The second was like Valerie and me when I call to collect Lila.'

He laughed. Then he put his arms around her and kissed her again, this time tenderly and softly. Without the passion, but with a gentleness that made her feel safe and secure within his arms.

'So,' she said, when they'd retrieved their clothes and she'd finally made tea for herself and coffee for him. 'I guess we should talk.'

'Are we back on a break or not?'

'Oh, Rafe, I'm sorry you feel I shut you out. But I had to make choices and I couldn't think straight when you were part of it.'

'Eden, sweetheart, it's important that you think about yourself and make choices for you and Lila. I'm . . . well, I'm here, but I've only been around for a short time. I'm not the one who matters.'

'Of course you matter,' she said. 'You matter to me. You always did. But . . . you were a complication. I was trying not to base any choices I made around the fact that being with you is so unbelievably enjoyable.'

'Can I just say that making choices based on unbelievable enjoyment seems good to me.'

'I was taken aback by Dunleary,' Eden told him. 'They've built an entire extension for me and Lila to live in. It's stunning. It's fantastic. It's . . . it's the perfect home for us in so many ways.'

'You can't turn down a great opportunity because of me,' he said. 'If that's what you really want.'

'It would be difficult for us to keep enjoying ourselves, unbelievably or otherwise, if I was there,' said Eden. 'Not only because of the distance. No matter how I try to spin it, I'd be living with the in-laws.'

'Yes.'

'What they've done is absolutely amazing,' she said. 'It's hard not to be grateful to them even if they might have ulterior motives.'

'I get that,' said Rafe, 'but are you supposed to be grateful for the rest of your life?'

'I've a lot to be grateful to them for,' Eden said. 'They

343

helped us out financially when we were first married. When I told them I was pregnant, they rallied around. Then, after Lila was born, I ended up with mastitis and it was agony and I couldn't breastfeed her and I felt so utterly, utterly useless. I had postnatal depression and I wasn't coping very well, so I ended up living with them again for a while. Valerie was wonderful. I would've been lost without her and Sean. It can't be OK to live with them when it suits me but to turn them down when it doesn't.'

'There's a big difference between living temporarily with someone because you're ill, and moving in with them permanently.'

'Valerie kind of joked that Lila and I could be around to keep an eye on them in their old age. She said that perhaps we could switch then – she and Sean could move into the extension and Lila and I could have the house. And Michelle made the point that it would be a relief for the family to know I was there. So that if and when they became infirm, I could look after them.'

'Are they all mad?' asked Rafe. 'Are you? You surely don't think they've a right to suggest that? Besides, your in-laws are in their sixties, aren't they? Mum and Dad are around the same age, and there isn't a hope in hell that they want any of us living with them in case they become ill. In fact they're aching to get Noelle *out* of the house!'

'It's for the future,' said Eden.

'How long into the future? Ten years? Twenty? Until they're a hundred? Is that what you want? To live there waiting for one of them to have a heart attack or a fall?'

'You're not saying anything I haven't thought about myself. There are all sorts of reasons why this move is as good for them as it is for me.'

344

'Then move,' he said. 'Do it with a good heart and be happy. Live the life you deserve.'

'I think about that a lot,' she said. 'The life I deserve. I wonder if there was a life for me and I messed it up.'

'How?'

'When my parents died, everything changed. What if my best life would have happened if they'd lived?'

'Oh, Eden!' Rafe's voice was full of sympathy. 'I knew you felt somehow responsible for your parents' deaths, but—'

'Huh? How d'you know that?'

'You told me,' he said. 'The day afterwards. You said you'd wanted them to be late home because that way you could stay at ours for longer, and it was your fault that they weren't coming home ever because you'd prayed they'd be late but God must have got it wrong. Don't tell me you can't remember.'

'I honestly don't.' She shook her head and looked at him in disbelief. 'I . . . I must have buried that memory. I don't believe it.'

'I know you said you had counselling, but did you discuss this with them, Eden? Because your parents dying wasn't your fault.'

'I accept that now. I really do. But sometimes logic goes out the window, doesn't it? Actually what I struggled with most was not telling Andy I loved him before he left for work that day. I nearly always did. But we were running late, he asked about dinner, I said "fish and chips" and then he rushed off. If I'd known . . . if I'd told him I loved him . . .'

Rafe put his arms around her as the tears slid down her face.

'His family keep telling me what he'd want.' She reached for a box of tissues and wiped her eyes. 'And I feel like I owe him too. But I know that I'm seriously messed up for thinking that way. You've had it as bad as me, if not worse, but you're doing great. Your family are fantastic. They support you without being on top of you all the time.'

'You're wrong there,' said Rafe. 'Truth is that ever since Jewel's murder, they worry incessantly about me. They weren't very keen on my relationship with her in the first place, not when they heard her story. My mother, who watches far too many documentaries about dysfunctional families and relationships, always thought we were on track for a disaster. I'm not sure what her definition of disaster actually was, but the shooting confirmed her suspicions that Jewel was a ticking time bomb. And then, of course, there was the whole situation with Poppy. On the one hand, everyone felt so sorry for her. On the other, there was a feeling that she was the daughter of a murderer and I was taking on more than an ordinary child. Which is bonkers – the children of murderers aren't murderers themselves. And Mum was very careful to say that the sins of the father shouldn't be taken into account. But it was something to add to the mix of concern and confusion. That's why they think I need constant monitoring. That's why Petra comes to Dublin so much. She says it's for recordings, but I know that part of it is to check up on me. As though I didn't cope on my own in Seattle. I know I struggled there, but I could still function as an adult human being. In Galway, after you left, they were checking up on me all the time. Asking me how I felt about you. What your purpose in my life was. What I intended to do about you.'

Her eyes widened.

'And what did you tell them?'

'To butt out,' he said. 'That I didn't know how I felt. That you didn't have a purpose in my life. That I didn't

346

intend to do anything. Which,' he added, 'wasn't true, because I intended to keep seeing you and sleeping with you and having fun with you for as long as you wanted.'

'And then I told you I needed space. But when I texted you, you came without a second thought.'

'I'm not good at playing hard to get.' He smiled at her. 'Even if it's only for a short time, before you go to Wexford.'

'While I was there, I wanted to say yes,' admitted Eden. 'And I can't believe I'm turning down the opportunity to live in one of the loveliest places in the country, but . . . Dunleary isn't home. This is my home. I have to say no.'

'Are you sure? You're not saying that just because I'm here?'

'Rafe, you may not always be here. I understand that. This decision isn't really about you. It's about me and Andy's family. It's about standing on my own two feet. Which I can do, and am doing.'

'I'm very glad you've decided to stay,' said Rafe. 'Poppy will be too. She misses Lila and I've missed you.'

'We should organise a play date for the girls.' Eden wiped her eyes again.

'And us?'

'We've already had a play date,' she said. 'I was actually wondering if you'd like a sleepover?'

He laughed and put his arms around her.

'Sounds like a plan.'

They went upstairs together.

This time she brought him into her bedroom.

When Eden turned up to Elizabeth's next physiotherapy session, the older woman noticed the change in her immediately.

'You're positively glowing this morning,' she said as she settled into her chair.

'Must be my new face cream,' said Eden. 'I got it in Galway.'

'If it's that, I want some.' Elizabeth said. 'But something tells me it's more than face cream.'

'Well . . .' Eden gave in. 'Rafe came to see me the night of your barbecue.'

'Ah.'

'We talked.'

'I hope you did more than that!' exclaimed Elizabeth.

'The talking was very important,' said Eden, even as she felt herself blush.

'And did the talking come to a satisfactory conclusion?'

'Yes. Though it wasn't about me and him. It was about me and my decisions. I'm not moving in with the in-laws.'

'Probably wise.'

'I'm not sure how to tell them,' admitted Eden. 'But I'll find the right moment.'

'Good for you.'

'Rafe dropped by with Poppy yesterday too. We all went to Howth and walked along the pier and had fish and chips afterwards. Then he and Poppy came back to my house and the girls played in the sandpit while we sat and chatted. It was lovely.'

They'd talked for hours. Filling each other in on more details of their lives with Andy and Jewel, with talk of the happy times they'd had, the trivial things they'd done, the major decisions they'd made. They'd steered clear about future decisions that would have to be made, deciding there was time enough for those.

'I'm very glad we met that first time at the seafront,' Rafe said, before he lifted Poppy, who'd fallen asleep after dinner, into his arms to bring her home. 'It seems like it was meant to be.'

Eden kissed him then, but because Poppy was in his arms, with simple affection.

'Drop over to me after you leave Elizabeth's tomorrow,' he said. 'I'd say drop in before, but I have a stupid Zoom first thing that has the potential to go on for ages.'

The house had felt very empty when he left.

'So you're going to race through my physio in order to get over to number four?' Elizabeth's eyes twinkled.

'I'm a professional,' said Eden sternly. 'I'll be a hundred per cent committed to your care while I'm here. Anyhow,' she added, as she switched her attention from Elizabeth's ankle to her shoulder, 'I'm not the only one with news. I believe you went public with William at the barbecue. How did that go?'

'We sat as far as possible from the loudspeakers and spent most of our time bitching about my neighbours. He loved it. He doesn't really know his neighbours. That's single men for you. They don't put themselves about. They take on a bunker mentality.'

'Not Rafe.' Eden smiled.

'Older men,' conceded Elizabeth. 'Widowers like William. He'd sit at home all day reading his newspaper and watching rubbish sport on the telly if he was let.'

'He played golf before his heart op,' Eden pointed out.

'True,' Elizabeth conceded. 'But obviously there's more to life than solitary golf, and we enjoyed ourselves tremendously.'

'I'm delighted for you. Are you going to have no-strings sex?' Eden grinned at her.

'We haven't quite got that far yet,' said Elizabeth. 'But I'm not ruling it out.'

Eden laughed.

'And you should have as much fabulous sex as possible with Rafe,' said Elizabeth.

'Andy was the love of my life,' Eden said. 'It's not the same.'

'It'll never be the same,' agreed Elizabeth. 'That doesn't mean it can't be great.'

'Would you still consider your late husband to be the love of your life?' Eden asked.

'It took me time to fall for him, but I did love him and there was never anyone else. So yes, he was the love of my life. But it was more a quiet-burn sort of thing. You're lucky if you've found love for a second time, Eden,' she added. 'Whether it's hot and passionate or something else. The same as I'll be lucky if I have another quiet-burn situation with William.'

'Oh, Elizabeth.' Eden put her arms around the older woman.

And as Elizabeth patted her on the back, she didn't complain that Eden was squeezing her dodgy shoulder.

Chapter 29

Elizabeth's words echoed in Eden's head as she sat in Rafe's kitchen drinking orange juice while he organised Poppy's breakfast. There was no doubt that the sex was hot and passionate, but her emotions were more difficult to define. The one thing she was sure of, though, was that being with him made her happy.

And she liked being happy.

That feeling of happiness, and a level of contentment with where she was in her life, stayed with her all day, and she was smiling to herself as she drove to Valerie's to collect Lila.

'Stay for a cuppa,' said her mother-in-law when Eden arrived. 'I've been boxing things up and I need a break.'

'When are you planning to move?'

'They've finished painting at Dunleary and we already have a tenant for here, so we need to go as soon as possible,' replied Valerie. 'It's all very exciting. Lila thinks so too. She's looking forward to moving with us.'

'You've told Lila.' Eden was aghast. 'But I—'

'Oh, come on, Eden,' said Valerie. 'You've been to the house, you loved the extension, you saw how well it would work *and* you'll be living with us for free. It's a great way to build up a nest egg. Everything's fine.'

'It's not fine, and I'm not going!'

Eden said the words in her head, but they didn't get past her lips. Because even though she wanted to, she simply couldn't say them out loud to Valerie yet.

'Moving is daunting,' conceded her mother-in-law. 'But you know it makes sense. And once you're settled in, you'll feel like you've been there forever.'

For all her talk about standing on her own two feet, thought Eden, as Valerie continued to talk, she was utterly unable to stand up to Andy's mother.

But, she promised herself, I'm not moving, and that's that.

It was after four o'clock by the time she got home, and she was still annoyed with herself for not being able to say what she wanted to Valerie. Meanwhile, Lila chattered about 'our new house', and Eden responded by saying that it was really Granny's house, but they'd have a place to stay there.

'She said Daddy would like us being with her,' said Lila.

'Daddy is happy if we're happy.' Eden felt her jaw clench as she spoke. Valerie had gone too far in dragging what Andy would've wanted into a conversation with Lila. She recalled other times when her mother-in-law had done the same with her. He would've approved of the arrangement where Lila stayed with Valerie instead of going to play school. He would have wanted Eden to cut back on her carer's hours. He would have wanted her to have a better life. An easier life. The life that Valerie was now proposing.

But Andy didn't know what she wanted now, did he? Nor did he know about Rafe. At least, he didn't know how things were progressing with Rafe, because she hadn't written to him to tell him. She hadn't written to him at all since her letter after Galway. It was the longest she'd gone without sending him something.

She walked up the stairs and into the spare room. Almost every item in it had belonged to Andy and was all stuff she couldn't bear to throw out.

I'm not that different from Valerie, she thought, as she looked at the fireman's helmet on the shelf, the hurley propped up by the wall and the half-dozen pairs of trainers piled on the floor. I haven't truly let him go either.

Maybe, despite everything, I can't.

She opened the wardrobe door and took out the lacquered box with the store of letters she'd looked through so recently. Nearly five years' worth. At first, one a week. Then, later, the gap had widened to fortnightly or monthly or even longer. But they were a constant in her life. Whenever she needed to think things through, she wrote to him. Whenever she was worried, she wrote to him. Whenever she needed to make a hard decision, she wrote to him. And afterwards, she always felt the relief of having shared a problem with him, a weight lifted from her shoulders.

She stood up and looked out of the window. Lila was sitting in the sandpit in the garden, building castles. Eden watched her daughter fill the red plastic bucket with damp sand, pat it down firmly and then, very carefully, turn the bucket over and lift it up to reveal the neat mound of sand beneath. Like her father, Lila was a perfectionist.

She took the box into her bedroom and emptied the letters onto the bed. She looked at the mound of correspondence before finally picking up her first letter to Andy and running her finger beneath the fold of the envelope, unsealing it. She took out the sheets of paper.

Darling You,

This can't be real. It can't. This morning you asked what was for dinner, and when I told you it was fish and chips, you gave me a thumbs up and said you'd see me later. Then you rushed off and I didn't even watch you leave.

I wish I'd followed you. I wish I'd hugged you and kissed you and told you how much I love you. But I didn't. I stacked the dishwasher instead. And then I sat in the kitchen and faffed about looking at pictures of kittens on Instagram. And when I went to work, I didn't think of you at all because I was dealing with kids who'd fallen off their bicycles and people who'd broken arms or legs and others who had vague symptoms of imaginary fatal illnesses who should have gone to the GP instead of clogging up A&E.

I wasn't thinking of you when you were rushed in, your body broken and burnt. When I heard the word 'firefighter', I still wasn't thinking of you, because you should've finished your shift and been home by then. I didn't know about the fire in the industrial estate. I didn't know you were there.

But then I saw you.

I saw Tony too, though I didn't give him a second thought. I feel bad about that, but not very bad, because Tony is alive and Tony will be OK.

I hoped you'd be OK too, even though I was sick with fear and worry. I knew we had a great team at the hospital and you were in good hands. I couldn't believe that they'd let anything bad happen to you.

And then you died.

Dr Morrison told me. She was kind and gentle and brought me to a quiet place. I knew what she was going to say before she said it. I've seen it done a million times. I know the look. I know the tone of voice. And even though the quiet room they brought me to wasn't the room they usually use to break bad news, I knew.

I didn't want to believe it.

I looked at Dr Morrison and said, 'Thank you for telling me. I'd better get back to my shift now.'

And she told me I couldn't go back to my shift and that there were people I could talk to if I needed and that my family had arrived a few minutes earlier. It was your mum and dad and Gene and Michelle. They hadn't asked for me. They didn't know I was working. They never really understood that I wasn't a nurse on a ward.

But then they were all shown to the room too, and your mum was distraught. I've never seen her like that before. Your dad was doing his best to be calm, but it was very hard when Valerie was wailing like a banshee. Michelle was supporting her. It was Gene who comforted me. I felt his arms around me and I wanted them to be yours. I leaned my head on his shoulder and I wanted it to be yours. I kept thinking that Michelle and Gene would go home together tonight, but I'd go home alone.

Except I went to your parents' house, because nobody wanted me to be on my own. I'm here now. In your room. In your bed. They wanted me to get some sleep, but of course I can't sleep without you. But even though there's nobody else in the room, I'm not alone. I'm not alone because of the baby. I haven't told your mum I'm pregnant yet. I whispered it to you and I want to believe you heard me. I want to believe you'll be with me on this journey. The one I'm taking earlier than expected and the one I thought you'd be with me for.

I want you to watch over us. To look after us. I want to be able to talk to you and tell you everything about us.

I want to love you.

To keep loving you.

To always love you.

There will never be another you in the world. I will never find another soulmate.

I made vows to you.

In sickness and in health.

And even death can't part us.

I won't let it.

I won't let you go.

You are mine and I am forever yours,

Eden xx

Although some of the writing had been smudged by her falling tears as she wrote, she knew exactly what she'd said. She'd read her love letter to Andy over and over, the words as fixed in her mind as they were on the page.

Valerie hadn't wanted her to return to her own house, especially when Eden told her about her pregnancy. Her mother-in-law had insisted she needed looking after and that she couldn't possibly go back to Artane alone, and Eden had agreed to stay for an extra couple of weeks. But she'd posted the letter to the house so that it would be there waiting for her when she finally went home.

And when she did go back (accompanied by Valerie and

Michelle), the first thing she saw was the envelope on the mat. She'd picked it up before anyone else spotted it and put it, unopened, in the lacquered box. Even though she was the one who'd written it, the fact that it was there, addressed to him, was a comfort to her. Seeing his name on the envelope kept him alive in her heart and in her mind. And writing to him, even about the most trivial of things, made her feel as though he was still part of her life, sharing the best moments, helping her in her worst.

She looked through the envelopes now, not remembering what every letter had been about, but knowing that some were long and some nothing more than brief notes. Each one, when it arrived, had lifted her spirits. She knew that people might think her crazy. She supposed the postman already did – after all, he had to know that Andy Farrelly no longer lived at Briarwood Terrace. But she didn't care. The letters were a lifeline to her husband, and they'd sustained her in the years since his death.

She opened another envelope. This letter was from the day of his funeral, her writing almost illegible. But she could remember the ache of forming the words.

You can't be gone. You can't leave me like this. You have to stay with me. In my life. For the sake of our daughter. Why didn't I text you as soon as I did the test? Why was I waiting? What was the point? Send me a sign, Andy. Send me a sign that you heard me, that you knew you were going to be a dad.

There hadn't been a sign. At least, not directly from Andy. But when she'd posted the letter and it had been delivered to their home, that was a sign in itself. As long as letters addressed to him landed on the mat, he wasn't really gone.

She opened another.

We have a daughter! She's so beautiful. She has your nose, definitely. And your lungs! You should hear her cry when she's hungry. So she has your appetite too. Oh, Andy, I never thought I could love again, but when they put her in my arms . . . She's perfect. I wish you could see her and hold her. She's amazing.

And then, a couple of weeks later:

I didn't realise how difficult it would be. You'd be ashamed of me. I'm failing our child. I love her but I can't take care of her. I can't feed her. I'm too tired and too sore and too hopeless as a mother. I feel awful. If it wasn't for your mum, I don't know what would happen. I can never repay her. Ever.

The next one was about the inquiry into the accident.

They tried to smear you, but they were proved wrong. I'm glad your name was cleared, but I don't really care how the accident happened. Nothing will bring you back . . .

And one on Lila's birthday:

I can't believe a whole year has gone by. After those first weeks, after everything your mum did for us, it got so much better. Lila is wonderful. I can't imagine my life without her.

His family's continuing care of her:

358

I'm so lucky to have them all in my life, your parents, Michelle, Gene, Stephanie, Gavin, Amanda – they've been amazing to me . . . I can never, ever thank them enough.

Her new job as a carer:

It's perfect for me, and the clients are nearly all wonderful – such interesting lives they've led, I'm quite privileged to hear their stories.

And one when she'd taken up calligraphy:

Don't laugh, it keeps me happy – I'll be practising on you . . .

She stopped counting them after a hundred. She'd written to him more than a hundred times. She'd told him more than a hundred times that she was his forever.

She'd also told him, over and over again, that she could never repay his parents and his family for the care they'd taken of her. Yet now, when Valerie wanted this one thing from her, she was going to refuse.

Because living at Dunleary wasn't about repaying her for anything. And saying no was the right thing to do.

Chapter 30

Anita

Booty alert. Have just seen smokin' hot woman leaving Rafe's house. Feel sure she was there all night

SandieC

You're kidding me! D'you know who it is?

Anita

Nope! Absolute babe tho ✹ Haven't seen her before – flaming redhead ♟ great body

FiadhFoley

Maybe it's another sister ✌

AAtkins

You wish ☺

JacinthaHarmon

It's his private life, ladies

SandieC
I thought I had a chance after you gave up on him Fiadh!!!!!

FiadhFoley
I haven't given up, I'm biding my time

AAtkins
Are you guys love rivals @FiadhFoley @SandieC?

Anita
They've been outmanoeuvred by the mystery redhead ☺

FiadhFoley
@AAtkins hasn't Poppy spent a few nights at yours? Has she said anything about a new woman?

KrystleK
Jacintha is right, it's his private life and we really shouldn't gossip

AAtkins
I wouldn't dream of gossiping. Poppy hasn't said anything but if she does I'll let you know

KrystleK
I don't want to interfere obvs but it's important we know who's coming and going on the Grove

Vanna West phoned Eden later in the week to ask if she could drop the place cards to Dalkey as soon as they were done. 'Tomorrow if possible,' she said, 'because Amahle wants to chat to you about a few bits and pieces and she has to go away for a couple of weeks.'

Eden still had half a dozen to complete, but she told Vanna that she could call by the following afternoon if she could bring Lila with her.

'No problem,' said Vanna. 'Look forward to seeing you.'

The next day they drove to Dalkey, where Vanna brought Lila to play with Dion and then showed Eden into a different room, where Amahle was chatting to a man Eden immediately recognised.

'Hozier!' She gave a squeak of excitement. 'I'm in fangirl heaven. I love you nearly as much as Amahle. I can't believe you're both in the same room together. And that I'm in it too.'

The singer laughed and told her he was honoured she liked his music, before telling Amahle that he'd be in touch with her soon but that he thought the new album was brilliant.

'I would've asked for his autograph but I was too embarrassed,' confessed Eden after he'd left.

'He'll be at the party,' said Amahle. 'Maybe he'll sign a menu. Anyway, to more important things. You've changed your hair colour! It's *totally* your shade. I mean, the grey was a lovely fashion statement, but goodness, Eden, you look stunning.'

Eden smiled. Her wavy hair with its rose-gold highlights was no longer grey. It was now closer to the burnished Celtic red of her youth, still with gold highlights but now reflecting hues of cinnabar and vermilion. It was bold and bright and changed her completely from the almost ephemeral woman she'd been into someone altogether more forceful and determined. When Rafe had first seen it, he'd swept her into his arms and told her that she was the loveliest, sexiest woman on the planet. And at that moment she'd felt that maybe she was. It was as though she'd suddenly changed back from a grief-stricken widow to the Eden she'd been before. And she loved the feeling.

She explained to Amahle that the grey had been a fashion choice forced upon her and found herself telling the singer about Andy's accident and how tough things had been after-wards.

'I'm so very sorry.' Amahle's voice was soft and warm. 'I'm sure it's not something you ever truly get over. But look at you now, working for yourself, bringing up a gorgeous girl and rocking your new look.' She fixed Eden with a critical gaze. 'It's not just the hair, though. You look different. Lighter. Brighter. Happier.'

'Didn't I look happy before?'

'I thought so,' said Amahle. 'But there's a bit of a glow about you . . . Oh!' Her eyes widened. 'Is there someone new in your life?'

'Can women only glow because of a love interest?' Eden asked.

'Totally not,' said Amahle. 'But am I right?'

Eden laughed, and told her that she was seeing a man and that it was going well, although there were complications.

'If he's good enough for you, then you can work out the complications,' said Amahle.

'I'm working them out by ignoring them at the moment,' admitted Eden.

'As good a way as any.' Amahle grinned.

'There'll be a reckoning,' Eden said. 'But I'm happy to put it off for a while.'

*

Elizabeth was also enchanted by Eden's new hair colour.

'You're a totally different woman,' she said. 'I hardly recognise you. Also . . .' she dropped her voice, even though there was nobody else in the house, 'I'm thankful it's you and not some other mystery redhead who was spotted leaving Rafe's house the other morning. Anita mentioned it to me when she came in with some chocolate, and I was concerned. Apparently the WhatsApp group is rife with speculation.'

Eden laughed.

'It's lovely to hear you laugh like that too,' Elizabeth said. 'I'm so glad it's working out. You have an aura of happiness about you, Eden.'

'I was happy before,' said Eden. 'But I'm extra happy now. And not because of Rafe. It's because I know what I want. I haven't quite figured out how things will go, but I'm OK with that.'

'Good,' said Elizabeth. 'I'm glad for you. But I hope Rafe is part of it.'

Eden smiled, but she didn't say anything in reply.

Whatever about other people making assumptions about her apparent glow, it hadn't been remarked on by the Farrelly family, although both Valerie and Michelle commented on her hair.

'Why did you change it?' asked Michelle when she called around to Eden's unexpectedly one afternoon. 'I thought you liked the grey.'

'It wasn't me any more,' said Eden.

'The red is you like you were five years ago.'

'If I've knocked five years off myself, that's all to the good.'

'You always look fabulous,' said Michelle. 'It's nothing to do with your hair colour.'

'Fabulous is pushing it. But I wanted to look a little less exhausted.'

'You never look exhausted.'

'Really? You and Valerie are always telling me I look tired and not to work so hard.'

'Well, it's hard work doing it all by yourself,' said Michelle. 'It'll be so much easier when you're at Dunleary.'

Sean and Valerie were moving at the weekend.

Eden still hadn't told them she wasn't moving too.

Angelina
I was in Wexford town today and I met Valerie. She invited me back to see the house. It's amazing. WHY haven't you said anything to me about the move?????

Eden
I'm not actually moving

Angelina
Huh? But Val showed me where you'd be living

Eden
Where she wants me to live

Angelina
What's going on?

Eden
Let's FaceTime later in the week

Angelina

OK. I'm intrigued

Valerie called around to Eden's house the following day and interrupted her work on Amahle's seating plan.

'We've decided to have a family celebration for Sean's retirement at Dunleary the weekend after next. We'll have moved in by then and we'd love it if you were with us too. Have you done anything about it yet?'

'Valerie, I don't think it's going to work out,' said Eden. 'I'm very busy here and—'

'I understand,' said Valerie. 'I realise I've been pushing you a bit. Don't stress, just come for the celebration.'

'That would be lovely,' said Eden.

'It'll be like old times,' Valerie said. 'With a new twist.'

It had been a while since Petra had stayed over at Rafe's. As she turned into Sycamore Grove, she saw him standing outside his house chatting to a man who was leaning on a serious-looking lawnmower. Rafe introduced him to her as Jack.

'Good to see you getting all suburban with the local dads as well as the mums,' she said when they were indoors.

'The barbecue was a good ice-breaker,' he admitted.

'Did Eden come?' Her question was casual.

'No,' he said. 'It was a residents-only thing. Besides, we were on a break at the time.'

'And are you still?'

'Not currently. But there's a chance she'll be moving to Wexford,' Rafe said.

Petra's eyes widened.

'To live with her in-laws.'

'Seriously?'

'She doesn't want to, and she says she won't, but I can't help thinking she might.'

'If she says she's not, why do you think she will?'

'There's a whole emotional blackmail thing going on with that family,' said Rafe. 'And she struggles to hold her own against it. Even when she tells her mother-in-law she's not going to do something, Valerie carries on regardless and somehow Eden always ends up falling into line.'

'How would you feel if she leaves?'

'It is what it is.' Rafe shrugged. 'I thought you'd be pleased.'

'I don't care either way,' said Petra. 'It's a little odd, though, isn't it? She's a daughter-in-law, not a daughter. I'm surprised they'd want her with them. Or that she'd want to go, to be honest.'

'It's all caught up in her head with a sense of obligation towards them and her late husband's memory. Apparently they've built a magnificent extension for her to live in, so it's difficult to say no.'

'Poor Eden.' Petra frowned. 'Letting the in-laws walk all over her has to be a mistake. Have you said that to her?'

'More or less. But it's not up to me.'

'Look, Rafe, I know I've been on your case about her, but it's only because I was concerned you were losing your heart to the first woman you've met since Jewel. Especially someone with her own traumas.'

'She isn't the first woman I've met since Jewel,' he said. 'She's the first who's mattered to me. And who doesn't have traumas?'

'Are you in love with her?'

'You're seriously asking me that question?'

'Why not? Are you?'

'She matters to me,' repeated Rafe.

'Does she matter because you love her or because you want to be in love with her?'

'There's a difference?'

'You know there is.'

'Why isn't it straightforward?' he demanded. 'Why don't you meet someone, decide they're right for you, marry them and live happily ever after?'

'If I knew the answer to that, don't you think I'd be living happily ever after myself?'

'Oh, Petra.' He was apologetic. 'Here I am getting myself in a twist over someone, and I haven't asked you about what's going on for you. Is everything OK? Is there someone? *Was* there someone?'

'Shut up, Rafe.' She shook her head. 'I'm fine. I'm perfectly happy. All I'm saying is that if life and love were that easy, everyone would find their ideal match and there'd be no misunderstandings and broken hearts and difficult relationships . . . Look, I think – thought – Eden Hall was wrong for you, but what do I know? If you love her and you want her to be with you, then tell her. Because she could make a decision to move based on faulty information, and that wouldn't be good for either of you.'

'Faulty information?'

'Such as that you don't really care.'

'She knows I care. I've proved that to her. I don't need to say anything. Besides, this decision is all about her and what she wants.'

'Rafe, for God's sake. You can't assume she knows exactly how you feel. You have to tell her.'

'I don't want to influence her.'

'This is another damn example of faulty information. She might think you care about her as no more than a friend.'

'She couldn't possibly think that.'

'Why . . . Oh!' Petra made a face. 'I don't want to know about your sex life. But sex and love, they're different. You know they are. *She* knows they are. If you don't tell her how you feel, maybe she'll think it's all about the sex, and that the love part . . . Oh, Rafe, you do bloody love her, don't you?'

'Ever since I was five.'

Petra stared at him. 'Seriously?'

'I didn't know it then,' he said. 'And I went away and I fell in love with Jewel, so it didn't matter. But now . . . I don't want to lose Eden. And I might.'

'Not if you tell her. Not if she loves you too. I'm a woman. I guarantee it. And if you do lose her, then she never deserved you and you've dodged a bullet the size of a ballistic missile and you should be heaving a massive sigh of relief.'

'You really are an amazing big sister, you know that?'

'Yes,' said Petra. 'I do.'

Chapter 31

Eden took the Friday of Sean and Valerie's celebration off. But instead of heading directly for Dunleary, she took the Enniscorthy exit and drove to Tony and Angelina's house, a detached four-bedroom home overlooking the river.

Angelina opened the front door before Eden was out of the car, and hugged her fiercely, saying how good it was to see her in real life again.

When Lila was happily playing in the garden with the toys Angelina kept for young visitors, the two women sat at an outdoor table, glasses of iced water in front of them.

Eden had FaceTimed Angelina after their WhatsApp exchange, and they'd had a long discussion about the proposal for Eden and Lila to move to Wexford, as well as Valerie's methods of making things happen the way she wanted.

'She definitely wants me to persuade you,' observed Angelina now. 'She was like an estate agent showing me around the extension and pointing out the benefits. It *is* gorgeous and I *would* like to persuade you,' she added, 'but only for the selfish reason that it would be great to have you nearby. But that's not the point, is it? The point is you'd be living with Valerie.'

'I know.'

'I love my mum. I moved here to be closer to her. All the same, I wouldn't live in her one-acre back garden, let alone in a granny flat, no matter how gorgeous, attached to her house. And she's my mother! Valerie is Andy's mother. Besides, you'll never find anyone new if you're living with her, you know that, don't you?'

'Well . . .'

'Eden!' Angelina stared at her. 'Is there someone? Are you keeping secrets from me?'

Eden took a deep breath and told her about Rafe.

'Why didn't you tell me any of this before?' demanded Angelina.

'Because it seemed like betraying Andy,' confessed Eden. 'Michelle thinks that me even knowing Rafe is all wrong.'

'For crying out loud!' Angelina shook her head. 'You're entitled to live your life, Eden. You've been a grieving widow for long enough. Andy would want—'

'Valerie is always telling me what Andy would want. Don't you start too!'

'I'm sorry if I'm sounding like Valerie, but for God's sake, you know he'd want you to be happy. He certainly wouldn't want you to miss out on a second chance at love because of a misguided sense of loyalty to him.'

Whatever Andy's advice would have been on the situation, Eden knew that Angelina was right about one thing.

He'd always wanted her to be happy.

Despite the contradictory thoughts chasing each other around in Eden's head, the usual sense of tranquillity at winding through the soft green and gold fields and leaving the cares of the city behind settled on her as soon as she turned onto the quiet road that led to Dunleary. It really was a perfect house in a perfect location. If Valerie had been in a position to make this suggestion a year ago, Eden knew she'd have said yes to the move without even thinking.

She parked between Michelle and Stephanie's cars, conscious that she was the last to arrive.

'Mama, I want to get out!' Lila's voice jolted her from her sudden daze, and Eden released the seat belt, allowing her daughter to clamber out of the car. Lila raced across the driveway and used the coving at the doorstep to reach the bell, while Eden followed at a more sedate pace.

When Valerie answered the door, she swept her granddaughter into her arms and covered her in kisses.

'Stop, Granny!' But Lila was giggling as she squirmed in Valerie's hold.

'We thought you'd never get here,' Valerie said to Eden, who was walking towards the house pulling her overnight case behind her.

'Sorry, I dropped in to Angelina's on the way. I didn't realise you were expecting us earlier. When did the others get here?'

'Michelle, Steph and Gavin came for lunch,' said Valerie. 'Gene won't make it until tomorrow, but it's lovely to have you all here to celebrate our move. Yours too, I hope! Do you want to leave your things in your room and then join us? Lila can go and play with her cousins.' Valerie turned around without giving her the opportunity to reply.

As soon as Eden finished unpacking, she took a photo of the sea from the long windows of the study and sent it to Rafe.

His reply came almost immediately:

Rafe
Great view. Better than from my window, that's for sure.

Eden
It's fabulous isn't it. But views aren't everything

Rafe
How's the mother-in-law?

Eden
Possibly peeved I was the last to arrive

Rafe
You don't have to stay. Come back. Stay with me instead.

Eden
It's just the weekend 😊 Wish you were here tho

Rafe
I'm not sure I'd be welcome! But I wish I was there too. Rx

She put away her phone and went into the garden. Lila was sitting in a wicker chair eating ice cream with her cousins. The adults were at the long patio table, champagne glasses in front of them.

'Thank goodness you finally made it,' said Sean as he popped the cork on a bottle of Prosecco and filled everyone's glass. 'We've been waiting to open this for hours.'

He clinked his glass against Valerie's. 'To us!'

'To you both!' cried Michelle. 'I hope you have the happiest of retirements.'

'You so deserve it,' said Gavin. 'You've been the best parents to us, and we couldn't be happier for you.'

Eden clinked her glass too, but she didn't say anything. Nor, she noticed, did Stephanie, who, despite Gavin's obvious enthusiasm, didn't look exactly thrilled to be there.

'You took an age,' remarked Stephanie after she'd taken a large gulp from her glass. 'We were all gasping for bubbles.'

Surely Stephanie wasn't in a bad mood because she was waiting for a drink, thought Eden, who nevertheless apologised again for dropping in to Angelina's on the way.

'How is Angie?' asked Michelle.

'On good form.'

'And Tony?'

'He was at work. He sells tractors, hard though it is to imagine.'

'Such a nice young man,' said Valerie. 'Well, not so young now.'

There was an awkward silence, and Eden knew they were all thinking, yet again, of Andy, who would always be young in their memories.

If only there really was a way of talking to the dead, she thought. If only Andy could answer her letters. Though obviously exchanging letters with her dead husband while having hot sex with someone else wouldn't exactly be the best of ideas.

Her phone vibrated in her pocket.

She took it out and glanced at the message.

Rafe
I forgot to mention I love you 🖤🖤🖤

She felt her face burn as her heart skipped a beat.

It was the first time Rafe had told her he loved her.

She hadn't said she loved him when Angelina had asked her earlier.

She hadn't ever said it to him either.

Her fingers tightened around the phone.

'Everything OK?' asked Michelle.

'Yes, yes, nothing important.' Eden looked up and put her mobile back in her pocket. 'Just work.'

'They're not trying to get you to cover for anyone this weekend?' This time it was Valerie who put the question.

'No, it's all under control.' Eden smiled brightly at her, and then Valerie said she planned to do a little gardening and asked if anyone was going to help.

'After Prosecco?' Stephanie raised an eyebrow. 'And the wine I had at lunch? I wouldn't be safe!'

'And you need to be careful with the shears, Mum.' Michelle laughed.

'I only had one glass of bubbles, and it's only a little light weeding.' Valerie stood up. 'You can all do whatever you like, I don't mind.'

'I'm going for a swim,' Gavin said.

'I'll join you,' said Sean.

'Bring the boys with you,' suggested Michelle. 'I'd say take the girls too, but I can't be arsed to move myself right now and the entire crew is too much for you to have to worry about.'

Fifteen minutes later, the men and boys were swimming,

while the girls were helping Valerie with the weeding and their mothers had opened another bottle of Prosecco.

'We should toast you too, Eden,' said Michelle. 'And your great new life in Dunleary. Just as soon as you can break free from the shackles of the home-care crowd.'

'Oh, look, I don't think that's going to happen,' said Eden.

'What d'you mean?' Michelle stared at her. 'I thought you were only part-time anyhow.'

'I meant coming here. There's a lot to consider, and—'

'Seriously?' Stephanie looked at her. 'They've practically built you a house and you're not dying to move into it?'

'It's a lovely idea, but there are some practical issues to consider,' said Eden.

'Have you said this to Mum?' Michelle sounded horrified. 'She's counting on you being here soon.'

'How could you even think of refusing?' asked Stephanie.

She's definitely pissed at me for something, thought Eden, hearing the hint of sarcasm in Stephanie's voice.

'I'd love to live here myself,' added Michelle.

'Why don't you?' asked Eden. 'Why don't you and Gene do what Valerie is suggesting to me? Rent out your house and move in with them?'

'Don't be silly,' Michelle said. 'It would never work.'

'Why?'

'Gene's job, for one thing,' said Michelle. 'Plus we have two kids. The extension was built for you, Eden. You only have Lila.'

'Gene could commute and work from home,' said Eden.

'Commuting wouldn't work for him,' said Michelle.

'Why d'you think it would for me?' asked Eden.

'Valerie showed me the desk she bought for you. It's perfect

376

for your calligraphy. You can do that and give up your carer's job.'

'And care for Sean and Valerie instead?'

'That's completely different,' said Michelle. 'What you need, Eden—'

'You all seem to think you know what I need!' Eden exclaimed as she pushed her chair back from the table and stood up. 'But you don't. So leave it. I'm going for a walk.'

'Hey, I didn't mean to upset you . . .' Michelle's voice trailed off as Eden strode rapidly down the garden towards the beach. 'Oh, for heaven's sake,' she said as her sister-in-law disappeared from view. She reached for the bottle and topped up her glass.

Rafe was in the garden, his phone on the table in front of him. He knew Eden had seen his last message, but she hadn't yet replied, and now he was wondering if he'd been really stupid in sending a soppy 'I love you' text with those ridiculous hearts. It was Petra's fault, of course, with all that 'tell her you love her' stuff she'd said. He shouldn't have listened to her. He looked at the message, hoping to see the little dots that indicated Eden was replying, but there was nothing. He wished he'd kept his big mouth shut. Or his big thumbs off the keyboard. Texting a declaration of love was naff. If he'd said it to her face to face, he'd have been able to see straight away if it was welcome, and he could have made a joke of it if necessary. But now . . . now it was out there and he couldn't take it back.

What had he hoped to achieve?

What did he want from her?

What did she want from him?

Was she ready to let him replace Andy Farrelly?

Was he ready to let her replace Jewel?

He looked at his text again.

Rafe

I forgot to mention I love you 🖤🖤🖤

He should've said it before she left.

Because he had competition for her heart, and the competition wasn't another man.

It was an all-enveloping family. It was a potential new life in a beautiful house in Wexford. And it was the legacy of her dead husband.

She'd said she didn't want to live with Sean and Valerie, but she'd gone there all the same.

If she wasn't sure what she wanted, how the hell could he know?

Eden let the dry sand fall through her fingers as she sat in the shadow of the tall sea grass and gazed out towards the water. The tide was high and so were the waves, delighting the bodyboarders who rode them in to the shore, and clearly delighting Sean, Gavin and the boys too, because their shrieks of laughter floated up to her on the breeze. She remembered running into that sea with Andy, and him catching her around the waist and throwing her against the oncoming waves. She remembered emerging spluttering and laughing, the water stinging her eyes. And she remembered the salt on his lips as she kissed him.

She didn't want to remember. But she didn't want to forget either.

She checked her phone again.

Rafe
I forgot to mention I love you 🖤🖤🖤

She started to type a reply, but she didn't know what she wanted to say. She deleted the words and started again. She deleted them for a second time. She was conscious that if Rafe was looking at his phone, he'd see that she was texting him. So she had to send something.

In the end, she sent three heart emojis herself.

They said everything and nothing.

He didn't reply.

Amanda and Bruno joined them for a Zoom chat later that evening. This time, Sean opened the bottle of champagne that Stephanie had brought as a retirement gift for him. Eden's head was buzzing with the unaccustomed amount of fizz she was consuming, and she hoped Lila would sleep through the night and not wake too early in the morning. Lila had been enchanted by her new bedroom in the extension, dragging her cousins in to bounce on the bed.

'All the renovations look amazing,' said Amanda. 'Especially Eden's extension. We can't wait to visit.'

'It's not—' Eden began to speak, but her voice was drowned out by Valerie saying that the other bedrooms had been done up too, and that when they arrived, Amanda and Bruno could have the dormer, which had always been Amanda's favourite.

'Ah, thanks, Mum,' said Amanda. 'We hope to be over in October. You'll be well settled in then, and of course . . .'

she turned to Bruno and smiled before beaming at them all from the screen, 'we'll be able to celebrate our great news with you too.'

'What great news?' Valerie's voice was hopeful and her eyes shone.

'You've guessed, of course! We're expecting a baby!'

Sean refilled their glasses with the remainder of the champagne as they all rushed to congratulate Amanda and Bruno.

'Another grandchild for you, Valerie,' said Stephanie.

'It's very exciting,' Valerie said. 'I'm blessed with all my grandchildren. My children and their wives and husbands too, of course.'

Even though they were all laughing and joking, Eden felt everyone glance in her direction.

'It's at times like this that we miss Andy,' whispered Michelle. 'I'm sure you do too.'

'I can still feel his presence, you know,' said Valerie, who'd overheard her. 'Especially at family occasions. He's delighted for Amanda and Bruno too, and he's wishing us all the best for the future.'

Did Valerie really feel some kind of presence? wondered Eden in the slightly uncomfortable silence that followed her mother-in-law's words. Or did she simply want to believe in it? Surely if Andy's spirit was with them, she herself would be the one to feel it.

'It's like a whisper,' Valerie added, 'telling me I'm doing the right thing. Reminding me that I have to look out for you and Lila.'

'And you've done that brilliantly,' said Eden. 'But quite honestly, Valerie, I'm a little spooked at the idea of Andy's presence looming over us.'

'Not looming.' Valerie looked offended. 'Just here. With us. Happy for us.'

'I feel him too,' said Michelle.

'You'd imagine *you* would, Eden.' Stephanie echoed her thoughts. 'You were the love of his life, after all. Everyone knows that.'

'Even so,' said Eden, 'I don't sense his presence. I'm not sure I'd want to.'

'It's a pity you're not receptive to it,' Valerie said.

'I'm as receptive as the next person.' Eden stood up. 'But I don't believe in spirits. I'm tired. I'm going to bed.'

She stood at the window of her new bedroom and looked towards the sea. Although it was too dark to make it out, she could hear the distant roll of the waves against the soft white sand. She recalled the wilder, stonier beaches of Galway, where her parents had brought her as a child. She remembered her mum and dad sitting on grassy verges while she scrambled around on the rocks, collecting seashells and pink coral and rushing back to deposit her finds with them before starting her search again. It wasn't until she was older that she learned the coral she was so proud of finding wasn't coral at all, but calcified seaweed. She'd kept her collection on her window ledge. She hadn't brought it to Dublin. She'd let Aunt Trudy throw everything away.

Why was I so keen to forget? she wondered. To put my childhood in the past and leave it there? Because it was easier? Less painful? And yet losing Andy was the most painful thing that had ever happened to her, and she hadn't left him in the past.

She took out the phone and looked at the message again.

Rafe
I forgot to mention I love you ♥♥♥

Eden
♥♥♥

There were no further texts.

The following morning, Rafe sent a video of a squirrel running along his garden wall and stopping to stare in the kitchen window. Eden responded with one of Sean's robot lawnmower cutting the grass at Dunleary, a task that had been happily supervised by Lila and her cousins. He sent laughing emojis in return. But no hearts.

She thought about phoning him, but even with the privacy afforded by the extension, there was too much going on in Dunleary for her to feel comfortable making the call. She stood at the window, looking out onto the freshly mown lawn, where until a few minutes earlier, the children had been chasing each other, shrieking with delight.

She turned away and walked into the main house. Although there was no sign of Valerie, three loaves of freshly baked soda bread were cooling on wire trays in the kitchen. The living room was also deserted, so Eden made her way to the conservatory at the side of the house. It was a favourite place when the skies were blue but cool easterly winds whipped in from the sea.

'Where's everyone disappeared to?' she asked when she saw Stephanie sitting in their mother-in-law's rocking chair, her legs curled up under her.

'Valerie and Michelle took the girls to the shop for ice

cream,' Stephanie replied as she unwound her legs. 'I'm trying to keep my kids to a healthy diet, but Val insists on stuffing them with sweet things, and of course, Michelle never says no to her. Meanwhile, the boys are building some kind of camp. Nothing like reinforcing gender stereotypes.'

'It is a bit,' agreed Eden. 'Oh, well, it's only for the weekend.'

'I wasn't planning to be here this weekend,' said Stephanie. 'I was thinking of a spa break with a couple of pals when Gavin sprung this on me.'

'Why didn't you say you had plans?' asked Eden.

'Are you mad?' Stephanie snorted. 'Nobody can say no to a royal command from Valerie. And of course, the kids love it too. There was no chance of me doing something I wanted when the alternative was something Valerie wanted.'

'We all seem to do what Valerie wants,' agreed Eden.

'She likes to think she's indispensable,' said Stephanie. 'But it's exhausting to be sucked in by the whole Farrelly vibe every time.'

Eden had never heard Stephanie say anything like this before. She'd always assumed that she herself was the only one who found Valerie overwhelming at times.

'She has them all twisted round her little finger,' said Stephanie, when Eden remarked on it. 'Nobody is allowed to be a dissenting voice. What Valerie wants, Valerie gets. Of course, it's hard for me to object to anything, because I'm the second wife.' She said the last words in a dramatic whisper, which made Eden smile.

'Seriously,' said Stephanie. 'It took a long time for them to accept that I wasn't a scarlet woman who'd enticed Gav away from Hilary.'

'I never met Hilary,' said Eden. 'What went wrong?'

'They married too young.' Stephanie shrugged. 'He'd only been going out with her a few months before they got engaged. Valerie loved her, so that probably had something to do with it. Then Gav and I met. We grew closer as they grew apart. Valerie's view was that if I hadn't been around "offering comfort", Gav and Hilary would've worked through their difficulties. She was wrong.'

'But you and she get along well now, don't you?'

'Once I had the children, her attitude changed,' said Stephanie. 'She adores her grandchildren.'

'Especially when she's feeding them jelly beans and ice cream.'

'Her heart's in the right place,' conceded Stephanie. 'All the same, she uses emotional blackmail on people to get them to do what she wants. Anyhow,' she added, 'you'll always be in her good books because of Andy. He was her favourite, you know.'

'I honestly don't think she has favourites. But a son who died a hero is a lot to live up to. Especially when the failed attempt to put the blame on him only ended up making him even more of a hero. Feck it, he's a lot for *me* to live up to.'

'But you have. That's why you've pride of place. The grieving widow and soon-to-be-live-in daughter-in-law.'

Eden's eyes narrowed. The resentment in her sister-in-law's voice was evident.

'I'm not the live-in daughter-in-law,' she said.

'In that case, why did they build you your own space?' demanded Stephanie. 'And why did we have a family meeting? Valerie put the plan in front of us as though it was agreed.'

'She never even asked me about it!' cried Eden. 'It was presented to me as a done deal. And I know she chatted to you over lunch one day, but I didn't realise it was quite so formal. Did anyone object?'

Stephanie shrugged.

'You did?'

'I questioned the wisdom of it.'

'So did I,' said Eden. 'It's why I can't do it.'

'Don't be daft, it puts you on the pig's back,' said Stephanie. 'Living here for free while getting rental on your house in Dublin. It's a no-brainer.'

'It's still living with Valerie and Sean,' said Eden.

'But separate,' said Stephanie. 'That extension is lovely.'

'Would you live here?' asked Eden. 'Extension or not?'

'My situation is different. But being here would certainly give you enormous influence over them.'

'To do what?'

'Whatever you wanted,' said Stephanie.

'Thanks for clarifying that you think I'd swindle them out of your inheritance or something.'

'Hey, I didn't mean . . . I'm not saying you'd do it deliberately,' said Stephanie. 'Only that if you were here all the time—'

'Oh, please!' Eden gave her sister-in-law a look of disgust, then got up and walked into the garden.

'Wait a second!'

She turned around.

'I'm sorry,' said Stephanie, who'd followed her. 'I'm being bitchy because I want to be on a massage table right now. I'm taking it out on you.'

'You made some valid points among the insults.'

'Yeah, but you know them already. The truth is, we're all manipulated by Valerie and you bear the brunt of it, because while the rest of us can duck out of some things, being Andy's widow will always give you a special status.'

Eden stayed silent.

'I liked him a lot, you know. But he's become a family icon. Nobody can say a bad word about him. His death has given Valerie the opportunity to guilt-trip us into being together more than we want because we're afraid of her bursting into tears and saying that you never know what might happen and that we should spend time together when we can because life is short and—' Stephanie broke off at the expression on Eden's face. 'Oh, shit, Eden. Sorry. It's like I'm blaming you too, and I'm not.'

'You're not saying anything I don't already know.'

'I should keep my big mouth shut,' said Stephanie. 'It's not your fault Valerie's put him on a pedestal. That she leaves space for him at the table.'

'She doesn't leave a space at the table for him.'

'Not literally,' said Stephanie. 'But he's always there, isn't he? She talks about him all the time. The son who can do no wrong. Nobody can replace him.'

'You might be right, but you're talking about my late husband and I'm finished with this conversation.' Eden began to walk away again. 'Don't come after me this time,' she said over her shoulder.

Eden spent half an hour sitting among the dunes again, gazing at the horizon without really thinking of anything at all. By the time she returned to Dunleary, the girls were back from their ice-cream run and all the children were playing chasing around the garden while Michelle lay on a lounger, flicking through a magazine while keeping an eye on them. There was no sign of Stephanie. Or Valerie. Eden took a few deep breaths, then went to the newly constructed extension and sat at the desk her mother-in-law had chosen. She took a sheet of paper from the in-tray, turned on the Anglepoise lamp and formed the letters.

Darling You

Usually the words flowed when she wrote to Andy, but she didn't know what to say next. Stephanie had spoken aloud some of the things that Eden had kept to herself, the most telling of which was that Valerie had put Andy on a pedestal and was using Eden to keep him there. Well, maybe she hadn't said that last part exactly, but it was true nonetheless. Whereas Stephanie had been awarded the title of femme fatale, at least for a while, Eden would always be Andy's widow. For as long as she was under Valerie's roof, she would never move past being a Farrelly. She would never truly be Eden Hall again.

She stared at the blank page. How was she supposed to say all this to Andy, a man who'd loved her so completely? A man she'd promised to love in return. To be forever his, as he'd promised to be forever hers.

Darling You

She would never stop loving him. She would never forget him.

She picked up her pen again.

Darling You,

We never talked about what would happen if one of us died. We never thought of it as a possibility – at least not while we were still young. We never told each other that we'd mourn forever. We never gave each other permission to find someone new. I'm trying to imagine how I'd feel if I knew you'd found another woman to love. I want to think I'd be happy for you, but I have a horrible feeling that I'd actually feel betrayed. That makes me a terrible person, doesn't it? I wouldn't want you to be happier with another woman than you were with me.

And yet I've found another man and he makes me happy. I'm not happier with him than I was with you, but I like being happy. It's a relief that I still know what happiness is. I don't want to betray you. I will always love you. But I haven't been entirely honest about Rafe. I've been honest about the sex. But not about how he makes me feel.

Yes, he makes me feel happy, but more than that, he makes me feel alive.

You made me feel alive too. When you died, I felt a light inside of me go out. But I did my best for Lila. This year, for the first time, I might be able to do my best for myself. Because of Rafe. It's not only him, though. It's other things. Like meeting Elizabeth, who's such a sassy woman and has made me look at things differently. It's the work for Amahle Radebe, which has made me feel more confident in myself and what I can do. It's as if I've opened a door to another life. And I like it. It has possibilities, and I'm ready for them.

I've spent five years mourning the life I lost and not

looking forward to the life ahead of me. Now it's time to do that, yet here I am in Dunleary with your whole family once again. They think my moving in is a done deal, but no matter how wonderful it would be for Lila, and no matter how much living in this area was a dream of ours, it's not my dream now. To be honest, I don't actually have a dream. But whatever it may be, it can't be focused on looking back. That's what Dunleary is and always will be.

I love Valerie, but I can't take responsibility for her future happiness.

I can only be responsible for mine. And, for the time being, Lila's.

Does that make me sound selfish? It shouldn't, yet I feel like it does.

No matter what, though, Andy, there's a part of me that will always be

Forever yours,
Eden xx.

Chapter 32

Eden's phone beeped. She picked it up and frowned at the unfamiliar number. Then she read the message and her eyes widened in shock.

Unknown number
Hello Eden. Trudy had a stroke last night. She's stable but poorly in hospital. I thought you should know. Kevin

She reread the message a couple of times before she grasped what it was saying. And even when she did, she found it hard to believe. That her aunt, vibrant, self-confident Trudy, was poorly in hospital. Eden had used that phrase herself many times in the past. It was a useful way of not saying how ill a patient might be. Poorly could mean the potential to get better. Or not.

She couldn't imagine Trudy not getting better.

But any possible recovery would depend on the severity of the stroke and how quickly she'd been treated. She typed the question to Kevin, who replied immediately.

Kevin
We were out to dinner but we were near the hospital when it happened. So she was admitted v quickly. I don't know prognosis.

Eden released her breath slowly. It might not be too bad. But even if it wasn't, the effects could still be marked. Trudy might be in hospital for some time.

Eden
Is there anything I can do?

Kevin replied that he doubted it. Eden asked whether she should come.

Kevin
That's up to you.

The fact that he hadn't told her not to bother worried Eden more than anything.

She went downstairs. Valerie was making tea in the kitchen.

'Hi, Valerie,' said Eden. 'I have to—'

'Who's Rafe?' asked Valerie.

Eden stared at her.

'Rafe?'

'You heard me.'

'Yes,' said Eden. 'I was wondering why you're asking me.'

'Because I want to know.'

'Rafe is a friend,' replied Eden. 'He's also the father of Lila's friend Poppy.'

'She said you went on holidays with him.'

'Rafe is the friend whose brother owns the B&B in Galway we went to.' Eden kept her voice steady.

'You told me your friend was a woman.'

'No I didn't.'

'You let me think it.' Valerie echoed Michelle's words. Eden knew that both of them were right. She was surprised that Michelle hadn't told Valerie about Rafe already. Deep down, she'd thought she would.

'It's not very relevant,' she told Valerie. 'Particularly now. I have to—'

'Of course it's relevant,' snapped Valerie. 'You've been carrying on with some man while I've been looking after you and my granddaughter and offering you a great lifestyle! How could you do this to me? How?'

'Carrying on? For heaven's sake, Valerie, I'm not a child. I'm entitled to have friends who are men.' She wasn't going to lie outright to her mother-in-law and pretend she wasn't in a relationship with Rafe. It was better to have things in the open.

'You've besmirched Andy's memory with your behaviour,' said Valerie.

'Valerie! My behaviour is perfectly—'

'I do everything for you.' Her mother-in-law continued as though she hadn't spoken. 'Everything. Has there ever been a day when I haven't backed you up? Has there ever been a time I haven't helped you out? I've practically built you a home of your own here in Dunleary, and this is the thanks I get?'

'I'm sorry I've upset you,' said Eden. 'And I'm sorry I didn't tell you about Rafe sooner, even though there was absolutely no obligation for me to share that with you. As far as the renovations to Dunleary go, they were entirely your decision. You didn't even ask me. We need to talk about that, but not now, because the thing is—'

'I don't care what "the thing is",' said Valerie. 'You've changed over the last few months, Eden, and not for the better. It's since you got that calligraphy job and started hobnobbing with celebrities in Dalkey. We're not good enough for you any more. Andy isn't good enough for you.'

'You are and have always been a rock for me and Lila,' Eden said as calmly as she could. 'She adores you. She'll always adore you.'

'Until you start pushing us out of your life.'

'I'm a grown woman and I'm entitled to have a life. That doesn't mean I'm pushing you out. Just that I'm moving on. You're getting this out of proportion, Valerie.'

'I'm not! You've been having your cake and eating it too. I can't even look at you right now.'

'Well, you don't have to look at me for much longer,' said Eden. 'Because what I've been trying to tell you is that I've had a message from Kevin Anderson. Trudy's had a stroke and she's in hospital. I'm going to see her.'

'What?' Valerie was taken aback. 'Trudy? Your aunt?'

'Yes.'

'But you don't speak to her,' said Valerie. 'You don't speak to either of them.'

'Not frequently,' agreed Eden. 'All the same . . .'

'She treated you terribly when you were a child,' said Valerie. 'You said so yourself. You were damaged by her. It wasn't until you met Andy that you began to recover. That's exactly my point, Eden. You needed him. After that terrible,

terrible night when he died, you needed us. And now it's like you don't care any more.'

'I'm very thankful that I had a husband like Andy,' said Eden. 'I'm grateful for all you've done for me too, Valerie. And of course I care about his memory and every single one of the Farrellys. But no matter how much I wish he was here now, he's not. My life with him is in the past. Everything that happened between me and my aunt and uncle is in the past too. In the present, *this* present, she's ill and I need to go to her.'

'But she's in France!'

'I know.'

'You can't go to France.'

'Why not?'

'How will you cope?'

'I'm a grown woman. I'm not helpless.'

'What about Lila?'

'She can come too.'

'Don't be stupid,' said Valerie. 'You can't bring a four-year-old to a medical emergency. She has to stay here.'

'Valerie—'

'I'm furious with you but I'm not going to take it out on my granddaughter. She should stay. There are plenty of people here to distract her.'

Eden hesitated. Annoying though it was, Valerie had a point.

'Go if you're going,' said Valerie. 'But use your common sense and leave Lila with me.'

'I wasn't planning to leave this minute,' said Eden. 'I have to check out flights first.'

'Let me know when you do. But I'm not letting Lila go with you. She's a child.'

Eden wanted to say that Valerie had no right to dictate to her about Lila. But for the sake of peace, she stayed silent.

'You know I'm right,' continued Valerie. 'However hurt I am by the fact that you've lied to me, I'll never take it out on my granddaughter. And an emergency dash to France to see a sick woman she doesn't even know is not the place for her.'

'Lila can stay.'

'I'm glad you've seen sense on one thing at least,' said Valerie, just as Michelle walked in and asked what the raised voices were all about.

Lila was unfazed by Eden telling her that she had to stay with her granny and her cousins while she went to visit someone sick in hospital. Eden was pleased that her daughter was so independent, she herself was the one who was anxious about them being apart for more than a single night. She gave Lila a hug and told her she'd see her soon, before getting into the car and heading back to Dublin.

She called Rafe when she got back to the house, apologising for not having been in touch sooner and telling him what had happened.

'Can I help?' he asked.

'Not right now,' she replied. 'I have to sort out a flight and somewhere to stay. Kevin texted me the name of a *pension* not too far from the hospital, so I'll try there.'

'I wish I could come with you,' said Rafe.

'It's probably better that I'm on my own,' said Eden. 'Who knows what the situation will be and how much time I'll spend at the hospital.'

'I'll drive you to the airport, though.'

'That would be great. I'll let you know when I've booked something.'

'Would you like to drop by for a while after that?' asked Rafe.

Eden hesitated.

'Only if it's not a hassle,' he added.

'It's definitely not a hassle,' she said. 'I'd love to, thanks.'

It was over an hour later by the time she parked outside his house. Elizabeth was in her front garden and waved at her as she got out of the car.

'Hi, Elizabeth.' Eden walked across the road. 'How are you?'

'Good as new,' said Elizabeth. 'And you? I've missed you.'

Eden updated her on her last couple of weeks, including the situation with Trudy.

'I'm sorry to hear that,' said Elizabeth. 'I hope she recovers.'

'So do I,' said Eden. 'I don't think about her that often, but she's always been there.'

Elizabeth nodded and then gestured towards number 4, where Rafe had opened the door and was now approaching them. He put his arm around Eden and gave her a hug, exchanged a few words with Elizabeth, then suggested to Eden they go back to the house.

'Take care,' said Elizabeth. 'Let me know about your aunt.'

'Thanks.' Eden gave the older woman a quick kiss on the cheek, then followed Rafe across the road again.

Alone together, she suddenly found herself unable to speak. She said nothing while Rafe busied himself with the coffee machine.

'Did you sort a flight?' he asked as he handed her a cup.

She gave him the details and he said he'd pick her up in the morning.

'Rafe . . . I didn't reply properly to your text.'

'Which text?' His voice was steady.

'The one where you said you loved me.'

'I shouldn't have sent it,' he said.

'So . . . you didn't mean it?'

'Of course I meant it. But sending it to you when you were with your mother-in-law . . . that was putting pressure on you and I shouldn't have done it. It was just . . . well, Petra said that if I loved you, I should tell you.'

'Petra did?' She looked at him in surprise.

'Seems that we both have families who want to tell us what to do.'

'Like you ever did what she told you before.' Eden smiled slightly.

'Only if she told me to do something I should have done ages ago.'

'Oh.' She looked at him and her eyes brimmed with tears.

'Now I've made you cry,' he said.

She was the one who moved towards him, and she was the one who wrapped her arms around him. And she was the one who was kissing him when Poppy ran into the kitchen and demanded to know if they were in love.

FiadhFoley
The hot redhead at Rafe's is Elizabeth's carer 😕

AAtkins
You're kidding! The old friend? The one with the GREY hair?

FiadhFoley
Yes. I saw her car pull up and park outside Rafe's. Then Elizabeth came out and spoke to her for a minute before she went into Rafe's. That's when I realised who she was 😊

SandieC
Old friends my arse!

AAtkins
Sorry girls. Looks like you've been relegated

SandieC
After all that cake!

FiadhFoley
I knew there was someone 😕 I never expected it to be her

JacinthaHarmon
Maybe you're getting it wrong. Maybe she's bringing him his house-warming invitations

KrystleK
I met her at his early one morning. She said she'd come to talk about the invites then. It might suit her to drop by early . . .

FiadhFoley
He had his arm around her when she was talking to Elizabeth. It's more than a house-warming she's giving him

What Eden Did Next

SandieC
Want to meet for 🍷 later?

FiadhFoley
You're on

Chapter 33

A wall of heat hit Eden when she stepped outside the airport at Nice, where the sun was high in a cloudless blue sky. It was so long since she'd been anywhere that she was taken aback by the ferocity of it, and she peeled off the long-sleeved blouse she'd been wearing over a white vest top, tying it around her waist as she made her way to the taxi rank. All around her, people in shorts and T-shirts were laughing and joking, clearly looking forward to their holidays. Despite having removed the blouse, she was melting in her jeans. She wished she'd thought to bring a baseball cap for some shade, but at least she had a decent pair of sunglasses to protect her eyes from the glare.

The journey from the airport to the Pension Cinq Coquilles took nearly forty-five minutes, but Eden didn't mind being stuck in traffic on the Promenade des Anglais, with its magnificent views of the sea. It occurred to her as she sat in the thankfully air-conditioned cab that being near the sea was important to her. She liked being a mere ten minutes from the coast in Dublin. She'd liked being near the Atlantic Ocean when she'd stayed at Dommo and Becky's, and she loved the proximity of Dunleary to the beach in Wexford. Seeing the water always lifted her spirits. The intense blue of the Côte d'Azur made those spirits soar, even if her reason for being here was upsetting.

She over-tipped the driver, who'd stayed silent for most of the journey, then checked in to the pretty *pension*, with its shell-decorated facade and blue-shuttered windows. An estate agent would probably have said the room she was brought to on the second floor had a sea view, even though only a small triangle of water could be seen through the hotchpotch of tiled red roofs in front of the building. The room itself was small but pretty. Its old-fashioned iron bed was covered in a white quilt with a blue seashell design, which was matched on the tiles in the adjoining bathroom. On a small table near the window was a vase of multicoloured flowers, along with a bottle of Evian water. There was no air-conditioning, but a ceiling fan spun lazily over the bed.

Eden changed into a pair of denim shorts and a fresh vest top. She took a selfie at the window and sent it to Valerie with a message to Lila to say that she loved her and she'd see her soon. Then she sent the same photo to Rafe. His reply was immediate.

Rafe
Looks lovely. Such a shame your reason for being there isn't happier. Thinking about you and your aunt and uncle. Rx

She sent a heart in return.

She waited for a few moments for a reply from Valerie, but when nothing came, she left the room and ordered another taxi to the hospital, which Kevin had told her was about twenty minutes away.

She'd rehearsed what she needed to say in basic French so that she could ask about Trudy at reception, but when she arrived, her uncle was standing outside the main door. Even though he was thinner than she recalled, and somehow seemed shorter, his mane of thick white hair was instantly recognisable.

'Kevin.' She waved at him.

'Eden. You came.'

'Of course I came. How is she?'

'I don't know. The doctors are telling me not to worry, which is ridiculous, because all I'm doing is worrying. They seem to think that it could've been worse. But she's dazed and confused and spends most of her time asleep. At least, I'm guessing asleep and not in some unconscious state.'

'Can she speak?' asked Eden as they walked into the hospital and Kevin pressed a button for the lift. 'Can she move?'

'At the moment, all she's doing is lying there,' said Kevin.

As they waited, Eden looked around her. Other than for Lila's birth, she hadn't been in a hospital since she'd given up nursing, but now the sense of familiarity with her environment and the constant activity of doctors, nurses and patients returned. She knew that many people were stressed the moment they walked into a hospital building. She was at ease.

They exited the lift on the third floor and walked along a corridor until they reached Trudy's ward. Curtains were closed around the beds, and Kevin led her to the one nearest the window.

'Trudy,' he said softly. 'It's me. And Eden.'

Eden caught her breath as she looked at her aunt. Trudy was propped up on pillows, her face pale, her eyes closed and her long grey hair lank around her face. She was hooked to a drip and various monitors, which Eden took a moment to check. She'd dealt with many stroke patients in the past and she was relieved to see that her aunt's vital signs were reasonably good.

'Hi, Aunt Trudy.' Her voice caught in her throat. 'How are you?'

'She doesn't answer, not even when she's awake,' said Kevin. 'They said she would when she was ready, but they won't tell me when ready is. I've been sitting with her ever since it happened, but even when she opens her eyes, she doesn't see me.'

'I'll stay with her for a while,' said Eden. 'You take a break.'

'I don't want to leave her,' said Kevin. 'We've never spent a night apart before.'

Eden knew how that felt. Until Andy's fatal accident, they'd never been apart for a night either. But they'd only been together a couple of years. Trudy and Kevin had been together for more than fifty. She remembered her mother once saying that nobody believed it was a relationship that would last. And yet it had. Despite the bad feeling from her grandmother and the rest of the family, Trudy and Kevin were a proper love story. And regardless of the rancour that had still existed, they'd stepped up to the plate for Eden when it mattered.

'I can't tell you everything will be all right, because I don't know,' she told Kevin as she took his hand. 'But what I do know is that Trudy is a strong woman. She must have been to leave home and do what she wanted all those years ago. She was strong when you set up the restaurants, and strong when you lost them. And she was strong for me, even though I was a nuisance. She'll want to be strong for you too.'

'You weren't a nuisance.' Kevin waited a moment before releasing her hold on him. 'You were a ten-year-old girl who'd lost her mother. We had no idea how to deal with you. We probably didn't do a great job.'

'You did your best,' said Eden. She told him about her trip to Galway and Mrs McConnell saying how scared Trudy had been at the idea of looking after her. 'I didn't realise it then, of course,' she said. 'I thought you were being mean to me, taking me away. But when Maggie said what she did, I realised that it was hard on you too.'

'We must have done something right all the same,' said Kevin. 'You've turned into a lovely person. You came here without a second thought.'

'I wanted to come. And now that I'm here, you should have some rest.'

Kevin reached for his jacket, which was slung over the back of a chair. 'I'll go home, have a shower and then come back. I didn't suggest you staying with me because the apartment only has one bedroom, but if you need anything . . .'

'I'm fine at the Cinq Coquilles,' Eden assured him. 'It's lovely.'

'OK.' He gave her shoulder a quick squeeze. 'See you later.'

She waited until he'd left the ward before sitting beside her aunt. Trudy hadn't moved. Eden took her hand. Then she closed her eyes and drifted.

It was nearly an hour later when she felt Trudy's fingers squeeze around hers. She opened her eyes and looked at her aunt. Trudy's eyes were open too.

'Aunt Trudy?' Eden stood up and leaned towards her. 'It's Eden. I'm here and everything's OK. How are you feeling?'

'Tired.' Trudy's voice was a whisper.

'But you can hear me. And you can speak.' Eden beamed at her.

'Yes, I can,' whispered Trudy. And she closed her eyes once more.

Even though Kevin hadn't yet returned, Eden left the ward for a short time to call Valerie, who hadn't replied to her photo text. She thought it was going to ring out, but then she heard Valerie's breathless voice saying, 'Yes?'

'It's me,' said Eden. 'How's Lila?'

'She's fine,' said Valerie. 'We're all at the beach. She's swimming with the others.'

'Did you show her my photo?'

'There hasn't been time. I didn't spot it straight away and they've been in the water for ages. How's your aunt?'

Eden gave her an update.

'My friend's husband had a stroke and you'd hardly know,' said Valerie. 'He's had a slight limp ever since, but that's it.'

'Hopefully Trudy's recovery will be as successful,' said Eden. 'Is Lila still in the water? Can I talk to her?'

'I'll tell her you called when they've finished their swim,' said Valerie. 'She's having a great time and we'll be having a picnic on the beach later.'

'You were right to keep here there,' said Eden. 'But I miss her.'

'I'm not often wrong,' said Valerie. 'Anyhow, she's happy as a sandboy and I'm taking good care of her. Don't worry.'

She didn't have to worry about Valerie's care of Lila,

thought Eden as she went back to Trudy's room. But she did worry about what her not-often-wrong mother-in-law might be saying to her.

She went to sit by her aunt's bed again.

Kevin arrived an hour later and was pleased to hear that Trudy had opened her eyes and spoken.

'Typical of her to do it when I wasn't here,' he said.

'It's always the way,' said Eden.

'Thanks again for coming.' Kevin rubbed his eyes. 'It's nice to have someone else here. When I sent that text, I'd completely forgotten that you were a nurse. The staff here are great, but it's good to have that extra support.'

'I doubt I'll be any more use to you than them, but I'm glad to be here.'

'I'm sorry we didn't come to your husband's funeral.' Kevin looked at her. 'We would have done, but it was my turn to be unwell then.'

Eden remembered Trudy phoning to say that they couldn't travel because Kevin was having a minor procedure. She hadn't elaborated any further and Eden hadn't asked. A convenient excuse, she'd thought at the time.

'Stents,' he told her now. 'I'm fine.'

Eden had cared for many people who'd had coronary stents inserted, and she felt bad for doubting Trudy.

'To be honest, I hardly remember anything about the funeral,' she confessed. 'Least of all who was or wasn't there.'

'I'm sure it was a very difficult time. I'm sorry.'

'I'm . . . Well, it's been five years,' she said. 'I'm OK now.'

'And your little girl?'

'Lila. She's wonderful.'

Eden took out her phone and showed him some photos. He stopped at one she'd taken on the recent trip to Galway. Lila was standing on a rock, the sea behind her, her hair lifted high by the wind.

'Great shot,' said Kevin. 'You're a natural.'

'Hardly,' she said. 'But I like to take photos of her. She'll probably hate me for them when she's older.'

He smiled, then told her she could take a break if she wanted.

'I'm happy to stay as long as you need me,' she said. 'But if you want to be on your own with Trudy, I'll come back later.'

'Take some time out,' he said. 'Have a stroll around the town. Get something to eat. I'll call you if I need you, but otherwise come back in a couple of hours.'

'OK.'

She got up and leaned towards Trudy again.

'See you later,' she said, and kissed her on the cheek.

There wasn't a direct bus that left her near the *pension*, so she got another taxi, although she asked the driver to drop her at the coast. He left her on a cobbled street, outside a row of cafés and restaurants with brightly coloured awnings and terraces with views across the bay.

She looked at the blackboard outside one of them, and almost immediately a handsome waiter appeared wishing her a good afternoon and asking if she was English.

'Irish,' she said, even though she realised his question probably related to the language she spoke rather than her nationality.

'I'm from Wexford myself,' he said, his barely there French accent disappearing immediately. 'Just outside Ferns.'

'I know it well.' She beamed at him and told him about Dunleary, and they spent a happy couple of minutes comparing the charms of the Irish east coast and the Côte d'Azur.

'In fairness, this is spectacular.' He waved his arm to embrace the sea and the sky. 'But there's nothing like a bag of Tayto crisps and a pint of Guinness.'

She grinned and ordered tea with lemon, and tarte Tatin.

The apple cake was soft, crumbly and bursting with flavour, and, she had to admit, a step up from crisps and beer. But it was all about time and place, she said to the waiter when he returned to ask if there was anything more she needed. And this was the time and place for tea and cake.

She asked him if he'd take a photo of her with the sea as a backdrop, which he did. She sent it to Rafe with a message that she was having a break but would be heading back to the hospital later.

Rafe
Looks amazing. Wish I was there.

Eden
Wish you were too

A moment later, her phone rang with a video call.

'How are you doing?' asked Rafe.

She filled him in on Trudy's condition. 'Kevin is exhausted, but he wants to be with her as much as possible,' she added. 'The hospital encourages family to stay with patients. Even if Trudy is only partially aware of what's going on, it's good for her to have him there.'

'How long will you stay?'

'A few days at least,' she admitted. 'I don't want Kevin to think I only came to show my face. He needs a break.'

'It must be awful for him.'

'Given that Trudy is becoming more aware of her surroundings, I'm hopeful we'll have a better idea of her condition soon. The next set of scans will show us how she's recovering.'

'When will they be?'

'Today or tomorrow, I reckon.'

'OK,' said Rafe. 'Keep in touch.'

She ordered more tea, then FaceTimed Valerie.

'They're playing in the sand dunes,' her mother-in-law said when Eden asked if the children were out of the water.

'I'll wait while you fetch her.'

'Hold on,' said Valerie.

A few moments later, Lila's face filled the screen. Her hair was tangled from her swim and her cheeks were rosy.

'We went into the sea and we built sandcastles and Granny said that this is my forever house!' she cried.

'It's certainly your forever house while I'm away,' agreed Eden. 'But I'll be home soon.'

'Tomorrow?' asked Lila.

'Not tomorrow. But soon.'

'I want you to put me to bed later.' Lila's chin wobbled. 'And sing my song.'

'I can't put you to bed,' said Eden. 'But when Granny does, tell her to call me and we'll sing "Feed the Birds" together.'

'OK. Oh! Amber wants me!' And Lila ran away through the sand, Eden and lullabies forgotten.

*

Kevin texted her later to say that Trudy had opened her eyes again and now recognised him and understood where she was. She'd been taken for more tests, he said, and would be back on the ward later. Eden said she'd see him at the hospital, and forty minutes later, they were sitting together in the cafeteria. Kevin had a coffee, but Eden, still replete with tarte Tatin, didn't bother with anything.

When they went back to the ward, Trudy's face seemed less pale than before.

'Trudy, sweetheart, how are you?' asked Kevin.

'I don't know,' she replied. Although her words were slow, her speech was clear.

'You know who I am?'

She nodded.

'And look who's here.' He gestured towards Eden.

Trudy looked at her without speaking for a moment, then whispered her name. 'You must have thought I was a goner to have come to see me.' She smiled faintly.

'You had us worried,' said Eden.

'I don't remember,' said Trudy.

'Don't try,' advised Kevin. 'Take it easy.'

'Am I going to be all right?'

'Of course you are,' said Kevin.

'I was asking the nurse of the family.' Trudy turned her head slightly so she was looking at Eden.

'In my professional opinion, you'll be fine,' said her niece.

Trudy was a little better the next day, although it was clear that she found speaking tiring and she struggled to remember the names of everyday objects. But the dullness behind her eyes had disappeared and she looked more like herself, even if she was an older, paler version of the woman Eden remembered.

Eden opened her bag and took out the Clarins Joli Rouge lipstick she'd bought in the airport. She smoothed it over Trudy's lips and then held up her phone so her aunt could see herself.

'I look wretched,' said Trudy.

'You look lovely,' said Eden. And she was telling the truth. Because even with her illness, the spark that lit up Trudy's eyes, so like Eden's own, was evident.

Eden picked up the brush from the bedside locker and ran it through Trudy's hair. This time when she held up the phone, Trudy gave a grudging nod.

'I'll do. When can I go home?'

'You'll be here for another week,' said Kevin. 'They want to run more tests and then, if they're happy with you, there'll be a schedule of therapy to help you with your movement and balance.'

Trudy had been allowed out of bed that morning, and although she was walking well, if slowly, she kept veering off to the left instead of keeping to a straight line.

'She'll overcome that,' Eden promised Kevin when he told her. 'It'll take time, but she will.'

She knew that Kevin was depending on her to tell him things he thought the nurses on the ward wouldn't, but Eden insisted they weren't hiding anything from him. Stroke patients could make remarkable recoveries when treated as quickly as Trudy had been, she assured him, and although her stroke had been scary for everyone, it had actually been quite mild.

'I was sure she was going to die,' Kevin said. 'I know it's

411

not exactly an unexpected event at our age, but I wasn't prepared for it at all.'

'Even when you think you're prepared, you're not,' said Eden.

They were in the cafeteria again, and he leaned across the table and put his hand over hers.

'I truly am sorry about your husband. I'm sorry we didn't visit you after I'd made my own recovery. That was wrong.'

She shrugged.

'You're here for me. We should've been there for you.'

'You were there when I needed you most.'

'All the same.' Kevin sat up straight again. 'We haven't been the best family for you, Eden. Trudy and I prided ourselves on being independent spirits. We wanted you to be independent too. But even independent spirits need someone to fall back on from time to time. I'm so glad we have you right now.'

'I'm glad to be here,' said Eden. 'Everything else is in the past.'

'And you?' asked Kevin. 'Do you have someone you can fall back on?'

She explained about the Farrellys and then told him about Rafe. She outlined the situation about Dunleary too.

'But you don't want to go,' said Kevin, 'so what's the problem?'

'Valerie for one thing. She's so quietly domineering.'

'You never let yourself be dominated when you were a kid,' said Kevin. 'You drove Trudy and me crazy because you wouldn't listen to us. We admired it, but it was very frustrating.'

'It's not just Valerie,' she said slowly.

412

'What?'

'Rafe told me he loved me.'

'And that's not a good thing?'

'I thought Andy was forever,' she admitted. 'We told each other it was forever. And now, by loving Rafe, I feel like I'm letting Andy down. I know he's dead,' she added quickly. 'I realise that. But I don't want to lose the feelings I had for him.'

'You won't,' said Kevin. 'Loving one person doesn't dilute the love you have for someone else. What will happen, Eden, is that you'll layer what you now feel for Rafe over your love for Andy. And that love will always be a part of you, because we have an infinite capacity for it. You were unlucky to lose Andy, but you're lucky to have found Rafe. To have found love twice. Don't let that go.'

She looked at her uncle in astonishment. She'd never expected anything like this from him, but his words, delivered so warmly, touched her.

Layering one love on top of the other. It was a comforting idea.

'But what about Valerie and the rest of the family?' she asked. 'She definitely sees me as a link to Andy. I can't be that forever, but I feel obligated towards her because she's been so kind and protective to me and Lila.'

'You can reassure her that you and Lila will always be part of her life. Sometimes people struggle to let go,' he added. 'Trudy felt that was the case with her own mother. It was why she left the way she did. She couldn't talk it over with her because she knew she'd crumble. Your grandmother wanted her children to be close all the time. She thought that them being near her proved they loved her. But letting go can be just as much an act of love as keeping someone close.'

'Granny never did let Trudy go,' said Eden. 'She talked about her all the time. None of it particularly flattering,' she conceded, 'but she brought her up in every conversation anyhow. My mum felt the terrible burden of being the daughter who stayed home.'

'I'm sorry about that,' said Kevin. 'But Martina could have left too, if that was what she wanted.'

'She couldn't.' Eden shook her head. 'It would've broken Granny's heart.'

'Or did your grandmother make her think that?' asked Kevin. 'Did she make her feel obliged to stay, in the same way you're feeling obliged to do what your mother-in-law wants?'

Eden looked at him thoughtfully.

'I never looked at it like that before,' she said. 'You might have a point. And it's weird to think that I feel obligated to Valerie when I never once felt obligated to you and Trudy. Even though you gave up your lives for me.'

'We didn't give up our lives,' said Kevin. 'We adapted, but we were still doing what we wanted to do. So the question is, Eden, what do *you* want to do? Are you in love with this Rafe guy? Do you think it's a long-term relationship?'

'It already is.' She smiled. 'I knew him when we were children. He's Rafe McConnell. His family lived opposite us.'

'His mother talked to Trudy,' Kevin recalled. 'You wanted to move in with them.'

'Yes.'

'And now it's come full circle.'

'Though it's not plain sailing with him either.' Eden gave

her uncle a brief run-down on Rafe's history. 'So,' she concluded, 'there's a feeling in both our families that we've clung together because of our tragedies but that we don't really know what we're doing.'

'You're a clever, capable woman and you must know that's nonsense,' said Kevin. 'However, perhaps I can put your mind at rest, at least partly. It always bothered your aunt that nobody believed she knew her own mind. That they thought she was foolish and flighty and that I'd turned her head. That it was a short-lived fling, built on shifting sands. And yet we've been together for a long time. Because our love is about her and me and nobody else. Once you find the right person, everything else falls into place.'

'I never thought I'd ever have this kind of conversation with you,' said Eden.

'Life is full of surprises, isn't it?' Kevin smiled.

Her phone buzzed. They both looked at it. She picked it up and opened the message, a GIF of a cup of coffee, sent by Rafe.

She typed a reply:

Eden
Missing you

Rafe
And you. How's your aunt?

She looked at Kevin. 'Do you mind if I make a call?'

'Not at all.'

She walked out of the cafeteria and stood beneath the shade of a tree as she phoned Rafe.

415

'Things are looking positive,' she said. 'I'm getting to know Kevin better too. It feels right to be here.'

'Good.' Rafe's voice was soft and warm.

'But I really do miss you,' she said. 'And . . .'

'You still there?' he asked when she didn't go on.

'I love you too,' she said.

Rafe got out of the cab and paid the driver. In the heat of the early afternoon, the street was quiet and deserted. The blue and white sign of the building in front of him swayed in the gentle breeze, creaking slightly with every movement. Then the door opened and Eden stepped outside.

He'd never seen her looking better. In her lilac sundress and pink espadrilles, red-gold curls pinned up on her head, she'd already taken on the air of a stylish Frenchwoman. He was about to say this when she put her arms around him and kissed him hard on the mouth.

'I couldn't believe your text from the airport,' she said when they came up for air. 'I'm in shock.'

'After we talked, I called Petra and she offered to come and stay with Poppy, who's undoubtedly milking her for everything she can.'

'Petra seems to have transformed from someone who thought I was excess baggage to your personal matchmaker,' said Eden with a laugh.

'She realises how much you mean to me.' He kissed her again.

'Come on,' said Eden as they finally broke apart. 'Let's get your case upstairs. I told Madame Levine you were coming.'

Madame Levine, who knew all about Eden's aunt and the

arrival of the man she called Eden's 'lover' (in an accent so very French that, Eden remarked afterwards, she made him sound like a character in an erotic novel), welcomed Rafe warmly and waved them upstairs.

'It's so chic,' he remarked when Eden showed him into the room. 'And you're looking very chic too. As well as which . . . you seem different somehow.'

And she did, he thought. There was something altogether lighter about her. Despite the strain of her aunt's illness and missing Lila, she looked happier than he'd ever seen her.

'Because you're here?' she suggested.

'Really?'

'It's part of it. And it's the part I want to celebrate.'

'Sounds good to me,' he said, and he pushed her gently onto the blue and white bedspread. The afternoon sun, slanting through the window, lit up her face. She smiled and put her arms around him.

Their lovemaking was so energetic that Madame Levine, who'd stopped outside the door to ask if there was anything they needed, walked away immediately, knowing there wasn't.

Chapter 34

Rafe insisted on accompanying Eden to the hospital that afternoon. He told her he'd wait in the cafeteria if Trudy didn't want visitors, but when Trudy heard he was there, she insisted on seeing him.

'Look after my niece,' she said, after they'd spent ten minutes talking. 'She deserves the best.'

'I know. But I'm hoping she'll put up with me instead,' said Rafe.

'He's a charmer.' Trudy smiled at Eden.

'It's my strength,' said Rafe.

'Speaking of strength . . .' She gave Eden an anxious look. 'D'you think I'll be able to paint again?'

'Paint? Like painting walls? Or pictures? I don't remember you painting either before.'

'Pictures,' said Trudy. 'I took it up when we retired. I'm not that good, but it relaxes me.'

Eden took a pen from her bag and handed it to Trudy. At first it slipped through her aunt's fingers, but on the second attempt she was able to hold it.

'You'll need to work with the community nurse or whoever it is who's going to do therapy with you,' Eden said. 'I can't honestly say that you'll be back to how you were before. But there's no reason you can't paint.'

'Good.' Trudy smiled and closed her eyes.

Eden and Rafe sat with her until Kevin arrived. Eden did the introductions again.

'I want Eden to have one of my paintings,' said Trudy. 'Let her choose.'

'OK,' said Kevin. 'Perhaps a photograph too.'

Trudy nodded.

'We could meet at the apartment later,' said Kevin. 'Have something to eat? There's a lovely restaurant nearby.'

Rafe, who'd hoped to spend the evening alone with Eden, said he'd be delighted. Eden glanced at him and smiled.

'I know you weren't keen,' she said when they left the hospital later. 'But you're a decent man to say yes.'

'Your uncle is a decent man too, and I'll have you all to myself later, so it's the least I can do.'

Eden had expected her aunt and uncle's apartment to be a quirky studio in a quaint old building, but in fact it was on the top floor of a block that Kevin said had been built in the seventies. The building was painted pale yellow, and each apartment had a large balcony with white railings, most shaded by yellow and white awnings.

'They're big by today's standards,' said Kevin, as Rafe and Eden stepped inside. 'But back in the day they weren't considered much. And of course they're third line back from the sea.'

'But . . . but this is wonderful!' exclaimed Eden as she looked around the large living and dining room. 'And oh, Uncle Kevin – your photos!'

A complete wall was taken up by Kevin's photographs, which were a mixture of black-and-white portraits and brightly coloured landscapes. Eden walked over to study them. She recognised some from when she was younger, particularly the ones of Trudy that Kevin had taken fifty years earlier: her aunt turning cartwheels on the beach, or perched on a rock, or sitting at a waterside café, a wicked gleam in her eyes. She caught her breath at photos of herself, ones she'd forgotten that Kevin had taken, some she didn't remember him taking at all. There she was as a ten-year-old, eating an ice cream, an expression of pure joy on her face. And another of her looking serious at her school nativity play, where she'd been a shepherd, with no dialogue but a role in keeping the wooden sheep-on-wheels moving. There were some of her as a teenager too, a moody expression on her face as she turned to look at the camera. And a colour one of her school graduation, her hair up, wearing a crimson dress that Trudy had helped her choose.

'These are amazing,' said Rafe.

'Thank you.' Kevin smiled at him and then turned to Eden, who was now gazing at the opposite wall, where half a dozen of Trudy's abstract paintings were hung. There were others stacked against the wall too.

'Choose whichever one you like,' said Kevin. 'I can always take it out of the frame for you.'

Eventually Eden selected a swirl of reds, blues and greens that reminded her of the sea. When she said this, Kevin grinned and told her it was titled *La Belle Mer* and that she was clearly good at interpreting Trudy's work.

'I'm not sure about that,' said Eden. 'But I love how vibrant it is.'

'I wanted to ask you a favour,' said Kevin, when he'd rolled the canvas and put it in a tube for her.

'Of course.'

'I want to take your photo again.'

'Where?' She looked around. 'In here? On the balcony?' He shook his head.

'At the Poisson Rouge,' he said. 'It's the café where I took so many of Trudy's. I'd like to reprise one of them with you, if you don't mind. This one,' he added, pointing to a photo of Trudy sitting on a low wall in the shade of a large parasol. She was wearing a chiffon scarf over her head and was holding a glass of champagne, raising it to the camera, a wide smile on her face. It was a very sixties image, thought Eden.

'I don't think I could look like that,' she said.

'I'm not asking you to *be* Trudy,' Kevin assured her. 'I want to recreate the same photo with you, that's all.'

'I don't have a scarf,' said Eden.

'Trudy has lots.'

'You'll look fabulous,' Rafe assured her.

'If you say so,' she said as she gave him a doubtful smile.

The Poisson Rouge was a five-minute walk from the apartment, and although it had clearly been modernised since the day of the original photograph, the location was instantly recognisable. Kevin was greeted by the owner, who was happy to allow him the space to set up his equipment.

'I thought it was just a quick photo,' said Eden, as her uncle opened his case and took out an impressive camera. 'And I wasn't expecting you to need anything else either.' This last comment was made when he unfolded a light diffuser. 'I'm not a model.'

'You're *my* model.' He smiled at her, suddenly more at ease than she'd seen him since she'd arrived. 'Right, let's fix the scarf and then you sit here . . . no, here.'

She was part of a family of perfectionists, she realised, as he asked her to move her position, re-drape the scarf, hold her head a certain way . . . and then asked Rafe to hold the diffuser so the light was reflected where he wanted it.

'And to think I just point and click with my phone,' she murmured when he fired off a few preliminary shots.

'You'd pay good money for this normally,' said Rafe.

She stayed patient through all the different poses that Kevin wanted until he finally declared himself happy with the shot. He showed it to her on the camera, and she gasped. Because she *was* Trudy. A younger, more modern version, but Trudy all the same.

'That's . . . astonishing,' she said.

'It's your bone structure,' Kevin told her. 'And your eyes. And even your hair. You're both very photogenic people. I'll print a copy for you too.'

'Thank you,' said Eden.

'Would it be possible for you to take one of the two of us?' Rafe looked at him enquiringly. 'You wouldn't need to take too much time over it.'

'I think by now you realise I always take my time over it,' Kevin said. 'But I'd be delighted.'

Once again he spent a while setting up the shot, telling Rafe and Eden to face each other, then him, then away from each other, then turning back towards each other. When he was satisfied, he showed them the pictures.

'Oh!' cried Eden. 'They're lovely.'

'They capture your happiness,' said Kevin. 'That's why they're lovely.'

He was right, she thought. Because her joy and contentment at being beside Rafe McConnell shone through. And
she could see the same emotions in him. There was no doubt.

She had layered one love on top of the other, and it was
even stronger than she could have imagined.

They arrived back in Dublin late the following night. Although
she would've liked to go to Dunleary immediately and see
Lila, Eden knew that at this late hour, her daughter would
be asleep. But she resolved to get up early the next morning
and drive to Wexford so that they could have breakfast
together. And then she would tell Valerie and Sean that she
wasn't going to take up their offer to live with them, because
she wanted to stay in Dublin. She wanted to live in her own
house with her daughter and she wanted to be close to Rafe.

She said this to him as they lay in bed together in her
house.

'Are you sure about this?' he asked. 'You won't regret it?'

'How can I regret loving you? I'm sorry it took me so
long to be sure about it. But something's shifted in me, Rafe.
I loved Andy from the moment I met him until the day he
died. I still loved him afterwards. I felt it was important to
keep loving him because otherwise he'd sacrificed his life and
it meant nothing. But now . . . now I love you and I have
to believe and hope he'd be happy for me.'

'I fell in love with you the day you delivered the flowers
from Elizabeth,' he said. 'It was something deep inside, something telling me that you were important. When I realised
who you were, I knew why. You were always important to
me, Eden Hall. And I know that Jewel would be happy for
me. She wanted people to be happy.'

Eden pulled him towards her and rendered talking unnecessary.

'The other thing is,' she said breathlessly some time later, 'the sex with you is absolutely brilliant. I was afraid that bringing love into it would change it.'

'Seriously?' He laughed.

'I thought that just being friends might mean it was more . . . well . . . raunchy.'

'Oh, Eden.' He laughed again, then kissed her, and they both said, at the exact same time, that bringing love into it had actually made it better.

And then they slept, wrapped in each other's arms.

Chapter 35

Valerie was in the front garden weeding the flower beds when the silver Audi pulled into the driveway and parked behind the two other cars already there. She stood up and readjusted her yellow visor to protect her eyes from the glare of the sun. The doors of the car opened and Eden stepped out, followed by a tall, rangy man with dark hair. Both of them were wearing T-shirts and shorts. Valerie noticed that Eden's normally pale skin had a hint of a tan, and that she was wearing a selection of pretty necklaces and bracelets. She looked young and happy and glowing.

She felt her stomach lurch as the man put his hand on the small of Eden's back.

'Hello, Valerie,' Eden said. 'It's good to see you again.'

'I'm glad your aunt is OK,' Valerie said. 'I didn't realise you were bringing someone with you.'

'This is Rafe,' said Eden.

Valerie gave him a cool look.

'And are you expecting me to invite him to stay?' she asked.

'Of course not, Mrs Farrelly,' said Rafe. 'I drove Eden down. She wasn't sure if she was going to stay herself.'

'This is her home,' said Valerie. 'She'll stay.'

'No, it's not.' Eden spoke gently. 'It's your home, Valerie. Yours and Sean's. And I really hope I'll be welcome, whether it's for a day or a week, but I can't live here with you and you know that.'

'This isn't the place to talk about it,' said Valerie. 'Come inside.'

She walked to the back of the house. Eden and Rafe followed her.

'Mama!' Lila, who was in the garden, spotted her mother at once and raced towards her, throwing herself into her arms and squealing with delight when Eden picked her up and covered her with kisses. 'I've been a very good girl for Granny,' she said. 'I've helped her tre-men-dously around the house.'

'What an excellent word,' said Eden.

'We've been learning words,' Lila said.

'A new word every day,' Valerie told her. 'She's very clever. Gets that from her father.'

'Indeed she does.' Eden kissed Lila again and put her back on the ground, where the little girl transferred her attention to Rafe. 'Is Poppy here?' she asked.

'Not today,' said Rafe.

'Why can't she come?' Lila's lower lip wobbled. 'We could go swimming.'

'Next time,' promised Rafe.

'I see Michelle's car is still here,' said Eden.

'She came back down for the day. She's at the beach with the children,' said Valerie. 'Lila stayed here to wait for you. We weren't expecting anyone to come with you.'

'Rafe kindly offered to drive,' said Eden.

'I'm going to fetch Michelle.' Valerie finally took off her

gardening gloves and dropped them on the table. 'Sean should be back shortly too. He went for a walk.'

Alone together, Eden and Rafe exchanged glances.

'I see what you mean,' said Rafe.

'She's actually a decent woman and she'd do anything for me,' said Eden.

'We just have to figure out what part of doing anything for you is really doing everything for herself,' said Rafe.

'Oh, God.' Eden wiped the glistening sheen of perspiration from her brow. 'This seems so very grown-up and I feel like a naughty child.'

'You've done millions of grown-up things already,' Rafe assured her. 'You're a proper adult, don't worry.'

Eden smiled, and then her expression grew serious as she saw Valerie come through the gate to the beach followed by Sean and Michelle and Michelle's two children.

'Sean was on the beach too,' said Valerie. 'Which was useful.'

'Hello, Sean,' said Eden. 'Michelle, you've met Rafe already.'

'Michelle, will you help me make some tea. I'll bring it out to the patio,' said Valerie. 'Iris, will you supervise Lila in the paddling pool? I'm sure Darragh would like a splash too, it's so hot today.'

Iris nodded, and while the adults sat around Valerie's brand-new rattan table, the children began splashing about in the pool.

'Nice table,' said Eden when Michelle and Valerie returned with the tea. 'Lovely chairs too. Good choice, Valerie.'

'We're not here to discuss furniture.' The cups rattled as Valerie placed the tray in the centre.

'I'm not sure there's anything to discuss,' said Eden. 'Generous and wonderful though your offer to live here with you is, Valerie, it's not something I can do.'

'Because of him?' asked Michelle.

'Rafe has a name.' Eden spoke sharply. 'There's no need to be rude.'

'I'm not sure I'm the rude person here,' retorted Michelle. 'You're the one bringing a stranger into our midst.'

Eden took Rafe by the hand. 'He's not a stranger.'

'He is to us,' said Michelle. 'And we didn't invite him.'

'Michelle.' It was Sean who spoke. 'Manners.'

'I brought Rafe to introduce him to you because he's become important in my life and in Lila's,' said Eden.

'So important that you can forget your family?' asked Valerie.

'I haven't forgotten you. How could I ever forget you? You'll always be family to me,' said Eden. 'But things have changed over the last few months. I've met Rafe, and you and Sean have made decisions about your future life by moving here. A great move and I hope you're really happy. And like I said, it was generous of you to offer me a place to live with you, but Lila and I belong in Dublin.'

'And you, Rafe?' Sean looked at the other man. 'Are you planning to move into Eden's house with her?'

'No.' Rafe shook his head. 'I have my own house, where I live with my six-year-old daughter.'

'Because your wife died in mysterious circumstances. I feel it's something we should know about.'

'I have a feeling you already do,' said Rafe. 'Though the circumstances weren't mysterious. Just tragic.'

'What?' asked Valerie. 'What should we know?'

Michelle started to tell Rafe's story, but he soon interrupted her to correct her, telling it himself in a stark yet humanising way that left everyone, including Eden, unable to speak when he'd finished.

'I'm lucky to have found Eden as a good friend,' he added. 'And lucky that we care about each other and have a relationship with each other.'

'I'm lucky too,' said Eden. 'Because I more than care about Rafe, I love him. Which doesn't at all diminish my love for Andy. How could it? But it does mean that I have someone else in my life and I'm happy.'

'Do you love Eden?' Sean asked Rafe.

'Of course I do,' he said. 'How could I not?'

There was silence around the table.

'Seems to me that you two will be sharing a house soon no matter what you say,' remarked Michelle eventually.

'Maybe,' agreed Rafe. 'Who knows?'

'But you're from Galway,' wailed Valerie. 'You could take Eden and my granddaughter back to Galway and out of our lives, and I can't have that. I can't.'

'I've no desire to return to Galway,' said Rafe.

'Or Seattle,' said Michelle. 'You could go to Seattle.'

'I've even less desire to return to Seattle,' Rafe said. 'But truthfully, who knows about the future? It's not written. Anything can happen. Andy and Jewel's tragedies prove that. All I can say is that right now, my life is in Dublin, with Poppy, and it includes Eden and Lila too. Eden has already assured you that she's part of your family. Trying to guilt her into being some kind of archive for the dreams and hopes you had for Andy is unfair on her. You have to accept that.'

'We love Eden for herself,' said Valerie.

'Do you?' asked Rafe. 'Or do you love her because she was Andy's wife?'

There was another silence.

'Eden is my friend,' said Michelle eventually. 'No matter what. And I'm sorry, Eden, if I somehow tied up the loss I felt about Andy with wanting you to live as though he was still alive.'

'That's OK,' said Eden.

'Seriously,' said Michelle, 'I wasn't thinking straight. We've always got along well together. That shouldn't change. I won't let it if you don't.'

'Why should it?' asked Eden.

'You might get closer to Rafe's family,' Michelle said.

'Don't you think that the more love in the world there is to go around, the better?' asked Rafe. 'If Eden is close to my family *and* yours, how much nicer is that for her? And for Lila too.'

'You're making us seem very shallow,' remarked Sean.

'Oh, look, I can be chill about it because I don't really know you,' said Rafe. 'It's not always plain sailing with my own relatives either, you know.'

'Didn't you bring Eden to meet them?' asked Valerie.

'She knew them from before,' Rafe reminded her. 'She practically lived in our house when we were kids.'

'Are you sure this is what you want, Eden?' asked Sean. 'Because your happiness means a lot to us. It really does. This chap here might be right about us investing a lot of Andy's memories in you. But that doesn't mean we don't want you to be OK.'

'I'll be fine, Sean,' said Eden. 'Nothing is changing between

430

us, you know. And I'd love it if Lila and I could stay here from time to time.'

'With him?' asked Valerie.

'No,' said Rafe and Eden at the same time.

'I can't honestly say I'm happy,' said Valerie. 'But if you are, Eden, I suppose that's all that matters.'

'It matters that Lila is happy too,' said Eden. 'She loves her grandparents so much. And you're the only ones she has.'

'Rafe's mother and father . . .'

'Are lovely people, but not her granny and grandpa,' finished Eden.

'So are you taking her home tonight?' asked Valerie.

'Yes,' said Eden. 'But we'd love to come back later in the summer.'

'We got a desk for you and everything.' Valerie sighed. 'It was going to be great.'

Eden didn't say that it could still be great. But she knew that she'd honour her promise to keep a good relationship between Lila and her grandparents, because those connections mattered. And she wanted to have a good relationship between herself and her parents-in-law too. Families were complicated, but at least, with the Farrellys, they nearly always had each other's backs.

'So that wasn't too bad,' said Rafe as they prepared to drive back to Dublin later in the day. 'I liked Sean. I liked Michelle too, but she likes being in charge, and so does Valerie. I can see why they've been tugging you one way and then the other.'

'I suppose they've all been used to tugging me and bossing

431

me and generally organising me,' said Eden. 'It's hard for them to stop.'

'And you?' he asked. 'Are you OK with bossing yourself from now on?'

'Don't be silly.' She turned and gave him a big smile. 'I'll be bossing you.'

Chapter 36

Elizabeth and William were the first to arrive at Rafe's house-warming party. The invitation, designed by Eden, stated 6 p.m., and Elizabeth rang the doorbell at exactly 6.05. Poppy opened it and shouted to Rafe that people were here before leading them through a house decorated with balloons and streamers to the back garden beyond.

'Good to see you, Rafe,' said William as he held out a six-pack of beer. 'Where can I put these?'

'I'll take them,' said Rafe. 'D'you want one of them yourself, or will you try one of my special cocktails?'

'What would that be?' asked William.

'It's a summer punch,' said Rafe. 'Sparkling wine, vodka and fruit juice.'

'Just the one,' said William. 'Otherwise your girlfriend or mine will start lecturing me on the evils of drink.'

Rafe grinned and poured him a glass of punch, while Eden took the flowers that Elizabeth had brought and put them in water.

'It all looks fabulous,' observed Elizabeth. 'I didn't think Rafe had it in him.'

'It's an English country garden,' said Eden. 'It was Fiadh's idea in the end.'

'Oh?'

'She'd offered to help before, and he asked her if she had any thoughts when he picked the date. She's a good neighbour, even if she did once try to jump his bones. Anyway, you look very English country lady yourself, Elizabeth, so you're totally into the spirit of it. Your dress is fabulous.'

'Meghan got it for me online.' Elizabeth smoothed the skirt of the sky-blue dress with yellow flowers she was wearing. 'I never bought clothes online before. And now I think it's a great way to shop. You're looking very lovely too,' she added.

Eden's light organza dress was the palest pistachio green, with a wide skirt and a narrow belt around the waist. To highlight the English garden theme, she'd added a short cardigan with a multicoloured butterfly design that echoed her favourite butterfly clips holding up her hair.

'More people,' cried Poppy, guiding Krystle (in stunning vintage gold lamé) and Sandie (a white short-sleeved broderie anglaise blouse and pink skirt) into the garden.

From that point, people arrived continuously, until the entire street, with the exception of Jacintha, who'd given birth to a baby girl the previous night and was still in hospital, was gathered in the garden. After Eden's reminder that the children needed to be catered for too, Rafe had organised a magician to entertain them, and even the older ones were enthralled by his tricks.

'Brilliant theme,' Eden said to Fiadh when the two of them were standing side by side watching people tucking into the daintily cut sandwiches that had been delivered earlier in the day by a local café. 'Everyone's having a great time.'

'Thank God it wasn't last night. We'd have been washed out of it.'

'I know. I was keeping my fingers crossed the forecast was right for today. You put in a lot of effort to help Rafe. He really appreciates it.'

'I'm not trying to lure him away from you, if that's what you think,' said Fiadh.

'If he's the sort of man who can be lured away by a cucumber sandwich, I'm not interested anyway.' Eden smiled at her and Fiadh laughed.

'He was such a good prospect,' she admitted. 'But he's mad about you, anyone can see that.'

Both women glanced over to where Rafe was drinking beer with William and Bert Atkins. As though he sensed her looking his way, Rafe turned towards Eden and raised his can. She lifted her glass of punch in return.

'Sickening actually,' said Fiadh, although her voice was warm. 'Also, the fact that your kids get on together is a bonus.'

'Hello, ladies.' Krystle came to join them. 'What a lovely party and what a nice time to have it, before autumn really sets in and our Halloween Howlers night in October. Will you be at that, Eden?'

'I don't know,' she replied.

'I do hope so,' said Krystle. 'It's so much easier to get the men on board when the women are involved. And of course, we have trick-or-treating and games on the green for the children.'

'Sounds amazing,' said Eden. 'Can you excuse me for a moment? I need to welcome someone.'

'She'll be an asset to the Grove,' Krystle said to Fiadh when Eden had gone.

'I guess she will.' Fiadh took a slug of summer punch.

Eden walked over to Michelle, who'd arrived alone, having decided that one representative from the Farrellys was enough.

'I'm glad you came,' she said.

'How could I not?'

'You didn't have to.'

'Oh, look.' Michelle shrugged. 'I was madly curious to check out Rafe's house and see him with other people.'

'Did you think he'd be different with other people?'

'I dunno.'

'Let me get you a drink,' said Eden. 'Summer punch or a massive G&T?'

'Would you think badly of me if I had the massive G&T?'

'Not at all,' she said.

'They make a lovely couple,' said Anita to Sandie as Eden diverted towards Rafe and gave him a kiss on the cheek before getting Michelle's drink.

'Fiadh was bitterly disappointed,' Sandie said. 'She was so sure she'd win him over.'

'A man with a child might seem like a good idea, but it's probably far too much trouble,' said Anita.

'He's a decent guy, though,' said Sandie.

'Ups the stakes for the rest of them on the road,' agreed Anita.

'Back to the drawing board for Fiadh and me, though.' Sandie sighed. 'Oh well, I guess it's the dating app again.'

Michelle saw Eden kiss Rafe and felt her entire body stiffen. She knew she should accept her sister-in-law's new relationship, but it was hard. Because it made Andy's death so very final. It wasn't as though she'd expected him to walk in the door one day like the hero in a crazy TV soap and say that they'd got it wrong, he'd just been badly injured and kept away from everyone for five years, but somehow Eden and Andy had been such a strong couple that she couldn't let the idea of them go. She knew her mother felt the same way. Valerie was still devastated that Eden had rejected the idea of living in Dunleary, and had tried hard to make her reconsider, even suggesting that Eden could invite her boyfriend to stay from time to time if he wanted, an offer that Eden immediately turned down.

'I'm sorry, Valerie,' she'd said, her voice strong and steady. 'Dunleary is your home, and I know it'll always be a place I want to visit. I'm sure Lila will love to stay there too. But it's not *my* home and it never will be. I know you still think of me as Andy's wife,' she continued, without giving Valerie a chance to speak, 'and being his wife has been an important part of me. I'll never forget him. I'll always love him. But he's gone, Valerie, and I'm here. I have to keep living. It's easy for you to tell me what Andy would want. You've done it lots of times. But I'm pretty sure he wouldn't want me mourning him forever. I'm pretty sure he'd want me out there doing my best. For me and for Lila.'

Valerie had cried after Eden's words, and Michelle had been the one to comfort her. But she couldn't help feeling that Eden was right, and that all their efforts to hold her close within their circle were misguided. Nevertheless, it was hard to accept that Eden and Andy no longer existed, and that Eden and Rafe were a thing. But she smiled brightly at her sister-in-law when she returned with the gin and tonic, then waved her away to deal with the crisis when Amelia

Atkins came to ask where Rafe kept his kitchen towel, because Rory had spilled juice all over the kitchen floor and she couldn't find anything to wipe it up with.

She was leaning against the side wall, watching the neighbours, when a woman she didn't recognise materialised beside her.

'Hello,' she said. 'I don't really know too many people here, and I feel a bit of an eejit, so I thought perhaps you'd talk to me. I'm Rafe's sister, Petra.'

'Oh.' Michelle's eyes lit up. 'I'm Eden's sister-in-law, Michelle.'

'He's spoken about you,' said Petra.

'Really?'

'He said you were like me.'

'I don't know if that's good or bad.'

'Nor do I.' Petra grinned. 'I get on well with my brother and I look out for him, but I got it all wrong about him and Eden.'

'D'you really think he loves her?'

'Oh yes,' said Petra. 'I think he always did.'

'You've done well there,' Mark Keneally told Rafe. 'She's a cracker.'

'You're right.'

'Krystle is both pleased and disappointed.'

'In what way?' Rafe pulled the tab on another can of non-A beer. He planned to have a few alcoholic drinks later, but not while the entire neighbourhood was in his house.

'She wanted to mother you,' said Mark. 'And to organise you. It's her thing and she feels like her wings have been clipped.'

438

'Too many people have tried to organise me over the last few years,' said Rafe. 'I'm happy to organise myself.'

'That'll never happen if there's a woman around,' said Mark. 'We think we're in control, but we're not.'

'They have skills,' agreed Rafe as they watched Fiadh and Krystle clear away empty plates and replace them with bowls of sausage rolls. 'They keep the threads of social life together. They organise stuff like this. They're a civilising force.'

'Ah now,' said Mark. 'We're not total Neanderthals without them.'

'God, no.' Rafe grinned. 'I'm your totally woke single dad, after all.'

'Fair play to you, mate,' said Mark. 'But well done on getting the girl all the same.'

He held up his can and bumped it off Rafe's. 'To women,' he said. 'And beer!'

'I'm quite enjoying this,' William said to Elizabeth. 'Even if we're the only people sitting down.'

'Eden said there'd be dancing later.'

'I don't dance.'

'You don't come to parties either, yet here you are. And you were at the barbecue.'

'I know more people on your road than on mine,' acknowledged William.

'And they're all good people. A bit nosy sometimes. But there for you if you need them.'

'I've never bothered to find out about my own neighbours,' he admitted. 'I suppose they'd be good too. But I live on a long, straight road. There isn't the same sense of community as here.'

'Oh well, you can share mine,' said Elizabeth.

'I'd like to share more than that,' William said.

'Like what?'

'Like the lots of years I hope we have left. I'd like us to spend them together.'

'O . . . K . . .' said Elizabeth slowly.

'What I'm saying,' said William, 'is that I'd like you to marry me, Elizabeth Green. I want you to do me the honour of becoming my wife.'

Afterwards, Elizabeth said that everyone had heard William's proposal because he was shouting over the music and the constant stream of chatter, owing to being a little bit deaf himself and thinking everyone else was too. Anita, who was closest to them, squealed with excitement, sparking off a chorus of shouts and applause.

'Oh, for heaven's sake, look what you've started,' said Elizabeth, but she smiled as she spoke.

William looked at the crowd that had clustered around them.

'I didn't mean it to be this public,' he said.

'Then you shouldn't have asked me in a public place.'

'I couldn't help myself. It seemed the right thing to do.'

'So if I say yes, do you have an engagement ring for me?' asked Elizabeth.

'Actually, I do.' William took a box out of his pocket and opened it. The ring inside was a narrow silver hoop with a small sapphire and ruby set into it. 'It's antique, but not from my family or anything, so you don't have to worry about it having some deep significance. I bought it in town myself.'

'Oh, William.' Elizabeth looked from it to him. 'It's beautiful.'

'So are you,' he said.

It didn't fit perfectly, but, she said, it didn't matter for now, and she wasn't going to take it off because she was an engaged woman and she didn't want to be pestered by any other man who was thinking of making a move on her. The neighbours laughed even as they applauded them and then raised their glasses in a toast.

'I'm so happy for you,' Eden said to her. 'Your slow burn wasn't such a slow burn after all.'

'And your no-strings sex seems to have come with a whole heap of strings.' Elizabeth grinned.

'Good strings,' Eden said.

'So . . . are you looking after him or is he looking after you?'

'Gosh, Elizabeth, I hope we're looking after each other.'

'Just like William and me,' said Elizabeth, and there was a touch of satisfaction in her voice.

Later, when most of the neighbours had gone home and only a few diehards remained chatting in the garden, Eden went upstairs and sent some photos of the evening to Trudy.

Trudy
It looks fun

Eden
It was. It still is. How are you?

Trudy
OK. Doing lots of physio but feeling the benefit of it

Eden
And Kevin?

Trudy
He's good too

Eden
Perhaps you can visit sometime

Trudy
Perhaps. But I'd love to see you here again with your lover

Eden
Trudy!

Trudy
He is your lover though

Eden
Yes

Trudy
Good. We all need lovers. They make the world go round

Eden smiled as she put her phone away. Despite her age and her stroke, her aunt would always be the woman who'd left home to do what she wanted to do. And that was a good thing. Because Trudy living any other life wouldn't have been Trudy.

And Elizabeth living any other life wouldn't have been Elizabeth.

And Rafe without the life he'd led before she came into it again wouldn't have been Rafe.

And she without Andy wouldn't have been the person she was now.

A person who was ready to take another step.

Her own person. Doing things her own way. But with someone she loved by her side.

AAtkins
Hi everyone – did you see a For Sale sign has gone up outside number 12?

KrystleK
They're getting a divorce – guess Rach isn't getting the house tho

HealeyLauren
I'm sorry for the kids

KrystleK
These things happen

SandieC
Wonder who'll buy?

AAtkins
Nobody as lovely as Rafe that's for sure

FiadhFoley
Damp squib in the end tho 😢

SandieC
From your POV

FiadhFoley
Turns out he wasn't my type

AAtkins
I'm sure it'll be a family in number 12. It's a 4 bed house after all

KrystleK
No matter who it is, we'll give them a warm Sycamore Grove welcome

SandieC
Hope they have a house-warming!!!!

FiadhFoley
Oooh. I'll have to think of a theme . . .

Chapter 37

Darling You,

It's a long time since I last wrote, but there's been a lot going on. Your mum and dad are well settled in Dunleary now, without me and Lila, although we were there last weekend and I think they've forgiven me for turning down their offer. Actually, no, they haven't, but they realise there's no point in having a fight with me. And it's not that I'd ever stop them from being with their granddaughter, but I did say to Valerie that I'd be less inclined to visit if she was going to freeze me out or spend her time making barbed remarks about me and Rafe every time we met.

Oh, Andy, this is why I haven't written. I've been trying to work up the courage to say it to you. (There's a part of me that does realise I'm writing letters to someone who will never read them and so I don't really need courage, but writing to you has been such a help to me over the past five years that I can't quite believe you don't somehow know what I'm saying.)

Anyway. Rafe.

We're a couple now. We outed ourselves properly at his house-warming party and it felt so good to be part of it with him. I told you already that he makes me happy. I make him happy too. We love each other, Andy. He's brought the sunshine back into my life. I feel bad saying this to you and yet I don't feel bad any more about loving him. I did, of course, at the start. I didn't want to admit I loved him because it was so hard to believe that after you I could love anyone. But I do love him. Madly.

When we were in France together (Trudy had a stroke, so I went to see her. She's recovering well, thank goodness) – anyhow, when we were there, Kevin said something to me and it really made me think differently. He said that loving Rafe didn't mean I loved you any less, simply that I was layering one love on top of the other. He said we had an infinite capacity for love. And you know, Andy, he's right. That's exactly what's happened. Loving Rafe has locked away my love for you. It's still there, always a part of me, but beneath the surface now. And that's OK. Loving you helped me to overcome so many things. And loving Rafe has helped me to overcome losing you.

Lila is crazy about him and he's an amazing dad to both her and Poppy, neither of whom are biologically his. Lila knows he's not her actual dad – she knows exactly who you are and that you were a fireman, which she thinks is 'super-cool'. That's her new phrase at the moment. She learned it from Poppy, who is the best sister she could possibly have.

It seems like I fell on my feet with Rafe. I hope you're happy for me. I want to think you're cheering me on.

You can cheer me on in other ways too! I've got a heap of new calligraphy commissions and I'm taking a break from being a carer to deal with them. Remember I told you about Amahle Radebe's party invites? Well, she actually invited me and Rafe along, since I'd done so much work for her. I couldn't believe it. I told her that we'd love to (I didn't even make excuses about not being celeb enough, because feck it, Andy – Amahle Radebe's party!!!!), and we had the most fantastic time. My place cards and menus looked fabulous, and when Amahle got up to make a speech, she actually name-checked me. Afterwards she asked if I'd do the lettering on her new album cover. Can you imagine??? I'm sure it's going to be a massive hit, and my art will be on it. I'm so excited! Also – and here's the extra work bit – one of her celebrity friends is creating a fitness clothing line and asked me to do the logo for her. She hasn't gone to some well-known designer, she's asked me! I've sent her some samples and her reply was 'They're all so brilliant I don't know which to choose. Maybe I'll have to launch a line of something else too!!' AND I'm being paid really good money for it. If that wasn't enough, I'm doing wedding invitations for one of the other guests. Someone from Amahle's music label and very well known in those circles, though I hadn't a clue who he was. But it's going to be a massive wedding with five hundred invitations!!! My hand will be falling off ☺

You would've loved Amahle's party. I didn't say anything to Rafe, of course, but I thought of you when I was dancing with him. It was late and the stars were out, and when I looked up, I saw three of them in a line together. I know it's fanciful and I know Trudy would be annoyed if she thought I was thinking like this, but I wanted to believe they were you and Mum and Dad looking down on me and giving me your blessing. I think you would, Andy, because I know you only wanted what was good for me. I feel safe with Rafe, just as I did with you. And I love him, just as I loved you.

Oh, I nearly forgot! Lila started play school in September and she's loving it. She's so smart and clever and really good with her drawing and writing. Sometimes I look at her and I see you. Sometimes I see me. And sometimes, because it had to happen, she'll do or say something that's so like Poppy you'd never believe they weren't actual sisters.

We're becoming a blended family, I guess. And I think you'd be happy to know that Lila has the sister we would have wanted for her, and that she has a father figure in her life, as well as Sean and Valerie and all your family and another family in Galway who love her as much as I do.

Love isn't about one person or one family.

It's about everything and everybody.

This is my last letter to you, Andy, and when it's delivered, I'm going to take all of our letters and burn them.

I don't need to write to you any more and I know you don't need to hear from me.

But you'll be forever in my heart, one layer of my love.

And I know that a part of me will always be

Forever yours,

Eden xx

Acknowledgements

I never thought I'd be writing a second book during a pandemic, and I wouldn't have been able to do it at all without the support of so many people, most particularly my wonderful agent, Isobel Dixon, and her team at Blake Friedmann; and my equally wonderful publisher and editor, Marion Donaldson, and her team at Headline Publishing. I am extremely lucky to have two exceptional women offering advice and encouragement even in the toughest of times. Thank you also to the fantastic people at Hachette Ireland, Australia and New Zealand and my new friends at Mobius Books in the US who have brought my books to readers all around the world.

I'm always nervous about putting names in the Acknowledgements because of the terror of omitting anyone, but hopefully I've got you all – Eli, Rosanna, Jo, Alara, Ellie, Yeti, Breda, Jim, Joanna, Bernard, Elaine, Siobhan, Ciara and Ciara, Ruth (my guardian angel), Sian, Tia, Hana, James, Lizzie, Daisy and Giuliana.

Thanks to Jane, my copyeditor, who spots all the mistakes, and Colm, my husband, who reads the final draft to make sure that I've corrected them.

As a writer, it's a real privilege to hear from readers who've enjoyed my books, who've identified with characters or situations, and who tell me how important reading is to them. Many of us met again on social media this year, and it's always a pleasure to chat with you at the different events. To everyone who has joined me for 'Live' sessions this year, thank you for your company.

Of course, I'm a reader as well as a writer, so a massive thank you once again to all the booksellers and librarians who got books into readers' hands, and who helped us to keep our reading mojo going over the past months. Thanks for your recommendations and your enthusiasm and for reminding me – over and over again – why I love the book community so much.

More than ever we've come to realise the importance of the people closest to us, especially when we can't be with them. My family is my enduring support in good times and bad. Thank you for always being there.

Part of Eden's story deals with her mourning the life she should have had. I think many of us have felt that way over the past years as we've seen milestones go by without the customary celebrations, as reminders of cancelled events popped up on our timelines, as we were forced over and over again to isolate ourselves from the people we love. So we need to thank each other, too: for doing the right thing, for the support we've given each other and for the courage so many have shown in the face of hard times. Most especially, thanks once again to our frontline workers in every sector, who have kept the whole show on the road. We, and I, couldn't have done it without you.

Don't miss Sheila's stunning first historical novel, coming in April 2023

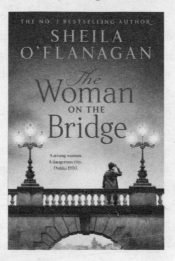

Dublin. The 1920s. As war tears Ireland apart, two young people are caught up in events that will bring love, tragedy – and the hardest of choices.

In a country fighting for freedom, it's hard to live a normal life. Winnie O'Leary supports the cause, but she doesn't go looking for trouble. Then rebel Joseph Burke steps into her workplace. Winnie is furious with him about a broken window. She's not interested in romance. But love comes when you least expect it . . .

Ireland's tumultuous independence struggle is the backdrop for an unforgettable story of courage and heartbreak, in which heroes are made of ordinary people. Inspired by the story of Sheila O'Flanagan's grandmother, *The Woman on the Bridge* is the unmiss-able, compulsive new novel from a bestselling author.

Available to order now from

REVIEW

One summer, three weddings, and a phone call
that changes everything . . .

At the first wedding, there's a shock.
Delphie is enjoying her brother's wedding. Her surprise last-minute
Plus One has stunned her family – and it's also stopped any of them
asking *again* why she's still single. But when she sees all the missed
calls that evening, she knows it can't be good news.

The second wedding is unexpected.
Delphie has been living her best life, loving her job, her friends, her
no-strings relationships and her dream house by
the sea. Now she has to question everything she believed
about who she is and what she wants.

Is it time to settle down? Or does she want to keep on
trying to have it all?

**By the third wedding, Delphie thinks nothing could
surprise her. But she's wrong . . .**

Available to order now from

REVIEW

Lose yourself on one truly unforgettable journey with. . .

Deira isn't the kind of woman to steal a car.

Or drive to France alone with no plan. But then, Deira didn't expect
to be single. Or to suddenly realise that the only way she can get the
one thing she wants most is to start breaking every rule she lives by.

Grace has been sent on a journey by her late husband, Ken.

She doesn't really want to be on it but she's following his
instructions, as always. She can only hope that the trip will help her
to forgive him. And then – finally – she'll be able to let him go.

Brought together by unexpected circumstances, Grace and Deira
find that it's easier to share secrets with a stranger, especially in
the shimmering sunny countryside of Spain and France.

**But they soon find that there's no escaping the truth, whether
you're running away from it or racing towards it . . .**

Available to order now from

REVIEW

Her husband has betrayed her. Can she forgive
him – and should she?

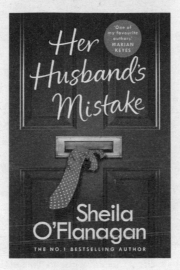

Roxy's marriage has always been rock solid.

After twenty years, and with two carefree kids, she and Dave are still
the perfect couple. Until the day she comes home unexpectedly, and
finds Dave in bed with their attractive, single neighbour.

**Suddenly Roxy isn't sure about anything - her past,
the business she's taken over from her dad, or what her
family's future might be.**

She's spent so long caring about everyone else that she's
forgotten what she actually wants. But something has changed.
And Roxy has a decision to make.

**Whether it's with Dave, or without him, it's time for Roxy
to start living for herself . . .**

Available to order now from

REVIEW